ENTER
EVIL

Also by Linda Ladd

Die Smiling

Dark Places

Head to Head

ENTER EVIL

LINDA LADD

PINNACLE BOOKS
KENSINGTON PUBLISHING CORP.
www.kensingtonbooks.com

PINNACLE BOOKS are published by

Kensington Publishing Corp.
119 West 40th Street
New York, NY 10018

All Kensington titles, imprints, and distributed lines are available at special quantity discounts for bulk purchases for sales promotions, premiums, fund-raising, educational, or institutional use. Special book excerpts or customized printings can also be created to fit specific needs. For details, write or phone the office of the Kensington special sales manager: Kensington Publishing Corp., 119 West 40th Street, New York, NY 10018, attn: Special Sales Department; Phone: 1-800-221-2647.

This book is a work of fiction. Names, characters, businesses, organizations, places, events, and incidents either are the product of the author's imagination or are used fictitiously. Any resemblance to actual persons, living or dead, events, or locales is entirely coincidental.

ISBN-13: 978-0-7860-1888-8
ISBN-10: 0-7860-1888-7

First Printing: August 2009

10 9 8 7 6 5 4 3 2 1

Here Comes Trouble

The son was trouble. Some people suspected there was a little mean streak in him but no one said a word to the parents, of course, because most of the time he seemed so sweet and loving. But there was something that came out now and again, something unsettling, something they just couldn't put their finger on. A tragedy was bound to happen one day but nobody at the big family get-together knew it yet, not even the kid himself.

As for the son, sometimes, not often, he, too, found himself doing truly horrible things, things he did not understand and could not explain when he asked himself why. Today, however, he was doing okay; nothing much weird was going on. Actually, he was pretty happy-go-lucky at the moment and having an awesome time with all his kinfolks. It was hot summertime; a real heat wave bore down on them. Lots of American flags were flying everywhere; everybody acting real patriotic and stuff. Flapping on the flagpole at the corner of the back deck was their big nylon American flag, and his mom had stuck tiny American flags inside her flowerpots full of yellow marigolds and red petunias, and just about everywhere else. She'd hung puffs of red, white, and blue bunting on the edges of the deck and the picnic table sitting out on the grassy lawn and some more around the pool house eaves. His mom loved holidays.

The afternoon was really sultry and humid, bringing sticky sweat rolling down people's necks after a few minutes outside, and the sun broiled down and sunburned everybody. The concrete around the swimming pool was hot as hell, but the kid didn't care. He loved being outside, loved summer the best, and tonight was the night he'd been waiting for a long time. Tonight his team was matched up against the number-one team in Park League baseball.

Yeah, him and his Bearcats, they were going to tangle with the Wildcats at seven o'clock for the big brass first-place trophy with the swinging batter on top, and they were gonna kill 'em because he was gonna get to pitch, and he was the best pitcher in the whole league, everybody said so, even the other team's coach, Mr. Manning. The boy wanted to be number one more than anything, and he always got to be, in just about everything he did. Best yet, all his aunts and uncles and cousins were gonna sit in the stands and see how hard his fastball was and how far he could hit homers, all the way out over the left-field fence, lots of times. Yeah, he was real good, *real* good, and he couldn't wait for people to pat him on the back and tell him how special he was, like they always did after his games. Because he *was* special. It was easy to see that.

Best of all right now, though, were the relay races and diving contests they'd been having in the swimming pool. Naturally, he was winning everything, and that was what was important. To win, every single time, every single place, always come out on top and get all the glory. Not that he was a bad loser or anything; he always shook the winner's hand and stuff, if somebody should accidentally beat him. He didn't like doing that, but nobody could ever tell how steaming mad he was inside his chest.

Right now, he was in the pool. It was way too hot to get out and put on his shorts and shirt for dinner. Swimming was his favorite thing to do when he wasn't practicing his sports, and he was in the pool constantly when he was at home. He was the best athlete of all his brothers and sisters and cousins and could swim like a fish. That's what his dad always was saying to people. He liked it when his dad and mom praised him like that, you know, went on and on about it, and they did it a lot. He was their favorite, big-time, hands down.

His mom told him that he was the best, the smartest, the most loved, even over the other kids. He always just beamed when she did that, 'cause she was right, he definitely was. Mom and Dad both whispered stuff like that in his ear, low enough so his brothers and sisters didn't hear and start blubbering and being jealous. His mom was especially proud of his grades in school, and she'd come home from the end-of-the-year conference with his counselor and told him that he'd scored at genius levels in the spring IQ tests. He'd already figured out that he was smarter than nearly everybody else already, even her, but she sure was pleased. She said that with a keen mind like his, he could do anything and be anything he wanted when he grew up.

The younger kids in the family were okay, though, he guessed, especially Lyla. She was just four years old and had the most beautiful long blond hair. It hung all the way down past her waist and curled up in these little fat ringlets like his did and shone like golden fire in the sunlight. She was his favorite sister, way favorite, and he had a lot of sisters. For some reason, he just loved being around her and hearing that funny little giggle she was always spilling out. The other kids were okay, too, sometimes, but they weren't like Lyla. He loved her so much, even more than his mom and dad loved her, so much sometimes that it expanded up inside his chest and hurt him and made tears well inside his eyes. Usually that was when he thought about how sweet she was and how much she looked up to him. He was her special hero, and he liked that. She always drew pictures of him wearing a red cape on the coloring sheets she brought home from preschool, like he was some kind of superhero or something. She always put his first initial on the chest of her superhero.

It was getting late, almost time to eat. All his dad's relatives had brought lots of good food for the annual cookout. The kids had been in the pool, but they'd all gotten out now to play Wiffle ball with their dads and uncles and romp around the yard with the dogs. His family had three dogs: Cocoa, Puffs, and Cheerio, and at the moment, Cheerio, the little beagle, had six itty-bitty newborn puppies. Most of the kids were inside now, in the mudroom, watching the puppies frisk around and play inside the cardboard box with an old red and white patchwork quilt inside that his mom had made for their bed.

The boy liked to watch the puppies roll around, too, but right now, he was kinda glad to be alone with just him and Lyla. He was tired of shooting basketballs into the floating hoop, anyway. He rarely missed, and it really wasn't much of a contest going up against his cousins. Now he and Lyla could be by themselves and dive after the shiny new pennies his dad had thrown into the pool. Just like him, she swam like a little fish. He taught her himself when she was just two years old and made sure she did it right, in case she ever fell in the pool or got a stomach cramp, or something, when he wasn't around to save her.

"C'mon, Lyla, let's go down in the deep end. I'll hold you up high so your head won't go under."

Lyla was clutching onto the top step of the shallow-end ladder, and she took off and dog-paddled to him. She was really a pretty good girl to be so little. She was always belting out that funny laugh. She did it now as she reached him and grabbed him around the neck so tight that he nearly choked. He laughed, though, liking her little chubby arms around him, then he transferred her around and onto his back and started swimming them out into deep water with his perfectly executed breaststrokes. He had his junior lifeguard certificate and knew exactly how to perform every single stroke. He'd been the youngest member of his Red Cross Lifeguard class and the very best swimmer with all the highest scores. When he reached the heavy twisted white rope dividing the shallow and deep ends, he held on with both hands and peered through the thick red rosebushes to see if the grown-ups were keeping an eye on them.

His dad was busy cooking hamburgers and Cheesy Jumbo hot dogs on his fancy new grill. It was green and shaped like a big egg. Mom had bought it at some special store for his dad's birthday, and his dad loved to cook on it. His dad had six brothers, and each of them had a bunch of kids, so there was quite a crowd milling around in the backyard. His uncles were all standing around and drinking beer and listening to his dad tell them all the fancy stuff his new grill could do. His dad was wearing a big white chef's hat and an apron that said EMERIL, EAT YOUR HEART OUT. But none of the adults were watching them swim around in the pool, and the son was glad because his parents didn't like for him to take Lyla into the deep end. But she loved it when he did, and it was their secret fun thing to do, and he was always extra careful and held onto her really, really tight.

After he'd flipped the rope over their heads and was treading water to keep their faces out of the water, he put Lyla's fingers around the rope and made sure she held on with a tight grip. "Okay, there you go, Lyla, you hold on hard, got it? Real tight, you hear. You know the drill. Don't let go for anything, okay?"

"I wanna dive after the pennies!" Lyla cried, and then she smiled that big wide grin that everybody loved so much. She was just the sweetest little thing ever. She had these huge blue eyes, just exactly the color the sky was high above them right now, but her eyelashes were real dark and long, even though her hair was blond, which was kinda odd, actually. He really, really loved her. More than just about anything, even some of his smaller trophies. Her hair looked darker now, all wet, and it was floating all around her shoulders on top of the water like a sleek, shiny cape.

"Okay, Lyla, I'm goin' down to the bottom first. See all those pennies layin' around down there? Hold still so the water'll calm down and you can see where they are. Dad threw them in this morning and said he'd give us kids a dollar for each one we bring up. It's supposed to happen tonight after we eat dinner, but we'll get a jump on the other kids."

"I wanna dollar, I wanna dollar!" Lyla was holding on to the rope, but she was yelling pretty loud, so he glanced up at the deck again, but nobody was paying a bit of attention to them. They trusted him alone in the pool with his younger brothers and sisters, anyway; sometimes they even called him their own personal Junior Lifeguard. He liked it when they did that, because it made him feel all grown up and important. And now he was trained to be one; that's how good he was.

"Okay, Lyla, I'll take you down with me, but you gotta help me kick, 'member? And if you run outta breath you gotta pull on my hair and I'll swim you up as fast as I can, okay?"

"Let's go down deep, all the way to the bottom, I want to, I want to!"

The boy laughed at his little sister's excitement, and that brought out her funny little squeal. She always wanted to be with him, constantly, every day, all day. And he usually didn't mind having her around, except when all his buddies came over and wanted him to go down the street and Rollerblade in front of Kevin's house. Then Lyla was a big pain, and his mom would have to hold her and make her stay inside the house so she wouldn't follow and get herself lost in the woods along the road. But she always cried and threw a little hissy fit until he was out of sight.

"Okay, you ready, Lyla? You gotta hold your breath a real long time, but if you want to come up, remember, tug on my hair, okay? Not too hard, though, okay?"

"Okay! Let's go down and get the dollars. I wanna new Barbie!"

He laughed some more. "The dollars aren't down there, goofy, just the pennies. Dad's gonna give us real dollars when we bring up the pennies."

"I'm gonna buy us some suckers. The kind with the chewy good stuff in the middle. I'm gonna get a red one."

"Those're called Tootsie Roll Pops. Okay, ready? Take a deep breath and let's go down!"

He made sure she took a good one and held it, because sometimes she forgot to hold it and got to coughing, and that always scared him. This time she got it right, and they dove down together, Lyla holding tightly to his shoulders. But her eyes were open, and he could see her face clearly through the yellow swimming goggles he wore. The pennies were scattered all around the bottom, but most of them had landed near the drain, so he headed there first. They began to pick them up, and he had to keep batting Lyla's long hair out of the way because it kept getting in front of his goggles and he couldn't see where the pennies were. Lyla had managed to pick up three, and he got about five more real quick because he was running out of breath. Her hair was waving out toward the drain, and he pulled it back because his mom had warned them about hair getting caught in swimming pool drains.

Suddenly a thought occurred to him, and he took the wad of hair he had in his hand and wound it around the edges of the drain. Lyla was still grabbing up pennies, but after a second, she turned to him and pulled on his hair. He stayed where he was a moment, then he let go of her and rocketed back up to the top. When he broke the surface, he gulped air, but all the adults were crowded around the picnic table and bringing big platters of food out from the kitchen. Nobody was paying any attention to him at all.

So he dove back to the bottom and grabbed hold of the drain to keep himself down. Lyla was struggling desperately now, and her big pretty eyes were open real wide and looked all panicky and stuff. She grabbed him, jerking his hair frantically in their signal to surface, and he held on as long as his breath lasted, waiting for her to run out of air. A few seconds later, Lyla gave up and let go of him. He watched her mouth open and then she swallowed water, and then a bunch of bubbles came rolling out of her mouth and nose and she didn't struggle anymore but drowned right in front of him until she was just staring at him out of those great big blue eyes that looked so surprised at what he'd done to her. Then she was quiet and dead, a long strand of her hair caught tightly to the drain, the rest of her pretty hair waving around in the currents left over from her struggles to get loose. Gradually, her feet began to drift upward and she floated upside down, and he thought she looked beautiful and peaceful, just floating there like that, dead and gone forever.

When his air ran out, he surfaced and filled his lungs again. He went down several more times to stare at her, for some reason enjoying the way she looked. He wondered why he had done such a terrible thing. He really didn't know why. He loved her. He was gonna miss her a lot, but he did have lots of other brothers and sisters and cousins to hang around with, so it probably wouldn't be that bad without her. Mom and Dad were gonna be really upset, though. She was their baby.

Oh, well, he was their favorite, after all, so they'd get over it, even if they did blame him. And they probably wouldn't blame him; they'd probably feel sorry for him for having to be there and see her when she got caught at the bottom and got her little lungs all filled up with water. And now, after it was all over, it had been a pretty bad thing to watch; he was glad his mom hadn't had to see it.

Once he got tired of watching Lyla float around upside down, he swam underwater to the nearest ladder and climbed out. He could still see her down on the bottom, and he wanted to watch her float around some more but knew he couldn't waste any more time.

"Mommmmmmmmmmmmmmmm! Dadddddddddddddddddd!

Lyla's hair's caught in the drain! Help, Mom, Mom, hurry, hurry! I can't get her loose!"

The adults standing around the table all froze for a second, and then they dropped what they were doing and ran hard to the pool. The men dove headfirst into the water, all of them at once, and so did his mom. A couple of his aunts ran to him and held him tightly against them, holding his face into their red American flag T-shirts so he wouldn't have to see, and he thought that was a nice thing for them to do. So he started bawling, real hard. He'd learned early off that he could fake tears, any time he wanted, to varying degrees, without anybody suspecting that they were false. He could make himself look so pitiful. He'd practiced the look in the mirror lots of times. His mother always fell for it, his dad, too, but sometimes it took longer to get his dad to feel sorry for him.

The men in the water kept resurfacing, gulping air and plunging back to the bottom, trying to get Lyla's hair loose, and the women were all screaming and crying and saying oh God, even the ones trying to comfort him. Several of his aunts ran back into the house to keep the other kids from coming out and seeing how Lyla looked dead and drowned. He kept up his weeping and yelling, impressing even himself this time with the amount of tears he managed to pour down his cheeks.

But the funniest thing, suddenly the fake tears turned into real, honest-to-goodness tears. Because he *did* love Lyla! So much! She was his favorite person in the whole wide world. And now she was drowned and lying all limp and dead on the concrete at the other side of the pool, while his youngest uncle, who was a paramedic and rode in ambulances, was pressing on her little chest while his dad wept and blew air into her mouth. But it was too late, way too late. She was deader than dead. He sobbed louder. He was gonna miss her so much. And now he wouldn't get to pitch against the Wildcats tonight! None of them would get to go to the game and see him play. Why did he have to go and tie her hair to the drain? It just wasn't fair!

ONE

Okay, my name is Claire Morgan, and I'm a homicide detective with the Canton County Sheriff's Department right here at the beautiful Lake of the Ozarks in mid-Missouri. At the moment, I'm on a undercover surveillance assignment for probable drug dealing in a lovely cove cradled by the most beautiful green wooded hills you can ever imagine. Unfortunately, the idyllic spot is marred a bit by about fifty runabout boats full of practically nude young college coeds and their horny boyfriends. Various and sundry other under-age kiddies are also out in the hot summer sun, drinking and flirting and trying their best to hook up with the next good-looking thing that happens by. Ah, Party Cove, the place to be on a sultry summer day. There is plenty to watch, believe you me, some of which could definitely be called X-rated, or even in the triple Z range.

In fact, as I lie here on my stomach in the prow of Nicholas Black's shiny and magnificent Cobalt 360 cruiser, training a high-powered, telescoped digital camera on yon distant shore, I'm getting quite an eyeful of boozed-up, sex-crazed kids in action. My own very special honey, the aforementioned Black, who is also a filthy rich shrink to the stars and all manner of other celebs, is sitting in the pilot's chair behind me talking psychobabble to somebody who'd called from his posh London clinic. No doubt there's a Brit in a straitjacket on the loose in Piccadilly Circus.

It's late August, and the lake is dark olive green with not a breath of wind to ripple the glassy surface. Calm as death, as they say. Not that I want to think about death at the moment. I've had enough narrow escapes with the Grim Reaper of late, so many in fact that the Dreary Dark Man with the Scythe probably has my name tattooed on his palm for easy reference. Nope, I sure don't want to think about my last case, or the one before it, or any of them, actually.

So instead, I fixed my attention on my partner, Budweiser D. Davis, a good-looking, silver-eyed Southern drawler from Atlanta, Bud for short. He is hiding in a honeysuckle thicket on the nearby shore, no doubt enjoying the fragrance and buzzing bumblebees, while similarly scoping out the wild goings on all around us with a video camera running, the incriminating tape of which we someday hoped to share with a judge and jury.

Although a charm-meister extraordinaire for sure, Bud hasn't done a lot of that sort of thing lately, not since our last case when his girl, Brianna, got herself in some very deep trouble. She's gone away now and nobody knows for how long, to live in Europe, Rome to be exact, where she's trying to get over the injuries she sustained and the severe psychological trauma she suffered. Truth is, she's doing pretty good under the circumstances, and Bud thinks she'll be back one of these days, and they can start up where they left off.

Frankly, I have my doubts about that one, but who knows? My world's a strange, dangerous place, and it has a tendency to rub off on my friends. Actually, a lot of us went through a pretty hairy ordeal along with her and still have our own ugly scars to prove it. Bud took her departure pretty hard at first, still has his sad moments of guilt and depression, but he is coming out of it slowly. How do I know? He's once again ogling good-looking women and making wisecracks and telling me the origins of phrases from a book I bought him, the latter being pretty annoying. A sure sign of healing, however. His appetite has picked up, too.

"Nabbed any bad guys yet?"

That was Black, now off his private line, but trust me, it'll ring again, give it three minutes. He is an important man, a buyer of five-star hotels and owner of exclusive psych clinics, a writer of best-selling self-help books, even, and last but not least, one helluva good lover and good-looking guy, to boot, with that black hair and those bluer than Montana sky-blue eyes. He actually drives a Humvee, believe it or not, and has a motor yacht moored mid-lake that is so magnificently apportioned it could earn its own article in the July issue of *Yachts Only Aristotle Onassis Could Afford.* He calls it the *Maltese Falcon* since he's such a big Dashiell Hammett fan. That's probably the reason he's spending so much time with me, my being a so-called primo homicide detective, and all. But I do enjoy his company and vice versa, it seems. In fact, things are pretty hot and heavy between us and have been for quite a while now. Indeed, we're from vastly different social and economic levels, but we rarely talk anymore about how we met, that being when he was my prime murder suspect and I was out to get him, come hell or high water.

I said, "We're not trying to nab, Black. We're trying to surveil and identify who's doing what. So far I've seen lots of drunk college kids playing loud music and making out, but no blatant drug exchanges. More like spring break at South Padre Island meets *Girls Gone Wild.*"

Black did some looking around, no doubt for the girls gone wild in question. "How much longer is this going to last? I'm getting hungry."

"Did I not see a big fridge down in the galley? Filled up with all your favorite gourmet foods? Make yourself a caviar sandwich or something to tide you over until we get done here."

Black lounged down beside me, all six foot three, deeply tanned hunkiness of him. He's part of my cover today, you see, we're yet another drunken couple playing loud music and getting touchy-feely at Party Cove. Only problem is, Black has his top-of-the-line satellite radio set on some kind of rhythm-and-blues station. I daresay we're the only kids today at Party Cove blaring Koko Taylor's "Piece of Man."

Otherwise, however, Black is playing his part exceedingly well indeed. With one hand, he took a drink from his icy long-neck Dixie Lager, imported by the truckload from his home-town, the Big Easy, no less, and groped my bare flesh a bit with the other. When he stopped the massage long enough to hand me an icy Wild Cherry Pepsi in a frosted crystal goblet, I decided that, yep, this guy knows my weaknesses. All he forgot was the frozen Snickers bars that I usually request, preferably the miniature kind.

Leaning back and resting his head on a dark blue boat cushion, he adjusted his aviator sunglasses that he bought when last seen skiing in St. Tropez. Not by me; I've never been there, of course, but somebody on those frosted vener-able slopes must've seen him, I'm sure. He shut his eyes and said, "Forgot to order your Snickers. Sorry."

See what I mean? This guy's hard to resist. He's wearing black swim trunks and nothing else, so I removed my eyes from my camera viewfinder long enough to admire all that sun-brown skin and nicely ridged six-pack. I'm on duty, right, but I'm not comatose and unresponsive. Later would come soon enough, but a quick peek doesn't hurt to tide me over.

I said, "Something gone awry at Buckingham Palace, I take it?"

Black kept his eyes closed but smiled, dimples galore, I tell you, the man's smile gives me tremors in the solar plexus, not to mention other delicate places. "They've got a problem with a patient. He's waking up from some very bad nightmares screaming bloody murder."

"Oh, yeah? I can relate."

"Right, but you've usually got me in bed to calm you down. This guy gets up and attacks the nearest woman."

"I see your dilemma."

That was true about him being in my bed, or lately, we've been waking up in his Sealey Posturepedic mother of all beds, custom designed, and I mean huge bed, over at his big lake resort called Cedar Bend Lodge. At least we sleep there together on the nights Black's at home and not off gallivanting around the globe doing very important things as he's wont to do. Truth be told, I'm glad to have him nearby when I wake up, all sweaty and shaky, or I might get up and attack some woman, too. The handguns we both keep handy under our pillows are a mite reassuring, too. Yessiree, our bed's a veritable shooting gallery waiting to happen. But better safe than sorry, I always say. That's why I have my big Glock 9 mm and .38 snub-nosed revolver right here on the deck beside me, mere inches from my right hand. I would've strapped them both on over my bikini, but that might give me some strange tan lines and my drug targets might notice.

Getting down to work again, I returned my attention to the myriad of drug-peddling suspects guzzling every imaginable kind of booze and raising hell all around us. "Keep down, Black, and put on your cap. You're too well known around the lake. If any of these guys recognize you, you'll get me made."

Unperturbed, Black lifted his head and snugged on his black fiber-optic cap. It had a gold New Orleans Saints logo on the crown that lit up at the touch of a tiny switch. Bud gave it to him as a thank-you for a great big life-or-death favor Black had done for him a couple of months back. He said, "They'll recognize you before they do me, Claire. You're the one whose picture keeps popping up in the papers for getting the bad guys."

"Ergo, that's exactly why I'm down here behind this rail with this nifty visor hiding my face."

"That visor's just about all you're wearing, too. Maybe you ought to keep down, just for modesty's sake."

Black, Black, getting a bit possessive now, yes, he is. I didn't care for that remark much, but he didn't push too hard about that kind of stuff, so I swiveled my camera back to where Bud was hiding with the departmental video cam. He was still hunkered down in the bushes, and I wouldn't be able to pick him out if I didn't know his location. I just hoped to hell he didn't rub up against any poison ivy. He's allergic, big-time, but never sees it soon enough. I addressed Black's crack about my skimpy apparel. "If I recall, Black, once upon a time you bought me this very string bikini and insisted I wear it day and night."

"That was at my private beach on Bermuda when you had casts on your arm and leg. It's different out here with a hundred guys on the lookout for visual stimulation."

More psychiatrist talk there. I felt his hand enjoying itself on my lower back, then farther down into my bikini bottom, what there was of it, also looking for stimulation, which it found pretty damn quick. After an enjoyable minute or two, I pushed his hand away, but not because I wanted to. "Later, Black, I'm working, remember."

His sigh sounded annoyed, almost reached the grumble level, but he relaxed back beside me with nary a profane mutter. "You're getting burned. Let me rub some lotion on you. Your skin's too white to stay out in the sun this long."

"Cut it out, Black, I'm slick as a seal, already. We can get our jollies tonight after Bud and I get this surveillance over with."

This time Black did mutter a low oath in the dialect of his New Orleans Cajun youth, which he didn't usually reveal but frustration sometimes brought out in him, then he got up and headed back into the square of shade thrown by the black canopy over the pilot's chair. When one of his three cell phones chirped softly, he carried it down the steps into the galley, no doubt looking for Beluga and French baguettes to munch on while analyzing a new batch of bizarre British dreamscapes.

Fully concentrated on my job now, I zeroed in on one boat that I found a trifle more suspicious than the others. Three Caucasian males lounged around, two young guys, one older, and by that, I mean late twenties/early thirties. All wearing knee-length swim trunks and baggy white T-shirts with American flags on the front. They had Old Glory on their baseball caps, too. How patriotic can drug dealers get? Or maybe that's how their strung-out clients recognized them.

All were drinking Budweiser beer and ogling half-naked women flaunting their stuff along the rocky beach and in the nearby boats. They were lounging around in a sleek black-and-white Tahoe Q8i with a MerCruiser 5.0, plenty fast enough to outrun most police boats but couldn't hold a candle to Black's Cobalt. Their craft was floating near a flotilla of about twenty boats tied together in the middle of the cove. College kids home for the summer and looking for action aka public nuisance citations. Our suspects had not tied on with the rest of the crafts. No doubt ready for a speedy getaway, just in case any cops such as myself and Bud were lurking around, just waiting to catch them when they whipped out a bag of crack cocaine to entice scantily clad beauties aboard. Of course, they could do that with beer, too, and probably already had. I clicked five or six photos, zooming in on their faces, tacky tattoos of various patriotic eagles and naked women holding lightning bolts, and one with the name of their boat. *Siren's Call*. How appropriate is that.

After that, I relaxed my tense shoulder muscles, rolled them around a bit, took a deep breath, then wiggled into about a two-inch spot of shade cast by the railing, where I did have an excellent position from which to observe. I swung the camera to the other end of the flotilla. A busty, half-naked girl was doing some kind of hoochie-coochie dance on the prow of her boat. She had on tall red cowboy boots with black fringe and a ten-gallon red cowboy hat with a black leather hat band about the same size as her bikini bottom. She whipped off her bikini top as I watched and swung it around like a rodeo porn star. I guess she forgot her lasso at home.

I restrained myself from taking a picture, then changed my mind and snapped a couple of her, just in case. But I do declare, what's the matter with these gals? Other than the fact that she was obviously drunk out of her mind, which could be a considerable factor, she wasn't breaking the law, other than an indecent exposure charge, maybe, which would break my cover if I busted her, so I guess she's gonna get to show off her wares. Which she did with a great deal of abandon and jiggly mammary pride.

I was a bit surprised, however, that the young man in the boat with her, obviously a boyfriend of sorts, was blatantly encouraging such behavior in his own personal girlfriend, but he seemed to be enjoying her gyrations as much as everybody else. Or maybe he was just her brother. I daresay Black wouldn't be so obliging if I flung off my top and did a jig, considering that jealousy thing he flares up with now and again. All around, I began to hear male catcalls floating in from every direction and boat horns honking with the old, approving "Oh yeah, take it off!" message. My, my, this girl must work at Hooters. If not, she should. And Bud, no doubt, had gotten it all down on film for posterity or to share in the squad room with the other guys, probably the latter.

I continued to surveil, not impressed with the size of her breast implants in the least, but now the sun was slowly dropping behind the tree line, ready for some downtime while the moon did its thing, I guess, but this party on the water was not going to break up until the wee hours of the morn, trust me. The boats might change their order, some kids might untie from the flotilla and speed away to barely make Mom and Dad's curfew, but just as many others would show up, dock on, and join in the fun. Nope, Party Cove was just getting started, and the longer it went into the night, the drunker and rowdier everybody got. That's why the sheriff had some of our deputies on undercover duty here each and every night all summer long, and I was just glad it wasn't me. I prefer the afternoon surveillance any time.

I spent a few minutes perusing the two honky-tonk bars inhabiting the cove, trying my best to luck upon a drug deal in progress. There were two bars, side by side, Manny's and the Kangaroo Trapeze, and let me tell you they sold more beer than Busch Stadium during the World Series. With dusk quickly approaching, it didn't appear as if we were going to get lucky and bust any criminal types, so I shifted a little, sat up, and drained the rest of my Wild Cherry Pepsi. It tasted sweet and cold, really good going down my dry throat. It was still humid, despite the fading day, and Black was right, I was sunburned all down my backside. That was gonna be great tonight in bed. Guess we'd have to get creative. What I really needed to do was hang it up for the day, jump off the stern platform, and cool off my bright red skin in the water.

I stretched cramped neck muscles a few seconds, then regained my position and refocused on my targets. The boat with the three white males had now picked up the cowgirl with the red boots and naked breasts, knowing something classy when they saw it, I suppose, and had just slid their boat into the sand directly in front of Bud. They were stowing gear and getting ready to jump to the beach and head on foot to the nearest bar. The girl was still topless, and she was not a gal who needed to go topless, believe you me, uh uh, and she was just so elegant with that giant tattoo of Dog the

Bounty Hunter on her right breast. I swiveled my telephoto lens to Bud and found him standing up in plain sight with the video camera in his hands, probably thinking that Dog tattoo was just too tempting not to get a close-up on tape.

Damn, it didn't take a genius to figure out he was filming them from the bushes and the reason why, and geniuses these three guys were not. They also weren't above beating Bud to a bloody pulp with a flag-painted baseball bat for ogling their foxy lady, so I decided to save Bud's bacon yet again. A bit of distraction was called for, so I jumped up, switched Black's radio on to a blasting rock station, then hit the Cobalt's horn a few times to get their undivided attention. All three guys and Dog's biggest fan turned around and stared at me, so I jumped up on the prow and began a rather clumsy, spraddled-legged rendition of Tina Turner's "Rollin' on the River" routine.

I'm not exactly Bojangles but I had enough naked flesh showing to make up for some pretty ugly dance steps, and it was too far for them to be turned off by the big hatchet scar decorating my shoulder. Luckily, the three stooges stood transfixed on the shore and watched me so I gyrated my hips as provocatively as I knew how and pretended that I was going to take off my top like the other girl had done. Catcalls erupted from a couple nearby boats, so I kept it up for a few minutes, doing a little kicking and strutting like I saw one of the girls at the Mustang Ranch do on an HBO special and feeling pretty much like an idiot.

"What the hell are you doing?"

That was Black, now up from below, frown on his face, cell phone still at his ear.

I looked to shore, found Bud safely out of sight, so I stopped and jumped down. "Don't be rude. I had to distract those guys over there because Bud blew his cover."

"Where did you learn something like that? What exactly was that, anyway?"

"It wasn't that bad."

"Yeah, it was. Remember that old *Seinfeld* episode when Elaine tried to dance? That's what you looked like."

Well, now, that was downright tacky and uncalled for. Dancing wasn't my thing and I knew it. But they hadn't picked up Bud filming them, and that's all I cared about. I watched until the foursome entered the front door of the Kangaroo Trapeze, which ended our surveillance and put it officially into the hands of our undercover colleague lurking at the bar. My little *Dancing with the Stars* routine had brought too much attention to me anyway. Time to go home. Shift over.

Black was still staring at me. "As horrible as that was, Claire, it still turned me on."

"So it wasn't all that bad, huh?"

"It doesn't take much where you're concerned. Even something like that is arousing."

I smiled. He smiled. My eyes lit up. His eyes lit up. My cell phone started up with "The Mexican Hat Dance" song. I smiled wider. He frowned, no doubt knowing his romantic plans were about to hit the dirt.

Caller ID identified Bud was on the line, so I picked up quickly and said, "Bud, that was a helluva dumb stunt. They almost made you."

Bud provided me with an earful of gut laughs. "I saw you tryin' to dirty dance. Cool. I didn't know you had it in you. I got it on film. The guys at the station are gonna love it."

"I humiliated myself in public so you wouldn't get beat up, Bud. Please don't ever make me do something that gross again. Why the hell did you show yourself?"

"Saw a snake. Thought I better get the hell out."

Well, now, that explained it well enough. Bud just got done with a serious, up-close-and-personal encounter with a nasty slitherer, not too long ago, either. I'm surprised he didn't run like hell. I suspect the topless Calamity Jane had something to do with that.

Bud said, "You looked sorta like Elaine did on that *Seinfeld* rerun."

I frowned. I was going to have to look up that show and see what they were talking about. "I wasn't that bad."

Bud laughed some more, but then he sobered and said, "Hey, I'm gettin' a call from dispatch. Hold on a sec."

He clicked off for about a minute, then he came back. "We gotta body. Somebody just called in a suicide at the Grand Glaize Bridge."

"Water patrol there?"

Black cursed under his breath, knowing the score from experience, but I was ready for a new case. And a suicide didn't usually shoot back. But who knows, the way our cases had gone lately, this one just might.

"Yeah, but the guy didn't jump. They found him hangin' under the bridge."

"You kidding me? He hung himself instead of jumping off?"

"Yep."

"That's a novel approach."

"Who hung himself?" asked Black.

I ignored him. "You gotta name on the vic, Bud?"

"Nope. They've got the bridge cordoned off, waitin' for us to get there."

"Where are you?"

"Just now gettin' to the Bronco."

"We'll meet you there." I glanced at Black for confirmation. He nodded, and now he looked interested, too. His blue eyes were all intense and excited, just like mine. We have that in common, you see.

Bud said, "Last one there buys Krispie Kremes, chocolate with nuts on top."

Now that sounded more like my old Bud. Food on the mind, competition in the blood, donuts on the breath.

"Get ready to eat our wake, Bud."

Bud hung up, and no doubt stomped the gas pedal.

Maybe we'd get lucky and he'd run into a traffic jam on his way across the lake.

I looked at Black. "We got a bridge suicide and I need to get there in a hurry. You up for it?"

"You bet."

Sometimes Black liked my job better than I did. I guess sitting around listening to people lying on couches and whining about their problems got old sometimes.

As Black expertly maneuvered the powerful Cobalt out of the cove and thrust the throttle to full speed, I jerked on a pair of jeans and black T-shirt over my bathing suit, laced up my high-top Nikes, strapped on both my weapons, looped the chain with my badge around my neck, and felt whole again. I stood next to him in the cockpit and enjoyed the speed and wind blowing through my short and sun-streaked blond hair, and the beautiful red and purple sunset swirled in an Impressionist painting above the trees on the far horizon as we skipped and roared our way across the lake at way too high a speed, but that's Black and his big, expensive toys for you.

Yeah, I was going to enjoy the ride over while I could because I sure as hell wasn't going to enjoy cutting down a suicide victim and telling some family their loved one was gone forever, in the blink of an eye, just like that, never to be seen alive again. Nope, not in my top ten list of fun things to do.

TWO

Minutes later we hit the channel and sped off toward the Grand Glaize Bridge, which carried Highway 54 through Osage Beach and over the Grand Glaize arm of the lake, one of the heaviest traveled areas of the county. Lots of rubber-necking Sunday boaters were there ahead of us, floating around the perimeter of the crime scene and trying to see what the police were up to. Water patrol had already cordoned off the area directly underneath the bridge and about thirty yards down each shoreline, but the contingent of the curious continued to gather gleefully as close as they could get, bobbing in the bouncing wakes of arriving police boats. At least twenty pairs of binoculars reflected in the setting sun like cat eyes glowing in a dark alley.

As we slowed to approach the sandy bank under the bridge supports, a water patrol officer cruised from gawker to gawker, breaking up the party. Luckily, not a single reporter was in sight, but that wouldn't last long. Black killed the motor and slid the Cobalt up onto the sand. As the hull scraped to a gradual stop, I climbed over the side, jumped out onto the bank, and peered up the hill, where a couple of our deputies were gathered around a concrete support, way, way up from us. I could also see the victim's body, swaying in a stiff breeze that was now blowing in over the water.

I said, "Better wait here until I know exactly what's going down."

Black didn't argue, just took a seat in the pilot's chair and twisted open another Dixie. He didn't get to take time off like this often, leisure hours when he could just loll around on a boat all day with me, not with all his business irons in the fire. Even though he was constantly on the phone, I think he was enjoying himself.

Picking my way around some large limestone rocks, I began the steep climb to the suicide scene. I could see Bud now, up top, looking over the side of the bridge. He'd made good time, too. He waved down at me, pointed to the crime site, and then disappeared from view. Every so often, we got a jumper in Canton County, but nobody had ever hanged themselves off the underside of a bridge, not since I'd been with the department. There's always a first time for everything, though. I sure had learned that the hard way.

Our other female deputy, Connie O'Hara, was on the scene ahead of me. She was short and blond and a killer shot with a rifle and a new baby boy named Tucker at home. She was a good cop, one who did her job well and by the book without a lot of drama going on. I liked her. When I approached, she nodded at me and said, "Bud comin'?"

"He's on his way down from up there." We both looked the forty-some-odd feet above us. "You got any ID yet, Connie?"

She shook her head. "Nobody's touched the body. But it looks like he's been out here since at least noon, maybe longer. He's in full rigor. He did it way up under there, so it's hard to see the body from the highway. Nobody reported him from the water, either, believe it or not."

I looked down the hill to where Black sat in the beached Cobalt. He was on the phone again but watching me through his high-powered binoculars. I turned back to O'Hara. "Strange place for a suicide, don't you think?"

She shrugged. "Yeah, I guess. You'd think he'd just take the leap and get it over with. It's far enough down to kill him and a helluva lot quicker."

We both judged the distance, and I wondered what it would feel like to fall that far and hit a solid sheet of water. Not good. Probably break a lot of bones, at the very least. "Has anybody called Buckeye Boyd?"

"We were waiting for you to get here before we called the ME. Want me to give him a call now?"

"Yeah, do that, would you? Tell him we got a body down here and ask him how fast he can get out to the bridge. You got his cell number?"

Connie nodded. "Okay, I'm on it."

As she started trudging up the nearly vertical incline, Bud was winding his way down through the big rocks and clinging brush toward me, sliding now and then on the loose gravel. Yeah, he's a bit of a klutz. Frowning, I moved to a spot where I could get a better visual on the body. The man hung suspended from a concrete crossbar, so far up under the bridge that he was more over solid ground than water. From the looks of it, the bottoms of his feet were no more than four or five feet off the steeply inclining hillside. I picked my way across the precarious slope to just underneath the victim and found that the rope around his neck was attached to a concrete shelf above him. Probably tied it up nice and tight, stood up, placed the noose around his neck, then jumped into hell. It probably would've broken his neck instantly.

"Whassup, Claire? I just heard Connie callin' in Buck."

That was Bud, almost to me now. He ran down the last few yards and pulled to a stop a few feet from me. He stared up at the victim and gave a long, low whistle. "Man, why the hell would he wanna end it this way?"

"Who knows? Wife left him, he lost all his money gambling,

was lonely, probably one of the usual reasons. Take your pick. Unless he left us a note and explained everything all nice-like in black-and-white. Now that'd be sweet, wouldn't it?"

"He's just a kid. Pretty young a guy to kick himself off. He's gotta be in his early twenties, maybe, twenty-five tops."

We moved in closer and gazed up at the dangling corpse. I avoided looking at the purple-blue color of his face. He was in rigor all right; his body was as rigid as a window mannequin. He wore a pair of navy blue Dockers and a yellow polo shirt, both neat and clean and pressed with creases in the sleeves and the pant legs. I could see the earring in his right ear, a large diamond stud that kept winking and blinking as he swung stiffly back and forth in the gusting wind. There was a cell phone on the ground about six feet below him.

"He dropped his cell. See it there, on the rocks?"

"Maybe he made a good-bye call. That oughta be helpful."

"Let's leave it until forensics get here. Maybe it'll give us a next of kin."

Bud said, "He looks like a clean-cut kinda kid. Clothes brand new by the looks of it and pressed up nice and neat, and that looks like a Ralph Lauren logo on his shirt. I'm guessing that's a Rolex watch on his wrist."

I said, "His tennis shoes aren't even scuffed, white as the day he bought them, not even much wear on the soles. He's no blue-collar workingman, believe me."

"Maybe he's a student down at Missouri State in Spring-field. Up here to off himself so we'd have something to do tonight."

"Just our luck. What's all that stuff on his arms?"

"Looks like a bunch of bracelets. What is it, blue and white beads? Man, I bet he's got twenty on each arm."

"What's up with that? Have you ever seen anybody wearing that many bracelets?"

"Hell, no. I've never seen anybody wearing even one that looks like those."

My cell phone erupted into song, and I jerked it off my belt and read Black's name on caller ID. I punched him on and peered down at him where he now stood in the stern of the boat. He had me focused in again with those high-powered binoculars. Made me feel like an amoeba under a microscope.

He said, "You ID'd the victim yet?"

"No. We're waiting for Buck to cut the rope and lay out the body."

"I'm pretty sure I know who it is."

Okay, now that hit me like a king-size wallop. "How'd you know who he is? Can you see him that well?"

"Yeah. I'm looking at his face right now, poor kid. He looks exactly like a boy I treated several years ago. If it's who I think it is, his name is Michael Murphy. He's probably around twenty-one or twenty-two now."

"Michael Murphy? Why does that ring some kind of bell for me?"

"Could be because his father is Joseph Murphy, one of the chief political advisors to the governor. He's on the news all the time, loves the cameras. If you'll recall, he was the chief strategist for Governor Stanton's last campaign, the one he won big-time, in a landslide, remember? Another thing, the Murphy family is old money. They own most of the real estate in downtown Jefferson City. They've got a lot of holdings in Kansas City, too, and they own some properties around the lake. That's how I got to know them. We had a couple of investment projects we worked together."

"Oh, that Joseph Murphy. A big politico honcho, huh? Sleazy, maybe? Great."

"That's the rumor but I never saw anything unethical going on. The press hates his guts, and vice versa, so they'll jump all over this. Just thought I'd warn you."

"Gee, that's wonderful news, Black. Bud's gonna be thrilled." Bud noticed my sarcasm; he has an ear for it after several years as my partner. I said to him, "Black says this guy's name is Michael Murphy, son of the great Joseph Murphy, best bud to the governor."

"That the rich guy from Jeff City? The one who's always on TV? He comes off as a real creep."

I nodded. "Black says he's pretty sure it's that guy's son." I spoke to Black again. "Can you be certain, Black? Without coming up here for a closer ID?"

"You used these binoculars, Claire. It's like I'm standing right next to him. It's Mikey, I'd bet my life on it."

"Mikey?"

"That's what he liked to be called. Insisted on it, actually. His family called him that, too."

"You remember his address?"

"I can get it for you quick enough. Want me to call Miki on her cell and have her look it up for you?"

"Yeah, we're gonna have to notify next of kin ASAP. He married?"

"Not when I treated him. He'd just gotten dumped by a girlfriend and was depressed about it. That's why he came to see me, but I referred him to a colleague."

"Why?"

"His parents asked me to. They wanted him to receive therapy up in Jeff City at a clinic specifically designed to treat teenagers. They knew one of the doctors there."

"What doctor?"

"Martin Young. He's one of the resident psychiatrists and the name of the clinic is Oak Haven. It's sort of an old-fashioned-type sanitarium for teenagers. They specialize in young people suffering depression and anxiety, especially those who come in with suicide attempts or suicidal tendencies. It's a residential program with intensive counseling and academic classes, so they don't get behind in their studies while they're there. It's got a good reputation in the state. Pricey, though, but they get good results, at least that's what I hear."

"The results weren't exactly spectacular this time, I'd say. Okay, we'll check it out. Here comes Buck and the guys. Go on home and get something to eat, and I'll call you later. Bud and I have to notify the family. What time do you fly out for New York?"

"Tomorrow before noon. I'll hang out here a little while, then I'll take off. Call me if you want me to pick you up later."

"Gotcha."

Silence for a second or two, then Black said, "This's a damn shame, Claire. I thought Dr. Young could get him through his problems."

"Yeah, this kid's way too young to die. See you later."

"Duck and weave, baby. Don't call me from the hospital again."

Black's way of telling me to be careful. "Check. Talk to you later."

I flipped the phone shut and waited for Buckeye Boyd to navigate the rough terrain down to us. His bushy white hair looked uncombed and messy, probably because the wind was having its way with it, but his beard and mustache were black and close shaven and always impeccably groomed. He was still gimpy from a fall he'd taken on a slippery dock at the last bass fishing tournament he'd entered. He'd won the first-place trophy and lined it up with all his others, but had limped around for weeks. He was scowling big-time at having to negotiate the steep slope, no doubt because he was going to miss *American Idol* or *Survivor*. He really dug all those reality shows. Connie was right behind him.

Shaggy was right behind her, toting his aluminum case. He was limping, too, because he'd gotten shot up pretty bad a few months back, which happened in the same hairy situation with Bud's girlfriend, but he was getting back into the groove now. He'd made some stupid decisions and paid dearly for them, and he wasn't the same any more, not the crazy, easygoing surfer pseudo beach boy of days past. At least, he wasn't back to his old ways yet. I hoped he would be there again one of these days. But he gave me the old grin, and I returned it. Behind those eyes, though, there was this haunted look that wasn't going away, not anytime soon, anyway.

Truthfully, I was beginning to wonder if we all weren't wearing that same expression lately, at least people who hung around me too long. Maybe all the death and destruction in my job was finally getting to me. Maybe I needed to get out of homicide for a while and become a patrol cop and stop speeders, but I knew I wouldn't do that. I couldn't let go of the hunt. I lived for finding the killers I pursued and really got off on putting them behind bars, if they didn't end up six feet under first.

Bud and I stood back and said nothing as the forensics team joined us one by one. We watched Vicky, the department photographer, do her thing from every angle, fast and efficient as usual. Nobody said much. Maybe we were getting pretty fed up with finding and tagging dead bodies. Even though this wasn't a murder but a suicide, it was just as hard to stomach when the vic was little more than a teenager.

Once the body was cut down and lowered to the ground, Buckeye searched through the victim's preppy clothes and found in his front pants' pocket a current driver's license and a small metal ring with three keys, two neatly labeled with white tape: car and front door, the third left unlabeled. No wallet, no good-bye note, no money, nothing, just empty pockets and the driver's license and keys. Odd thing, though, were those bracelets. They were made out of blue and white beads, some with black dots in the middle that looked almost like eyes, the kind of bracelets made from elastic that stretched over your hands. I counted twenty-six of them. Thirteen on each arm. That number could not be coincidental.

Buck examined the driver's license, then held it up between two gloved fingers. "Name's Michael Murphy. Twenty-one years old. Photo matches, so do vitals."

I said, "Black was right on."

Buck said, "The cell phone's brand new. No outgoing, no

incoming. It's one of those phones you buy minutes for. We'll see if we can find fingerprints for you."

"Good."

Bud said, "Wonder why the kid didn't leave a note?"

"Maybe he didn't expect to be found. Maybe he thought nobody would ever find him. That's why he came up so far under the bridge support. Maybe he left it at home."

"Who did find him?" I turned to Connie O'Hara for that answer.

"Some kids playing basketball over there on that playground." She pointed to a little park off to our right, one with a basketball court surrounded by a twelve-foot chain-link fence. "They were playing one-on-one and the ball went through a gap in the fence and rolled down this way. When one of the boys came down the hill searching the brush for it, he saw the vic hanging over here. Scared him to death, so they all ran like hell to where one of their moms worked at the Applebee's just down the road. She called in to 911."

"Okay. Buck, let us know what you find out. Bud and I need to go check out this guy's house. Hopefully, we'll get a note."

Below I heard the Cobalt crank up, and I waved to Black and watched him ease the boat from the bank and speed off toward Cedar Bend Lodge. Then I turned and followed Bud up the hill to his Bronco. I was not particularly looking forward to telling this kid's parents what he'd gone and done on this beautiful summer day.

As it turned out, Michael Murphy, Son of the Great One at the Capitol, ran a pizzeria called Mikey's Place in Osage Beach on Highway 54. It was located in the Stonecrest Shopping Center, and we assumed he lived in the apartment right above the restaurant. Bud pulled up and stopped right in front of the pizzeria's front door. The Stonecrest Book and Toy store was a few doors down, and I knew some of the ladies there because I shopped for presents for Bud and Black at that store once upon a time. We'd have to check them out and see what they knew about Mikey Murphy. There was also a Starbucks out in the center of the parking lot, which made us both crave some latte and cinnamon rolls, but we decided to put the brakes on that idea until after we had given notification of the death. Only problem with that is we probably won't be able to stomach any by then. My own personal kind of diet.

The front door key on Murphy's key ring fit the front door of the pizza place, labeled appropriately, for our convenience, I guess. The pizza parlor was closed up and deserted. We knocked a couple of times anyway, just in case he had a roommate or live-in girlfriend asleep upstairs or tossing pizza dough in the back. Traffic was still going strong on 54 in front of the Stonecrest Shopping Center, and we stood waiting for a few minutes. I was hoping there wasn't anybody inside to break this horrible news to. I wasn't good at notifying next of kin, loathed every minute of it, would rather have ten root canals in a row, oh, yeah.

Bud said, "Somebody must be in there. I smell food cooking. Barbeque, maybe."

Looked like my hopes weren't panning out. "Yeah, but this is a pizza place and the closed sign is sitting right there in the window."

"Doesn't mean somebody can't be cooking dinner for when this poor guy was supposed to get home. Or maybe he likes Crock-Pots. Let's go in."

Bud pushed open the door, and we entered the dark interior of the restaurant. Cautiously, of course—we weren't stupid. I didn't pull my gun, either of them, actually, because I neither sensed nor expected danger. At least not until my sixth sense quivered alive and poked me in the back and said something to the effect of *"get the hell out of here quick."* At that point, I decided to stop just inside the door and take weapon to hand. When I did that, Bud did, too. We're a team, you see. We both looked around. Bud called out a guarded hello.

It was dark and gloomy inside, not a large place but probably nice and cheery when open for service, with lots of tables with red-checked vinyl tablecloths and red booths along each wall. Baskets of red and white checked napkins and crocks of silk red geraniums on every table and white candles melting down over empty Chianti bottles. There was a long bar at the back with lots of neon signs advertising Busch and Bud Light and Coors, but it was very quiet except for some low and steady electronic beeps emanating from somewhere in the back.

"You hear that, Bud?"

"The beeping? Yeah."

"What is it?"

"Dunno, but it's comin' from back there, behind those black swinging doors. Probably some timer goin' off in the kitchen, maybe?"

We headed for the swinging doors off to the right side of the bar that probably led into the kitchen. Suddenly I felt another little warning chill and waited while it crawled its way up my spine and made the back of my neck feel all stiff and icy. The smell of cooking meat was even stronger now. I looked at Bud, and he nodded. We held weapons ready and entered the kitchen like it was Daniel's lion's den. The room was as big as the dining area, but clear of danger. The oven light was blinking red and making the steady beeps. There was a big metal oven rack lying on a large center island topped with black granite, and I moved around the counter, then bent down and peered inside the glass door of the giant pizza oven.

My stomach rolled, heaved up some bile. I backed up, stunned, not sure I believed my eyes. "Oh, my God, Bud, tell me that's not what I think it is in there."

Bud said, "What? Lemme see."

"Look inside there and tell me what that is."

Bud rounded the island but didn't peer inside anything. He grabbed the oven handle and jerked the door down. Oh yeah, nightmares incomin'. Horrified, we both stared at what lay inside. Someone had stuffed a body in there. A woman, small and naked, bent, almost folded into a fetal position. The oven control was set on low, and by the looks of it, she had been roasting inside for a long, long time. Her skin was brown and crusty and I could smell the singeing of her long dark hair. I felt more caustic sting of acid in the back of my throat and gagged reflexively.

"Turn it off, Bud, turn it off, quick, oh my God! I'm gonna be sick!"

Bud slammed the door and switched off the control, and we both rushed outside, away from the odor and the awful sight, hands shaking and sick to our stomachs. Out in the fresh air, I bent over with my hands on my knees and took some deep breaths to stop the nausea that was tossing around that Cherry Pepsi inside my stomach. Oh, God, I was gonna throw up. I was used to gruesome crime scenes, but this? This was depraved, inconceivable. Bud paced off down the sidewalk, stood ten yards up from me alone for several minutes, dragging his palms down over his face, clearing his throat, over and over, then he came back, pacing back and forth in front of me, trying to walk off the horror we'd just discovered. He shook his head, put his hands on his hips. "Who the hell do you think that is in there?"

I rubbed my fingers over my mouth, still almost tasting the odor of the woman's roasted flesh. I swallowed hard, trying to get a grip, but this time it was hard. I finally said, "I don't know. How could somebody do that to somebody else? Stick them in an oven and cook them like that. God, who could do that?"

Bud said, "Some sick, psycho, sonofabitch, is who. I'm callin' Buck. He's gotta get over here and get her outta there. I can't stand havin' her in there, slow cookin' like that."

Now that we knew what the smell was, it was unbearable. We both backed away from the front door, and I waited while Bud got the crime scene tape out of his Bronco. We strung it up around the front. Neither of us spoke. Neither of us wanted to go back inside.

I finally said, "We've gotta check out the apartment. There might be somebody up there, another victim, maybe. Maybe one who's still alive."

Bud looked at me like I'd suggested going inside and ordering a pizza. He didn't want to see that body again. And I sure as hell didn't. I'd probably never want to eat in any restaurant again, I can tell you that, much less a Pizza Hut. But we had to check out the second-floor apartment, had no choice, and God only knew what we'd find up there.

Here Comes Trouble

It took forever for his parents to get over Lyla drowning. Much too long, the son thought, downright irritated. Jeez, what was with all the crying and carrying on and mourning, like it was gonna go on for years? He tried to divert his family's attention away from Lyla's death by winning medals and trophies and that kinda stuff, but no, no, it was always poor Lyla, poor Lyla died so young, poor Lyla, poor Lyla, poor Lyla. It really did just make him sick to his stomach.

Time went by, dragged, in fact, and eventually his mom had a new baby, another girl, and they named her Destiny. He thought they went overboard with that lame name, but hey, they thought God had given them a new little daughter to make up for taking dear little Lyla away. His parents could be so naïve.

Sometimes he wonderèd where he got his brains. Both his parents were dumb as rocks. Heck, he could pull about anything over on them, anything at all, including his sister's murder. Not that he particularly looked at it as murder; she just had to die young, that's all, no real reason why. It was just in the cards for her. Her predestined life plan. He was just an instrument in it, that's all. Sometimes things happened that were just plain inexplicable. But still, he was a lot more intelligent than anybody else in his family. And they were easy to manipulate. After all, they idolized him, and for very good reason.

One summer when he had grown older, his dad decided to take the whole family on a vacation to Arizona. Unfortunately, after Lyla drowned, they had closed up the pool for good, even filled it in with dirt, and never had another family barbeque in their backyard. That seemed a bit extreme to him, but hey, what could he do? He was still a minor and they could boss him around. The drive out west was pretty uneventful and boring, but they took his mom's big Dodge van so all the kids could have a seat belt. She was really paranoid about keeping all the kids safe now. All the younger kids bickered constantly, but it didn't bother him much. He had earphones and an iPod and he'd downloaded hundreds of songs that he liked, so all he did was listen to music.

The son loved music. His favorite rock band was one from Germany because they had these really dark and disturbing lyrics. They were right up his alley. He loved to read books, too. He liked geography and learning about other countries and cultures and what the people who lived there did. He loved learning about everything. His dad said he had a photographic memory, and he was dead on. All the son had to do was read something one single time, and he had it forever. Could almost quote it verbatim, even. Talk about smart; he'd cornered the market.

Now they were all out sightseeing at the Grand Canyon because his dad and mom loved to hike trails with beautiful scenery around to look at, and the son found it awesome to the extreme. His dad had gotten them all tickets on this cool old-fashioned train that took them up to the Grand Canyon from their hotel in Phoenix, which was the old, fancy one called the Biltmore. Right now they were hiking down one of the canyon's narrow, dusty trails with a bunch of other people. The place was really something, with all those high drop-offs and craggy cliffs that shone in the bright sun with beautiful, horizontal bands of reds and yellows and coppers and browns. Far, far away, and way down on the floor of the canyon, he could see the Colorado River, and it looked like a shiny ribbon in the sunlight. He loved it here. For once, his parents had chosen a really awesome place to visit.

Avidly, he listened to the guide who was telling them all about the history of the Grand Canyon, but he lagged behind the group with his mother, a little concerned about her health. She was a good athlete, too, that's where he thought he probably got his skills, but she was still a little out of shape from giving birth a couple of months ago, so she had to stop a lot and rest. He worried that she was gonna poop out and not be able to finish the hike, so he decided to give her a hand.

"Hey, Mom, let me carry Destiny some. You're tired. I can tell. She's gotta be getting heavy."

"That's okay, sweetie, I like holding her. I just need to rest a minute, 's all."

His mom sat down in the shade of a little scruffy pine tree that was growing out the side of the canyon. His dad was already about ten or fifteen yards ahead of them down the twisting trail that ran precariously along the edge of the cliff, and the son yelled down to him.

"Hey, Dad, Mom's gotta sit down and rest for a sec. I'll stay with her. You go on ahead with the other kids. We'll be along in a few minutes."

"You sure, honey?" his dad called back to his wife.

"I'll be fine. Go on, but watch the kids around that guard-rail."

The son pulled a bottle of Ozarka water out of his back-pack and handed it to his mom, and then while she unscrewed the cap and drank about half real quick, he stood looking out over the vast vista of wind- and water-carved canyon and marveled at how deep it was, and how pretty. It almost took his breath away. His mom put down the bottle and cooed at the baby, who was crying and squirming around, as usual.

His mom said, "Thanks for waiting with me, sweetheart. You've really been great on this trip."

"Yeah, I know," he answered.

They laughed together at that, and she smiled fondly at him. He stood and watched her deal with the fussy baby. She carried the kid in one of those mesh sling things that held the baby tightly against her chest. It looked hot, and so did she. Her face was flushed scarlet with the heat and the exertion of hiking the trail in her weakened condition. She hadn't slept much the night before because of the baby having colic, and her eyes were bloodshot with sleep deprivation. New babies were such a big pain in the butt.

"Here, Mom, let me hold her for a while. You look really hot."

"She's just hungry. Do you see anybody coming down from above?"

He glanced up the trail behind them. "Uh uh, we're the last ones in the group. The next one doesn't start for forty-five minutes."

"Then I'm going to feed her while I sit here and rest. Then she'll be quiet for the rest of the way down."

"Okay."

The son watched her open her sleeveless white blouse, open this special bra she wore, and put her breast up to the baby's mouth. The child grabbed at her nipple and began to suckle like crazy, and he looked away, repulsed. That was just so gross. It made him queasy in the pit of his stomach. He couldn't believe his mom would do something like that out in public, and in broad daylight, too. He looked both directions again and was glad nobody was in sight. He sat down at the overlook point and gazed out over the panorama, wishing she'd get done with that nursing crap.

His mom said, "Don't get too close to the edge, honey."

"I won't."

"Are you enjoying the trip?" his mom asked him then from where she was still sitting on the ground nursing Destiny in the shade of that little tree.

"Yeah. Sure."

"You don't seem very happy lately. You know, you've been kinda quiet the last few days."

"Just listenin' to my music."

"What are you listening to?"

"Marilyn Manson. I like him pretty good. That's who I've been playing today."

"I'm glad we got you that iPod. You're sure putting it to good use."

"Yeah."

The son looked back at his mom and said, "Come on, Mom, let me hold her for a while. I like to hold her. That contraption you're wearing looks real hot. You've gotta be uncomfortable."

His mom laughed again. "It is hot. She feels like a little heater up against me."

Walking over, he waited for her to lift the strap over her head, and then he took the little baby and held it in one arm. She was about the size of a St. Bernard puppy. She probably didn't weigh ten or twelve pounds yet. Destiny was quiet now and looked up at him out of dark blue, unblinking eyes.

As his mother leaned back against the rocks and closed her eyes, he examined the baby's face. Destiny really didn't look much like Lyla. She was kinda cute, though, he guessed. Her hair was darker, but it was hard to tell because all babies looked just the same to him. He really hadn't paid much attention to her before. She was pretty useless, but it was kinda neat how people started out like little lumps of nothing and grew tall and strong and athletic like him.

His mom was dozing now, so she must've been really exhausted from keeping up with Destiny. He walked back to the very rim of the canyon and gazed out over the vast and magnificent hole carved into the earth. Then he held the little baby up so she could see all the pretty colors. "Lookee out there, Destiny, that's the Grand Canyon. See that little bitty ribbon down there, that's the river that carved this place out like this. It took it millions of years."

The baby gurgled a little and waved her little arms, and he glanced at his mom. She was lying back on the ground now with her forearm over her eyes. Who was she kidding? She was really tired. Having another baby sure had taken it out of her. It suddenly occurred to him to hold the kicking child over the guardrail to see if it would know to be afraid. The baby just hung there from his fist and looked around. Actually, it calmed down a bit. It sure was a stupid little thing. One slip of his hand and it would fall fast and hard, straight down. Or it was so little, he could just throw it out over the drop with his perfectly executed spiral football pass. Heck, he bet it was one or two hundred feet to the bottom. It'd be dead on the first bounce against all those sharp rocks.

"Omigod, what are you doing?"

His mom was awake now and on her feet flying right at him. He brought the baby back over the ground and handed it over to her, glad to get rid of it. His mom grabbed it and glared at him.

"Are you out of you mind? What were you thinking? You could've dropped her!"

He thought his mom was overreacting a bit, but she was its mom and she didn't know how firm a grip he'd had on it. He could have held on for ten or fifteen minutes before he had to let it drop. That's how strong his biceps were from lifting all those weights.

His mom was still pretty pissed off. "You know better than to pull a stunt like that! Are you crazy?"

Well, he didn't like that crazy crack much. "It's not that far down, Mom. There's a little shelf right under this cliff that would've stopped her, if I'd dropped her, but I didn't, now did I?"

"Now don't you get smart with me, young man. You just did a very stupid, irresponsible thing. I can't believe you did that. And I'm going to tell your dad, you better believe it!"

She was acting so upset that she nearly dropped the baby herself, and the kid's blanket came out of the mesh cradle thing and fell in the dirt. When his mom bent over to get it, Destiny in one arm, he snatched Destiny away from her, then shoved his mom hard in the chest with his palm. She went over the cliff backward, her face so shocked by what he'd done that she didn't have time to put up a struggle at all; she just gave a short scream and fell like a rock down through the air.

A few seconds later, she hit that first outcropping of rocks, glanced off it, and somersaulted like a rag doll about halfway down the canyon before she came to a stop on a narrow ledge. She was probably already dead. The baby was crying now and he rocked it gently in his arms. He had an urge to toss the little kid over, too, and he started to do it, but then he decided that might not look right. He'd seen the crime shows on television where the CSI people could tell if a mother had been holding a baby when she fell by how far apart they landed and stuff like that. Maybe he ought to hold on to the baby and tell everybody he'd saved Destiny's life when his mom tried to take the baby down with her. Yeah, that sounded really good. Liked she'd jumped and committed suicide. It would make him come off as a real-live hero.

Belatedly, he glanced around, afraid somebody might have appeared at the top bend of the trail when he wasn't aware of them, but nobody had. He was pretty lucky sometimes. He looked down the cliffs again and saw that his mom still wasn't moving and her arms and legs were all twisted around in impossible angles. There was blood on her, too. All was quiet, so he guessed she really was dead. He thought about that a second and wondered if he shouldn't have done it. She *was* his mother, after all. Then he thought, well, so what? She shouldn't have threatened to tell his dad. He sure wasn't about to get grounded for holding Destiny over the drop, not with the baseball championship play-offs coming up as soon as they got back home.

Dad had enough kids anyway, and he'd saved Destiny for his dad to have. And his dad could find a new wife easy enough with all his money. Maybe a younger and prettier one. A tragedy like this would probably bring him and his dad closer together, anyway. It would be the best for everybody, except his mom, of course. But now she'd be with Lyla in heaven. She'd like that better than being alive, anyway, the way she'd been carrying on since Lyla died.

Standing there alone for a moment, he thought about how he was going to explain this one, and then he decided to just tell everybody that she'd tried to kill her baby but he'd grabbed Destiny in time, and she'd just jumped off in despair and committed suicide before he could stop her. He'd heard of postpartum depression, and he'd heard his dad ask her if she was having that once when she'd been crying and getting all hysterical up in their bedroom. She'd told him that she was thinking about Lyla, but hey, this idea was gonna work out just fine. Who in the world would ever suspect him of killing his own mom?

Mustering up a suitable amount of tears, he started down the trail at a run, yelling hysterically for his dad.

THREE

"Okay, Bud, we gotta check out Mikey's apartment, so let's just do it and get it over with."

Bud did not look enthused, to say the least, and I sure as hell wasn't champing at the bit to go inside and climb those stairs, either, uh uh, no way. But we needed to go up there and make sure no other victim was frozen solid in the freezer or slow cooking in a Crock-Pot or anything else equally grotesque. Ever heard of Jeffrey Dahmer, anyone?

Donning latex gloves and protective booties, we reentered the silent pizzeria and found the staircase that led to the second floor at the rear of the restaurant. The door at the base of it was unlocked and standing open, which I considered a good sign. Nobody locked in, nobody not wanting to be found, nobody hiding in a closet with a machete, I hoped.

Bud said, "I'll take the lead."

He was probably itching to shoot whoever had done this, but I didn't argue. I stayed right on his heels as he inched slowly up the narrow steps to the door at the top. It was closed but also unlocked. We both drew our weapons, just in case, not about to become some psycho's next baked entree.

Bud went in high and fast, me low, through a clicking, clinking curtain of red and blue Oriental beads that hung from the top of the door frame. It sounded like a bunch of scorpions scratching in a box, which I'd heard before, believe it or not, and it was loud enough to herald our presence to any lurking maniacs. Luckily, the apartment was as empty and silent as the restaurant below. Mikey's living room was dark. In the deep gloom I made out a table lamp, headed for it, switched it on, and beheld Shangri-La.

Bud said, "I do believe our little Mikey might've been a Chinaman underneath all those preppy clothes. Don't know why, just a hunch."

I agreed. It appeared we had entered the Chinese Pavilion at Epcot Center or Scheherazade's harem, take your pick. Silk adorned the walls, Chinese red, lots of black enameled tables, low ones, close to the floor with ornate carved designs. A thick, aromatic scent, strong incense, to be exact, hung heavily in the air, almost, but not quite, blocking out the horrible odor of roasting human flesh rising from the kitchen below. Maybe that cloying sweet aroma was coming from Mikey Murphy's giant incense burner, one that had about a dozen sticks of incense sticking at various angles in some white sand, all still smoking and burnt about halfway down. More like a bloodred oriental urn, it sat inside the hearth and was about the size of a small microwave. An even bigger and shinier black statue of Buddha sat beside it, and the lush red satin panels with intricate black embroidery that draped the fireplace turned it into an altar and uncontested centerpiece of the room.

"That smell is sandalwood," said Bud.

"How do you know? Got a pagoda down in the Georgia woods somewhere?"

"I used to date this girl from the Philippines. She always smelled just like this. Her apartment, too. She told me it was an aphrodisiac."

Well, that was a new one on me. "No kidding?"

"That's what she said. Worked for me, I can tell you. Ready to check this place out?"

"Yeah."

In our usual tandem effort, we edged around opposite walls toward the next room. He took the hallway leading deeper into the apartment, and I took the dining room. They were clear, and when Bud called an okay from somewhere in back, I sheathed the Glock in my shoulder holster and examined the place. Michael Murphy had a nice little dining room, same red silk walls, no windows, but a big black lacquered table and china cabinet with a single blue and white Oriental tea set on a woven wicker tray sitting behind the glass doors. There were some bamboo place mats on the table, four in all and replete with place settings, black square dishes, and chopsticks. A real live orchid sat in the middle. In full bloom and well cared for.

Lots and lots of various sized Buddhas sat around looking fat and happy, and a particularly beautiful midnight blue silk hanging of Buddha in front of a lake with snow-capped peaks in the background decorated nearly the whole wall at the end of the table. A bit incongruously, there were lots of amulets hanging around on the walls, too, one about every four feet on a parallel line, made of the same blue and white beads with black dots, twins of the multiple bracelets on Mikey Murphy's stiff, dead arms.

I walked over, pulled one of them off the wall, and examined its fine craftsmanship.

"Looks like something ugly went down in the kitchen," Bud said from the doorway.

"You find another body?"

"No, but something happened in there, believe me. Come see."

I held up the amulet and said, "First, take a look at this, Bud. Look familiar to you?"

Bud walked over and took it from my hand. "What'd you

think? A good-luck piece? Maybe the guy was superstitious. Thought somebody was after him."

"Yeah? Well, I'm beginning to think he was right. Look around. He's got them hanging up everywhere."

"Maybe they're just the opposite, maybe they're evil amulets fighting off good. Makes more sense, judging by what's gone down around this nutcase."

"But why so many? He's got them everywhere. I bet there's fifty or more. That's pretty much overkill, don't you think?" I winced at my own terminology. Overkill was an understatement for the poor girl downstairs.

Bud shrugged. "C'mon, I want you to get a load of this guy's kitchen."

"Oh, God, the stove's not on, is it?"

"Just come and see for yourself."

I pushed through another shiny black swinging door and looked around. It was clean, modern, but turned completely upside down, stainless steel pots and pans thrown everywhere, on the counters, floors, in the sink. The oven door was open but nothing was inside, thank God, and every other cabinet door stood open, everything inside out on the counters, as if somebody had been scrubbing down the kitchen shelves. The refrigerator door was hanging open, fully stocked with all kinds of food. Not exactly the sign of an impending suicide. The weirdness of the scene was punctuated by a big spotlight pouring down on a white Buddha fountain in the middle of the center island, its quiet tinkling and soft splashes the only sounds in the silent apartment. More bamboo, silk embroidered hangings, and many, many strange silver-threaded, blue and white beaded charms hanging on the cabinet knobs. But no Crock-Pots, pressure cookers, or stockpots steaming with human body parts to be seen. God was good, or Buddha, in this case.

Bud said, "This place looks like a cyclone hit it."

"Or somebody looking for something."

Bud nodded. "There's just one bedroom. Through there."

I kept thinking some evil Mandarin overlord dressed in a long crimson robe was gonna jump out and get us with a curved scimitar, then dance through the air on tree branches, because that's the kind of thing that's been happening to Bud and me of late, but my stomach wasn't quivering, my nerves weren't on edge, and more important my trigger finger wasn't twitching. I kept my hand on the butt of my Glock anyway, just in case my sixth sense was taking a break, you understand. Or Jackie Chan showed up.

We entered the bedroom, which was also ransacked, and I looked at the large round bed covered by a lush black velvet spread that had been thrown onto the floor. A giant Chinese symbol was embroidered in the middle, one that I am sure means something really gross. Red silk sheets were torn off the bed, too, and lots, and I mean LOTS, of velvet and silk tasseled pillows were scattered around all over the place. I wondered where the hell this guy found huge round red satin bedsheets at Lake of the Ozarks. But then again, his father was purportedly as rich as Oprah, so maybe he'd gotten them in his Christmas stocking or the Buddhist equivalent of Bed Bath & Beyond. Or maybe Oprah gave them to him at her favorite things show.

"Think he's got enough freakin' pillows?" Bud asked.

I looked back at the bed. "I'd say thirty or forty at the most, but that's just on the bed. Gotta be twenty over there on the floor for emergencies."

"I have a feeling overnight guests here don't get to leave in the morning. Not in one piece," Bud said.

I tried to force a smile, but it didn't quite come off. We were trying, but making light of the situation wasn't gonna happen. This crime was too horrific. I doubt if I'd be laughing any time soon, either, not that I ever did much. When I heard a vehicle pull up outside followed by the slamming of doors, I moved to the living room window, pulled back a silken drape, and saw Buckeye Boyd hustling his team inside the front door.

"Buck's here."

"Good, now they can get that girl outta that oven."

"Okay. Let's look around some more and see what turns up."

There was a closet in the bedroom, actually more of an old-fashioned freestanding wardrobe. I opened it and found men's clothes, many torn off the hangers, but all the same: preppy and pressed. Nary a black silk Marco Polo gown in sight. No tasseled silk hats, either, or woks, for that matter. He probably kept those in the kitchen, anyway.

Bud was going through the dresser and finding nada of interest. I poked through some drawers that had been left open in a bureau with a big round mirror. There were four blue and white beaded amulets hanging on the mirror; many, many more were tacked around on the walls. This guy had some serious issues. Trust me on that.

I said, "Mikey had a real problem with keeping his home protected, if that's what these things are for. He should've just called Brink's Home Security. Lot less gaudy."

"Maybe he was trying to keep his victims' ghosts at bay. Maybe he hung up one of those things for every victim he offed."

"Well, that's a pleasant thought, Bud. If I were some girl he brought up here, I'd start whistling psycho the minute I clicked my way through those beaded curtains."

Bud said, "Yeah, but you're not strung out on dope like they probably were. Take a look at this."

I turned around. Bud was holding up a gallon Ziploc bag of fine white powder. He said, "He's got to be a dealer with a stash this big."

"Where'd you find it?"

"In that big red ginger jar."

"What's a ginger jar?" He pointed to the thing. I said, "How the hell do you know what it's called?"

Bud said, "Mom made me one at her china painting class. I keep my bullets in it. Not into ginger much."

"I keep my ammo clips in a walnut bowl on my bedside table."

"That's handy." Bud was reaching down into the jar again. "Oh, boy, look what else Mikey's got hidden away. Lots of little plastic Ziplocs to make up all his little eight balls. I think we got a drug thing going down here, Claire."

"Looks that way. But why wouldn't whoever tossed this place take the drugs? It stands to reason that's what they'd be after."

"Good question," said Bud.

For some reason I was more intrigued by the amulets, or whatever the hell they were. I had a hunch they played a big part in this thing, whatever it turned out to be. I turned over the beaded charm in my hand and didn't find a label or signature, but I didn't give up. When I got to a very large one hanging on the wall over the bed, presto, there it was.

"This was made in Branson."

"You gotta be kiddin'. A Chinese bracelet maker in little ole Branson, Missouri? That's a new one."

"Ever heard of a head shop or a New Age place down there? That's probably the kind of place selling this stuff."

Bud laughed. "What'd you think? I don't think Andy Williams or Jimmy Osmond would stand for it. Not to mention all those buses full of senior citizens. Downtown Springfield, yeah, maybe. It's gone a little bohemian lately."

"We'll check the phone book. And any head shops in Springfield, too. I'm guessing this guy is a regular customer wherever he bought this stuff. Maybe whoever sold it to him can tell us why he wanted so many."

"Hell, he probably kept the place in business, all by himself."

As Bud went downstairs to get Vicky up to shoot the photos, I nosed around some more in Mikey Murphy's desk, trying not to disturb anything. It was black lacquered, too, quite beautiful, and very, very pricey, if I had to guess. There was a hidden well underneath the writing surface, I knew that because Black had a similar desk in his house in Bermuda. I found the latch, pushed it back and voilà, there were a couple of photographs lying in the bottom, facedown.

"Aha, we got pictures here. Maybe it's our victim."

"Bingo," said Bud, back already with Vicky in tow.

She said, "I'm going to start in the living room."

We nodded, but we focused on the picture of a young girl smiling back at us so innocently. I said, "This could be the girl downstairs."

"She's got long black hair like the vic."

"She's Asian."

"That fits with Mikey Murphy's tastes, all right."

Bud said, "Okay. She's got on a Missouri State University sweatshirt. Maybe she's a student down there. We oughta be able to find out her name at the registrar's office."

"*Was* a student over there, you mean."

"Yeah. She looks too young to be in college. She's petite like the vic."

"Could be her. My gut says she is," I said

"She's pretty. Too bad she ever met up with Mikey Murphy."

"If he's the perp," I reminded him.

"You thinkin' it's a different perp?"

"I don't know. There's something strange about this whole thing. He meant us to find him and come here. Nearly left us a map, for Pete's sake. Maybe somebody else wanted us to find him and blame him for the murder. Make us figure it for a murder/suicide. Maybe somebody offed him, too, and made it look like Mikey did it to himself."

Bud did not look convinced. "Could be, I guess. Unlikely, though, if you ask me."

"We'll find out. Let's get the guys up here to process this place. We need to canvass the stores around here and see if anybody heard or saw anything."

"Good, I'm ready to get out the hell of here. This place gives me a serious case of the creeps."

Downstairs, Vicky had already shot the victim, and Buck had his team processing the kitchen. The girl was still in the oven, cooling before they could load her onto the gurney. To my surprise, my boss, Sheriff Charlie Ramsay, had shown up, too, and stood across the black granite-topped island from the body.

"What the hell's this world coming to?" Charlie asked me.

I shrugged. The question was rhetorical, and way over my head, too.

"You positive the bridge suicide is Joseph Murphy's kid, Claire?"

That didn't bode well. Charlie on a first-name basis with the governor's guru. And he was well connected up Jefferson City way, too, politically and otherwise. This case was going to get sticky as road tar and that would make my job a lot harder than I wanted it to be.

"Yes sir. We believe so. Black happened to be with me when I got the call, and he recognized the victim right off as a former patient. Buck found the vic's driver's license on the body at the scene. The photo appears to be a match. Buck gave us the official ID and we're ready to notify next of kin."

"No. I'm gonna have to do it myself. Joseph Murphy's an old friend of mine. We haven't always seen eye to eye politically, but I owe him that courtesy. I'll drive up there tonight and break the bad news. You and Bud can follow up tomorrow with his interview, and I guess you'll have to interview all the family members, too. Joseph's got a bunch of kids."

"Yes sir. That'll give us time to interview the people who work around here and see what they can tell us about the vics."

Bud and I exchanged glances, both very, very happy we weren't gonna be the ones to tell mom and dad that their lives are changed forever. We usually got that assignment, and trust me, it was not a barrel of laughs. We would take a bye on that unpleasant duty any time we could get one.

Charlie stared hard at me. He had a tendency to do that, not just look at me, like everybody else, but search my face, the depths of my soul, even. "Any ID on the burned vic?"

He didn't look over at her, but I glanced at the oversize pizza oven. Several techs were trying to remove the body now with silver metallic hot pads on their hands. If it wasn't Mikey who'd done this to that poor girl, I was gonna prove it and then I was gonna take down the freakin' sicko. Whoever it was didn't deserve to walk the face of the earth with the rest of us.

"We found a picture upstairs of a young Asian girl. No name, but it could be the victim. She was wearing a Missouri State sweatshirt, so that's a lead we can pursue."

"Don't do anything until Buck determines identity one hundred percent."

"Yes sir."

"This is shit. Joseph and Mary Fern are gonna be devastated. Dadgummit, I am sick of these psychopaths murderin' my constituents."

Oh, yeah, dadgummit, that's one of Charlie's Southern Baptist adaptations of more vulgar profanity, which is colorful and different, if not downright peculiar. But far be it for me to judge one's choice of swearwords.

Charlie said, "Okay, both of you get outta here and check out this shopping center. I wanna know who did this, and I want him sittin' in prison for the rest of his life or strapped to a table gettin' a lethal injection. Don't matter to me which it is."

"Yes sir," Bud and I said. Almost together but not quite, more like a faint echo.

We got out of there, more than pleased to do so. I, for one, would never eat pizza again, not even a real one in Italy if Black ever took me over to Rome for a look-see, which he was threatening to do. After today, I was beginning to think that skipping the country for a while might not be a bad idea.

FOUR

Outside, Bud headed down the sidewalk toward the east end of the shopping center, and I walked in the other direction, my destination Stonecrest Book and Toy, my favorite bookstore at the lake. When I entered the front door, I caught sight of Sarah, one of Stonecrest's managers. At the moment, she was ringing up a stack of books on astrology for a teenage girl who looked about fifteen or sixteen. The teen was wearing a cut-off T-shirt that barely covered her breasts and was very Britney Spears–esque, not a good thing. Her short shorts accomplished their mission, too, but barely, and I use that word literally.

"Hey, Sarah."

Sarah looked up and gave me a quick smile. She was an attractive redhead and a very nice one, too, and she'd gone out of her way big-time once to help me figure out what to get Megabucks Nicholas Black for Christmas, so I liked her a lot. She helped me pick out a book for Bud, too. One of her former coworkers named Sherry sold really cool jewelry on the side, stuff called Lia Sophia, and at the moment Sarah had on a beautiful filigree cross adorned with cut crystals. It hung around her neck on a thin tan leather cord. Maybe I'd give Black a hint about some Lia Sophia for my birthday, not that I ever wore any jewelry except for the St. Michael's medal he gave me once upon a time. I always wear that now because St. Michael is the patron saint of police officers and I figure it's good luck, which is something I have decided I need about a bushel of every day. Okay, it's true, I'm getting superstitious, not to mention paranoid. But live my life for a month, and you'd armor yourself with whatever cropped up, too.

Sarah finished with the Britney clone, turned to me, and said, "How'd your partner like that book you got him on the origins of popular sayings?"

"He dug it a lot. That's all I've heard about since. And Black liked me making him that custom-bound book on Louisiana bayous, too. The binder you recommended was great. Black didn't have anything like it, which is the trick when it comes to him. He's got a zillion of just about everything."

Her grin was wide and amused. "Wish I had that kinda problem."

"Yeah, me, too."

"So what brings you in? Dr. Black's birthday coming up?"

"Not for a few more months, but I'll be in as soon as it does, so keep your eyes out for something he'd like. Unfortunately, this time I'm here on official business. You got a minute to answer some questions?"

With a look of surprise, Sarah glanced around the store. Only one customer was browsing in the recently expanded used books section. He was dressed in tan pants and a red button-down collar shirt, and was looking at a large book titled *Napoleon and Josephine*. The romantic type, no doubt.

Sarah said, "It looks like it'll be pretty slow till closing time. What's up?"

"Do you happen to know a guy named Michael Murphy? His friends call him Mikey."

"That the guy who owns that pizza parlor a few stores

down? Yeah, sure, I see him around now and again. He's come in here a couple of times and bought some New Age books. He likes stuff about the Orient. Seems to be really into that kind of reading. He likes Indian music, you know, flutes, and he wore a lot of beaded jewelry. Can't say I know him much better'n that, though. Why? What's the deal with him?"

Sarah's sole customer was sitting down now at a table, thumbing through his French love story, so I lowered my voice. "We've got a crime scene at his place, but I can't really get into the details. Sorry."

Her curiosity turned into a frightened look, and she said in a whisper, "Oh no, was there a break-in here at the center? I've been really nervous about that kind of thing lately."

Now that got my interest pumped up a notch. "Nervous? Why? Something happen around here to spook you?"

"Uh uh, I don't know, really, just bad vibes, I guess, and lots of late nights closing up by myself. Sometimes I get a little freaked out when I'm here all alone after nine o'clock. I really shouldn't, I guess, there's a security guard who comes around every night and checks on all the stores. Carman gets nervous, too, when she closes up."

Carman was the other co-manager, a lovely lady with brown curly hair and a friendly disposition, and both of them were really gonna be freaked when they found out Mikey might have cooked his girlfriend like a well-done filet mignon, and just a short walk down the sidewalk at that. "I can't get into the details right now. What else can you tell me about Michael Murphy?"

Sarah shook her head. Nervously, she fingered the cross she was wearing and glanced at the man in the red shirt like he was gonna whirl around and pull a gun on us. She was spooked, all right. Can't say I blame her. So am I. I'm just more used to it.

She said, "Not much. He seemed like an okay guy, maybe a bit on the eccentric side. I do know he had lots of girlfriends, and the girls here were saying that they thought some of them looked like hookers. He hit on Carman once when he was in here, but she wasn't interested."

And lucky Carman might still be alive because she had the sense to blow him off. "What makes them think he spent time with hookers?"

"The way his girls dressed, mostly. Sort of like that last customer I waited on, but worse. You saw that girl's black thong under her shorts when she turned around, didn't you? Kids nowadays don't know what modesty is." She smiled, but her eyes remained serious.

Unfortunately, I had seen the aforementioned thong, but had tried to block that disgusting image out of my mind. As far as that goes, most young girls nowadays dressed more like hookers than hookers themselves, and it was hard to tell them apart. Bud usually could, though, had a real knack for it, actually. Usually the hookers were loitering on street corners and the teenagers had iPod earbuds in their ears.

I said, "You mentioned that he wore beaded jewelry? Can you describe it?"

"If I recall, he wore some bracelets made out of blue and white beads. I noticed it because he wore so many at a time. I thought that was more than a little weird, for a guy like him, anyway."

"Do you happen to know the significance of the bracelets? Where he got them, maybe? What they meant?"

"No. I just noticed because he wore five or six on each wrist. I suspect it's something to do with his New Age interests, but I haven't seen anybody else wearing them."

"How does his pizza restaurant do? They get a good business?"

"Oh, yeah. I usually run down there for lunch myself and fix a salad at their salad bar, but most of the time, I bring it back here and eat in the back with Carman. I haven't seen Mikey out front much with his customers, though. I think he does the cooking."

Yeah, you can say that again. Well done, too. "So the restaurant is crowded most of the time. Not in danger of going out of business or having any kind of financial trouble that you know of?"

"Oh, no. They do real well down there. Especially at lunch. Lots of people who work around here either stop in there or go to the Steak and Shake a couple of blocks up the street. Mikey's gets a good crowd at dinnertime, too. Has lots of birthday parties for kids, stuff like that. They've got good pizza, better'n most the chains, at least I think so. It's the thick Chicago style with lots of different kinds of toppings, and the salad bar's really good, everything real fresh. Saturday night is the busiest, I guess. Sometimes there's a line, with customers waiting outside on the benches. They're closed on Sundays, which is a little unusual nowadays."

"What about his employees? Do you know any of them personally?"

"A couple, I guess. He hires a bunch of high school kids to work on Saturdays, I think. Carman might know some of their names."

"Carman's not here, I take it." Sarah shook her head, and I said, "Could you have her give me a call, if she can identify anybody by name working down there? Anything else you can tell me, Sarah?"

"Well, one of the waitresses down there might've been his girlfriend. She came in here with him once, I recall, and she had on a Missouri State jacket, so she might be a student down there. A lot of MSU kids come down here on weekends in the summer to work in food joints when the tourists are all here because of the big tips or just to party."

"You don't remember the names of any girls he might've dated? Did you ever see a girl of Asian descent?"

"Yeah, actually, that one I just told you about from MSU looked Asian." She frowned. "Yeah, and now that I think on it, there was another one I saw hanging around with Mikey, too, a pretty little thing, who was from China, or somewhere."

"You know her name?"

Sarah shook her head. "She came in here not long ago and bought some romance novels. She usually comes in on Fridays, after she gets paid. She likes the historical ones set in England, you know, the knights and ladies, that kind of book."

"Okay. I guess you don't know where she lives, do you?"

"Can't say I do. She pays in cash and we've never talked about personal stuff, just about the various romance authors and who we like the best, you know."

"Okay, Sarah, I really appreciate your help. I'm going to ask you to keep this conversation quiet. The scene's being processed now and forensics should be working for most of the night. If you think of anything else, give me a call, okay?"

"Sure. Gosh, this's pretty scary. That guy, Mikey, was kinda odd in some ways, but he was pretty nice. I hope nothing too bad's happened."

If she only knew, but I wasn't going to tell her the gory details. I didn't even want to remember them myself. My phone rang at that very moment, so I thanked her and gave her a good-bye wave and headed out the front door.

Black said, "You about done?"

I merely laughed. He got the message loud and clear. "How much longer?"

"All night, maybe."

"You're kidding me."

"I wish."

"And you're frowning, too."

I stopped walking and glanced around the parking lot. It didn't take me long to find his gigantic black and silver Humvee sitting under one of the lampposts. He blinked his headlights flirtatiously. Glancing at the pizzeria and crime scene van just down the sidewalk, I turned gratefully and made a detour to his impressive tank. I got in, clunked the door shut, and immediately smelled something delicious. Black was all cleaned up and dressed in khakis and a black linen shirt and smelled really good.

"I brought you dinner. I've already eaten but thought you'd probably be hungry."

"I'll never be hungry again. You won't believe what we found over there in that pizzeria."

"I see that Buck's here with his team. Do you think Mikey was murdered? Did you find a note?"

"No note, but he did leave us a girlfriend cooking in the oven."

Black frowned. He even looked good when he frowned, I'd found, which wasn't often. We got along pretty good thus far. "I hope you don't mean that literally?" He gave a little uncertain grin. He'd been with me well enough to know bad things had a tendency to happen when I was around. Grotesque and stomach turning, even.

"Unfortunately, yes, it's true. Bud and I found her. It was not a lot of laughs, believe me." Inside my mind I saw again the charred, smoking corpse and decided to pass on whatever goodie he'd bid his chef cook up for my dinner.

Black said, "No way."

"Way. Oh, yeah."

"Are you actually telling me that Mikey Murphy put his girlfriend in the oven of that restaurant over there and turned it on?"

"That's exactly what we think happened. Probably just before he tripped off to the bridge and hanged himself, which would give him one helluva good motive to kill himself as soon as he found a strong enough rope. I'd have some trouble carrying on, too, after doing something that awful to somebody."

"Holy Mary, Mother of God." Black said, being a good Catholic boy from the bayous. He stared at me as if I'd just told me something truly revolting, and then said, "I treated Mikey long enough that I can't see him ever doing anything even remotely like this. He was shy and retiring and didn't appear to have any violent tendencies. He had lots of issues, mostly involving drug use, brought on by insecurities and low self-esteem, maybe a bit of paranoia, too, but I can't see him doing anything this sick."

"I don't see anybody doing anything this sick. It takes a special kinda person."

"Have you notified his dad?"

"Charlie said he'd do it and more power to him. He knows the guy."

"Think he'd let me come into the restaurant and take a look at the crime scene?"

"You don't want to, trust me on this."

"Are you heading back over there right now?"

"Yes. We haven't even gotten started."

"I won't touch anything. Charlie's pretty much given me carte blanche on your cases in the past. Maybe I can help, especially since I treated Mikey for a while."

I sighed. But he was right. Charlie always wanted Black's professional opinion on my more psycho/sadistic/godawful kind of cases, probably because the department got expert opinions pro bono. I nodded and got out of the Humvee. I could see Bud now under the streetlights edging the sidewalk. He was striding down the parking lot toward us. We met up with him in back of Buck's crime scene van.

He said, "Charlie just called. Joseph Murphy and his family are now wingin' their way home from England and are probably somewhere midway over the Atlantic Ocean. Comin' back from vacationin' in London, no less, so we get to do the notification, after all. Charlie's gotta leave for Washington, D.C., early tomorrow so he can't do it in person."

"Great, we're just so lucky. Find out anything else?"

"Not much. Everybody who worked in the shops along here knew who Murphy was, but nobody really associated with him, not socially anyway. Thought he was a nice weirdo who made awesome pizza, especially the one called Mikey's Special."

Oh, yes, yes, there was a cruel joke in there somewhere, but none of us wanted any part of it. "Same here. Sarah at

Stonecrest Book and Toy knew he dated some Asians but no-body by name. Sounds like he had a long list of honeys."

"So what now?"

"Let's go back in and take another look around. See if Buck's found anything relevant."

The three of us entered and not one of us acknowledged the stench of burned human flesh still hanging malodorously in the air. Forensics were too busy dusting for prints and taking videos and crime photos to notice us. I was glad to see the victim's body was long gone, already bagged and delivered into the ME's van. That was one autopsy I wasn't looking forward to, not that I ever looked forward to them.

A minute later, Buck caught sight of us and immediately pointed a forefinger up at the ceiling just behind us. We all turned and followed his direction. "Vicky discovered a well-hidden security camera when she was filming in here. You might want to get back upstairs and see if you can find some monitors. There aren't any down here. We've already looked. If you're lucky, you just might have yourselves a live action account of that poor girl's murder."

Now that was good news, to be sure. I peered up in the corner he'd indicated, but didn't see anything. It was well hidden, all right. Why would anyone hide the security camera focused in on a restaurant's kitchen? Afraid the cooks would steal the pizza dough? I said to Bud, "Did you see any monitors when we were upstairs?"

Bud said, "Hell no, but I wasn't looking for them, either."

Black spoke up and joined the fun. "He's probably got them hidden in some cabinet or closet. I do that in some of my buildings."

I said, "Well, it looks like we might've gotten a break, after all, fellas."

We wasted no time hightailing it back upstairs and found that the security monitors were well hidden, all right. It took about ten minutes for us to find them. Turned out there was a hidden room behind the giant midnight-blue painted silk hanging in the dining room, the one I'd admired so much but never considered that it might be keeping secrets. It concealed a doorway that led into a large walk-in closet, about seven feet by nine feet, and where, not only did we find the camera focusing on the kitchen island and ovens, but five more cameras, all top-notch quality and functioning just fine.

Camera one focused on the cash register at the end of the mahogany bar, number two showed the inside of the stairwell from above, and all the others were outside the building, two focused on the front door and front parking lot, two more on the rear door and alley behind the building. Since Bud and I didn't notice a single one of them, all must be very cleverly hidden. Something that I thought sort of defeated the purpose, you know, like being a deterrent for criminals loitering about outside waiting for Mikey to come outside with the day's cash intake, and all, but Mikey must've had his reasons.

Bud said, "Hallelujah, God is good. We're gonna get this guy in spades."

I said, "Only bad thing is we've got to watch this girl get put into that oven." We all looked at each other in turn, none of us relishing that idea. In fact, I was looking forward to that like a hole in my head.

Here Comes Trouble

Everyone believed his sob story, of course; he was really that good. They were just so glad he'd been able to save poor little Destiny from being murdered by her own mother. People were just so damn gullible, especially his own relatives. But he laid it on pretty thick for them, too. Lots of pretend throwing up in the bathroom, weeping hysterically, and even some keening, which he threw in after he saw an Arab funeral where all the black-clad women were making high-pitched sounds that really got on a person's nerves after about two minutes.

Also, he locked himself in his room periodically and refused to let his dad come in and check on him. He refused to go to the funeral, sure not wanting to see how bruised and cut up his mom looked after getting all busted up on the rocks. Sometimes in the weeks that followed, he pretended to get up in the night and call out his mom's name down the hall, really loud so his dad would hear and believe he was having nightmares and grieving. That was pretty upsetting to the younger kids, but it pretty well convinced his dad that he was suffering and had gone slightly cuckoo after having to watch his own mom commit suicide and try to kill her own baby. The more he'd thought about it afterward, the more he decided that his mom probably would have done it herself, sooner or later, if he hadn't helped her along with it first. She really did suffer that postpartum depression thing and was unhappy down deep inside, being alive and all, without Lyla around anymore. Mom was better off and so was he. The whole family was, really.

At present, as an extra touch, he had landed himself in the hospital. Cleverly, he had decided to do a mock slitting of the wrists in a fake suicide attempt, just to concrete everybody's belief that he was an unwilling victim that had to be the one to watch his mom and Lyla die. And in a way, that's exactly what he was. But he'd been smart about it. He'd researched on the Internet on how to make the cuts, and then he made sure both were superficial and shallow and totally missed any veins or arteries. Didn't hurt much, but would it ever pay dividends with his dad. Did he ever love the Internet.

At the moment, he was lying in bed in his own private room in the psych ward of the local hospital. Leaning back against the pillows, he placed his hands behind his head and smiled. This last stunt had really jolted his dad, nearly put him over the edge. Now he was really freaked out big-time and didn't know what to do . His dad was depressed himself, anyway, and very concerned about his son doing himself in, while everyone was still grieving over his mom.

On top of that, his dad was all stressed out because he had to take care of a newborn infant, too, and had finally given up on that one and turned Destiny over to a sister-in-law till things settled down at home. All the other kids had totally taken a backseat to the son and Destiny since the Grand Canyon incident, and that's exactly the way he liked it. Now he was riding high. His dad would do just about anything he wanted, anything at all. The whole suicide idea had been brilliant. He could coast on it for years, probably. People were just so, so stupid.

And the nurses here, whoa, they were hot, a couple of them, anyway. Especially one with huge boobs and long dark red hair that she wore back in a bun. He was getting to the age now where he noticed the way the nurses' breasts looked pressed up against their pastel scrubs, and when women wore skirts how their legs disappeared up underneath them to their female private places. They all felt so sorry for him, too. Coddled him and hugged themselves against him when he cried. It was freakin' perfect.

When he heard his dad's voice out in the hallway, he took off his iPod and stuffed it under the pillow. He put on his morose act, oh, so sad and pitiful. The one that usually made his dad end up crying, too. But it served its purpose. He wanted attention and sympathy, and he was getting plenty of it.

His dad had stopped just outside the door to speak with one of the doctors. He looked terrible. Dark circles under his eyes, skin white and sallow, new lines all over his face that hadn't been there before, but the son decided to make him feel better, so when his dad came into his room, he said, "Hi Dad. I'm sure glad to see you. I miss being with you and the other kids."

"How're you feeling, son?"

"Okay, I guess, a little better."

Taking hold of a chair, his dad dragged it up close beside the bed. He reached out and took hold of his son's hand. He touched the clean white bandages on his right wrist with a gentle finger, and then he said, "I'm so worried about you. God help me, I can't believe you actually tried . . . to hurt yourself like this. You've got to remember that you have so much to live for. You're special, son. You've got such a bright future. You've got to remember that."

The son kept his voice low, made sure it sounded tortured. "I just keep seeing Mom . . . seeing her fall like that . . ."

He stopped, as if overcome, and made himself shiver. When his dad squeezed his fingers, he said, "I couldn't stop her, Dad. I tried to, but I couldn't."

"Of course, you did, son. Everybody knows that. And we all know you saved Destiny. Don't blame yourself for what Mom did. I shouldn't have gone on and left you and Mom behind. Oh, God, and you had to find poor little Lyla, too. You saved the baby, and we're all so grateful you did. Thank God for that."

"Yeah. Destiny would be dead, too, if I hadn't waited there with Mom."

They both looked down, and the son made himself appear very sad, but he was smart and perceptive, and he sensed his dad was hesitating. Something else was going on here, something important. He waited, wondering what it possibly could be.

Finally, his dad cleared his throat and said very softly, "I've been talking to your doctors, son."

"Yeah?"

"Yes, they're good, you know. They say you need to get some therapy to help you deal with all you've been through. They say you have to come to terms with your grief and loss and what you tried to do to yourself."

The son had been expecting this, so he nodded. "Okay. It's just going to take me some time to get used to Mom not being around. I miss her so much. I miss talking to her." He forced up some tears and made a show of wiping them off with the hem of the crisp white hospital sheet.

"Don't cry, son. There's this clinic for kids your age. Oak Haven. The doctors want to send you there for a while so you can talk all this through with professionals. They say it'll get your life back on track."

Uh oh, he wasn't expecting to have to go to a loony bin. "For how long?"

"They don't know. Not long, I promise. I couldn't deal with that, but I think this's a good thing, that it'll help you, so

I'm giving permission. They say it's in your best interest, and that's all I care about. Home isn't a good place for you to come back to right now, not with your brothers and sisters so torn up about Mom."

"But I want to come home, Dad."

"I know, but I have to listen to the doctors. They know what they're talking about. It's temporary, I promise. This place is a residential clinic, and you can take classes there so you can graduate on time. They'll help you cope with all you've been through."

Tears were running down his dad's cheeks again, and he wished the guy would get some guts and pull it together. He was a man, for Christ's sake. Step up to the plate. Lots of guys had lost a wife and a daughter. His dad looked really old now, too, wasn't shaving every day anymore, and his whiskers were turning white. In fact, he looked about fifteen minutes from a massive stroke.

"Okay, Dad, if you want me to go there, I will. Don't worry about me. You've got enough to worry about."

Relief flooded his dad's face, man, he was so easy to read, but he couldn't quite muster up any kind of smile. He said, "Oak Haven's got a nice gym and tennis courts and a swimming pool, all the amenities. You'll like that, I bet, and the kids are all around your age."

"That sounds good."

Actually, it really did; it sure beat the hell out of hanging around his own house with all the whiny kids going nuts about not having a mom to tuck them in at night. Maybe there would be some hot girls there, even hotter than that redheaded nurse who liked to comfort him. He wanted to have sex with a girl. He hadn't done that yet; he'd been biding his time, but now he was going to find a way to do it, and this psycho clinic sounded like a place that could serve him up a smorgasbord of chicks to hook up with.

His dad said, "Oak Haven's close to home, so we can come out and see you a lot."

"When do I go?"

"As soon as you heal up some and get out of here. I'll drive you out there myself." He reached over and laid his hand on top of his son's. "I'm going to miss you, but this is for the best. I'm convinced of it."

It sure was. Maybe the son could have some laughs for a change. Nobody in his family ever wanted to do anything fun since his mom had made him kill her.

FIVE

"Okay, I've got the tapes rewound and ready to go," said Bud.

I looked at him and said, "This is not gonna be fun."

Black said nothing, just leaned against the wall behind Bud's swivel chair. He knew how to keep out of the way. Or maybe he was standing there so he could close his eyes and not watch that poor girl get cooked to a crisp. Maybe that's what I should do, too. Shut my eyes. Wish I could.

I said, "Let's go with the kitchen camera first. Start it this morning, early, and fast-forward until you hit something."

Bud had done this before, many times, and he hit a red button on the console, and presto, we were fast-forwarding through a day in the life of a closed pizza parlor. The tape had no sound, and none of us said a word while we watched the hours fly by. No relevant action occurred at all until around noon.

Bud said, "There she is."

He punched another button and the film slowed to normal speed.

I watched the girl walk into camera view near the base of

the steps. I couldn't tell where she had come from, probably from upstairs but I couldn't be sure. She was very small, couldn't be much over five foot, if not less than that. Stark naked and barefoot, her raven-colored hair was very long, waist-length, and covered her bare breasts. She took a few steps toward the center island, then stopped and stared straight ahead. It appeared she was not looking at anything in particular, just staring at nothing. Then she started to move again, like a sleepwalker, and stood next to the sink. We could not see her face at all clearly at this point—no way a vidcap would be used for ID—but she looked like she was probably of Asian extraction. We watched her open a cabinet over the sink and take out a clear glass tumbler. All her motions were slow and deliberate.

"She's definitely drugged up." That was Black. He was right.

The girl filled the glass with tap water, then she opened her left palm, revealing a handful of white—maybe pills. She tossed them into her mouth all at once, drank some water, and swallowed them down with a backward jerk of her head. Very carefully, she placed the glass in the top rack of the dishwasher, shut it, and then stood a few minutes staring at the brick wall in front of her. She kept both palms pressed flat against the countertop.

I said, "We need to make sure Buck dusts that drinking glass. And what's she doing that for? See how she's pressing down with her hands?"

Bud shrugged then said, "Think she's waiting for somebody?"

"Nude?"

Bud shrugged again. Black stayed quiet but leaned forward and closely watched the monitor.

After a good five minutes of apparent daydreaming, the girl seemed to come alive. She moved suddenly, took a few steps to her right, and picked up a cell phone off the black granite counter as if she'd heard it ring. She put it to her ear and listened a moment but didn't say anything. A moment later, she turned around and faced the big wall oven. I swallowed hard, knowing full well what was coming next. She pulled down the door, removed a heavy cooking rack, and placed it on the counter where I'd seen it, and then boosted herself agilely into its depths and out of sight, still holding the cell phone in her hand.

Bud said, "Oh, God, is she gonna do it to herself?"

Black and I didn't answer, just watched with horrified eyes. And that was exactly what our victim did. She folded her body up into that impossible position in which we'd found her, then she pulled the door closed behind her.

Black said, "She couldn't do that in a hot oven; no matter how drugged up she was. That oven's not on yet. See, there's no light. It's cold, and she didn't turn it on before she got inside."

Bud shook his head. "Why the hell would she just climb in there like that?"

I said, "Maybe she's the suicide. Maybe she did herself, then Mikey came in and found her and went crazy and hung himself on the bridge out of despair."

No one answered. So we waited, watching for her to get out or turn it on, but nothing happened. Nobody showed up, and the girl just lay inside the cold oven, unmoving as far as we could tell, maybe even asleep.

"Fast-forward it." I didn't really want to watch the rest of this gruesome crime, but we had to, so I grit my teeth and kept my gaze fastened hard on the monitor.

The film continued to run, but nobody else showed up in the kitchen. Then I realized with some shock what was going on. "Wait, stop it there, Bud."

Bud pressed the button, and Black said, "I see it now, too. Look, now the oven light's on. It's a timer. Somebody set a timer to come on after she got inside."

I said, "Of course, it was going off when we got here. Rewind, and see when it came on."

We found the exact frame when the light suddenly blinked on, and the digital time read 1:30 P.M.

My stomach took a tidal wave, forward roll, and I felt nauseous. "My God, how could she stay in there when the heat kicked on?"

Black said, "She either drugged herself into a deep enough sleep not to be awakened or she took a lethal dose of those pills and was dead before the burners lit up."

"God, I hope to hell she was dead first," said Bud.

I said, "Buckeye can tell us cause of death. Run it some more, Bud. Let's see if anybody else shows up in the kitchen."

Silent now, we watched the film flicker by until Bud and I showed up on the screen, checking out the kitchen, guns drawn. I watched Bud pull open that door, and then both of us backed away, the expressions on our faces not easy to take. We got out of the kitchen pretty damn fast after that, and I wanted to escape this place again. This was so sickening and terrible; it was hard to get my mind around it. I was still having trouble believing it could have actually happened. I'd never in my life heard of anything like this, and I had heard some pretty gruesome things, I can tell you.

I said, "Okay, so who set that timer?"

Bud said, "The girl?"

Black said, "So she took sleeping pills or intentionally overdosed, then climbed inside an oven and cooked herself. That's bullshit. Nobody would do something like that."

Sometimes Black came right out with it. I said, "Yeah, my sentiments exactly. I don't think she'd have the guts to do it, either. Somebody else set that timer."

Bud said, "Nobody in their right mind would climb inside a freakin' oven like that. She was wide awake when she got in there."

I said, "Maybe she wasn't in her right mind. Maybe she was suicidal, too."

Black said, "I'm telling you that no woman would willingly commit suicide this way. It just wouldn't happen."

Bud stood up. "Hell, Nick, no man would, either. This is loony tune time."

Black's eyes met mine. "She almost looked like she was hypnotized."

I considered that, and it made sense to me.

Bud said, "Yeah, that'd have to be one helluva potent hypnotist to make a pretty young girl climb inside an oven and take a nap, never to wake up again."

I said, "Let's run the other tapes. See who else was hanging around here today. We just might get the killer on tape."

We stood and watched Bud fast-forward through footage from the other cameras, anxious to find out who set that timer and when, but that happy little Disney wish just didn't pan out. Nobody showed up on the film. Nobody, nada, so crap. We went back further on the tapes. The previous night's crowd at the pizzeria looked normal, a bunch of families with kids running back and forth from their booths to the bank of video games in the corner, young men and women on dates sitting in the same side of the booth and sharing garlic kisses, and a few single people out for a lonely sausage pizza all by their lonesome.

"Bud, we're gonna have to interview every single employee and anybody else we can identify on the surveillance tapes."

"Tell me about it."

The girl appeared several more times on tape, once arriving late last night, close to midnight, according to the camera's digital reading, but as far as we could tell, Mikey Murphy had not been in the restaurant at all yesterday or today. And if he'd been upstairs all that time, he would've had to fly out the windows like an apparition to avoid all those security cameras surrounding the place.

When the crime scene team finally wrapped up downstairs, it was well past three in the morning. Black and I left by the front door, the smell of the victim still heavy in the air, an acrid, awful reminder of what had transpired that day.

I was dead tired, so I asked Black to head home, not overly thrilled by my life at the moment.

Unfortunately, tomorrow wasn't gonna get any better. Black was still scheduled to take off for that seminar in New York City, leaving me in bed all alone with my Glock nine and some creepier than creepy, Rachael Ray Yum-o kind of culinary pizza nightmares. Even worse than that, Bud and I had to drive up to Jefferson City in the morning and tell Michael Murphy's family that their son no longer walked among the living.

SIX

Early the next morning I spent some time in bed saying one lively and erotic good-bye to Black, which was probably gonna be the highlight of my day, hands down. Around eight o'clock, after an Irish Spring shower of mutual sudsing and other delights, Black bopped off to check on his Cedar Bend patients before he boarded his own personal Learjet to fly to New York. Less worldly, I drove over to Bud's apartment in my black Explorer and picked him up for our coming ordeal in Jefferson City.

And away we went to notify the Murphy family, which was not exactly in our *wowee-look-what-we-get-to-do-today* category. We hadn't called the parents yet and neither had Charlie, so they were still blithely unaware that in approximately one hour their world was going to explode in an impact closely resembling the Big Bang theory. Charlie had given me their telephone number, but no way was I going to break this kind of bad news over the phone.

Then again, I had to know if they had made it home from their European tour, so I punched in Joseph Murphy's private home number and was told by a haughty, *I'm-better-*

than-you-even-if-I-have-to-wait-on-people-all-the-time
maid that they had arrived home from London but that neither Mr. or Mrs. Murphy were presently in the mansion or
inclined to receive visitors. Wow, a mansion, even. Also according to the Murphy's unseen but unlikeable house help and
after some official prompting aka threats of arrest, she let loose
with the fact that they'd slept on the transatlantic flight then
dropped off Joseph Murphy at the airstrip so he could get a
limo to the capitol building for a powwow with the guv. The
wife and her daughters apparently had remained on the private
plane for a quickie jaunt over to the Plaza in Kansas City to do
a bit of last-minute shopping for upcoming summer soirees but
would return soon. The rich and powerful just really had a
tough row to hoe, I declare. Guess London shops didn't have
an expensive enough inventory to wow said Murphys.

I thanked the maid, whom I had already nicknamed Bee-
otch, and just off the top of my head, too, then I flipped the
phone shut, and said to Bud, "Head straight for the capitol
building. That's where daddy Joe is."

"Maybe we'll get to meet the big guy."

"By that, you mean Governor Stanton, I take it."

"Yeah, maybe he'll remember us someday in the future
and present us with some kind of state distinguished service
medal for cracking a big case."

"Oh, yeah, I'm sure that's gonna happen. He won't think
we're good enough to mop his floors, if he's like most politi-
cos I've met up with. Or Murphy's maid."

"I bet Nick knows this Murphy guy, right? Probably real
good friends. Hell, they probably get together and talk about
who has the most money. Stuff like that."

I glanced at Bud. "I thought you liked Black."

"I do. You know I owe him big-time for what he did for
me, but you gotta admit the guy runs in high circles."

Yeah, high circles were his stomping ground, okay, except
where his own family was concerned. Those circles were
more like Corleone/Soprano/Capone mafia stomping grounds,

all very well hidden so Black could keep all his important celebrity patients and governor friends. Of course, he didn't stomp on those kind of grounds himself, lucky for me. He was as straight an arrow as they come. Somehow, and unfortunately, however, I just kept running into those selfsame wiseguy friends of his and thus complicating my cases, which I found more than irksome. Yes, it had caused some friction now and then between Black and me, but our hormones and better sense had helped us weather those storms, at least for the time being.

Bud glanced over at me. "Oh, c'mon, Claire, don't get all pissy. I like Nick. Maybe I'm just jealous you spend all your time with him. We used to go to the shooting range together and eat cheese bread and guzzle pitchers of beer at Pizza Hut. No more. You cut me out of the picture, just like that."

"I spend more time with you than I do with him. It's just that time flies when you're with me because I'm so easygoing."

That met with a sarcastic guffaw. "Yeah, right. But you shoot straight and you got me to the hospital in time when that snake bit me, so I guess I'll keep you."

The Missouri State Capitol building sits high on the banks of the Missouri River and is pretty much a scaled-down replica of the Federal Capitol building in Washington, D.C. Lots of steps, lots of tourists snapping digital cameras, lots of kiddies on tour, and lots of self-important people strutting around. The latter being the hardest to take.

Bud said, "Shit, there must be a hundred steps out here. Let's find a ground-floor entrance."

I concurred, not in the mood to climb Mount Everest, or its concrete ilk. We strolled over to one side of the massive stairs, admiring all the shade trees and green lawns and beds of blooming marigolds and purple and red petunias, where we found the much-sought-after entrance sans steps with lots of state workers loitering around outside, women mostly, and all of them dressed in black suits, white blouses, and sturdy heels. Must be a state law to dress staid. Plus, they apparently knew about all those steps out front and avoided them like the plague.

Inside the entrance, we flashed our badges at a security guard and asked directions to the governor's office. He was a young guy, clean cut, right out of the highway patrol academy, if my guess was correct.

He told us where it was and how to get there. "You can't miss it," he added as an extra dose of encouragement.

"You know a man named Joseph Murphy?"

"Yes, ma'am."

Make me feel old, why don't you, kid? I looked for peach fuzz on his chin. "Has Mr. Murphy signed in with you today?"

"Yes, ma'am. About an hour ago."

"Okay, thank you very much."

Bud said, "You got an elevator in this place, man?" Bud wasn't exactly into unnecessary exercise, although he could run a five-minute mile when he had to, like when a hatchet-bearing freak was chasing him. Don't laugh; it happens. I speed up, too, under such circumstances.

The smiley young man directed us to the elevator, and we rode up with more secretary types dressed in dark suits, although all their nameplates identified them as legislative assistants. The word secretary must be passé in Jeff City. Most of them held matching Starbucks Styrofoam cups, and the aroma of vanilla latte almost made drool run out of my mouth. I forced myself not to snatch the nearest one, flash my badge, and gulp it down before she could claw it out of my grip. Guess I'm caffeine deprived.

"I'm hungry," said Bud, as we stepped out into an impressive marble corridor.

"Maybe we can bum a donut from the guv," I said, but I was watching the people strolling around us, all of whom were headed somewhere, very, very fast and efficiently, too, and all with a studied air of importance with a capital "I." Hey, maybe all capital letters, now that I think about it. More of the clone assistants, who at least looked pleasant and spoke to us, and a lot of males, who looked either harried or pompous. Both, sometimes. The latter were probably the state legislators themselves, although I know one or two from my own district who aren't half bad once you get to know them. The harried ones here, however, were so busy kowtowing, they were backing into each other.

Another security guard stood outside the guv's door, and we stopped politely, flashed our badges politely, and he examined them politely and peered at us as if we were gonna jump out of a *Mission Impossible* movie and tear off rubber face masks and become Osama bin Laden or Tom Cruise Dancing on a Couch before the guy could get off a shot.

"Okay, detectives. What can I do for you?"

"We're here to speak to Joseph Murphy. We were told downstairs that he's meeting with the governor this morning."

"That's right. He came in roughly sixty-five minutes ago."

That's roughly for you. I wondered what precisely amounted to. The guard went on, raising one hand to scratch his neatly trimmed brown sideburn. He had a military buzz cut, big brown eyes the color of that vanilla latte I was craving, and was in full uniform, hat held in his hand. I wondered if he burned up outside in this kind of heat.

"You'll have to talk to Debbie Winters. She's the governor's personal assistant."

Debbie Winters was sitting inside the guv's spacious outer office at a gargantuan desk that made her look even smaller than she was. She was a good-looking, petite blonde with big blue eyes, and Bud couldn't help but notice. He smiled. She smiled. I smiled. It seemed the thing to do.

"May I help you?" she said to Bud. Forgot about me, I guess. Like most of the women Bud and I met up with. Since it appeared I was just along to help him charm the ladies, I let him do the talking.

Bud moved closer, looked her over pretty good. She had on one of those expensive black suits, too, a pantsuit with a white tee underneath it, a very subdued elegance. Then Bud said, "Yes, ma'am, you sure can."

They both beamed impressive white-toothed wattage, and I wondered what kind of help they were talking about.

Bud said, "Debbie, right?"

"Yes, that's me. And you are?"

More coy smiles. I declare, set a wedding date, already.

"My name's Bud Davis. I'm a detective in Canton County down at the lake."

"Is that so? My mom, Dorothy, used to live there, not too far from Ha Ha Tonka. She really likes that area. So do I."

"Awesome," agreed Bud, but we all knew who he was talking about and it wasn't any lake views.

I decided to interrupt their suggestive, but not yet indecent, sexual innuendo. "We're here to see Mr. Murphy. It's urgent." I held up my badge to show I really meant it.

"And you are?"

"Detective Claire Morgan. Is Mr. Murphy available?"

Debbie did give a quick glance at my badge, but she appeared to like Bud's better, along with some of his other things. But shortly afterward, she got hold of her tango-dancing hormones and said, "He's in conference with the governor and asked not to be disturbed unless it was urgent."

Didn't I just say that? "It's not only urgent, ma'am, it's *very* urgent." Sometimes throwing in certain adverbs helped with recalcitrant guardians of important doorways.

"In truth, Debbie, it's a matter of life and death." That was Bud. Handsome face all concerned, waxing dramatic for pretty Deb's approval.

"Oh, then, in that case, I'll call him right away." She picked up the receiver, but then she hesitated, put it down again, and looked at her Bud. "Maybe I should go in and tell him myself. There's an important meeting going on."

She dragged her eyes off Bud's goofy smile and looked less impressed with my expression. "Could you possibly tell me what this involves? I know he'll ask me, and he doesn't like to be disturbed."

Her blue eyes were talking to me now, woman to woman, and they were saying loud and clear, "Joseph Murphy can be a real jerk, and he's gonna jump all over me with both feet if I go in there and interrupt his important gubernatorial business without a helluva good reason." I am exceptional at interpreting secret feminine eye codes, as you can see.

"We'll take all responsibility for this interruption, Ms. Winters. Trust me, he's not going to reprimand you after he hears what we have to say. It's extremely important that we see him as soon as possible. It's a personal matter."

"I see." Her expression told me she believed me a little bit but wasn't totally sure of my motives. She gazed at Bud again. He nodded, backing me up, and her shoulders sagged with reassurance. "Will you need a private conference room where you can talk to him without being disturbed?"

"Yes, ma'am. That would be a very good idea."

Debbie Winters smiled at Bud, and she did have a very nice smile, I had to admit, then she rose and crossed over the plush purple-and-red Persian carpet and passed into the sacred inner sanctum where white tapers were probably burning on governmental altars made in the shape of Missouri. Bud watched her every movement until the door closed softly behind her, and I didn't interrupt his lusting until the latch clicked and his eyes became clear again. I do believe he likes her looks.

"Okay, Bud. This is gonna be difficult, so let me do all the talking. I sense this guy might turn out to be a real jerk."

That got his attention. "Really, what makes you think that?"

See what I mean? Men don't have that little intuition vibe that women do when dealing with other women. Debbie of the Blue Eyes sent me a nice little warning sign, one that said *Tread Carefully with JM and Nobody Gets Hurt.* I'd gotten it, loud and clear, and I heed those kind of messages, you know. I skid to a stop and look both ways, just like I do at train crossings.

"Just a hunch I got, Bud."

Debbie returned, face all flushed and angry. She'd gotten reamed out in advance, it seemed. I felt her pain. She said, "Please follow me, detectives."

Bud followed her with earnest attention, and I trailed along for the ride. She led us down a long hallway and around a corner then over the bridge to grandma's house. Maybe Mikey's dad, Joseph, was gonna be the big bad wolf. She stopped and opened a tall mahogany door. Inside, we found a good-size room, replete with a long shiny conference table, mahogany, too, covered with glass with lots of little notepads and pens sitting at each of the thirty swiveling black leather chairs. The walls were painted a pale peach color, and two 50-inch plasma televisions hung on one wall. Along the other wall were lots of portraits of earlier pompous politicians. All the maroon drapes were closed nice and tight, but I think my expertise at geography put us in a room overlooking the east side of the capitol grounds.

"Well, this must be the break room where all the legislative assistants watch *Bold and the Beautiful*," I commented to Bud, after Debbie had hastened back to her duties at the guard desk.

Bud said, "Or where they plan up ways to tax us all to death. I hate taxes worse than poison." Bud had gotten rooked on his last tax return and was still fuming.

"You shoulda taken it to Coffman and Company in Springfield like I told you. I got money back this time. Black told me about them, and he came out smelling like a rose, too, of course."

"I will take mine there next year, trust me. I will drive them there myself and beg them to take me on as a client on my hands and knees."

"That should do it."

Our titillating tax talk was interrupted when the corridor

door opened behind us, and we both turned to see who was popping in to say hello. A man entered, tall and dark, imposing, even. He frowned at us, stern as hell, I'd say, then he shut the door, then frowned at us some more and all the way across the room, too. Okay, we get the picture. You are pissed. We have offended one of the great ones and we will have to pay a severe penalty of irked looks and dented brows.

"I'm Joseph Murphy. How can I help you, detectives? I'm very busy at the moment, so I can't give you much of my time."

Maybe, maybe not, but if my guess was right, he was going to change his tune in a New York minute. "I'm Detective Claire Morgan with the Canton Country Sheriff's department, and this is my partner, Detective Bud Davis."

"I know who you are. Ms. Winters told me." Mr. Murphy didn't reach out to shake our hands, but then he paused, and uh oh, he recognized our names. He was pretty easy to read, too, for such a self-important ass. He looked at me. "You're that detective down at the lake, right? The one who keeps almost getting killed."

Well, that's one way to describe me, I suppose, not the way I prefer, of course, but one way. Almost was the operative word in that assessment, but I was already beginning to share Debbie's tacit opinion of this joker. Sometimes when on a sorrowful mission like this, Bud and I acted lighthearted as long as we could, mainly because we didn't want to think about what was coming when we met the parents of a deceased murder victim. But now, we were here and whether we liked this man or not, it was time to get serious and show some respect.

"Mr. Murphy, you might want to sit down. I'm afraid I've got some very bad news."

"Oh, my God, is it Mary Fern? Is she okay?"

I knew that to be the name of his unfortunate wife. "This concerns your son, Michael, sir."

"Mikey?" His worried expression metamorphosed to anger pretty damn quick, so quick, in fact, that I had to blink to keep up with it. "What the hell has he gone and done this time?"

He didn't really want to know that, nor did he want to play the angry father. He just didn't know it yet.

Bud said, "Why don't you sit down, Mr. Murphy?"

"I don't want to fuckin' sit down. What has Mikey been arrested for this time? C'mon, get to it, like I told you, I'm very busy."

Well now, the F bomb and everything, right here in the innards of the sacrosanct capitol building, too. I stared at him a short moment, then I said, "Your son is dead, Mr. Murphy. We found him hanging from a bridge support in Osage Beach last night. We suspect at this point that he took his own life. I'm very sorry."

Murphy just stared back at me for one beat, then two, then he looked at Bud. Bud nodded. Murphy shook his head back and forth. "What do you mean? Mikey isn't dead. No. I don't believe you."

I said, "I realize this comes as quite a shock, sir. Please, sit down, and we'll tell you what we know about your son's death."

"Mikey's not dead. He can't be dead."

Bud and I merely stared at him. We'd done this before, more times than we'd like to remember. Then we watched in silence as the stark realization and horror dawned in his dark eyes. I tensed at the anguished look that twisted across his lined and deeply tanned face, and I remembered, remembered the day, the hour, the worst moment of my entire life, when I'd been standing in an ER in Los Angeles, when I'd been given a similar message about my own little boy, Zachary. I swallowed hard, felt the internal tensing of my stomach muscles, and I forced the grief rising inside me back down, down, down into that dark, dank corner of my mind and locked it there as I had learned to do over the years. I knew exactly what Joseph Murphy was feeling, but I didn't want to know or remember or relive it.

I watched him fall on his knees on another expensive Oriental carpet beside the table, this one blue-and-forest green-and-burnt orange, all his pomposity and arrogance drained out of him like air from a punctured air mattress, the loss of a lifetime, the kind of horror that never ends. He was groaning deep in his throat, making awful choking sounds, and Bud gave me a *what-should-we-do-now* look. I didn't know what to do, but neither of us moved to touch him or lay a comforting hand on his shoulder as we sometimes had done in other cases.

"Oh, my God, my God, my God . . ." Murphy was moaning out loud now, his words only half intelligible, and then he burst into a blubbering sort of crazed tears, his imperious facade in tatters, his mind destroyed by the mere magnitude of the unthinkable. I knew, I knew, only too well did I know.

I said, "Please take a chair, Mr. Murphy. I know this is terrible for you."

Murphy heard me somehow and managed to struggle up into the nearest chair. He folded his arms on the table and lay his head down atop them then bawled like a neglected baby. We waited for him to calm down, uncomfortable, you bet we are.

Murphy didn't get over the shock quickly, or easily, and he wasn't quiet with his grief, either.

After about ten minutes, Bud said quietly, "How about I get you a glass of water, or cup of coffee, something like that, sir? It might help a little."

Murphy raised his face to us, pale and blotchy now, running with tears, then he shook his head back and forth some more. His precisely barbered light brown hair was no longer manicured into place, his gold-framed glasses were off, tossed down on the table, his life destroyed. Finally, he mopped the wetness off his face with a crisp white handkerchief that he pulled out of the chest pocket of his navy suit. "Oh, God, no, did you say it's a suicide? Mikey committed suicide? Oh, God."

"That appears to be the case, sir, but we have just begun our investigation. There is a possibility that your son's death could turn out to be a homicide, but we can't tell you what happened until after all the evidence is collected and examined by the medical examiner. That is being done as we speak."

Murphy heaved in some deep breaths, but it didn't seem to help much. His hands were trembling, his whole body collapsed in the chair, all self-control gone. "Oh, my God, this can't be happening. This can't be true."

We all turned as a door at the far end of the room opened, and who should appear but the Honorable Governor Edward Stanton himself. He was a distinguished looking guy in his early fifties, had won his last election big-time with about 70 percent of the vote. I didn't vote for him, thought he was too slick and self-assured. Bud didn't, either, but he just forgot it was election day.

Stanton was the father of all politicians, according to Black, who claimed to know him personally. Today, he was wearing a pinstriped gray suit and white shirt, and the obligatory little American flag on his lapel like Barack Obama learned to do the hard way. His eyes were black as coal and glowed with inner intensity, and his hair was graying at the temples or he had them bleach it out in some fancy salon to affect age and wisdom. But that impression could be the result of my extreme and ultra distrust and/or dislike of all politicians, great or small.

Eddie Boy had a nice white smile on TV, but he wasn't smiling now. He strode down the room toward us, tall and trim, very athletic for his age. I bet he was into golf and something else like cross-country skiing in Vermont at his vacation home. He kept his gaze fastened solely on his distraught adviser. "Joseph? Are you all right? What the hell's going on?"

Murphy tried to pull himself together for the boss man, didn't quite execute it, and looked up at me with weepy agony in his eyes. I got his message, too.

I said, "Governor Stanton, Mr. Murphy has just gotten some very bad news of a personal nature."

"And you are?"

Well, now I know where Debbie Winters got it. "We're detectives from Canton County at Lake of the Ozarks. My name is Claire Morgan and this is Bud Davis."

"You're Nick Black's girl."

Well, hell, I sure didn't like the sound of that one little bit. I wasn't anybody's *girl*. In fact, I wasn't a girl. I was a woman, a policewoman. He might as well have added Friday on the end. I didn't respond. A glance told me Murphy was openly sobbing again, and Bud wasn't saying anything, so, crap, I had to speak, even after that rather insulting and sexist remark. So I said, "Mr. Murphy's son, Michael Murphy, was found dead at the Grand Glaize Bridge in Osage Beach. It appears to have been a suicide."

That rocked the guv back on his heels. "Oh, my God, Joseph, I'm so sorry."

In the next few moments, the governor seemed to be a pretty good guy; at least he didn't mind touching a suffering employee. He put his arm around his friend's shuddering shoulders. "Oh, Joseph, this is just terrible, terrible news."

Yeah, that pretty much summed it up, all right.

"Well, you have to go home immediately and be with your family. Don't worry about a thing here. Does Mary Fern know?"

Murphy just groaned some more and looked at me. I began to feel like a ventriloquist's dummy.

"We were told by Mr. Murphy's housekeeper that his wife is on a shopping trip in Kansas City. She's expected home any time now. We can call her for you, Mr. Murphy, if you prefer, but I thought you might want to inform your family yourself."

"Yes, oh, yes, thank you, Detective. I will. I have to, oh, God, I have to be the one who tells her."

Then the governor said, "Joseph, listen to me, you need to get home right away. I'll order around my limo. Maybe the officers could follow you there?" He looked at me for verification.

"Yes, sir. We would be glad to follow him. I'm afraid we'll have to ask a few questions of both parents before we leave."

The governor frowned at that but didn't forbid it. Good thing, too.

Murphy said, "Yes, yes, I'll take the limo. I need some time alone to get a grip before I face everybody. Oh, how am I going to break this to her, to the kids? They'll all be home, too. Oh my God, I can't tell them Mikey's dead. It'll kill them." His voice had risen higher and higher, precipitously shrill in pitch, then finally petered out in a helpless moan.

Bud found his tongue. "We'll be glad to follow you home, sir. And we'll break the news to your wife, if you think you're not up to it. Sorry, sir, but we'll have to ask her some questions. As soon as the two of you feel up to it, I mean."

"Oh, yes, please, please help me. I don't know what she's gonna do."

Apparently, Joseph Murphy wasn't quite the strong, in-command type everybody thought him to be. He was not exactly displaying innate courage at the moment, but who could blame him? He'd lost his son and a hole had been torn in his heart that could never be filled but would lie deep and gaping for the rest of his life.

Governor Stanton turned back to us. He was a commanding man, even I felt his presence, and he hadn't gotten my vote. "Yes, officers, if you'll be good enough to escort Joseph home safely, I'd be indebted." His gaze left Bud and his eyes zeroed directly in on mine. "Joseph's not himself."

No kidding, Sherlock, I thought. "Yes sir," I said.

We turned to leave, and the governor walked us to the door, a real polite gentleman, and everything. "He's been under a lot of pressure with Mikey the last few years. He's a fine man, but this is a very stressful time. He's hit the end of his rope."

I thought that a rather ironic, and yes, unsuitable, metaphor, considering, but then again, Governor Stanton didn't know yet that Mikey was found swinging from a noose. Both the governor and Joseph Murphy were really going to freak out when they heard about what their little Mikey left roasting in the oven for us to find.

Here Comes Trouble

As it turned out, the psycho ward was a pretty sweet place. It was way out in the woods, truly out in the middle of nowhere, with rolling green pastures surrounding it, and lush stands of cedar and pine trees and giant red and white oaks with spreading branches. His dad was right, too, about all the sports being available to the patients. They had just about every sport and leisure activity for the kids to play. He'd soon be known as the best athlete in the whole damn place. And it sure wouldn't take long until all the other kids looked up to him and were just dying to be his friend. He'd never found it hard to control others; in fact, he was an absolute master at manipulation and thought it was fun to mess them up in the head. And lucky, lucky him, he found the absolute perfect victim when he met up with his skinny new roommate, a kid straight out of the *Revenge of the Nerds* movies.

"Oh, hello," his new roommate said. He was lying on his back propped up with a bunch of red and white striped pillows. He didn't sit up, just turned his head.

"Hi," the son replied. Politely and with that odd embarrassment of complete strangers suddenly forced to live together, they exchanged names and towns and shy grins.

"That's my real name," the roommate said, "but everybody around here calls me Buddy. We go by aliases here, if we don't want people to know who we really are."

That seemed a cop-out. Weren't the doctors trying to get everybody used to living in their own skin? He said, "No kidding. That's pretty messed up. But I'll call you Buddy, if you want."

The son glanced around, then took the bed across from Buddy's. It was a nice size room, not as big as his at home, though, with lots of pictures hanging around with lame inspirational messages on them, like HARD WORK PAYS OFF. Sure, it does, he thought, unless you can get somebody else to do it for you. A framed message above the door said SUCCESS IS 10% INSPIRATION AND 90% PERSPIRATION. He wanted to laugh. He'd always found that to be just the opposite.

"What are you in for?" Buddy asked him, then quickly amended it with, "You don't have to tell me, if you don't want to."

"That's okay. Everybody knows that my family thinks I'm a nutcase and will kill myself, or something, if the doctors don't get inside my head and fix me."

"Yeah, I know, that sounds like me."

"I saw my mom kill herself," he said to Buddy then, curious if it would shock him. He watched the other boy closely to see if that triggered any emotions. It didn't, or if it did, he couldn't see them.

"Gee, that's tough," said Buddy after a moment, and oh, so earnestly, too. "Bet that sucked for you."

The son nodded. "Yeah, real bad. She fell off a hiking trail and died right in front of my eyes. She almost took my little baby sister with her."

Buddy's face looked horrified. "Man, that's awful."

"Yeah, but I managed to save the baby. Mom was carrying her in a sling, but I pulled it off just in time before she jumped. The baby's just a couple of months old, and it was still nursing and everything, so now she's gotta be on a bottle. My aunt's taking care of her for my dad."

"You don't have much trouble talking about it, do you?"

"No. Do you have trouble talking about your stuff?"

"Yeah, I guess. Most of us here do."

"You gotta tell me why you're in here. I told you."

"My sister died a few years ago. I can't quit thinking about it. I think about her all the time and how stiff and white she looked at the funeral in that little box."

"What happened to her?"

"I don't wanna talk about it anymore."

"Okay, whatever. Just tryin' to be friendly."

Then Buddy turned over and faced the wall, pretty much dismissing his new roommate, and the son went on unpacking his clothes and putting them in the drawers underneath his bed. He would have preferred to have the other bed because it faced a window that looked out into some big tree limbs. Those branches so close to the building might present a pretty cool way to skip out after hours if he ever needed to. But that's okay, he'd probably be able to talk Buddy out of the other bed before too much time passed. Buddy came off pretty much like a wimp and a pushover. He was already crying and trying to hide it by muffling his sobs in the pillows. Gee whiz, what a baby and he hadn't even told him what happened to the sister. Some kids didn't have any backbone. He began to wonder what exactly had happened to Buddy's sister. It must have been pretty gory and gruesome, even worse than what happened to Lyla. He couldn't wait to hear all about it. Maybe some of it would come out in the stupid group therapy sessions he heard they were forced to go to.

"Hey, Buddy. I got a box of chocolate-covered cherries here. Want some?"

The son waited, but he knew Buddy would. Buddy was a little chubby around the waistline. He had already decided that the way to Buddy's heart was through his stomach, and it didn't take two minutes for Buddy to prove him right.

Rolling over, Buddy lay on one side and stared at him. His eyes were red and watery. "I love those things."

"Me, too. Here, take one, it'll make you feel better. Take all you want, Buddy, 'cause my dad'll send me more any time I ask him. He feels real bad about me seeing my mom die. He feels guilty, and all that. So he gives me whatever I want."

Buddy said, "My dad just says quit being a stupid moron and get over it."

The son walked over to Buddy's bed and offered him the candy. "Here, you go, Buddy, take as many as you want to."

Buddy dug three out of the holes in the plastic liner that held the cherries in place.

"I take it you don't get along with your dad too well, huh, Buddy?"

"No. He wants me to play football and basketball and stuff, but I like being in the band better. I play snare drums, real good, too, but he said everybody'd call me a band fag, if I joined the band."

"Did you?"

Buddy nodded, chewing on a chocolate-covered cherry and acting like it was the best thing he'd ever put in his mouth. "Yeah. I got first chair right off, over some of the older kids, too. Our band director really liked me. He said I got the cadences down real good."

"Did kids call you a band fag like your dad said?"

"Yeah."

He laughed at Buddy's expression, and then Buddy looked pretty surprised but he grinned a little but uncertainly.

"Now, don't you worry about those jerks back home, Buddy. You can practice those drums and end up bein' as famous as Ringo Starr was with the Beatles but what're those dumbass football players gonna be? Nothin'. Just big fat ex-athlete losers who don't know how to do anything but push people around when some coach blows on a whistle."

Buddy sat up. His grin was slow but very pleased. "Yeah, that's what I've always thought about those stupid jocks, too."

"Did you tell your dad that?"

"No. He wouldn't listen, anyways. He was a big star when he was in our high school, you know, made lots of touchdowns and stuff."

"What's he do now?"

"He's a mechanic in the Shell station back home."

"Well, la di freakin' da, a mechanic. Bet they never asked him to go on the Jay Leno show, did they?"

Buddy laughed. "No. He sings karaoke at the Fifth Street bar sometimes, but he sucks at it. He likes to sing "Born to Be Wild." He didn't even have the money to send me here. Grandma had to pay."

"See what I mean? Nobody's gonna remember him anymore, but take a real good musician like you, you can get a job lots of places and make a big name for yourself. People will pay to come in and see you play the drums."

"Yeah, that's my dream, all right."

"Tell you what, kid, I'll help you. My dad's got some connections here and there. Maybe I can get you a gig with a real-live band when you get a little older."

"You think you could do that, really?"

"Sure I could. Just stick with me, Buddy, and we'll go places together. Once we blow this place, we can hang out, have some fun."

Buddy popped another chocolate-covered cherry into his mouth. He chewed on it pretty good, but he was smiling so much that some cream filling oozed out his mouth and rolled down his chin. He licked it up with his tongue, still grinning.

Yep, the son thought, if everybody in this place was this much of a pushover, he was really gonna love it here.

* * *

A couple of hours later, the new roommates walked down a long carpeted hallway together.

"Is this therapy stuff pretty bad?" he asked Buddy.

Buddy said, "Nah, not really. The doctors watch you like you're a ticking time bomb, but nothin' much ever happens around here."

"Like you're a lit cherry bomb at Fourth of July, huh?"

"Oh, yeah, that's exactly the way they look at us. I just look away when they do that and don't say nothin'. I don't trust 'em. I know they're gonna tell my dad stuff I say."

"Maybe you should talk. You know, say whatever comes into your mind. Maybe it'd make you feel better. I think that's what I'm gonna do."

"I don't like to talk in front of people." Buddy stopped in front of a dark green door. He knocked on it instead of going right in. Inside, a voice called out, "Enter."

The son thought that was a pretty funny thing for somebody to yell out, instead of just saying come on in or jumping up and answering the door. Buddy held it open for him and let him walk inside first. The entire therapy group was already there, sitting around in a circle in black metal folding chairs. When he did a quick head count, he saw there were twelve kids there, eight girls and four boys. He immediately scoped out the girls for the prettiest ones.

"Oh, there you are, boys. I guess Buddy's showed you around the place a little," the doctor in charge said to him, standing up. He was a lot younger than the son had expected, much younger than the shrinks in the hospital who had ordered him out here. He was wearing a white T-shirt and jeans and wore some large black sunglasses. He looked like an older guy who was trying to look cool with the younger kids. He didn't fool the son for one single second. He introduced himself to the son, and then introduced the son to the rest of the group.

"Go ahead and sit down, fellas. We're just getting ready to go around the circle and tell everybody how we felt today when we woke up. You know, the first thing we thought about, and how we felt. Just for fun, you know."

Yeah, right, thought the son, just for fun. What did this guy take us for, morons? He sat down beside a good-looking Asian girl, the best-looking one by far, and who was just the littlest bittiest thing imaginable. He thought she looked hot and like somebody he'd like to have sex with. He wondered if she was a virgin and how easy it would be to get into her pants. He smiled at her, slightly turned on, just thinking about it.

She had the longest black hair, and she had it tucked behind her ears. She kept her eyes downcast but watched him sidelong out from underneath some real long black lashes. She wore white shorts that came just above her knees and he liked the color of her legs. She had on some white sandals, too, with shiny silver trim, and her toenails were painted black. So were her fingernails.

Around the circle they went, with most of the kids just saying they felt nothing at all when they woke up. Some of them said they were too sleepy to think about anything. He almost laughed at what a failure this little shrink exercise was turning out to be, or therapy, if that was what the hell it was. It wasn't working for Mr. Cool, that was for damn sure. So he decided to liven things up a bit.

When it was his turn, the doctor looked at him in kindly fashion, even put his hand on his shoulder to make him feel welcome and comfortable. "So what about you? And by the way, nobody here is forced to go by their real name, if they prefer not to. It's completely up to you. We protect our patients' privacy in every possible way. Of course, you can give it to us, if you want to. Or you can make up something for us to call you that you feel comfortable with. It's your decision."

"Well, then okay. My name is Trouble. Always has been. But everybody can call me Tee for short."

Complete silence. He thought that would get him a couple of laughs. Nobody even smiled. God, what a bunch of dumb losers.

The doctor said, "Then Trouble it is. Tee, for short. Hope you don't live up to it, though."

No response. The group did not think the doc was funny, either.

"What did you feel, Tee, when you first opened your eyes this morning?"

If they wanted something to react to, he'd give it to them, by God. "Well, Doc, when I woke up this morning, the first thing I saw was the way my mom's head looked all busted up on the rocks at the bottom of the cliff. Just like a muskmelon tossed off a truck on the Interstate."

Dead silence.

Doc crossed his legs. "Indeed," he said without missing a beat. "That must have been a very painful thought for you so early in the day."

"Oh, yeah, it was painful. It even made me want to commit suicide again. So see, I have this little pocketknife, see, and I got it out and opened it up and put the blade against my wrist right here." He showed them with his forefinger. "See, it's still not healed from last time. But my dad came in and stopped me in time. Too bad, or I'd be in the morgue right now, instead of here chewing the fat with you guys."

Nobody said anything for a moment, and then a big, gangly boy who had on a T-shirt with Good Charlotte on the front said, "Bullshit. You're just trying to get attention with that stupid-ass story."

"Yeah," said the hot Asian girl beside him. "You think you're hot shit, don't you?"

Tee said, "Is there any other kind?"

That brought a few chuckles from around the circle. He

grinned. He was getting to some of them, but surprise, surprise, this little episode at the psycho clinic was gonna be more of a challenge than he had expected. There might actually be some kids with brains stuck in here with him. Hell, that's probably why they were in here. They were too smart to want to do the same old things everybody else did, like go to proms and drive around in cars and go to the movies, and all that crap. Maybe he would even like one of them. That would be a first. But maybe psychos made the best friends. He'd soon see.

Doc said, "Does anyone else wish to comment on Tee's remarks? Please be sure and identify yourself so Tee can remember you better."

"Sure," said one kid who was dressed like a real dork in a white dress shirt with a button-down collar and black dress pants. He looked like he'd just gotten home from a wake and taken off his jacket. "My name's Moses, and I think Tee needs to find the Lord and he won't have to try to impress us with his silly, immature lies."

Tee looked at Moses and said, "What're you in here for? Parting the baptism water?"

Everybody laughed at that, and the dork aka Moses said, "That's not the least bit funny. It's sacrilegious." Moses looked around for nods of agreement but didn't get any. All the other kids just stared at Tee. But they looked interested. This was probably the most excitement this group had seen in months.

"Anybody like to play basketball around here?" Tee asked, looking around at his fellow patients.

"I play," said the little tiny China doll beside him. Several others indicated that they played, too.

"You're too short to be good," Tee said to her.

"Ever heard of three-pointers?" she said to him.

"I was leading scorer on every team I ever played on."

"Me, too."

Tee eyed her with new respect. Yeah, he was gonna bang

her, all right. If she didn't want to, he'd make her. He was big and strong enough to do her, even if she fought back.

"You know, Tee, that's not a bad idea. Maybe we could form a little league, of sorts," said Doc. "Just for the fun of it. The gym's open every night. It'll be good exercise for the group."

"You're dead meat, Mr. T," said the girl.

He didn't like the Mr. T crack; he'd seen reruns of *The A-Team*, but he rather liked the sassy girl. "You're too pretty to be a basketball player," he said to her and gave her his most charming grin.

"You're lame and retarded," said the girl, and gave him her most scathing sneer.

"You sayin' something's wrong with that?"

"You're so done for. Please don't sit by me again. You make me sick."

The doctor said, "Lotus, be nice. Tee's new to our group. We should welcome him and try to make him feel comfortable."

"Yeah? Maybe I'll give him a bigger, sharper knife as a welcome-to-the-nuthouse gift."

Tee was really beginning to like her. A lot. He couldn't wait to hold her down and force himself on her.

SEVEN

"Well, lookee here, Claire, seems our man, Murphy, lives in the second friggin' White House."

I had to agree with Bud's assessment of the Murphy estate, or mansion, if you preferred maid speak. We followed the governor's big black limousine through an ornate, spiked wrought-iron gate that had to be opened from the house or with remote controls carried by family members, and drove up the sweeping curve of the blacktopped driveway. Far away and up to our left, atop a hill with jade-green, manicured lawns, stood the Murphy abode aka Palace of Versailles. Oh, yeah, old Joseph and his clan were rolling in money, no doubt about it.

Bud said, "Think they'll let us in without puttin' on a friggin' tuxedo?" Then he said, "This joint looks like something Nick Black might live in."

"He's rich, but he's not this obnoxious about it. Anyway, his digs are mostly the penthouses in his hotels."

"Oh, yeah, he's only got penthouses, poor guy."

Bud was teasing me, and I knew it, so I let it go.

I said, "Doesn't look to me like the kind of family that would produce a suicidal son who'd broil his girlfriend."

My remark hung in the air between us. Neither of us cracked a smile. Hell, I could still smell the roasting flesh, and I tried to clear that memory out of my head. Once more, I decided I'd never cook a roast again, not of any kind, not that I ever had. Once more, I asked myself what kind of whack job could possibly do something so inhumane? Or was it a horrible accident? The poor girl climbs into an oven in a drugged-out daze for some unknown reason, and uh oh, somebody accidentally left the timer on. Sorry, that just didn't pass the sniff test with me, uh uh, no way Jose. But why the hell would she climb inside that oven? She had to be so strung out that she didn't know what she was doing. That's the only explanation I had been able to come up with. Except for Black's hypnotism theory, which seemed a little screwy, too.

The buffed-up doozy of a shiny limousine slowed to a stop in front of the house under a massive pillared portico. The huge house, oops, I mean mother of all mansions, was quite the sight to behold. Red brick with pristine white trim. Colonial architecture that looked straight off Boston Commons. There was a glassed atrium on the south end, a screened porch on the north, and maybe fifty windows facing the giant fountain in a circular drive heralding the great big double front doors.

Across the rolling fields of grass I could see the muddy Missouri River meandering and gurgling its path to its eventual rendezvous with the mighty Mississippi. This guy might actually give Black a run for his money in a giant moneybags marathon.

We watched the uniformed driver jump out and hurry around to open the backseat door. Murphy slumped out and glanced back at us, where we still sat in my Explorer behind the limousine.

I said, "Well, Bud, I can tell you one thing, I would rather drink acid than walk inside that house."

Bud said, "Ditto, double time." He glanced at a deer that suddenly appeared at the edge of the woods to one side of us. I hoped it didn't charge out and attack us. That would top off our morning.

Bud said, "You think it's weird he wants us to come along and help him tell his wife?"

"Yeah, the thought occurred to me."

"You'd think he'd want to do it himself in private, locked up in their bedroom or somewhere, maybe, you know, give her some time to deal with it a minute or two before she faces the police."

"Yeah, but everybody's different. He's not strong emotionally, that's pretty evident, but he's not faking it, either. He's devastated about his son, definitely, without a single doubt. C'mon, let's get him inside, he's not going anywhere near that front door without us."

Reluctantly, we climbed out of the Explorer as the guv's limousine sped off with a quiet, expensive purr and ever-glinting wax job. Joseph Murphy stood on his doorstep like a lost waif, his facial muscles lax and morose, his eyes bloodshot, his life over. He said nothing when we reached him, just turned and started up the semicircular bricked steps to the front door. We followed, also silent. Over the front door was a gigantic fanlight made of cut glass that probably came from Tiffany's a hundred years ago and was transported to Missouri from Tara, or another plantation like it. In other words, it was worth plenty. Painted scarlet, my dear, the door was unlocked so the master of the manse ignored the huge brass door knocker shaped like a crown and walked right in, his two police escorts skirting in his wake.

Once inside, we were met by complete and utter silence. Mausoleum size foyer, by the way, if not larger. I bet I could yodel like Heidi's grandpa and get some super good vibrations off the giant crystal chandelier. No uppity butlers hanging around. No snotty maids, either; probably off some-where on the telephone offending callers. But there were lots of large beautifully decorated Chinese vases and gilded baroque mirrors. A few burgundy velvet chairs and a match-ing tufted settee were positioned at the base of a long curv-ing flight of stairs. Not bad for our little old Show-Me State. Black would want to buy it, no question. However, it seemed as cold as ice, deserted and lonely. Maybe Murphy just wanted us here for the company and some human warmth.

"Mary Fern's probably in the family room. She feels more comfortable in there."

Murphy was speaking in a low monotone now. Saying as little as he could get by with. We followed him some more. Down a couple of halls with double doors opening into great big grandiose rooms on either side. Nobody said anything, and there wasn't a sound to be heard in the house, except for our echoing footsteps. It could've been "The Night Before Christmas," sans the mouse.

At the extreme rear of the mansion we entered a huge room that actually looked lived-in. At least there was a frosted glass sitting on the top of a glass cocktail table, mak-ing a ring, even, God forbid. But it was a fancy goblet and it was made of Waterford crystal, so there you go. I know it's Waterford, because Black has some in his penthouse. Trust me, I do not. I use empty jelly jars at my house. Disney World ones. Once I got one that had grapes on it because it was Smucker's Concord Grape and that's my favorite.

Lo and behold, a woman was sitting alone at a beige mar-ble bar with mirrors behind it. Down an adjacent wide hard-wood-floored hallway, I could see glimpses of an equally giant chrome and black kitchen. The floors were all shiny polished dark wood that was almost black. I was beginning to believe Shaq and his team lived here, just for the head-space alone.

The three of us stood by the door and said more nothing. Murphy looked at me like a helpless little kid who had lost his way, and he was. He was mute, to boot. Bud was looking at me, too, so I guess that's my cue to get this show on the road. I said, "Mrs. Murphy?"

The woman jerked around quickly and looked at us, rather unnecessarily startled. She was middle-aged, late thirties, early forties, but slender and tanned and pretty in her black and white striped capris and spotless white sleeveless blouse made of fine linen, if I was any judge of expensive garments, and I wasn't. She stood up immediately and walked slowly toward us. She was a graceful woman. Her hair was highlighted with ash blond and expertly done. Inside she was probably giving him hell for toting home uninvited company wearing T-shirts and jeans.

"I'm sorry, Joseph, I didn't hear you come in." She looked me and Bud over pretty good with undisguised curiosity, then focused her attention on her husband, her expression faintly quizzical. "Honey, you're home awful early. Is everything all right?"

Joseph Murphy stared at her with a horrible look on his face, then he started to weep. Presto, that brought his wife alive quick enough.

She went to him and put her hand on his arm. "What? Tell me. Are you sick?"

Joseph grabbed her by the upper arms, held her back, and stared down into her shocked face, then lost his nerve and lay his head on her shoulder, sobbing. Confounded, she looked at us for help. She kept saying, "What's wrong, Joseph? What's wrong? What's happened?"

I didn't want to break the news, either, but I finally said the usual, "I'm afraid we've got some very bad news, Mrs. Murphy. I think you should sit down."

"Oh, my God, what is it? Is it one of the children?"

I nodded and said gently, "I'm afraid so, ma'am. Please, sit down here on the sofa and let us tell you what happened."

Although obviously terrified, Mary Fern Murphy led Joseph to one of the long white sofas and they sank down on it together, very close, but she wasn't going to wait any longer to hear the bad news. "All right, this has gone on long enough. I want to know right now what has happened to upset my husband like this. Please tell me. Now."

So I just said it. "Your son was found dead last night at Lake of the Ozarks. It appears at this time that he hanged himself under the Grand Glaize Bridge. I'm very sorry, Mrs. Murphy."

Her eyes went wide, blinked, and stayed closed for half a second, then opened and stared straight at me. She was ignoring her husband now, who was sobbing even louder against her shoulder. Then she seemed to relax, got a very calm look on her face, and said, "Which son?"

That surprised me for some reason, but I didn't have to answer. Her husband finally spoke up, his words barely intelligible. "It's Mikey, oh, God, Mary Fern, he finally did it. He killed himself."

Bud and I watched her face turn the color of cold ashes, as if the blood had rushed down to her feet in a gush, but she didn't burst into tears. She patted her husband's back and tried to comfort him in that way, but her eyes, a very bright, unusual color of green, probably tinted by designer contact lenses, remained fixed on me. "Was he alone?"

Now that was a surprising remark, startling even. Bud thought so, too, I could see it in his face.

"Yes, ma'am. As far as we know."

For a fleeting moment Mary Fern Murphy's face took on a look that I could only describe as heartfelt relief, then she said, "I was afraid he'd made a death pact with a girlfriend. He tried to do that before. Once, that we know of."

Bud said, "He's tried this before?"

"That's right. He and his girlfriend at the time."

Whoa, now. I said, "Mrs. Murphy, we really need to interview you. Are you gonna feel up to it today? We need you to tell us about prior suicide attempts, and there are other questions we need answered before our investigation can proceed."

Mary Fern had still not shed a single tear. I guess her husband was crying enough for both of them. She said, very politely, "I'd like a moment alone with my husband before we sit down with you. Would that be permissible?"

Permissible? That sounded more like something out of the mouth of a suspect. "Of course, ma'am. Take all the time you need."

"Thank you. Why don't the two of you go on into the kitchen and wait for us there? Fix yourselves something to drink, if you like. There are soft drinks in the fridge, and there are cookies under a glass dome on the center island. It's down that hallway." She pointed it out to us, still dry eyed and calm.

It appeared Mary Fern was quite the hostess, even when shocked and in mourning for the death of her child. We made ourselves scarce and entered the wide, bright, spacious kitchen, all done in black and white, a cooking area that Paula Deen herself would envy. Outside on our right, a long expanse of multipaned windows revealed a large kidney-shaped swimming pool with fake stone waterfalls and lots of flora and greenery, and a couple of hot tubs disguised as natural rock pools. About six or eight children of various ages were splashing and lazing about in the sun, the rest of the Murphy brood, I suspect.

Bud lowered his voice. "Did she take this really well, or is it just me?"

"I'm right there with you."

"Maybe she's a Steel Magnolia like we have down south?"

"Like in the movie?"

"Yeah. Bet she runs this place like a regular Nurse Ratched."

"Bet she is Nurse Ratched." I decided to be slightly more magnanimous. "Or maybe she's just in shock and wants time to comfort her husband in private."

"Somebody sure needs to." Bud looked around the elaborate kitchen. "How about a Pepsi? I'm dying to open that double icebox. I've never seen one this big outside a restaurant."

Yeah, Bud still calls them iceboxes, but so does my Aunt Helen. His remark brought a couple of horrific visions to mind concerning Mikey's Kitchen of Horrors, so I followed him across the shiny black-and-white tiles to the giant refrigerator. He opened both doors and took out a couple of cans of Pepsi and handed one to me.

Popping the tab, I turned and looked through the windows at the pool. It was surrounded by more perfectly sodded grass with lots of cushioned lawn chairs and padded chaises sitting around. A bath house with red and white striped awnings sat at one end. The kiddos were having fun out there, all right. Seemed to be getting along fine with each other. How had Mikey Murphy fit in around here? What the hell was wrong with his mom? I had a feeling it wasn't exactly a Bill Cosby/Huxtable kinda family.

"Okay, officers. Please come back now. We're ready to sit down and answer your questions. Feel free to bring your soft drinks with you."

Mom was back. Cool as a cucumber, too. Dry-eyed. Wow, it took her a whole ten minutes to get over the shock. Something was just wrong with this picture, oh yeah, you betcha.

Frosty Pepsi cans in hand, we trailed her back to the family room and found that her husband had bucked up considerably during our mini-absence. He still looked a bit shell-shocked, but he wasn't weeping and gnashing his teeth any more. He wasn't saying anything, either. Probably under direct orders.

Mrs. Murphy took a seat beside him and gestured for us to sit across from them on the matching snowy sofa. We sat. I looked at Bud and gave him my famous, *you-take-the-reins-for-a-while* look. So he took the reins for a while.

"I'm Detective Bud Davis, ma'am, and my partner's name is Claire Morgan."

"Claire Morgan? That name sounds vaguely familiar. Do you work on the governor's detail?"

"No, ma'am. We're both with the Canton County Sheriff's Department. I'm quite certain we've never met," I said, not wanting to talk about me and the miserable newspaper articles that everybody seemed to love to read about me.

"No, I suppose not." Since you're a peon, I finished for her. She looked back at Bud. Both her hands were entwined with her husband's now. She was patting the back of his left hand. His hands were trembling. Hers were not. "You said that Mikey hanged himself. Are you absolutely positive that it's a suicide?"

This woman was full of surprises and unexpected remarks when she wasn't playing White House First Lady/hostess. Grieving Mom strikes again and shocks the cops.

Bud said, "As my partner said, it appears that way at this time, but it could turn out to be a homicide. We'll know more when the medical examiner tells us how your son died."

"I should think it would be a homicide," Mikey's mom said calmly. "He didn't really have the guts to kill himself, or it would've happened a long time ago. Like I said, he's tried before."

Her husband stiffened and more tears erupted. Mom of the Year comforted him as much as she knew how.

"I'm afraid there's something else," I said. "We found a second body, not at the bridge with your son, but inside your son's pizza restaurant. It was a young woman, one we haven't been able to identify yet."

"Oh, my God," said mommy dearest. "I was afraid of that."

"Do you know who the second victim might be?"

Dad looked up at that, but Mom was quick to do the talking. "You think this woman was murdered then?"

"It's a possibility," I said, but thought that was the understatement of the millennium.

"How was she killed? Can you tell us?"

"We're not sure yet. The ME will make that determination, as well."

"I see."

Bud said, "Can you give us any information about your son's female friends? Did he have a steady girlfriend?"

Dad struggled to speak and said weakly, "Not that we know of. You see, we've been estranged from Mikey for about six months."

Mom said, "Mikey had lots of girlfriends, one after another. Many were absolute whores and weren't welcome in this house."

Well, okey doke, don't sprinkle Equal on it, lady. "Can you give us any names? It's important that we identify the body and notify next of kin as soon as possible."

"Are you asking us to go to the morgue and view this girl's body?" That, of course, came from Ice Water in Her Veins.

Bud said, "No, ma'am. That's not possible."

"What do you mean?"

I didn't want to get into that discussion and had decided to keep the details under wraps, anyway. The press was going to feast on this like the starving, gorging vultures they were. They weren't going to know about the oven crime scene, though, no way, not in a million years. The chief was going to make some phone calls.

"We can't really divulge the details of our case, ma'am. But it is important to know who your son was seeing, both his male friends and his girlfriends. Is there anything specific you can tell us?"

Dad sat up and spoke, almost eagerly this time. "I think he was dating a girl that went to Missouri State in Springfield. But I don't know her name."

"How did you know that, Joseph?" Mom didn't like him knowing that, not at all.

"He called me at my office at the Capitol three or four months ago."

"What did he want?"

"He just wanted to say hello and wish me a happy birthday, Mary Fern. For God's sake, our son is dead. Don't you get that?"

Amen, Joseph. But she apparently did not get it. She frowned at her presumptuous husband, then turned to me, "Joseph's not himself."

You think? Seemed everybody was stating the obvious, of late.

"I can see that you think I'm cold and unfeeling," she said to me.

"No, ma'am. I don't think that at all." Liar, liar, pants on fire.

"Yes, you do, but you just don't know what that boy's put us through. We tried everything, every single thing we could to get him off drugs, out of the low-life crowd he associates with. Nothing worked. He's just a bad seed. You've heard of that, haven't you? A bad seed."

"What sort of things was he into, ma'am?"

"Meth. Other drugs, too, of course, but meth was what did him in. He's been to psychiatrist after psychiatrist, but nobody could get through to him."

Now we're talking. "Was he seeing a psychiatrist recently?"

Dad said, "Yes, he was under outpatient treatment at the Oak Haven. That's a clinic here in Jefferson City. Martin Young runs the place. He's quite a genius with these kids."

That checked out with what Black had told me. "We'll have to talk to your son's doctors, of course. Maybe they can tell us who the female victim is."

Dad said, "The girl he was dating was Asian. Chinese. I think. Maybe Korean. Mikey said so on the phone. Said she was little bitty, a lot shorter than him, and he isn't very tall."

"Did he say anything else that you can remember, Mr. Murphy?"

"I think he said something about her hair being really long, down to her knees, I think he said. Said she was teaching him to speak Mandarin Chinese. He ended the conversation by saying the Chinese word for good-bye. I don't remember what it was."

"I doubt if our other children will know anything about this," Super Mom said. "I didn't like them talking to him because he was such a terrible influence on their behavior, but sometimes they disobeyed and saw him anyway. They'd go over to that little pizza place of his and hang out. I'd ground them for it, but they did it anyway."

"Yes, we'd like to talk to them, if possible."

Mom said, "You'll have to come back another day for that. They won't take this as well as I am."

Nobody would take it as well as you are, lady, not even a stranger who'd never heard of Mikey Murphy.

"Okay, we'll call first and make sure it's a convenient time. Thank you for your help. Again, we are both very sorry for your loss."

"Thank you for coming," said Mary Fern. Ever heard the word *wooden*? That pretty much sums up her demeanor. Joseph just stared up at us, his eyes red, face patently miserable.

Outside on the front steps, double doors shut firmly behind us, Bud said, "I hope my momma likes me better than that. Mary Fern in there makes an ice cube look toasty."

"I couldn't agree more. No wonder the kid was suicidal."

"Let's get outta here."

I was glad to oblige. I didn't like either one of the Murphys much, and I had a hunch Mary Fern Murphy had a few secrets hidden behind that icy facade of hers. But I'd dig until I got them, even if I had to take a blowtorch to melt her out of her armor-coated iceberg.

EIGHT

Oak Haven Clinic was located in a heavily wooded area just outside Jeff City, quite isolated, quite exclusive, and yeah, most of the trees were oaks, thus the name, I guess. Maybe neighbors wanting a bunch of unstable, suicidal kids next door were hard to come by. Go figure. It all looked very upscale and classy, of course, as if to impress Richie Rich and his dad, Even Richier Rich and mom, Rich Bitch, who'd screwed up their children with money and neglect and big-time overindulgence. Not that I am opposed to wealthy people. I do have a fondness for Black, after all.

A low wall of tan stones worn smooth by rushing water edged the blacktop highway for several miles, marking the outer perimeter of the clinic's property. No doubt the local creeks were all depleted now, no longer gurgling and splashing over pretty rocks anymore but flowing silently and morosely over a naked muddy bottom. Then we came upon the entrance, and oh, my, my, how impressive it was. A large brass plaque the size of a double front door announced in fancy flowing script that we had reached Oak Haven, and therefore should give thanks and bow from the waist. I listened for a blast of brass trumpets, but didn't hear anything, so Bud and I passed uneventfully through the portals of heaven without even a minor kowtow to the shrink gods. We followed the double-wide blacktop road through a football-field-size meadow of high grass, or maybe it was just weeds, waving in the brisk breeze and giving off gold-green glints as the sun caught its swaying ripples. Five minutes later, we pulled up in the parking lot. It was filled to the brim with the likes of Beamers, Cadillacs, Lexuses, and Lincolns. Not a genuine Humvee was in sight, though. Black was not here.

Oak Haven Clinic itself wasn't nearly as large as I expected it to be, actually the place looked like some kind of eighteenth-century dairy farm run by Quakers, with lots of long outbuildings built exactly alike: two-story, bleached pine siding, identical multipaned windows, and red shingled roofs. There was a giant flower garden out in front of the main building, sporting a twelve-foot-high tinkling fountain, designed in the shape of two entwined fish. The sculptor had to be a Pisces, bet on it. I wondered what a couple of cozy fish symbolized at this kind of institution. The only thing that came to mind was the newspaper-wrapped fish that Tony Soprano and his ilk left on their victims as dire warnings. Maybe Bud and I should take heed. Or at least throw some pennies in the fountain for good luck.

"Bet it costs beaucoup dollars to lay yourself down before these guys and spill your guts," Bud said, as I pulled into a parking space at the main building and killed the motor.

"Ah, yeah, you can count on that, all right, but nothing's too good for our less-than-sane crème de la crème aristocrats hereabouts."

"Young crazies, you mean?"

"Pretty much. And this is in-house therapy, too. That means all the little tykes live here together, like one big happy nutszoid family."

"Sounds like fun in the sun. Bet the inmates here are happier than Mary Fern's kids. She probably feeds them broken glass for dinner." Bud had not gotten over Mom's reaction to news of poor Mikey's demise. Neither had I. She made the Evil Queen in *Sleeping Beauty* look like Mother Teresa.

I said, "If I had to hazard a guess, the woman's messed up in the head. I wonder if Black knows her well enough to certify her. I'll ask him when he gets back from New York."

I removed the keys, and we sat a moment in silence, looking the place over. Four buildings were in sight, all connected by canopied sidewalks. We could see a big gymnasium in the distance and what looked like a swimming pool/tennis court complex.

Bud said, "Okay, Claire, let's not mess around in here. Let's get down and dirty with Mikey's doctor. You do the talking 'cause you're probably gettin' pretty good at cuttin' through shrink mumbo jumbo, spending all your time with you know who."

"Thanks. But Black doesn't discuss his patients with me. You know, all those pesky confidentiality standards. He's so honorable."

"Yeah? That's where warrants come in. Let's hope this guy won't mind sharing his thoughts."

"He probably won't mind after he hears about the oven thing." Yet again, that was a sobering thought.

We got out and walked across the tarmac to the front entrance. It was canopied, too, probably for the arrival and departure of ambulances and straitjackets. It was eerily quiet, as if all the teens were in padded cells while their shrinks smoked cigars, drank martinis in the break room, and pretended to be Sigmund Freud's interns. The entrance doors were painted this odd chartreuse color and made out of metal. Not exactly a welcoming sight. There was a doorbell located just right of the door. It had a sign screwed to the wall above it which read: PLEASE RING BELL. Now that seemed like a no-brainer to me, but hey, they were used to parents who had their maids and/or flunkies press doorbells for them. There was a surveillance camera pointed down at us, so Bud looked up and gave a big toothy grin and a friendly wave. I gave a friendly wave with my badge held up for emphasis and to get things off on the right foot.

Two seconds later, an elderly woman, who wore her meringue-white hair in those tight curls that women in their seventies seemed prone to do, swung open the door. She was dressed in a green-and-navy blue plaid blazer and long black skirt. Yes, it is hot summertime, but the living isn't always easy. And yes, she looked dumb as a stump in her winter clothing. Not to mention, hot as hell. Bud gave me a questioning glance, and then we felt the wave of frigid air blasting out the door and understood the woman's plight. Hell, the patients here must hail from Antarctica. Or maybe they raised penguins as pets.

She had large brown, extremely expressive eyes. Her face had lots of lines etching her cheeks and forehead. She did not smile and tell us how welcome we were to visit Oak Haven but she did say, "May I help you?"

Bud said, "Yes, ma'am, you sure can." He grinned his deadly smile, apparently expecting big results. She stared at him as if he were a prop man at *The Jerry Springer Show*. She didn't find him nearly as attractive as Debbie Winters had. Didn't matter; she wasn't his type, anyway.

I decided the lady was mine. I read her nameplate, Mrs. Mary Macy, and decided some good old-fashioned manners were in order. "Mrs. Macy? How do you do? My name is Claire Morgan. This is my partner, Bud Davis. We're detectives from the Canton County Sheriff's department."

"I deduced that, young lady, from the badge you held up to our security camera."

Well, Mary Macy quite contrary. "Yes ma'am, we're here to conduct interviews on a homicide case."

Mary Macy had on these little black half-glasses that she wore perched on the very end of her nose, and quite a nose it was. She looked at us over them with not a lot of pleasure, or respect, or need of eyeglasses it seemed. She held a book in one hand. A romance novel with an Indian brave on the front who looked like Arnold Schwarzenegger in the sauna scene in *Red Heat*. Except her guy had a tan leather strap around his forehead and a scantily clad captive at his feet. No feathers, though. The name of the book was *Savage Savage*. Actually, it looked pretty provocative, if you liked racy westerns. Mrs. Macy took a moment to dog-ear a page and shut the book. I hoped it wasn't a library copy, or she'd get in big trouble.

"I don't remember having your names on my appointment book for today."

Bud said, "We doan need no steenkin' appointments." He laughed. She didn't. He explained. "That's from that movie *Blazing Saddles*, remember, the bad guy said it?"

"I'm afraid I haven't seen that one."

Often a ruder sort than Bud, I said, "Law enforcement officers don't need appointments, Mrs. Macy. We carry guns, so we can blaze our way in."

I smiled. So did Bud. To my surprise, Mrs. Macy laughed out loud.

"Well, I do hope you aren't going to blaze your way in today."

Ice broken, or at least, cracked a little, I said, "We'll try to restrain ourselves, ma'am. As long as you cooperate."

Mrs. Macy said, "You're quite the card, aren't you, Detective Morgan?"

I wasn't sure if I was, or not, so Bud said, "She's not always this funny. Sometimes she's a pain in the ass."

"Watch your language, kiddo," Mrs. Macy said, but she gazed fondly at him.

I said, "Yes, ma'am. Now that we're all acquainted and getting along. We need to speak to Dr. Martin Young. Is he available at the moment?"

Mrs. Macy stepped back and allowed us to enter her frosty igloo. No wonder she was reading a hot romance to warm herself up. I immediately began to shiver and long for my police-issue, fur-lined parka. She led us across some serious burgundy and pale yellow tiles to her desk, a big curving brown one with an expensive marble top. A telephone system was on a shelf, but there were no lights blinking. Everybody asleep, I guess. Not much else on the counter except her Pilot black fine-point pen and a coffee cup painted with red and yellow roses. It was busy keeping itself warm on a single-cup electric warmer.

Mary Quite Contrary opened a low drawer and pulled out a different book. She smiled at us again, real friendly all of a sudden and now looking somewhat sheepish. She lowered her voice. "You know what? I have a thing for detectives. I think they're delicious."

That was a pretty good compliment. Bud and I both liked it.

Holding up the second book, she said, "This is a suspense novel. It's the kind that mixes the detective's romantic life with gory, bloody, horrible murders."

Sounded familiar to me, all right. "Yes, ma'am. Looks like a good read."

Mary turned the book around and showed me the cover. It was a picture of a nude woman who looked pretty darn dead, but not as dead as our little Asian victim had.

Obviously eager to get things rolling, Bud said, "Did you say Dr. Young is here today?"

"Yes, detective, he is. He comes here every day for his group therapy sessions. He should be about to wrap up one of them, right now, as we speak." She checked her watch. It was silver filigree with a black face about the size of a dime. Now I knew why she needed those spectacles. "Well, it's scheduled to end in about ten minutes. Would you like to wait here at reception or down in his office?"

Oh, man, would we ever like to snoop around in his personal stuff when nobody was looking. "His office sounds good. We're in no hurry. We can wait."

Mary Macy smiled at us. We were her delicious detective

buddies now. She headed off at a quick clip down a pale yellow hallway with the same shiny Italian tiles, then at the far end, we left the building by outside, levered doors and proceeded down one of those covered walks, hanging with pots of begonias and red salvia to match the roof. Mary chatted with Bud about detective procedures, which she knew pretty darn well, actually, said she'd always wished she'd gone into detective work instead of secretarial science. Bud said it was never too late to achieve one's dreams. Mary laughed and punched him lightly on the arm and said, "Oh, you kids."

When we reached the building directly behind the first one, she poked in a code with her forefinger and led us inside. It was extremely quiet, and most of the doors had rather large, and trust me, unmissable, signs that said IN SESSION: DO NOT DISTURB!!!

"Here you go. Dr. Young's private office," said Detective Wannabe Macy. I can see it now, her new NBC series: *Cagney and Macy, The Senior Years.*

"Thank you, ma'am," said Bud. "We'll look forward to having you on our force someday soon."

"Oh you, you're a little stinker, aren't you?"

Well, it had taken a bit longer for the little stinker to woo her into submission this time, but his record was intact, unbroken among any and all female oncomers.

"You oughta be the hero in that book I'm reading," said Mrs. Macy, who was really coming out of her shell now.

Bud grinned, and then Mrs. Macy actually did a little trill of a giggle. They'd call it a titter in her Indian book, I'm sure. My, my, Bud's charm was worth its weight in gold. Debbie Winters better prepare herself; she had some serious octogenarian competition going on here.

Dr. Young's office looked like a study in casual disarray. As if he had found some dusty old tome in a psychiatric hospital's medical library with a tintype of Sigmund Freud sitting behind his desk with book-lined shelves all around. I looked for the obligatory picture of the Father of Modern Psychiatry and found it on a bookshelf near the door. That must be a prerequisite demanded in psychiatrist school. Even Black had one. Not to mention his Rorschach prints. I didn't see any of those. I guess Young didn't go for ye olde inkspot therapy.

After Mrs. Macy had departed with one last smile at Bud, Bud looked at me and said, "Don't know about you, but I've got this uncontrollable urge to sink down on this couch and tell you my life story."

"Don't bother. I've already heard it. Twice."

Bud grinned and instead slouched his big frame down into a huge tan leather armchair sitting directly in front of the well-oiled oak desk. There was a couch across from it, tan and brown striped chenille, and I sat there, in a spot that gave me a good view out the window. Knots of young people suddenly began to stream out the doors of the next building, laughing and talking, just like regular kids. They all looked between, say, maybe twelve and twenty.

I stood up and stretched my arms to unkink my neck. "Wonder if Dr. Young likes to videotape his patients' every word? Black does that, I think."

Bud said, "Yeah, maybe we can get a warrant for those tapes and catch Mikey professing a fantasy of baking girls."

I had a hunch that Young liked to sit in the deep comfort of Bud's chair, instead of his leather swiveling desk chair, and chances were he directed his patients to the two side-by-side chairs right across from him. According to Black, who certainly knew his stuff, nobody ever asked patients to lie down on a couch anymore. Passé, I guess, or made fun of in too many B movies. I walked across the room to large, ceiling-high bookcases built against the wall directly across from the couch. Chock-full of books, they were stacked in the shelves at every angle, with a few framed pictures hanging here and there. Lots of magazines, too, like *Psychology Today*.

Slowly, I ran my fingertips over the spines of the books

that faced the tan striped couch, the ones at sitting level. It didn't take long to find the fake one, half hidden by a silk philodendron plant. I pulled it out carefully, opened the hinged lid, and found a honey of a little digital camcorder inside. The tiny red light wasn't blinking, so we hadn't been recorded. But then again, Martin Young wasn't expecting us. I had a hunch he probably taped everybody that sat down in his office, therapy sessions and otherwise, us included.

"Bingo, Bud."

Bud opened his eyes and said, "Huh?"

I held the camera up for him to see, then carefully closed the cover and slid the book back into place. I edged around behind the large messy desk with its backdrop of plate-glass windows. "Black's got a button control under his desk. Bet this guy does, too."

I bent down, searched one side of the center desk drawer, and presto, thar she blows. Top-notch psychiatrists must all think along the same wavelengths. I heard the door open and stood up quickly, but not quickly enough.

The man in the doorway stopped, as if surprised to find two detectives lounging around his private space. Imagine. A handsome man, Young was tall, stood at least six foot, thin and well groomed, and looked like a shrink, all right. He had short blond hair, almost in a military cut, and very dark blue eyes that burned a hole through me. Decked out in a gray cotton sweater with an open-necked white shirt underneath, he wore Dockers of dark charcoal, dark socks, and black loafers with pretty little tassels. Obviously, he was personally acquainted with the arctic temperatures of Oak Haven, as well. There was a pair of tortoiseshell glasses with square lenses that he had hanging around his neck on a red cord. He had the deepest cleft in his chin that I'd ever seen, not counting Aaron Eckhart and Kirk Douglas, of course. Heck, he could have a lint trap in a hollow that size. He centered all his attention on me instead of Bud, being a man instead of a lady, and said, "Drop something, miss?"

"I was just tying my shoe," I said, recognizing his biting sarcasm right off the bat. Then he smiled, as if I was lying and he knew it. I smiled, as if I didn't give a rip.

"Since this is my office, I suspect you know who I am, but I don't think I can say the same."

Bud stood up, the courteous detective, and I walked around the desk, the snurly one. Bud said, "Ms. Macy was good enough to let us wait here, where it was warm."

Dr. Young didn't find that amusing, nor did he seem to think Ms. Macy had made a wise decision. He just stared at us for another long moment, then said, "I see. And may I ask the reason you are here?"

I said, "Sure thing. We're detectives from Canton County, and we're here to ask you some questions about one of your patients."

"Is that right? May I see your ID?"

Wow, he sure was picky. Especially since we both happened to have said badges hanging around our necks in plain sight, so I decided he ought to perch his glasses on his nose instead of letting them hang down on his stupid and less than manly looking cord. We held our official calling cards up in tandem to show we worked for the same sheriff.

"It would have been nice if you'd called first. So I could've prepared."

I said, "Do you think you need to prepare yourself to chat with law enforcement officers?"

Our gazes locked. He was really considering me now, and I had a feeling it wasn't for a good-conduct medal. Then he showed me a very agreeable smile, with teeth as white and even as the major network anchor women, or the News Barbies, as I call them. Then he laughed out loud, as if I'd cracked a helluva good joke. Bud and I stared at him, our innards not particularly tickled, even though we are both known far and wide for our keen senses of humor. Just didn't get it, I guess.

"Sorry that I'm so testy. I just had a bad session, and I

guess I'm taking it out on you. You know, displaced aggression, and all that. Please sit down, detectives."

Testy was right, though it's not a word I use often but one that describes me rather well at the moment. Bud and I sat down in our original spots and watched the doc walk around the desk. He glanced at my shoes on the way by, I noticed, checking for the recently tied laces, no doubt. Luckily, I had on my black-and-orange Nike hightops, so my shoelace story checked out.

"Would you like a soda? Coffee? Something else?"

"Sure, I'll take a Coke." Bud never missed the opportunity for free food or beverage.

"No, thank you," I said. "I don't drink."

Dr. Young didn't react to my rather dry comedic side, but moved to a small fridge hidden in a low oak cabinet, where he retrieved a can of Cherry Coke for Bud and a bottle of Ozarka water for himself, that normally being the premier brand in the Ozarks. "You sure?" he asked me.

"Got any hot chocolate?"

"Afraid not, detective. You can wear one of my sweaters, if you're really that chilly."

Now that was a fate worse than death. I'm sure not into 1940s argyle. I demurred on the sweater but changed my mind and agreed to a bottle of water. While he got it for me, I watched to make sure Bud's Coke can hadn't been tampered with. After only a couple of minutes, I didn't trust this guy. Of course, that was the way it was with me and most anybody. The good doctor handed the soda to Bud, the water to me, then sat down behind his desk as Bud popped the tab. "Okay, what can I do for you, officers?"

"We understand that you have treated a patient by the name of Michael Murphy."

"That's right. Is he in some kind of trouble?"

Yeah, I'd say. "Yes, sir. He was found hanging from a bridge support yesterday evening. He's dead. An apparent suicide."

That caused him to strangle briefly on his pure Ozarka water. "You've gotta be kidding me."

That didn't sound exactly like shrink-ese, but we had hit him with a heck of a tsunami. Or at least, it appeared that way.

"I'm afraid we don't make jokes of that nature. I'm sorry to be the bearer of bad news."

Dr. Young stood up, squared his shoulders, as if trying to get hold of himself. Then he turned his back on us and stared out at the lawn. When he turned around after a couple of minutes, he said, "I can tell you that I treated him, but I'm afraid I can't really get into any more detail than that. Legally, I'm not allowed to, you understand, because of patient confidentiality requirements."

"Your patient is now dead, doctor, and stretched out in our morgue. He might've been murdered, and he might've committed murder. We need your help to find out."

"What do you mean, he might've committed murder?"

"There's a second victim, a woman, as yet a Jane Doe. We hope you can help us identify her. Her family needs to be notified."

"Are you seriously considering the idea that Mikey killed this woman?"

"Yes, very seriously. But we don't know yet. I'd say it's possible. We're just getting started with our investigation. That's why we need you to cooperate fully with us. Michael Murphy is dead, so you are released from protecting his confidentiality. If you still refuse, then we'll have to get a warrant for his medical records. Either way, you're gonna have to turn them over to us. Your choice, doctor."

"Sorry, I'd like to help, but I try to protect the privacy of my patients for as long as possible. His parents may not want his records released to the public. Have you told all this to his family yet?"

"Yes, they have been properly notified. We spoke to them earlier today."

"How did they take it?"

"They were upset, of course." Well, at least one of them was.

"Mary Fern took it well?"

"Yes sir, she did. Do you happen to know the Murphys well, doctor?"

"Yes, I do, actually. Truth is, Mikey's my cousin."

Now that was damn interesting. Mom and Dad hadn't mentioned that familial connection. Wonder why?

Bud joined in the conversation. We play tag team, you see. I took this opportunity to test the cap of my Ozarka to make sure it had not been opened, verified that, then twisted the top and took a drink. Never can be too careful. It tasted good, though. I was thirsty, after all.

"You treated a relative?" Bud was saying. "I thought you shrinks frowned on stuff like that."

Black had treated his own niece, too, once upon a time, not to mention me, but I had an urge to poke this guy a little with my obnoxious stick.

I said, "Please answer the question, Dr. Young."

Dr. Young turned his eyes on me and held them on mine for a beat or two. "You know, I don't think I caught your names."

"My name's Claire Morgan. He's Bud Davis."

A slow smile. "Oh, yes, I've heard of you, and now I know why you look so familiar. Nick Black's an old friend and colleague. I've attended a couple of conferences when he was the featured speaker. Very informative. He's really quite brilliant."

"Yes, he mentioned that he knew of you. He seemed to recall that he referred Mikey to this clinic. Is that correct?"

"Well, actually, he did, but it was because Mikey's parents wanted me to treat him. They preferred to keep his problems inside the family, if you know what I mean. They were concerned about publicity, you understand, with Joseph being connected so high up in state government."

Bud said, "Yeah, that occurred to us, too, just right out of thin air."

I sensed sarcasm in that remark, yes, I did.

Dr. Martin said to Bud, "I get a sense that you find the need for privacy contemptible?"

My turn. "Not at all, doctor. Tell me, do you have time now to sit down and talk to us?"

"I'll answer whatever I can in accordance with the laws governing my practice, of course, but that won't be much, I warn you. I certainly can't get into the specifics of Mikey's condition."

Bud said, "Why don't you just tell us everything you can and then we'll rush right out to a judge and get a warrant for everything else."

Sometimes Bud could be blunt and brutal. Not as much as me, of course, but blunt and brutal enough. He didn't like Martin, anybody could see that, but that was probably because Young had his glasses hanging on that sissified red cord.

Dr. Young's lips curved upward just a tad, but his eyes remained a very cold, disinterested blue. He was doing an awful lot of smiling, or smirking, you might call it. Maybe a background check on him might be in the cards. Silent and unpleasant, we sat and waited while he took a dainty swig of water. Trying to formulate psychiatrist-sounding words that meant no, I suppose.

"Mikey came to me, almost two years ago, I guess it was. Lived here at the clinic for a while. Then when we got his meds adjusted and he began to feel better, he left and went home to his place in Osage Beach. He's been doing fine since, as far as I knew."

I said, "Not exactly fine, if you factor in his suicide."

"You think it was a suicide then?"

"It appears that way. But sometimes appearances are deceiving. I'm sure you know that, considering your line of work."

"Did he leave a note?" the doctor asked.

"No. Was Michael Murphy suicidal when he was under your care?"

"I can't divulge that information."

"Mikey is dead, sir. We are trying to find out if he was the victim of murder. You are his cousin. Give us a break here."

"I have my professional standards to consider. I'm sure Dr. Black would do the same with any one of his patients."

He sure would, but so what? "Is there anything else you're willing to tell us?"

"Perhaps, if we don't have to get into anything he revealed to me during therapy sessions."

"When did Michael first begin treatment here?"

"I guess it was about five years ago."

"Before Nicholas Black referred him?"

"That's right. He's had various problems through the years."

"Can you give me a general reason what these problems are?"

Young didn't answer directly. "His parents contacted me. They were concerned about him being depressed over some personal problems, one being a breakup with a girlfriend. Drug use being another. They thought that, as his cousin, I might be able to understand and treat him better than another doctor. It turned out to be true. After only a short time, he began to feel better."

"Did he ever relapse and have to come back?"

"Yes, he did. How did you know that?" Young obviously knew I wasn't going to answer that question because he plowed right on. "His condition worsened when he quit taking his prescribed meds. He came in-house and stayed awhile and really did a lot better once he joined my group therapy session."

"Was he suicidal at that point?"

"I can't get into that. I do hope you understand."

"I understand you're being difficult when it's unnecessary. We can get the records. You're just wasting our time and putting up roadblocks."

Bud took over. "When was he released from here the second time?"

"Last week."

"Last week, huh? And you haven't seen him or talked to him since then?"

"No."

"Have you heard from him?"

"No. He was eager to get back home and run his business. He loved that pizza parlor."

I said, "You're taking his death awfully well, doctor. Your being his cousin, and all."

"I'm devastated. Working with troubled people, I have learned not to show my emotions. But you can believe that I am very sorry about Mikey. He was a good kid."

I pulled the plastic bag with Michael Murphy's blue beaded bracelet out of my purse and the one with the unidentified key. I handed them to him. He nodded, as he looked at them. "Yes, I've seen him wear these things. He had lots of them. He never told me what it was all about, though. He even got some of my other patients in his therapy group wearing them. I have no idea about this key."

"And nobody told you the significance of the bracelets? What they meant?"

"No, but I can't say I questioned anybody at length about it, either. That's not how I run my sessions."

"Oh? How do you run your sessions?"

"It's a common method. Much like your Dr. Black runs his, I imagine."

I hated it when people called him my Dr. Black, even if he was. "My Dr. Black prefers one-on-one sessions, I believe."

"Yes, every psychiatrist has his own preferences. I have found that the teenagers I work with respond better in a group of their peers. They have a tendency to start trusting them before they let down their guard with me. I observe while they talk, and if I need to intercede or guide the conversation, I do so."

"Do you have any other colleagues here who have treated Michael Murphy?"

"Yes, a couple of my colleagues have filled in for me on occasion, but it's rare. I live nearby and try always to be available."

I stood up and sauntered nonchalantly around the room as he answered, but I really wanted to see if he had managed to turn on the camera without my being aware. I didn't get close to the camera, and the red light was not easy to see behind the leafy plant, but it was blinking. He'd turned it on without my seeing him, all right. Now why would he want to record our interview?

I moved away and asked, "Do you film your sessions, doctor?"

"Usually."

"Why do you do that?"

"Sometimes I like to watch them later and see if there were any nuances or indicators that I missed. It has proved to be helpful in my therapy."

Time to catch him in a lie. "Do you ever film sessions held here inside your office?"

"Occasionally, but I usually don't hold therapy sessions here. This is where I come to think and do my paperwork. It's my sanctuary, I guess you'd call it."

"Are you filming us now, by any chance?"

Bud looked at me in surprise. Dr. Young just looked amused. I guess I'm a real hilarious police officer. "No, although it might be a good idea. You're a good interrogator. I've noticed that you use some of my own techniques to get answers."

"Is that right?"

Bud said, "Is it possible for you to show us around the place? Maybe meet up with some of your patients? Possibly interview a couple of Mikey's friends?"

"I suppose so, but only with their written permission. I'd have to make the request myself in private and get back to you."

I said, "That would be very helpful, Dr. Young." See, how nice I am when people cooperate.

Dr. Young seemed pleased as punch that we were both playing good cop now. "I would be glad to show you around right now, if you like. My next session doesn't start for about twenty minutes. Maybe I can introduce you to a few of my patients, with their permission, of course. You know, pave the way for your interviews. Maybe some of them would talk to you today."

Boy, the doc was really being helpful now, which made me wonder why, not that I am an extremely suspicious type who trusted no one, or anything. "Okay. That would be great, Doctor."

When he turned to lead us out, Bud and I exchanged our *what's-this-guy-up-to* glares, but we followed the suddenly *good-and-eager-to-please-us* doctor outside and down the corridor again. This time there were lots of teens milling around, and they looked at us like we were old people who didn't fit in the place, which isn't exactly a great feeling. But none of them were sporting butcher knives or wearing funny hats or slobbering from the mouth. None of them were wearing blue and white beaded bracelets, either.

"This is where we have our group sessions."

Dr. Young opened the door, and several of his patients were already inside the room, drinking Cokes and Diet Dr Peppers out of cans and relaxing on the couches scattered around the room. Two or three of the kids had on earphones and completely ignored us and everyone else. Two more were off by themselves, also being openly antisocial. One guy saw us and came striding up and smiling like we were his best friends come to have a birthday party.

Dr. Young greeted him. "Morning, Pete. How's it going?"

"Fine, much better."

"I'm glad you could make it in for the session. You feel better?"

"Oh, yeah. I just got one of those migraine headaches I get sometimes."

I said to the doctor, "Is Pete, here, one of your patients?"

"Yes, once upon a time I was," Happy Pete said brightly, "but now I assist him. I'm new on the staff."

"Well, congratulations," said Bud. He grinned, all friendly like, too, but I knew that expression. He didn't trust this guy. Too toothy, too happy, and too sappy.

"Thank you, sir. I've worked really hard to prove myself."

"Yes, this is Pete Parsons, and he's doing a stand-up job for us."

Happy Pete said, "Are you here to observe someone in treatment?"

I said, "No, we're sheriff detectives here to interview people who knew Mikey Murphy."

"Knew? What's that supposed to mean?"

I looked at the doctor and let him handle that little technicality. He lowered his tone, looked all somber. "Mikey was found dead, Pete. A possible suicide, but they're not sure yet that it wasn't a homicide."

Pete's cheery face whitened to a natural vanilla ice cream hue, and it didn't look fake. "No, no. No way. You can't be serious."

We all nodded, real serious.

"Jeez, he was such a great kid. I thought we had him all straightened out."

Bud said, "Apparently not."

That Bud, he wasn't mincing words today, uh uh. He seemed to have taken an intense dislike to Poor Pete, too. That meant I had to play nice.

"I'm sorry for your loss, Pete. Were you close to Mikey?"

"Oh, yeah, actually we were in a therapy group together some years ago, when I was still a patient here. That's where we met."

That jibed with Young's time line.

I spoke to Pete. "How about us having a word with you while Dr. Young informs the group of Mikey's death? Maybe you can answer some of our questions."

Dr. Young said, "Yes, why don't you do that, Pete? I can handle the group on my own." Well, I hope so, I thought. Young turned back to me. "Let me see if any of the kids want to talk to you. Just be gentle when you talk to them. Some of them are fragile."

"I can do that." Not well, of course, but I can do it, when absolutely necessary, and if kids are involved.

I returned my attention to Pete. "Is there a private place where we can have that little talk without being disturbed?"

"You think I could take them into the observation room, Doc?"

"Sure, but make sure the sound to the classroom is off."

"Right."

Pete led us next door and into a small room, painted institutional gray with darker gray suede chairs and even darker gray carpet. Gray seemed attracted to Oak Haven. The observation room was not designed for the cheerful, no sirree. This was a place where people sat and watched the crazies chat together. Forget the daffodil yellow and tulip red. Gray, gray, gray. Lordy, I was already depressed.

Pete sat down and gestured to a duo of matching swivel chairs, but he kept his gaze on the scene transpiring in the other room. Bud and I sat down and followed his rapt attention. The doctor had the kids all sitting around in a semicircle in front of him. His face was somber, his body language relaxed. He knew how to give bad news. The three of us waited silently, because it was damn obvious that poor Pete wanted to see his fellow patients go to pieces when hit with horrible news. Problem was, it was hard to tell when he actually told them, because there was no reaction, just eight kids sitting there staring at him. Ooookay. Stoicism, at its best. Or braindead-ism.

"They seem to be taking it well," noted Bud.

"This group isn't very demonstrative," said Pete.

No joke, Pete. Catatonic was more like it. They looked like young, sloppily dressed mannequins in a Gap store. Except they had lots of piercings showing and probably a lot more not showing.

"We'll get into their feelings. It has to be a gradual thing. Dr. Young's very good with them."

Okay, as far as I was concerned the morbid show was over. "How well did you know the deceased, Pete?"

"He was one of my best friends when he was here. We didn't see each other as much after he left. I live here, you know, sort of like a house dad." He grinned. My, my, but the Oak Haven staff was a likeable bunch. Problem was, I didn't like them much, but that was nothing new. I loathed most people right off the bat. Bud usually didn't, though, so we balanced each other out.

Bud didn't say anything, just stared at the kid, so I guess I got to dive in first. "Can you tell me what kind of person he was?"

Bright smile, happy, happy Pete, even in the shadow of the valley of death. "Oh, he was great. A lot of fun, you know, joking around all the time. Clever, I guess, I'd say. Always quipping some silly thing that made everybody laugh."

I thought of Mikey's purple face after having hung by the neck in the heat for half of a very hot day and then I thought of his girlfriend in the oven. I didn't particularly think great, fun, or clever hit the mark in the adjective market, and neither did silly.

"I see. Can you tell me what he was being treated for when you first met him?"

"I guess it's all right since he's now deceased. Or maybe I should ask the doctor?" He looked into the classroom, where Dr. Young looked very serious and shrink-aroo, then he leaned forward in his chair toward me, his young hazel eyes intense, his voice lowered. "He had some suicidal thoughts after one of his family members died. Actually, all of us were here because we had considered suicide in one way or another. So are all those kids in there." He pointed at the one-way mirror.

"Oh. And you are a heck of a lot better now, I take it." I smiled, ha, ha, you're not going to off yourself with a rope or bullet or oven any time soon, are you?

"Yeah, I'm doing okay. Thanks for asking. I had a bad situation at home with my mom's new husband, but she finally got rid of him when she realized he was screwing the neighbor and knocking me around. I wish all these kids' problems could be so easily remedied."

"Me, too. Did Mikey talk to you much about his personal life?"

"Yeah, sometimes, he did. That's when we were roommates. Most of the time he was pretty closemouthed about some things, though. He always passed everything off as a joke. He hid his sadness under laughs."

"I see."

"Something else, he always preferred to see Dr. Collins one-on-one. The group sessions with Marty were compulsory, so he went to those, too. But he had a special kind of connection with Boyce. I don't know why, but he liked him better than he did Marty, even though they're cousins, and all." He shrugged, as if nonplussed.

First time I'd heard about another doctor. "And Dr. Collins is?"

"He's a new guy here, came a couple of years ago. I guess that doesn't make him too new. And he's good. He's had a lot of success with the kids out here." He smiled as if pleased by it.

Bud asked, "His first name's Boyce?"

"Yes sir."

"Is he here today?"

"No, sir, he's out peddling his new book. He writes about teens and group therapies, so he gives lectures around the country and does book signings."

"Where is he now?"

"He's in Memphis, but he'll be in Branson sometime in the next coupla days."

"You think we could get a copy of that book?"

"Oh, yeah. I've got a copy you can borrow. I'll give it to you before you leave. Or you can find it in one of the bigger book chains. It's pretty esoteric, though, I'll warn you."

Yeah, I do know what esoteric means. It meant Black might buy a copy, but nobody else in their right mind would wade through said dry tome.

"What's esoteric?" said Bud.

Pete said, "I didn't know, either. I had to ask. It sorta means it only appeals to certain people."

Bud said, "Well, that's not exactly a brain twister. Who reads psychology textbooks?"

I said, "You think you might get word to him to call me." I pulled out my card and handed it to him. "We need to set up an appointment to meet with him ASAP."

"Sure. He's easy to work with."

"Okay. Anything else you can tell us about Michael? Anything I haven't asked but that you think is important?"

Considering for a moment, Pete took a swig of his Coke. "Well, he had bad headaches, and dreams, too. Really bad-ass scary kinda dreams."

This was getting more Freud-like by the minute. Black was gonna hang on every detail. "You mean nightmares?" That was a subject I had a close relationship with, oh yeah.

"Yes. I can remember him jumping out of bed at night, screaming, then he'd shut it off really quick like and apologize." Shaking his head, he seemed upset by the memory.

"Did he ever tell you about these nightmares?"

"Not really. I think death was involved. He witnessed his mother's death, I think, or some family member."

"Oh, God," said Bud.

Yeah. "How did she die?"

"I think it was some kind of fall. No, I think it was in a car wreck. I'm sorry, I just can't remember."

"So Mary Fern Murphy is not his real mother?"

"No. She and his dad got married a long time after his real mom died. Some of their kids are stepbrothers and sisters, I think. Dr. Collins can probably tell you more of this stuff when you get to him. They were pretty good friends. At least that's the way it looked."

"Okay, anything else, Pete?"

"Well, he was into Asian stuff. You know, incense and Buddha, that kinda stuff. And he liked Asian girls. That's who he liked to date, I mean. I think it was because they're all smaller than him. He's pretty little, for a guy."

"Do you know any of their names?"

"No. I've seen him out and about with some of them."

"More than one."

"Yeah. All of them were little, though, with long black hair."

I showed him the bracelet and key. "You know anything about either of these?"

"I know Mikey got real superstitious and paranoid and hung these all around his place. He wore them, too."

Bud said, "Know where he got them?"

"Uh uh. He never said, and I never thought to ask. Probably some New Age place, if I had to guess. The key doesn't go to anything around here, I don't think."

"Okay, you've been very helpful, Pete."

"Hey, no problem. I think this bites, what happened to Mikey. I thought he was gonna be okay. It's hard to believe he really did it. We have a pretty good rate of survival around here."

Well, that's good. "What about failures? I mean, when a patient commits suicide, despite your efforts?"

Looking down, face getting all serious, Pete said, "More than we'd like. Through the years, there's been some we couldn't get through to, no matter how hard we tried. Those are the tough ones to think about."

"Is this a large number?"

"I guess it's how you look at it. I don't have access to the total number. I only know the ones I've worked with. And there were too many of those, I can say that."

"You think Dr. Young will give us a list of deceased former patients?"

"Probably not. But you can ask him." He stared into the classroom again. "Truthfully? I'm surprised he's letting you talk to any of them. He doesn't usually want to release any records to anybody. He's very, very protective of his patients."

Bud said, "We're not just anybody. We've got warrants to help him make those decisions."

"Yeah," said Pete.

The three of us sat silently for a time, thinking deep thoughts. Mine were pretty morbid, so I tried to think about solving the case instead of the victims. Bud and Pete were now best buddies, sharing marathon running feats.

"You ever run in a marathon, Detective?" That was Pete speaking to me.

"No. If I've got to get twenty-six miles in a hurry, I take my car."

Pete laughed, delighted by my wit. "You ought to give it a try. It's elating to run and run until you're exhausted, then keep on going. And it's the accomplishment, really. Just being able to say you can do it."

"I'd rather say I solved a difficult case and put a criminal in jail. Besides, Bud always gets blisters."

Amused, Pete gave me a little wink, but about that time my phone started up with the Mexican Hat Dance song. It was Charlie, wanting to know if we'd notified the parents and how they'd taken it. I said not good to the latter. He said to get back to the station and have the reports ready when he came in tomorrow morning. I winced, then said, "Yes sir, no problem."

"We need to interview any kids who are ready for it," I said to Pete. "Thank you for your help. We may need to talk to you again. That okay with you?"

"I'm happy to help."

"Would you get word to Dr. Collins that I'll get in touch and set up an interview?"

"Yes, ma'am, I'll sure do it. And good luck. I hope you figure out why Mikey did this. I still can't believe it."

"How about finding out if any of the kids are willing to talk right now?" I said. I looked around the room, wondering if there were microphones or cameras hidden in the walls. I figured there were, so I said, "Anywhere outside we can talk? It's a nice day."

"Okay. I'll see what I can do with the patients. There's a couple of picnic tables outside under some big trees, if you want to talk to them outside. It's hot out there, though. Why don't I bring you some bottled water?"

These guys were sure peddling the water. Must be shareholders in Ozarka. "Okay, sure, Pete. That sounds great."

We walked outside, and Bud's phone rang. He looked at Caller ID and said, "It's Brianna from Rome. Mind if I take it?"

I smiled. "No, give her my best. I'll wait and see if anybody shows up at the picnic tables, then I'll meet you at the car."

Bud answered the phone quickly and walked off toward the front of the clinic. As I made my way to the picnic area, I looked back toward the building where the poor, unfortunate suicidal teens were spilling their guts and wondered how many would be dead in their graves a year from now.

Here Comes Trouble

The night they were supposed to play basketball came soon enough. A lot of kids showed up, and Tee was pleased. Especially that little Asian girl named Lotus. She dragged in late and kept pretty much in the middle of a bunch of other Asian girls, two of whom were real pretty, even prettier than she was. One thing he noticed, however, was that Lotus kept an eye on him. She tried to hide it, and did pretty well, but their eyes met a couple of times and she always jerked her gaze away like she hated him. But that usually meant the opposite when dealing with hot girls, at least in his limited experience.

On this particular occasion, he realized that there were a good many Asians in treatment at Oak Haven, and he began to wonder why. Missouri wasn't particularly known for its Asian populations, not to his knowledge, anyway. One Asian guy was a counselor, and not a whole lot older than the patients. His name turned out to be Yang Wei, and he openly told everybody that was his real name. Yang Wei didn't choose any other name, but nearly everyone else in treatment had chosen to go the alias route. Something about him using his own name interested Tee, and he became intrigued as to why each of the kids had been stuck in this psycho ward. Especially that little Lotus, not that it really mattered. He was gonna nail her, even if she was flat-out bonkers.

After everybody had arrived and had warmed up with some free throws, Yang Wei threw the ball to Tee and said that to get things going they would pick partners and play each other in one-on-one challenges. After that, they would choose up teams. Tee laughed inside, because Yang Wei might be tall and thin, but he didn't know Tee's expertise at all sports or his incredible hand/eye coordination or how many trophies he'd won on the basketball court alone.

Tee whipped his ass, of course, but barely. Yang Wei was a hotshot, too. Afterward, Yang Wei walked up and said, "You're damn good, kid. Quick as lightning."

"Yeah, that's my nickname on the court. Lightning."

"Tee your real name?"

"Uh uh. I'm keepin' that to myself. You'll know when I play in the NBA."

"How about we sit down and have a Coke?"

"Sure."

They sat on the bleachers together and watched the other kids play. Lotus was playing Horse now, and she hadn't been lying about the three-pointers. He watched her sink six in a row, all nothing but net, but what he really liked to watch was the way her short top rode up and showed her muscular midriff each time she shot the ball. She had to be working out on weights to develop abs like that. Hell, her six-pack was almost as defined as his own.

Watching the others, Yang Wei popped the tab on a can of Coke and said, "What do you think about our happy little home here at Oak Haven?"

"It's not so bad. Not as bad as I thought it'd be."

Yang Wei smiled. "At least you're honest."

Tee noticed that Yang Wei's English was perfect. Yang Wei sounded just like a regular American. He wondered if he'd been born in the United States. But he didn't ask. Instead, he said, "Yeah. I usually say it the way it is."

"You're slated to be in my therapy group. Not all the time but now and then, for a change of pace."

"Good. You any good at this analyzing crap?"

"You are direct, Tee, my man. But to answer your question, I'm very good. I try to make the sessions fun for you guys. You know, not as intense as the others."

"But you're not a doctor yet?"

"Nope. Working hard on it, though. It won't be long now."

"You a Chinese American or you from China?"

"I was born in China." They both watched Lotus drop in another perfect trey. "I defected, along with Lotus out there. She's my little sister."

"No kidding. I didn't know that." And that might complicate my plans, Tee thought.

"Yes, we came over here to an international basketball competition in St. Louis and managed to escape our keepers."

Now this was getting very interesting. On the other hand, he knew that Yang Wei's friendly conversation was not without its purpose. He was trying to gain Tee's confidence so he'd open up himself later. Yang Wei had already underestimated Tee's intelligence, but that was a good thing. Tee said, "They try to come after you?"

"If they did, they haven't found us yet."

"How'd you end up way down here in the middle of nowhere?"

"Lotus had a hard time accepting the fact she couldn't ever go back home. She had some emotional problems when we first got here, and so the people that gave us asylum said she ought to come out here for treatment, and then they helped me get on the staff so we could be together. That was several years ago. They've been sending other defectors down here since then, sort of a way to decompress and get used to a new culture. A lot of us develop paranoia because the government does send out people to find us. Lotus's afraid all the time that some assassin's gonna show up. She was in training for the Chinese Olympic team. Women's basketball, one of the star guards, actually. Talk about a quick launch. Wait till you see her on a fast break."

"Wow. That's some major shit, Yang Wei. I think she's beautiful. I have some sisters, but they're all dogs."

Laughing, Yang Wei nodded. "Yes, she is very beautiful, but she's a troubled girl. Gettin' better, though. These doctors here are pretty good with her."

"Including you?"

"I'm not a doctor, but I'm good with her. She and a half sister's all I have now. The rest of our family is still in Shanghai."

They were silent for a while after that, and then Yang Wei said, "I read your file. Man, you've had a rough time of it, too."

At first Tee didn't say anything, then he decided to play along. He wouldn't have any trouble getting himself out of this place when the time was right, so he might as well lay the groundwork of his miraculous recovery right off the bat. "Yeah, my dad's real worried about me. Thinks I'm suicidal, and stuff. I'm not, anymore, though."

"You saw some members of your family die, if I recall. That must've been a pretty bad trip."

"Yeah. I couldn't stop my mom, but I tried."

"Bummer. You think about it much?"

Okay, Tee thought, now I get it. Yang Wei's job was to get him talking in a social situation, get him all relaxed and see what he had to say when he was unguarded. These shrink techniques were really transparent.

Tee said, "I don't wanna talk about it."

"Okay. Sure. Maybe some other time."

"Yeah, maybe. Hey, there's my roommate. Catch you later."

Yang Wei nodded, and Tee got down and walked away. Gee, what'd they think? He was some kind of chump. He was going to enjoy playing them. Matching wits would be fun, but first things first. Right now, his primary concern was getting Lotus off by herself.

Three nights later, Tee managed to do just that. She'd begun to warm up to him a little. At least, she wasn't calling him names. One night when he saw her studying outside at a picnic table under some trees, he decided to get rid of Buddy, who had started tagging around after him like some kind of freakin' remora fish feeding off a shark. Twilight had fallen, and he told Buddy to go back to the room and see if Tee had gotten any phone calls. Buddy was turning out to be just about the easiest person to manipulate that Tee had ever run up against, but truth was, just about everybody he knew was easy to manipulate. All you had to know was what buttons to push.

Sauntering out to the table as if he'd just happened upon Lotus, he sat down across from her, and said, "Hey, girl, you ever play Moonlight Tennis?"

"What?" She said it real haughty-like and gave him a cold stare.

"Moonlight Tennis. It's fun. You hit the ball back and forth in the dark and can't see the ball until it's almost on your racquet. It's good practice for hand-to-eye coordination."

"I suspect I could beat you at it, if I wanted. Or anything else, for that matter."

"Okay, prove it then."

The girl loved challenges; that was the key to her. And she liked him better than she let on, count on that, too. That was because he was so good looking and drew girls to him like flies to melted chocolate ice cream.

She hesitated. "I'm too busy."

"Oh, come on, it's fun. Finish that later."

Finally, she bit. She shut the book. "Okay, but you're going down, Mr. T."

"They keep the racquets and balls in a shed out there. I already asked."

The tennis court was way out at the far end of the gymnasium but most of the patients pretty much had the run of the clinic grounds. The lights were off, but Tee had found out earlier that there was a button on the light pole that turned them on. There was a light inside the shed, too, and Tee opened the door, turned it on, and got out a couple of racquets and a tube of new yellow tennis balls.

"It's almost dark enough. Let's wait a few more minutes and it'll be more of a challenge."

"Okay. Give me that Wilson. I play better with it."

"So you know how to play tennis?"

"Of course, I do, stupid. You think I'd take this bet if I couldn't beat you?"

"You're pretty slick, Lotus."

"Thanks, I guess."

"I like your brother."

"He's all right."

"You miss China?"

"You nosy?"

"Yeah, pretty much."

She gave an itty-bitty smile then, but it faded quickly. "Let's get going with this. I need to finish reading that chapter before I go to class tomorrow. We're having a test, and I always make A's."

So they turned out the court lights and played, hard and fast, and she was good. The moon came out, and it was almost full, with just enough light to see the ball about four or five feet from the racquet face. It was kind of fun, especially when they swung and missed. Even Lotus laughed a couple of times.

"Okay, you win," he finally called out. "I'm beat."

Of course, he'd let her win because that was to his own benefit. He could've beaten her soundly, if he'd wanted to.

"Told you I'd win," she said, as she handed him the racquet.

The time had come, and he didn't waste a second of it, either. Some of the counselors might get curious and come out and check on them. Quickly and suddenly, he grabbed her, one hand over her mouth and the other around her waist. Dragging her back inside the shed, he kicked the door shut with his foot. The light was out, so he couldn't see the fear on her face, unfortunately. She put up a pretty good struggle for someone so tiny and was stronger than he would've thought but no match for his strength.

"Just shut up and enjoy this," he whispered in her ear, laying full-length atop her body and pinning her to the ground. The way she was squirming around underneath him sent all kind of tingling sensations straight to his dick and made it get hard. He began to pant and rub his hand over her breasts, and then inside the top of her T-shirt.

Lotus struggled harder, but he kept her quiet with his hand over her mouth. When she kept up the fight, way too long, he held her nostrils together and shut off her air.

"Now, listen here, Lotus. We're gonna do this, one way or another. Got that? Just relax and you'll end up liking it as much as I do. Otherwise, it's gonna hurt you."

The girl lay still then and shut up with all the muffled screams and wriggling, so he jerked down her shorts and fumbled to get off her underpants. She didn't move. He went ahead and had his way with her and felt the most exquisite release of all the pent-up tension he'd felt since he'd first seen her. Afterward, he realized he wasn't a virgin anymore, and from what he could tell, she wasn't to begin with. When he was done, he zipped up his pants and backed off her, but she still didn't move, didn't respond, just lay there silently with her eyes shut. Not crying, or anything, just lying there, like she was dead.

"C'mon, now, Lotus, that wasn't so bad, was it?"

She said nothing. She was lying so still that he began to

think she was dead for a second or two, but when he put his hand on her naked chest, he could feel her breathing just fine.

"Okay, that's it, for now. Don't tell anybody, you hear me? Or I'll kill you. I've got a knife in my room, and I'll do it. And I'll make it look like it was those Chinese ninjas, or whatever the hell they are, those guys that are looking for you."

Lotus reacted to that. She began to shiver all over.

For emphasis, he added, "And I'll kill Yang Wei, too. When he's least expecting it. It'll look like it's an accident."

Lotus opened her eyes then and stared at him. He could see her eyes in the moonlight coming in from a crack in the roof. Putting both his hands around her throat, he pressed down a little but not too hard.

"Gonna tell?"

She shook her head, and he rolled away and stood up, then looked down at her. "Good. I might want to do this to you again one of these days. You be ready to do whatever I say, you hear me?"

Nodding mutely, she slowly got to her feet, righted her clothes, and walked away. She didn't run.

Tee was pleased. She was taking it better than he thought she would. Maybe she hadn't hated the whole thing so much after all. It was good to have a willing participant for his newly discovered sexual needs. She wasn't gonna be nearly as assertive and hateful now that they'd had sex. Maybe she'd learned already who'd be boss between the two of them. And now he was a man who'd had sex with a pretty woman. Nope, this place wasn't gonna be so bad. He was fitting in pretty damn well.

NINE

Sitting down outside in the fresh air and sunshine filtering through the spreading limbs of a couple of big oak trees, a hot, sultry breeze lifted hair off my neck and made me long for the cool dark corridor I'd just left. I could see Bud way off on the lawn, leaning up against a tree trunk and talking on his phone. I kept getting whiffs of roses, maybe because about a hundred of them were hanging off a trellis about two yards away. There were lots of flower beds and hanging baskets and urns around the picnic tables so therefore lots of spicy and plain flowery scents. Hope I wasn't allergic.

It was seriously hot, even in the shade, and I was glad to see Happy Pete tripping out toward me with a frosty bottle of Ozarka in one hand and Boyce Collins's book in the other.

"Here you go, Detective Morgan. Anything else I can get for you?"

"No. This'll hit the spot."

"Okay then, I gotta run. I'm late for a session."

"Thanks, Pete."

As he trotted off, I breathed in all the heavy, airborne floral perfumes, twisted off the cap, and gulped down some of the ice-cold water, as I thumbed through Collins's book and read some stuff about light boxes, and sound waves, and hypnotism, all of which was pretty technical and boring, so I took out my cell and hit speed dial for Black, who could probably explain it all to me in two minutes flat, thus ending the tedious factor.

Okay, now the natural colognes bombarding me were becoming cloying, if not downright stomach turning. I wondered then if I might be subjecting myself to some special, maybe even experimental aroma therapy for the poor disturbed kiddies wandering hereabouts, and probably without their knowledge, too. Hoped I wasn't inhaling any therapies, or even worse, allergens. I glanced around the grassy lawn as the phone continued to chirp at the other end, on the lookout for hidden bugs and security cameras zeroed in on me. This place had more cameras than a CBS reality show, except for maybe *Big Brother*, and I was beginning to wonder about the privacy rights for patients around this place.

Black finally picked up and said, "Hello, sweetheart. You get tied up or what? And I mean that literally, knowing you."

"What's that supposed to mean?"

"You were going to try to meet me for a late breakfast at the Lodge, before I flew out. Remember?"

Uh oh. "Oh, yeah. Sorry. I got distracted."

"I tried to call you, but you didn't pick up."

"I was in Jeff City breaking the bad news so I couldn't answer. I was going to call you back as soon as I got a sec."

"Dare I ask where you are?"

"Oak Haven Clinic, smelling all million of their zinnias."

"Seriously?"

"About the clinic or the flowers?"

"C'mon, Claire."

"We interviewed Dr. Young this morning, and now we're moving on to some of the patients. Where are you?"

"Somewhere over Ohio."

"Oh. Hey, by the way, what do you know about light box/

sound waves, all that hypnotherapy kinda stuff that Boyce Collins plays with?"

"Not much. It's highly experimental. I've read some articles about it in the psychiatric journals. He's got a book out about it."

"Yeah, I'm holding it in my hand. What do you think? Does his stuff work?"

"Maybe. Sometimes he's gotten some pretty good results. He's young and bright and on the cutting edge. Truth, though? I think it sounds like a gimmick he uses to sell books and make a name for himself. Young's involved with the procedures, too, from what I understand. They both swear by the techniques they use."

"Hey, maybe I'll let Young try it out on me. Just to see what happens?"

Silence. One beat, two. Alas, I began to sense disapproval. "You ought to be careful suggesting things like that, Claire."

Actually it had been a joke, one of my rare and puny attempts at levity, but I hadn't expected him to wax all serious and stuff. "Why? He gonna turn my mind into a marshmallow?"

At that, Black got huffy. "Because last time I looked, I am your doctor, and I don't want anybody else messing with your head. Or your body, for that matter."

I'm telling you this guy has a one-track mind. "You don't have to worry. Trust me, nobody's going to mess with my head except you. In fact, nobody in their right mind wants to take on a challenge of that immensity." Joke two. I must be in a helluva jolly mood.

"I guess you didn't leave out the reference to messing with your body for any particular reason?"

"You are so possessive with my bod."

"Damn straight."

We both laughed, softly but with lots of welcome-home promises woven in.

I said, "Don't worry, my body's intact and untouched."

Black said, "Just get done over there and drive carefully. I may wrap up my sessions in New York early, and that'll mean I'll get back tomorrow, and I'll need some serious distraction."

"Okay. It's a date. I can be a terrible distraction, when I set my mind to it. Count on it."

"Oh, I will."

A minute later, we disconnected when I observed patient numero uno walking out the door of the nearest dormitory and heading straight toward me. Young and cute and smiley, she had jet-black hair cut in bangs straight across her forehead and curved under at shoulder length. She looked to be about fifteen as she quick stepped across the grass. She had on long khaki walking shorts and a terra-cotta-colored baby doll top with tan beads in the shape of a diamond on the front. She had on black flip-flops, the kind affixed with lots of vibrant colored stones and sequins, and she wore about three toe rings on each foot that glittered in the sun as she walked. She was so thin that her bones showed. I had a feeling I knew what she was in for. Anorexia or bulimia, trust me.

"You a real detective?" she asked, sliding in at the bench across the table from me, where she looked like a hungry waif. Made me wish I had a Snickers bar or some animal crackers in my pocket to give to her. She had lots of freckles dusting her cheeks and neon pink lipstick.

"Yes, that I am. I'm with the Canton County Sheriff's department down at Lake of the Ozarks. My name's Claire Morgan."

"Yeah? I'm Cleo. That's cool, you bein' a cop, and stuff. I watch TV a lot." She kept nodding then, like that was supposed to mean something significant.

I thought about it a moment then gave up on making any kind of intelligent connection. "Is that right?"

"Yeah. I like that wicked cool girl on that *NCIS* show, the one that does all that computer stuff. I forget her name, but she's awesome. She's got style I like, you know her boots

and hair in piggies, stuff like that. She wears her hair sometimes like Cleopatra. She was a Queen of Egypt. I saw her
picture in my Ancient Civ book. That's why I have them call
me Cleo while I'm in here." Cleo's pixie-ish face sobered
big time, as if Cleo's coiffure was a very serious subject.

I looked suitably impressed by her Egyptian tresses, then
I said, "So you go by different names while you're here?"

"Yeah."

"Why is that?"

"The doctors just say it's up to us. That we can use our
real names, if we want to, but if we want to maintain privacy,
we can choose a nickname. But it's kinda fun getting to have
a cool name like Cleo. I really like the way that girl looks in
NCIS. Don't you?"

"I don't believe I've ever seen that show. I don't have time
to watch much TV. Busy fighting crime and all that." I
grinned. Ms. Cool and With It Detective.

"There's not a whole lot to do around here but watch the
big-screen TV in the lounge, unless you wanna play Ping-
Pong or checkers over in the rec room."

"Didn't I see a tennis court and swimming pool when I
drove in?"

"Sure, but I don't know how to swim or play tennis."

Okay, aimless chatter now acomin' to a close. "I appreciate your willingness to talk to me about Michael Murphy."

Her face crumpled into a free-falling, anxiety-ridden angst.
"Oh, God, I hate it that he's dead. He shouldn't be dead. That
sucks so bad."

I nodded. It did suck so bad. He shouldn't be dead. He
should be tossing pizza dough and the roasted girl should be
sitting in a booth watching him. They were way too young to
die, especially at their own hands. And I wasn't at all sure
they did. Something niggled my mind and made me think
something was definitely rotten in the state of Oak Haven.
"Did you know him well?"

"A little. I thought he was cute for an older guy. He liked

the girls from overseas, you know, the Japanese and Chinese ones."

"Were there a lot of Asians here?"

"Yeah, more than you'd think in a place like this. They're all real little and short. That's why I think he went for them. I'm too tall for him. I'm five foot seven. You're even taller than that, aren't you? How did he do it, ma'am? Kill himself, I mean. Can you tell me?"

"I'm afraid not." Her interest in cause of death was worrisome. Her eyes were latched on me, real intense and focused, and maybe just a little bit afraid. They resembled the color of wet Miami Beach sand. She hungered after the gory details. That was troubling, too. "Okay, Cleo. Can you tell me any of Mikey's girlfriend's names, where they lived, stuff like that?"

"Yeah, but they're hard to pronounce. You'll probably spell them wrong."

Cleo was a stickler for details, all right. "That's okay. I'll spell them phonetically."

"Phonetically?" She forgot her anxiety long enough to laugh like all get-out. "Well, one girl they called Khur-Vay, K H U R hypen V A Y, and she was real pitiful 'cause she lost custody of her kid. She cried all the time she was here. I could hear her sometimes in the middle of the night, crying in her room when I got up to go to the bathroom. They had a suicide watch on her."

Zach's little face welled up, smiling and happy, in his little red swimsuit, blond and summer tanned. Struggling to remain professional, I thrust the mental image out of my head, furious at myself for thinking about him. I had to lock him up again, somewhere deep inside where the pain went away. "Anybody else you can think of?"

"Li was the one that Mikey seemed to like the most. They held hands and went off together. You know, out there in the trees so they could make out. Before that, there was a girl named Sing. He paid a lot of attention to her, too, but she was hard to get to know. She tried to commit suicide twice while she was here, once she cut her wrists and then the other time she tried to hang herself off this very tree."

Following her pointed finger upward to a sturdy branch of our very own spreading oak tree, I decided they obviously needed more supervision here than they were getting.

Cleo went on. "I tried it, too, but I didn't cut deep enough." Almost proudly, she held out both her wrists for me to look appalled at. There were faint scars running horizontally across both her wrists.

"I'm sorry that happened to you, Cleo."

She smiled and donned an expression that made her look like she was about ten years old. "That's okay. I'm better now. The docs have helped me lots. My mom committed suicide. That's why I tried it, too. She and me were real close. My dad was a druggie, he's in jail now, thank God. Yeah, she got in the car in the garage and did the carbon monoxide thing. She did it right. Didn't hurt and didn't suffer, just went to sleep."

Okay, I'm depressed out of my mind. Stop, already. "I'm glad you're better, Cleo. Seems to me that you're a good kid with a lot to live for."

"Oh, yeah, I know all that now. Pete, you met him yet? He's been real helpful to me. You know, he builds me up and tells me I can do anything, tells me to stay on my meds and do what the docs say and I'll get outta here in no time at all. He's totally awesome."

Happy Pete rides to the rescue. Well, thank God, this girl needed somebody in her stable. "Good. I'm glad to hear you're on the right track. Did Michael ever try to commit suicide while he was here?"

She shook her head. "He was in here because his parents thought he was getting suicidal. He hated his mom. Told me he hated her so bad he could kill her."

Well, that was understandable, if what Bud and I had heard her say was any indication of his treatment at her hands.

"What about Pete? I understand he was a patient here for a while."

"Yes, everybody knows that. But that was before I got here. I heard somebody say he had lots of family problems, too, and freaked out and blamed himself. All that, you know. But he's great now." Her eyes glowed hot with admiration.

Uh oh, I thought. Not good, this little crush. "Is there anything else you can tell me about Michael that you think might help me?"

She shook her head and twisted a tan jade ring on her right forefinger. "He was superstitious, though. He wore lots of evil-eye bracelets and had people cleanse his room by burning sage, like the Indians used to do. Pete's part Apache, did you know that? His grandfather was a real-live shaman."

"No." Didn't believe it, either. "Did you know the girl named Li very well?"

"Nope. She was sweet but not very friendly. She spent all her time hanging out with Mikey. And Pete sometimes."

"Did she have a romantic relationship with Pete?"

"You mean, did they hook up?"

I nodded.

She said, "I doubt it. I think he was just counseling her, you know. Letting her talk to him when she got all upset."

"Do you know what troubled her?"

"She didn't like it that she was gonna have to go back to China. Said they didn't get to do anything fun there, and everybody tried to run their lives."

"So you did have personal conversations with her?"

"No, uh uh, she gave us all the scoop in our group sessions. We're supposed to tell personal stuff when we sit around in therapy circle. It's pretty hard at first to admit things, private things, I mean, but then after a while, we just began to talk to each other. When one person started it off, everybody else began to spill their guts. It was sorta cool, really, the way it worked."

"I understand." Unfortunately, I did. I'd suffered through

a couple of group sessions after my son died in LA, but not for long, because I quit the force and came to Missouri. Can't say I ever spilled my guts, though, not there, or anywhere else, not even to Black when he plays shrink.

"All right, Cleo. Thanks a lot. I'm going to leave you one of my cards with my cell phone number on it. You call me, if you think of anything, or ever just need some help."

Cleo took the card, read it, then looked up at me. "Thanks. That's real neat. You're cool."

Watching her stroll away, I wondered what it was like to live out here at this place, and if the doctors really did help these kids get their heads on straight. Once the girl disappeared inside, the next kid joined me, a boy named Roy Sutter, fourteen, pimply, and shy, and not afraid to use his real name. He wore his mousy brown hair long and straight, and parted in the middle. Earrings in both ears, thin gold hoops, but he was very sweet and nervous, told me he liked model airplanes and got into big trouble huffing glue and spray paint.

"That's bad stuff," I said.

"Yes ma'am. The doctor said it could've killed me or burned out my brain cells. They showed us a film once with a guy who lived in a cardboard box on the streets in St. Louis. He sniffed spray paint until he destroyed most of his brain. When they talked to him on camera, he had a big ring of silver paint around his mouth and nose. That's when I decided I wasn't gonna do that stuff anymore, no way."

This kid was politeness with a capital P. "That's good, Roy."

We exchanged smiles. I liked this kid. He seemed harmless and endearing. Made me want to take him to a Cardinals game and buy him a ball cap and ballpark hot dog, or something equally tasty.

"Maybe I'll be a cop, like you," he said then lowered his eyes like he was embarrassed.

"That'd be good. Keep up your grades. Keep your nose clean. You can go to the academy some day."

Grinning, he nodded.

"Do you like it out here, Roy?"

"Yes ma'am. It's nice and quiet."

"Do you like the doctors?"

"Yes ma'am. I work with Dr. Young and Dr. Collins both. And Pete, too, now."

"Have you tried out any of those therapies with light boxes and sound waves?"

"Yeah, they're way cool. Just like a kaleidoscope."

"Have they hypnotized you?"

"Yes ma'am. They said I was a good candidate, real easy to put under. They said some of us are real naturals. Mikey was. Poor Mikey. I was real surprised to hear about him. They said he was all cured when he left here, but I guess he fooled them somehow."

"Mikey used all these lights and whistles, too?"

"Yes ma'am. And the headphones, too."

I did some jotting in my notes. Mainly that I wanted Boyce Collins to show me this stuff and tell me exactly how it worked. "Did this treatment help you?"

"Yes ma'am. I felt like a different person after I did it four or five times. I quit wanting to sniff that glue, quit wanting to drink, too. I started studyin' and listenin' in class and in group. It's great. I'm real proud of Dr. Collins for thinkin' it all up."

I asked him some more questions, found out that Li and Sing and most of the other kids in his group had been treated with the same experimental techniques. Oh, yeah, that question had bumped up to number one in my repertoire, because somehow, it was connected. I just didn't know how yet. One thing I do know, nothing about this case is sitting well with me.

TEN

The following day, Bud and I spent most of our time at the department, talking about the case, studying crime scene photos, deciding which warrants to issue, mainly because Charlie was on our case big-time about getting the paper-work done and on his desk. He wanted the Mikey Murphy case solved, and yesterday, at that. Bud started looking up info on the girl we thought attended Missouri State in Springfield, while I finished typing up my reports, put them in Charlie's in basket, and then tried to get hold of Boyce Collins to set up an interview, but he was in flight and not answering his cell phone.

After several more unsuccessful attempts to reach Collins, I gave up for the moment, tidied up my desk, and headed for Harve Lester's house. Black was still in New York, so I was alone and ready to spend some quality time with my old friend Harve. A few years ago when he was my mentor and partner at LAPD homicide, he and I got in a jam that cost him the use of his legs. He has been in a wheelchair ever since, and I blame myself for what happened to him, but he's no victim. Not now, not ever. Yes, he is quite a guy. Right now he's my next-door neighbor, and my best friend in the world. I love the guy.

In his fifties, with a gray buzz cut and as strong as an ox in his upper body, Harve is also a computer genius with a lucrative business going on with research corporations, not to mention headhunting and other things he's added along the way. Of late, I'd begun to drop off my little pooch, the feisty French poodle, Jules Verne, at his house while I went out hunting for bloody, maniacal killers. Harve likes the company, and it is definitely mutual. Every morning, Jules's little curly tail starts the crazy wag thing the minute Harve's house comes into sight, and Harve's usually waiting on the front porch to meet us. I tell you, this dog of mine could charm a terrorist.

When I pulled up later, around six thirty, Harve wasn't hunched over his keyboard in his sun-drenched converted sunroom office but in his motorized chair down by his dock on the water, frying fish in a big propane-fired kettle. Hands down, he fixed the best fish dinners this side of Key West, and Jules Verne was sitting on the ground beside him, almost at point, as if the designated cook's assistant. All he needed was a French chef's hat and apron that said *Ooh la la*. Probably just hoping Harve would drop one of those crispy, batter-fried fish fillets, or better yet, a hush puppy. Who knows, maybe Jules was a helluva better fishing buddy to Harve than I'd been of late.

Climbing out of my Explorer, I walked down the sidewalk to Harve's dock. The smell of frying crappie sent my stomach into spasms of delight, oh yeah, I do love home-cooked fish, nice and brown and crispy. Harve likes to use peanut oil in which to fry his fish, and then he'd cut up thick potato fries and raw onions and drop those in the sizzling grease, too. Last thing that went in was my favorite, and Jules's, too, the hush puppies that turned out light and golden brown and tasted like oniony, puffy cornbread. No ban of cooking with fats at Harve's house. He was old-fashioned that way.

Uh uh, he liked to fry everything and then dip it in mayonnaise and fry it again, especially since he'd been watching Paula Deen's cooking show on the Food Network. Not that he needed any of her recipes. Down deep, I think he's in love with her.

The big Cobalt 360 that Nicholas Black gave him some time back was bobbing slightly and every third beat bumping up against the rubber tires attached to the pilings. Always on the alert for brash and obnoxious reporters, probably because they'd been dogging me for the majority of my life, especially the last couple of years since Black and I had hooked up, I leveled my intense distrust on a well-rigged black and red bass boat that was motoring its way slowly up the middle of our little cove. The driver was sitting at the helm, the fishing chair bolted high in the bow, empty, and I didn't see the flash of any binoculars lenses or TV cameras trained on me and Harve, so I let down my guard and stepped up onto the raised planks of Harve's dock. It was newer than mine and better maintained. Hey, I'm busy.

Harve glanced up as I approached him, my Nikes creaking on the boards. "Hey, Claire, 'bout time you happened by."

Jules Verne, on the other hand, made much ado about my arrival, jumping up like he'd stuck his nose in a light socket and heading at me like a hairy whirling dervish gone straight. He leapt into my arms from about three feet out but still hit me mid-chest and staggered me a step or two backward. He was an impressive track star for a miniature poodle. Maybe I should enter him in one of those canine shows where the dog runs a hundred miles an hour and jumps out in a pool after a ball. Nah, he'd probably only do that in the Seine.

Black had brought him to me from Paris last Christmas, and now the little poufs on his tail and paws had grown out into softly ringleted white fur that I had to brush out nearly every night. Not that I coddled the dog but sometimes he got cockleburs tangled up in his hair. Truth is, though, Jules has turned out to be a pretty good friend and loyal bed partner to keep me warm when Black is off on his important business jaunts, such as right now.

"I know, Harve, sorry, but Charlie's got us working pretty hard."

I sat down beside him and hugged the dog against my chest. He kept licking my neck and chin until I let him go. Then he ran up and down the dock for a while as if marking his ground, then got all tired out and plopped down beside me, breathing hard. I dipped up some water in my palm and he licked it long and hard and sounded pretty much like a hog at a trough. Not that I get that many hogs at a trough in my daily routine.

I said, "Smells good, Harve."

"You gotta stay and help me eat all this fish. I got me a good stringer this morning."

"You gotta deal there. Fried macaroni and cheese, too?"

"Of course. My menu's always the same, you know that. You've been gone a long time. New case?"

"Yeah. Another freakin' doozy, in fact."

Harve stopped rolling crappie fillets in cornmeal and wiped both hands on his apron. It was a long white one with a bib that tied around his neck and had *Paula Deen and Sons* embroidered across the front in red. He'd ordered it off her show. Maybe I ought to get him a Paula Deen cookbook for his birthday, maybe even an autographed copy. He said, "Got a bad one, huh?"

"Oooh, yeah, worse than bad. A double homicide, to be exact. At least I think it is. One might be a suicide, but I'm betting that it's not."

"Whoa, murders seems to be coming in waves nowadays."

I nodded. "Sorta like the old days in LA"

"It's hard to beat LA in total number of murders committed."

"We're getting way too many for this little hidey-hole burg on the lake."

"Maybe. I dunno, though, seems lots of weird crimes and ugly killings are cropping up all over the place. My God, it's on the news every damn night. People getting mad and killing their wives and children, goin' to work and massacring their boss and coworkers. Schools, too, my God, talk about psycho. It's sick shit, everywhere, everywhere you look." He picked up another thick fillet and drudged it carefully in cornmeal, then let it slide gently into the boiling oil. "Wanna tell me the particulars?"

I told him about it. If anybody had a good head for investigatory work, it was Harve. He was the best detective I'd ever known, and I'd known a lot of them. Even he looked a bit startled by our friend, Mikey, and the fun and games going on in his pizzeria.

"You still don't have the identity of the girl?"

"Nope. We got a lead from the parents about one of Mikey's exes. Sounds like the same kid, because we think the vic is Asian. Bud's looking into that now. She's supposedly a student at Missouri State. But we've also been told he's had numerous Asian girlfriends. This girl could be any one of them."

"The perp's another freak, sounds like."

I nodded, thinking that was a charitable description and that this guy deserved much worse. Leaning back on my palms, I watched Jules Verne sit up on his haunches and beg. I didn't know he could do that, but Harve was a helluva better cook than I. Jules sure never begged for my Special K breakfast bars. Harve tossed my pup a cooled piece of fish, and Jules sniffed at it as if unsure it was up to his culinary tastes. He probably wanted Hollandaise sauce smeared on it.

But hey, he's a Parisian dog, he was probably more used to eating fancied-up snails at posh restaurants. Black had ordered those things once at one of the fancier restaurants he dragged me to when we'd been on Bermuda and the dish had looked really cosmopolitan, and all, but the sight of it had turned my stomach, made me want to gag, actually, especially when he actually put a bite of it in his mouth. But then again, I'm a plain old detective type, not rich, not sophisticated. I had ordered plain broiled chicken and plain white rice and plain salad so I could actually tell what I was eating and get a little nourishment, which the fancy-smancy chef couldn't mess up. But he just couldn't stand it, I guess; he just had to line up little anchovies all over my lettuce, which are nasty little fishy things almost on the par with escargot and which I probably should've fished out and saved for Harve's bait box. I am not exactly experimental when it comes to foodstuffs that I actually have to swallow. But the salad was served up in a chilled crystal dish, though, and that was pretty cool.

"You go out on the lake alone today?" I was glad he could now. Black's boat was completely handicapped accessible, not that I consider Harve in that category.

"No. Joe McKay and Lizzie showed up on their way to your place and I invited them to tag along. We had a real good time, too. That little girl's a sweetie and she's startin' to talk some now." Harve looked at me. "I guess Black's gone off somewhere again and that's why you're here."

"Aw, c'mon, Harve. He's roughing it at the Ritz in NYC or somewhere equally uppity for a couple of days. Man, I'm telling you I can't wait to get a bite of that fish. I haven't had your fish in ages."

"You and Black are doin' okay, I suppose?"

Let me explain. Everybody at the lake is hideously obsessed with this romance thing that Black and I have going on. Don't ask me why. Probably making bets on when Black moves on to Naomi Watts or Gisele Bundchen. "Yep, still plugging along. That's a little hard to believe, right? Me, actually staying with somebody this long."

Harve shrugged. "He's more than a somebody. He's good for you, Claire. You're good for him. Sounds like a winning combo. I'm happy when you're happy."

I wondered if I was good for Black. Then I wondered if I

was happy. Seemed that way to me, a real shockeroo because I wasn't exactly used to being happy. No Happy Pete of Oak Haven was I. Always seemed to me that I got the best end of the Black/Me hookup. I did dig the guy, I must say. Even wished he was not away at the moment. The great big, black silk-sheeted bed that he also gave me last Christmas was gonna look pretty cold and empty again tonight. But I did have Jules Verne and two lethal weapons to keep me warm, and that wasn't so bad. At least, temporarily, it wasn't.

When the thunderous vroom vrooms of a giant motorcycle echoed out over the cove, Harve and I turned together and looked down the gravel road. I knew who it was, even before Joe McKay roared into sight from the direction of my own cabin just down the road. He had his little daughter with him, a child who'd figured into a past case of mine, one that had turned up creepier than most. She still wasn't right, not emotionally, not socially, not any other way, but I had to give McKay an A for effort, because he was as gentle with her as he could be, plus he'd had the sense to get Black professionally into the act. Black was being his regular good-guy self and seeing the kid pro bono, but the child still wasn't saying much. Hell, who could blame her, after spending some nightmare time with us down in a dank cave holed up with a couple of psychopaths. I'm surprised I hadn't been struck dumb by what had happened down there, too.

"You didn't mention Joe was coming for dinner," I said, as Joe brought his big Harley-Davidson to a stop at the end of Harve's sidewalk.

"Yeah, he and his kid helped me catch the fish. Least I can do is ask them to help me eat it. He went home to bake an apple pie."

I laughed, couldn't help it. "Oh, right, he baked a pie?"

Harve looked surprised by my surprise. "That's right. He said he's real good at making pies."

"Bull. I bet he bought it at Kroger's and put in his own pie pan."

"We'll see, once we slice it up. I know a Kroger's when I taste it. That's the kind you make, if I recall."

I laughed, but I always thought Kroger's pies tasted just fine. Truthfully, I couldn't see the sexy bad boy McKay baking anything, much less the All-American apple pie. He was so thoroughly the dangerous type, so drenched in sex appeal, that he almost rivaled Black in the "fighting off of willing women" category, I'm sure, but I'd found out the hard way that he was okay, a real stand-up guy. He dearly loved his daughter, that was the one thing I knew about him for absolutely certain. I respected him for that.

"Well, well, the sexy detective's joinin' us for dinner. My prayers are finally answered. Thank you, God."

McKay's deep voice was right behind me. When I turned around, he was grinning at me, deepening some impressive dimples. Not as deep and impressive as Black's are, of course. You see, I've got this thing for dimpled men, just can't help myself. The more they had, the more I liked them. McKay had his long sun-bleached blond hair pulled back into a low ponytail, and I noticed it was shorter than usual. He'd actually been to a barber. He was holding Elizabeth's hand.

I looked down at her, and she stared at me without the hint of a smile, or any other kind of emotion, and then set her large cornflower-blue eyes on Jules Verne. I was holding him by his bejeweled collar, also from Paris, France, and I let the dog go. When he ran to Elizabeth and jumped up on her legs, she actually curved that sober mouth into a big beautiful smile and knelt down to pet him. That was the first time I'd ever seen her smile, or give us any insight into her troubled mind. McKay's gaze met mine. He nodded and smiled. "Lizzie's gettin' a little bitty bit better every day, detective. Showin' some signs of comin' out of her funk. Guess I owe some of that to your better half, Mr. Super Shrink."

"I can see that. I'm glad."

I watched the child hug my dog, and Jules Verne ate up the little girl's attention, wagging his tail like crazy and rolling around on his back so she could tickle his belly, something he demanded regularly from me. Even Jules Verne had a run-in with a certain bogeyman once upon a time, but he was tough as a rottweiler and came out of it a lot faster than Elizabeth. Sometimes, though, he woke up, whining and yipping, and I had a good idea what he'd been dreaming about.

I said, "Maybe you oughta get her a dog, McKay. Something tells me she likes them."

"We're gonna get one. You bet. Until then, I thought we'd just mosey over and let her get a dose of little Curly here. I wouldn't mind playin' with yours now and again, either."

Again, our eyes locked, and his sexual innuendo came across loud and clear. He had been coming on to me big-time since the day we'd met on that prior case but not in a creepy, intrusive way. He was getting really good, though, at thinking up ways to hang around my place and spend time with my friends, so we'd have to run into each other. I guess I was flattered. McKay was one helluva good-looking guy, but I'd made it crystal clear that I was with Black, a plethora of times, at that. McKay was proving himself to be a good friend, and as much as I didn't like to admit it, I enjoyed being around him and listening to his slow drawl, not Georgia-soft like Bud, but North Carolina, maybe, with all those rounded O's. He liked to joke, and believe it or not, I usually thought he was funny. Me, who never joked around or thought anybody was particularly funny.

I said, "Like I told you, McKay, you're welcome to come over and fish and swim off my dock, play with my dog, whatever it takes to help Elizabeth get back on track. Just don't overstep your bounds."

"That's real nice, Detective. I've been takin' you up on it, but it seems you're never home anymore. You move in with your shrink? That it?"

"And say again, what's that to you?"

"You know how much you mean to me, Detective."

"Right. To answer your nosey question, we're spending a lot of time at his place lately. But I live at my house."

McKay smiled, as if delighted to hear the last part, and Harve said, "I hope you brought a big appetite, Joe. We caught enough fish for a brigade."

"And I brought us dessert, just like I promised. I ain't much at cookin', but I can bake a mean pie." He held up a large brown paper sack and balanced it on his open palm.

"I can't help but notice that's a Kroger's sack." I said.

"Now you've gone and hurt my feelings, Claire. That's one thing my momma taught me how to do. She made the best piecrust this side of Tokyo."

"Well, now, I'm looking forward to tasting it. I think."

"Well, I made two, one for you to take home and share with the shrink. You know, just my way of paying you back for letting us fish at your place and him seein' Elizabeth free of charge."

Harve said, "I'll get the rest of this crappie dipped up and drainin' on paper towels, then drop in some hush puppies, and we'll be set."

"Let me ask you something, Harve." I pulled the plastic evidence bags containing Mikey Murphy's beaded bracelet and the key out of my pocket. "You ever seen one of these before?"

Harve took the bags and examined them. "No, can't say I have, but I bet I can pick up something on the Net 'bout that kind of bracelet."

Joe McKay took the bags from him. "Lemme see those. This got something to do with a case?"

I nodded, not about to give him the details. Not that I didn't trust him, but I didn't, not enough to run a case with him like I did with Harve.

"Wanna let me see what I can conjure up for you?"

Oh, yeah, I forgot, Mr. Bad Boy McKay was also a purported psychic, especially in his own mind, but he had proved himself to be just that more than once, and I found that fascinating, if nothing else. Sometimes I dragged my feet a bit before asking him to hold my evidence and summon his inner magic voices, dreading what he was gonna see. Usually, when he had his little visions and I was the star, the immediate future didn't bode well for my health.

"Sure, go ahead." My voice didn't show the enthusiasm required, but I was all tensed up and feeling a little nervous from the oven thing.

"How about lettin' me take the bracelet out of the bag, so I can feel the real thing?"

"Sure. It's already been dusted."

I examined his face closely as he squeezed the bracelet into one closed palm. After a second or two, he passed it into his other hand. He shut his eyes and began rolling one of the blue beads between his thumb and forefinger. I waited, and so did Harve, probably as interested as I was. I have to admit, it is pretty damn awesome knowing a real-live psychic, even if he's come up with some pretty bad stuff with me right smack-dab in the middle of it. Better safe than sorry, I had begun to believe. Occasionally, he gave me something that I could use, or try to avoid, was the usual scenario.

McKay opened his eyes. "I'm not getting anything, but let me try something else."

He took my hand and held it, and I thought for a moment that was just another lame come-on, but less than a minute passed before he shook his head. "Nothin' at all, sorry, detective. It happens sometimes."

I felt both relief and disappointment. "That's okay. I know you're not John Edward."

"Hey, man, I'm as good as he is. Sometimes even better. He's just got that show, and all."

"Yeah. You can make that one of your goals. A real, live TV show where you help solve cold cases. You'd be a big star and make some serious dough."

Harve said, "C'mon down, Joe, and help me get the boat tied down for the night. I hear a storm's coming in."

"Okay, sure. Claire, keep an eye on Lizzie, will you? Won't be a minute."

I tensed. I did not want to keep an eye on Elizabeth. I did not want to be left alone with Elizabeth. It was too painful. I had lost my own baby boy when he was about two, not much different in age than Elizabeth was now. He had been killed the same night that bullet had sliced into Harve's spinal cord and taken away his career. Both tragedies were my fault, but I pressed that sick feeling back down into the dark places. McKay and Harve were just going down to the water, not six feet away. Elizabeth was playing with my dog. How hard can this be?

"Okay. Jules Verne seems to be keeping her happy."

I lounged down in a green and white padded deck chair, close to where Elizabeth was sitting on the deck. Jules was rubbing up against her, wanting more attention. The child wasn't smiling, but she didn't have that terrible glazed look in her eyes, either. Thank God, for that. I'd worn that look a lot in my life, and it wasn't easy to throw it off. I knew that much.

A short time later, we ate outside on the deck in the blue gray of summer twilight and shrill calls of at least a thousand insects. The lake lapped the pilings, lulling us to a false sense of security under hickory and maple trees that tossed wildly in the tops of the branches and made rustling sounds as if whispering secrets back and forth. Across the lake, I could see heat lightning brightening the dark clouds over the purple hills in the distance. The smell of rain was in the air, that and ozone and the smell of the fish guts Harve had yet to bury.

Harve had a couple of mosquito coils to keep away the biting beasts, and the rising breeze was helping keep the insects at bay and gave us the opportunity to sit outside, rather than inside Harve's small screened back porch. I watched as Elizabeth fed most of the food on her red-checked paper plate to Jules, who was acting like I hadn't fed him a single bite in two years. After a while, we moved to a circle of cushioned chairs and just talked and watched the storm roll in over the lake. I was surprised when Elizabeth yawned, then walked over to my chair and crawled up onto my lap. Uncomfortable, I held her awkwardly and tried not to think about Zach as she curled her warm little body against me. She looked up at me, her little brows dented with confusion, and whispered, but as clear as day, "Zach?"

My breath caught and I couldn't move, so shocked was I, but then she relaxed, her eyes drooped, and she didn't last long before sleep overtook her. I nearly held my breath, still stunned that she'd said my son's name, still trembling with reaction. When I looked down at her and she looked so very peaceful for a change, I said a little internal prayer that she wouldn't have nightmares, just this one night.

When Harve's phone rang inside the house, he motored his wheelchair inside, and Joe moved to the chair next to me. He smiled down at his daughter. "She likes you, Claire. I haven't seen her do that with anybody but me. Not even Harve, and she loves him."

I could only come up with what I always said to him when discussing Elizabeth. "I'm not good with children." I had to tell him then, had to ask. "Lizzie said something to me, something I can't explain."

"What? She never says much."

"She said, 'Zach.' That was my son's name."

McKay stared at me a second, then he looked through the big glass window where Harve was sitting at his desk and talking on the telephone. "I know about your son, Claire. Harve told me. I'm real sorry that happened to you."

Oh, God, let him stop. I did not want to discuss Zach. "Did she hear you talking about him?"

"No." He hesitated. "I think she's inherited some of my

ability. I've seen signs that she might be psychic. She probably felt your pain, if you were thinking about him when you held her. That happens at times with me." He was very reluctant now. "I saw him a minute ago, too, when I held your hand. Little guy, curly blond hair, blue eyes, real big ones, and he looks a lot like you, and he liked to run around a hundred miles an hour. I thought it would upset you, so I just kept it to myself."

Swallowing hard, I shifted in my chair and stared out over the dark water. This was a subject I never discussed, not even with Black when he was trying his darnedest to help me deal with it. I wasn't going to start now, especially with McKay, though I knew he was trying to be considerate. It was painful enough, feeling Elizabeth's soft little body snuggling up against me. She felt exactly like Zach had the night I held him until his big blue eyes closed the very last time and he was gone out of my life forever. Pain, pure and elemental, erupted; my heart burned with it.

"Sorry, Claire. I can see you're upset."

I couldn't speak. What was there to say, anyway? McKay got the picture, thank God, and changed the subject.

"Maybe you can hang around with us sometimes, Claire? Just so Lizzie will get used to havin' a woman around? Her mom wasn't exactly a good role model for her. She needs a female in her life that she can trust."

"Oh, c'mon, McKay, you've got women galore in your life, right? You don't need me."

McKay didn't reply. Thunder rolled like a shaken piece of aluminum, but Elizabeth did not stir. He took a drink of his Bud Light. "I don't have any women in my life. I'm spending my time tryin' to get Lizzie through this. Therapy's helping, but she needs more time. Makin' up to you tonight like this is showin' some progress. Thanks for holdin' her."

"No problem." Yeah, right.

Silence reigned. The stars were beginning to come out, one at a time. We watched the rain sheeting the water very far away, past the mouth of the cove, and waited for Harve to come back outside. He was working at his computer system now, probably answering a question for one of his clients. After a time while we silently listened to more crickets and the faint sound of Harve's voice and the restless tossing of the treetops, McKay got talkative.

"Know what?"

"What?"

"I'm thinking about movin' down to Springfield and startin' up my own business."

"No joke? What kinda business?"

"You're gonna laugh at this."

"Probably."

"I was drivin' around Springfield last week and I found this vacant Victorian house in the old part of town, on Walnut Street. Big old place. So I got to thinkin' that it'd make a helluva good place to live, so I'm thinkin' about putting a bid in on it. It's in pretty bad shape, yeah, but I'm handy with tools. I could paint it and fix it up to look pretty good."

"Really? Sounds kind of big for just you and Lizzie."

"That's the thing. I'm thinkin' of turnin' it into one of those bed-and-breakfast thingamajigs. I can cook well enough to make some breakfast stuff, eggs and bacon, stuff like that, and it's near a real good early childhood center. Or maybe I can get a live-in nanny. If I can find one that Lizzie takes to."

"So now I'm gonna have two friends in the hotel business, huh?" I took a swig of my beer and found it warm and unpalatable. Nothing worse than hot beer, in my book. I set the bottle aside.

McKay chuckled a little. He had a nice, genuine laugh. "Mine ain't gonna be anywhere close to Cedar Bend Lodge's league. It's really run-down now and I'll have to put in a lot of hard work on it, but I like that kinda work. You like to paint?"

"Aha. Now the truth comes out. You're pulling a Tom Sawyer on me."

"Hey, I need some help, that's all. I'm gonna beg for it everywhere I can."

McKay was being serious now, so I said, "Sure, I'll help you out when I can. Where you getting all the money for this stuff?"

"I have my military retirement and some investments I made while I was in. My parents left me a little."

"Sounds like you've got it all figured out. Good for you."

"Now all I need is a good woman to share it with."

Crap. Everything was going just fine, friendship all warm and platonic, and now he was looking at me, the way he did from time to time, all serious, sappy, and romantic, and that's the last thing I wanted to think about. "That shouldn't be a problem for a Romeo like you. How about Black and I fix you up with one of his drop-dead-gorgeous employees? He's got a whole pack of them."

"I want to share it with you, Claire."

Damn. This guy just couldn't see the light. "I think we've been down this road before, McKay. Maybe not this far, but it's still the same road."

"I don't happen to think you fit with Black and his lifestyle and don't think he'll make you happy in the long run. Don't get me wrong, I like the guy. He's cool. He's just not cool enough for you."

I had to laugh at his arrogance. "And you are, I take it?"

"Damn right."

I laughed again, and so did he. We did get along for the most part. I did like this guy. We could've gone out, had a few beers, raised some hell, if Black wasn't in the picture. But Black was in the picture, big-time and in CAPITAL LETTERS. I changed the subject.

"I gotta idea for you, McKay, why don't you give your B and B guests some of your hocus pocus, seance acts down in the drawing room before dinner. You know, hold on to their hand and read their minds. That oughta get you a no vacancy sign up real fast."

McKay didn't take my bait, just smiled. "That's exactly what I was gonna do. You must be a mind reader."

I ignored his humor. "No way.

"Oh, yeah. I heard about this other guy who's doing something like that out East, in Rhode Island, or somewhere like that, and is making a mint off it. No reason I can't do it, too."

"You'll have to score a little better than you did with my bracelet a minute ago."

"Give me another chance on that a few days from now. You were just too close and smelled way too good for me to keep my psychic edge goin'."

"That's Irish Spring soap and gun oil."

"Two of my favorite things, especially on a hot woman."

Our smiles met for a rather warm instant, and it was a heck of a good thing my phone rang. Elizabeth bolted upright and rubbed her eyes as I pulled the phone off my belt and read caller ID. "It's Bud. I gotta take this."

Lowering Elizabeth to the floor, I stood up and moved off the porch, I said, "Yeah, Bud, you got something?"

"There's a female student of Asian extraction that's gone missing over at Missouri State in Springfield. You up to checking out her dorm room tonight? I got permission from Springfield PD after I told them about our possible double homicide and unidentified vic."

"Where are you? I'll pick you up."

"Black won't mind?"

I frowned. Everybody was always digging into my love life. It was getting a bit old. "Black's still in New York. Where are you?"

"I just got home. Let me grab something to eat and we're good to go."

"I'll be right there. Harve's got a ton of fried crappie and hush puppies left over. I'll bring you a doggie bag, just sit tight."

"Hey, Claire, you know why they call them hush puppies?"

"Is this out of that book I got you?"

"Yeah. They call them that because back in the Civil War if rebels got wind of Yankees comin' too close, they'd throw hush puppies at their dogs to keep 'em from barkin'."

"That sounds made up."

"Huh uh. It's straight outta that book. And that book knows."

"Thanks for sharing. I'll be there in ten minutes."

We hung up, and I walked back to the porch. McKay was rocking Elizabeth back to sleep in Harve's oversize wooden rocker. He said, "Gotta go, right? Duty calls?"

"You got it. Tell Harve that Bud and I had something come up. Think he'd mind if I take all those leftovers to Bud?"

"Nope. And don't forget that pie I made you."

"You did not make that pie."

"Oh, yes, I did. Secret's to cook it in one of those Kroger brown paper bags. It makes it brown real evenly and takes care of the juices dripping all over your oven. My mom had all kinda tricks like that."

"Thanks. I'll let you know what I think." I picked up the leftovers and the pie and headed for the door. I turned back when McKay called after me.

"Hey, Claire, tell Bud I said hi." He stopped rocking and gave me a serious look. "And by the way, detective, you take good care, okay? I've got a paintbrush just waitin' at my house with your name on it."

His cheesy grin was a challenge, but I just said so long and pushed open the screen. I headed for my Explorer, just as the rain hit with a vengeance. Yep, Joe McKay was quite a guy. He was just courting the wrong gal.

Here Comes Trouble

Tee awoke with a start. Initially he wasn't sure where he was or what was going on. Then he recognized the shrill sounds for what they were. Screams, high and horrible. He jumped out of bed, shaken and still groggy. Buddy was on his feet, too, and they stared at each other for a second or two, then raced each other out into the hallway. The commotion was going on down to their left, where the corridor turned at the girls' restroom.

Night nurses were sprinting toward the yelling, and kids were opening their doors all up and down the corridor. Other patients were already outside and standing around in their pajamas and underwear. Tee took off toward the excitement with Buddy dead on his heels. To his surprise, nobody tried to stop him or even slow him down.

Everything was going down inside the girls' bathroom, and he eased himself past a couple of others and moved inside the big community restroom. There were about eight lavatories with a long mirror stretching above them, and ten or twelve toilet stalls, but there were also three private rooms with bathtubs for the girls to take bubble baths in.

Edging around a young white-coated orderly, who was standing against the wall, his mouth hanging open as he stared horrified at something, Tee realized the screams were not coming from a girl at all, but from his new buddy, Yang Wei. When Tee finally got to where he could peer inside the private bathtub room, he gasped, shocked to see so much blood. Man, it was everywhere, turning the bathwater scarlet where it was washing over the edge of the white tub and streaming down the sides and all over the black-and-white tiled floor. It was sickening.

More stunning, it was Lotus in that tub, in all that red water. Yang Wei was going nuts, holding her head out of the water and trying to push together the gaping wounds on her wrists, so deep her hands were flopping down. But it was way too late for that to stop the bleeding. Yang Wei's little sister was stone-cold dead. Her face was white as the wall behind her, and her eyes were open and staring at Yang Wei. Tee wouldn't have thought a girl so small could pump out that much blood. Holy shit.

One of the doctors arrived and pushed past Tee. He took one look at the blood-drenched room and yelled at the nurses, "Get an ambulance out here, now!" Then he said, "Yang Wei, get back now, let me see what I can do."

Yang Wei obeyed, white dress shirt wet and stained crimson, the glazed look of disbelief in his eyes terrible to behold. When a nurse took hold of Tee's arm and pulled him out the door, he went quietly, because he'd seen enough. She said, "You don't need to be here watching this. Go back to your room. The doctor's with her now. He'll take care of everything."

Not so, Tee thought, the doctor was way, way too late to take care of anything, but reluctantly he did as he was told. Truthfully, however, he was more than perplexed. Why in the world had she slit her wrists, the dumb little bitch? What they'd done together in the shed hadn't been all *that* bad. For God's sake, talk about an overreaction. In fact, he knew she had enjoyed it as much as he had. He hoped to hell she hadn't left a suicide note incriminating him. That brought on a wave of fear, and he decided that it was in his best interest to find out, and find out fast.

Tee knew where Lotus's room was, because he had scoped it out the first day he met her. She had a private room now because her last roommate had recently been released, and he had originally planned to make love to her there. That idea had been discarded quick enough. Just look what a scream had done when the nurse had found the body. As he moved toward her room, trying to look inconspicuous, everybody else was being pushed back into their rooms and told to stay there. In the distance, he could already hear the shrill blare of a siren heading their way.

Ducking into her room, he found the clothes she'd been wearing at the court scattered around on the floor, and he quickly took them and stuffed them inside his pajama top. He wasn't any authority on crime scenes, but he knew about DNA and rape kits from watching *The First 48* on A&E network. Nobody was gonna find out that he was with her last, uh uh. He glanced around for a note, found one propped on her pillow, and stuffed it inside his shirt alongside her soiled clothes.

Biding his time until a couple of paramedics rushed down the hallway with a rolling gurney, he managed to use the confusion that caused to return to his room undetected. Buddy was gone who knew where, so Tee opened the note Lotus had left and silently read:

> *Good-bye. It won't stop. Not ever. I can't take it anymore. Yang Wei, I love you and I'm sorry about this.*

That was all the scrap of paper said and was way too sketchy to figure out. He went back to the doorway and ran into Buddy a few yards down the hall. He was sobbing his head off. "She's dead. Dead. They can't revive her."

Tee took Buddy back to their room and watched him fall on the bed and weep like his best friend had just offed herself. He was such a little sissy of a boy. The girl had made this decision. Nobody else. What had happened was her own fault. Certainly not Tee's. He wasn't about to feel guilty for what she'd done to herself.

During the next few weeks, Tee settled into the clinic's routine and made damn sure everybody liked him so he wouldn't be suspected of any kind of wrongdoing in Lotus's death. It was easy as pie, too. But sometimes he was plagued by Lotus killing herself. Yang Wei had gone off and not come back, and nobody knew where he was. Tee grew more and more intrigued by the girl's sudden rash act, and that he was involved in a real suicide this time, not one he'd conjured up to explain the "accidents" he caused in his own family.

Deciding that the only way to find out what had driven the stupid girl to end her life would be an in-depth look into her medical files, he made his plans. By now, Buddy was wrapped around his little finger. Buddy just loved Tee, to the sick point even, but more important, Buddy loved the way he got to be both the constant companion and roommate of the most popular kid at the clinic. If Tee told Buddy to keep his mouth shut, the kid did it, no questions, and that did make everything so much easier.

So they made their little pact. Buddy got to be the lookout, his mission to distract the nurses while Tee snuck into the office wing, especially the one named Maggie, who had seemed to hate Tee on first sight. That part went off just fine, and Tee crept up toward the offices of the staff doctors. This late at night, that area of the clinic was all dark, except for a few night-lights positioned along the base of the corridors to lead people outside, in case of fire. Moving along, he tried every door all the way down to his own therapist's office. He had learned to pick locks a long time ago, when his mom hid her daily journal in a locked drawer and he'd wanted to know all her secrets. He'd found out lots of useful information that way, and he'd also found his dad's will in there; he was a little disappointed to find that the family's considerable wealth would be divided equally among all his children. That was a bummer and hit Tee hard at the time. Tee was the favorite and should get it all. And maybe he would someday.

The tumblers finally clicked into place, and he tiptoed inside and glanced around. All darkness and crouching shadows from the faint illumination of a dusk-to-dawn lamp affixed to the end of the building. He knew from watching his doctor that he kept his files in a locked cabinet hidden under one of the bookshelves. Tee moved to it and shined his penlight on the lock. It was even easier than the one on the door. He found Lotus's file listed under her false name and opened it up on the floor behind a leather couch.

Taking his time, he read through the whole thing with interest and found her medical history all laid out for him. He also found she had been sexually abused by her dad when she lived in China, so forcefully at times that she ended up damaged inside her womb and couldn't ever have children. She'd been raped again when she was on tour with the Olympic team, this time by her trusted coach. Gee whiz, that kid was a rape magnet. Of course, he hadn't really raped her. She hadn't struggled, had she? She had just lain there underneath him, as if she was secretly enjoying the whole thing but wouldn't admit it. Of course, she had been enjoying it. What girl wouldn't? Everybody talked about how good looking he was.

When he finished perusing the last page, he closed her file and clicked off the penlight. So that was the problem. Lotus had been traumatized by rapists her whole life, and his lovemaking might have pushed her over the top. She had probably gone into some kind of psychological state where she thought he was not Tee but one of her real rapists. Wow.

He felt a certain sense of power glow hot inside him and got really excited about such a revelation.

Was it possible that he could manipulate any of the kids around here into killing themselves? How handy would that be if they annoyed him or got in his way? Man, alive, what an awesome thought! He could control what they did, how they got well, or better yet, didn't get well. All without dirtying his hands or tying their hair to a swimming pool drain or pushing them off a cliff. The possibilities were splendidly mind-boggling.

Alive with the thrill of it all, he switched the light back on and pulled out Buddy's file. Aha. Buddy was paranoid, afraid everybody was out to get him. Now that was interesting as hell. And that kind of psychological problem would be incredibly easy to provoke. Tee smiled to himself. He had a feeling he was going to learn a lot at this place. He was gonna have a real good time messing up these freaks.

Thoroughly intrigued, he took some time to read through some other kids' files, just for future reference. Man, what a sick bunch of losers. There was no telling how much damage he could do to their eggshell psyches, and most of the kids were in here being treated for their suicidal tendencies anyway. He could probably make the whole lot of them kick themselves off, and nobody would be the wiser. Chuckling softly at the thought of how easy it was all gonna be, he turned off the flashlight and headed swiftly and silently back to his room.

ELEVEN

Missouri State University lies in the heart of the city of Springfield, Missouri. It is a great school in a great town with an enrollment of about ten thousand students. Bud's liaison officer at the Springfield PD, an old friend of his named Dak, identified the missing girl's dorm as Hammons House. It was pouring rain and had been all the way down to the university. We stopped out front, across Harrison Street from the eight-story, high-rise dorm, and waited for a couple of cars to pass by before we ran through sheeting rain and mist to the front doors.

On our mad dash, we passed about twenty coeds running hither and there in very short shorts and halter tops. Bud eyed each in turn, an equal opportunity leerer, and no doubt rating most of them a 10 in his trusty black book. Thus he became more rain spattered than I, because I ran like hell for the lobby. Actually, most of those young things were a 10 in anybody's black book. Where were all the MSU guys?

Once inside the building, I found out the answer to that question quick enough. There was a Cardinals baseball game on the big-screen TV, broadcast out of Atlanta. We'd heard on the radio on the drive down when Bud was scarfing down fish, hush puppies, and apple pie that the game was running late, due to a rain delay, but now the bad weather was apparently over. Lots of college boys attending the summer session, or should I say, young men, were lounging around, drinking sodas, and eating hot wings and pepperoni pizza. I guess their dates had to wait until after the ninth inning. I wiped some of the rain off my face with my sleeve, never big on umbrellas, and we walked to the front desk, flashed our badges, and nearly made the young woman manning it faint with trepidation.

"Hey, you're not in trouble, miss," Bud reassured her, "At least, not yet."

Well, that didn't help.

I said, "We're here about the Missouri State girl who went missing. The Springfield police gave us permission to enter her room and look around. They were supposed to call and pave the way."

"Oh, yeah, they did. A real cute guy named Dak told me to do whatever you want me to. Poor Li. I don't know what happened to her, but I bet it's not something good."

If Li was our gal, it definitely wasn't good. "Her name's Li? What's her last name?"

"Li He. But they say it the other way around in China, I think."

Li He. Sounded like a subtle chuckle. "Could you leave the desk long enough to escort us upstairs?"

"Sure, there's a girl in the back room who can cover for me. Or I can just give you a key to Li's suite and let you take a look around. Her suite mates are still living there, though, so you might ought to knock."

"Okay, we'll take the key and let you do your job. Thanks for your help."

She handed the key to Bud, because he was a hot guy and girls had a habit of giving him keys, I guess. But he was really hitting the jackpot in that regard on this case. Debbie Winters came to mind. We headed for the elevators, just as somebody hit a home run. Bud said, "Just a sec, I wanna see if that was the Braves or the Cards. Please God, let it be the Braves."

"Oh, for Pete's sake, Bud, watch the replays later on *Sports-Center*. It's getting late."

My idea didn't appeal to him, and I stood leaning against the wall beside the elevator as he hightailed it to the lounge and checked out the score. A true Atlantan, his face showed joy and so did the whoop he let out. I could've told him it wasn't the Cards who scored by the lack of uproar of young male voices. I heard a couple of jeers aimed in Bud's direction and was glad he was armed.

When he reached me, I said, "Being a Braves fan around here is not healthy, Bud. You gotta know that."

"Yeah, tell me about it. I thought they were gonna attack me, but I got big money riding on this game in the department pool. I am gonna win this time, just watch."

"What'd you call big?"

"Twenty bucks."

We rode up in a smudged stainless-steel elevator with a girl who had a cloud of perfume hanging off her that made me think I needed to prune some lilac bushes. She was carrying neatly folded clothes in an oval-shaped wicker hamper. Now there was a mother who taught her daughter well. Most of us saved our dirty clothes in a big smelly duffel bag for the next time we went home. I remembered that much about my brief college days at LSU, not that I ever had a real home to go to. I spent most college breaks in the dorm by myself, or with a couple of foreign exchange students from Zimbabwe or Kenya, but it was better than trying to survive some of my foster parents' holiday uncheer.

Li He lived on the third floor. Way down at the end. The corridor was dead silent, all the gals out baring their bodies and all the males whooping and hollering at the TV or Bud. Except for one room we passed, where some loud music blared out into the corridor. John Mayer, I think. Whatever happened to Quiet Hours? Probably nonexistent now, a thing of the past. Nobody came to college to study anymore. Or maybe iPods were alien devices and had taken over the campus.

Room 315 overlooked the street running behind the dormitory. I caught a glimpse of the Hammonds Tower in downtown Springfield, looming up in all its black-windowed glory. I always thought it looked like some evil monolith out of a science fiction movie, the kind that took over your mind if you touched its sleek dark walls. Maybe it did, who knows? I always heard there was this super exclusive eating place on the top level with only hotsy-totsy types imbibing of its salad bar. I heard you had to have a special key to gain entrance. How pretentious is that, I ask you. Probably served some of those gross snails, too.

Tapping a knuckle on the door, Bud blew on his palm and said, "Does my breath smell like onions? Harve put tons of them in those hush puppies."

"Who're you expecting to answer the door? Charlize Theron?"

"Man, I wish." Bud fumbled around for a pack of Juicy Fruit gum, his favorite breath freshener, found it, folded a piece, and popped it in his mouth. He stuck the wrapper in his jeans pocket with the rest of them.

When nobody answered after about five minutes, I knocked on the door and made it loud enough to wake up the dead. Not a good analogy. Sorry. We had a key, but we didn't want to walk in on anything x-rated. On a college campus, you just never knew.

Bud leaned against the door and I looked at a poster thumbtacked on a door just across the hall. It was Brad Pitt in his little loincloth/skirt thing from that *Troy* movie. Must be a girls' suite. He looked pretty damn hot, if I say so myself. I said, "Brad Pitt's from Springfield, you know that, Bud?"

"Yeah, I heard about it. You think he'll bring Angelina around here or better yet, up to the lake, and maybe we'll get to bust them for disturbing the peace, or jaywalking with baby carriages, somethin' like that, and then we'd get to sweat them at the station? I'll take Angelina. You can have Pitt. I think his looks are overrated."

"Yeah, right. Tell that to any woman you pass on the street and see how bad they beat on you."

"They've been seen around Springfield. It could happen."

"In your dreams. They've got way too many kids now to have time to create disturbances, unless it's for excessive baby crying."

"I heard John Goodman's from around here, too. You know, he's the husband on *Roseanne*. That true?"

I said, "No, he's from St. Louis, I think, but somebody said he went to school here on a football scholarship."

"Know what else? Jenna Fischer, that girl that plays Pam on *The Office*? She's from Missouri, too. I heard that her parents or somebody kin to her lives up around Camdenton."

"What's *The Office*?"

"Don't you ever watch TV, Claire?"

"Sometimes I watch *Dr. Phil*, but I've got to be really bored."

Tired of our rendition of *Inside Edition*, I knocked again. We'd be giving each other movie reviews next. I'd barely got my fist off the door before it swung open. A girl stood there in her underwear. The skimpy kind with both pieces made out of a single handkerchief. Bud was immediately attentive. He just might need that Juicy Fruit, after all.

"You guys are cops."

Yeah, we get that greeting a lot in the places we frequent with our big shiny badges hanging around our necks. Go figure. "Yes ma'am. I'm Detective Morgan and this is Detective Davis. We're here to take a look at Li He's room. Did we get you at an inconvenient time?" I joined Bud in looking pointedly at her less than attire.

She pointedly didn't get my drift. "Yeah, I guess, but it doesn't matter. I mean you can take a look at Li's room without bothering me. I've been studying Ancient Greek history and fell asleep. My other suite mate's not here. Mel went home for her cousin's wedding."

"Okay, then."

The girl kept standing there so I gave her a blatant hint, "May we come in then? Now?"

"I guess so." She stepped back.

"And your name is?" Bud asked, surreptitiously glancing down her body, while I looked around the living room of the suite.

"Delia." While Bud and I waited, poised breathlessly for her last name, she sighed deeply, yawned, then said, "Winston. Delia Winston. I'm just a freshman. Li was a sophomore."

Bud jumped on that, even before I could. "Was?"

"Yeah. I assume somebody got hold of her and murdered her. Like, why else would she miss her psych final?"

I stared at her. "Well, there could be other reasons."

"Yeah, like what?"

"Like she's been in an accident and is in the hospital in a coma or she took off with a boyfriend without telling anyone?"

"The police already checked out all that kinda stuff. I say she's dead, whacked by some psycho freak who probably buried her in a shallow grave in the woods where she'll never be found unless some hunter with a bird dog happens to find the hole he put her in."

All righty now. I suspected this kid was a criminal justice/abnormal psych major, or perhaps just a textbook example of the latter. Then I saw the Stephen King book lying open on the couch and wasn't sure.

Bud said, "We hope she's just run off with her boyfriend, like Detective Morgan said, something like that."

Delia said, "Well, I do, too. Duh-uh."

"Yeah, duh-uh." I pronounced "duh" with two syllables like she had in a rather sarcastic manner, but she only smiled and seemed pleased that we were in agreement.

Bud said, "Could we have a look-see in her room?"

"I guess so, but the other policeman already spent a lot of time poking around in there. You aren't going to find anything new. He was a real hottie, too. Name was Dak."

I said, "We won't take long, Delia. And we'd love to interview you, too, once you're more fully awake and have on a bathrobe of some type." Now that was pretty damn pointed, too, and a little flush of color moved up into her face, so I assumed she began to remember that she was nearly nude. With strangers around, and everything.

"Her room's right over there, that last bedroom. Mine's on the other end, and Mel's is the one in the middle."

"Thanks, Delia. You've been a big help to us."

Delia nodded, as if that were actually true, and flounced off to the couch, if one can flounce without any clothes on. She lay down on her back and opened her King novel, to hell with ancient Greece and Odysseus and his tormented life, and Achilles and all that rot. Back to vampires and/or transmitting cell phones. Bud and I snapped on our protective gloves and stepped into our cute paper booties, and Delia took note. She peered over her tome and said, "They do that on *CSI New York*, too."

"Yeah, that's where we got it from," said Bud.

"Yeah, I'm learning a lot from that show, too. You can call me Dee."

I said, "Thanks, Dee. That means a lot to us."

Bud grinned at me and shook his head. Dee turned a page and twirled a strand of hair around her forefinger, oblivious. Remind me to look for her robe while I'm rummaging around. Or a bath towel might do it. A washcloth, even.

We opened Li He's door and went inside. I closed it to stop needless criticism of our search techniques, which might not be up to snuff with the seven-million-dollar annual salary the pseudo detectives/actors on *CSI* make. Maybe we could learn something from them. Like how to never be in the line of fire but get paid loads of money for reading tough-cop lines off a script.

"Li was a very neat young woman." That was Bud. Of course, he'd notice that first, being the neat freak of the universe that he was. "That's always a sign of good moral fiber."

"Then what about obsessive compulsives? They're looney tunes in their own special way."

"Not all of them."

I looked around the nice clean dorm room with its neat stacks of books and papers, and carefully made bed, its pink and white polka-dot quilt all smoothed out and tucked in at the corners in military fashion, and said, "I hope this girl isn't our victim." I wondered why I'd felt compelled to say that. No matter who it was, it was a terrible tragedy. "Tell me again what info the SPD gave you on this case?"

"She's a sophomore here at MSU. She lives in Branson. They said her parents work at one of the shows over there, a thing called the Beijing Acrobatic Troupe. Don't know much about that yet, except that the cast is made up of Chinese nationals, includin' her parents, who're worried out of their minds about her and don't speak very good English. Accordin' to them, and Dak and his guys interviewed them both, she's never gone off alone like this, never gotten into trouble, never given them a minute's concern. SPD says she's got a clean record, no drugs, no prostitution, nothin'. Makes good grades, all A's. Makes friends easily. Everybody liked her. You know the type."

Actually, I didn't know many straight arrows, not in my line of work. All my arrows were bent in some way or snapped in two. "Except for getting mixed up with Mikey, if she did. Let's see what we can find out about her."

The suite had one bathroom that was shared by all three girls, but I headed for the sink and vanity located in one corner of Li He's room. The hairbrush I was looking for was sitting right there in plain sight, beside a matching pink comb and hand mirror. All lined up, nice and straight and orderly. I picked up the brush with gloved fingers, found out it looked pretty clean, and then was pleased as punch to see several long black hairs entwined in the bristles. "We got a hair-brush, Bud. Maybe Buck can get a positive ID of our vic off her DNA."

"Great. And here's a picture of her. Man, what a shame. She was a little tiny thing, look at that. She's a gymnast."

Bud handed me a color picture of Li He in a tight maroon and white gymnastic uniform with the MSU Bears logo across the front. I picked up a different framed photo, a closeup of Li, Delia, and a small girl who looked some years older than the other two and like she, too, had Asian blood. Mel of the Weekend Wedding, I presumed. Sitting together in a booth at what looked a pizza place, very likely Mikey's, aka the scene of the crime, the happy trio were laughing with their arms around each other. Better times, no doubt about it. Maybe Delia was just in shock today, or a cold-as-ice sociopath, take your pick. Or maybe Mel just went home to get away from Delia's gloom and doom predictions and penchant for wearing nothing. Unfortunately, if Li was our victim, Delia was probably right on target this time.

I said, "She's got the same body type as our vic, same length of hair. My gut's telling me it's the same woman."

I returned to snooping. Everything I looked at was neat to a highly unlikely degree. I spent some time shuffling through the papers on her desk. She had her schedule of classes tacked on an yellow bulletin board above her textbooks. I looked at more thick college books lined on the shelf above the desk. Physiology, psychology of the aberrant personality, physics, you name it. Only a thin blue golf manual looked a little out of place, but hey, doctors always played golf on the week-ends, didn't they? Except for Black. He played with me on the weekends, and more power to him.

I took hold of a knob and pulled open the long narrow desk drawer. Everything in its place. Rubber bands, paper clips, Ice Breakers mints—two tins, both spearmint—and a small pocket address book. I thumbed to the M section. Mikey Murphy, address Mikey's Pizzeria in Osage Beach along with a telephone number, and a little asterisk that said "hot guy" in parentheses.

"She knew him, Bud. She was attracted to him. It's written down right here in her own handwriting. Black-and-white."

Bud joined me at the desk, took the book, and started flipping through the pages. "Yeah, Dak mentioned this book might be helpful to us. She has lots of friends. Doofus Dee out there is from Independence, Missouri."

"What about Mel? You find her name? We need to talk to her, too."

"Melanie Baxter? Right here. She lives in Fenton, that's outside St. Louis. And guess what? Lookee here, Claire, our little psychiatric clinic's number is in here. It looks like she might've been a patient at Oak Haven, and if not, she's probably made a couple of calls out there."

"Could've been when Mikey was being treated inpatient. Could be they were an item even that far back."

"Could be. Could be a lot of things."

"We need to get this hairbrush over to Buckeye and put a rush on it. If Li He is our girl, her parents have to be notified, and the sooner the better."

My cell phone erupted with its perky south of the border refrain so I grabbed it off my belt and found Black's super-secret, personal number glowing on Caller ID. I did love Caller ID; it took the suspense out of my calls. And I didn't have to talk to anybody I didn't like. I picked up in a hurry.

I said, "Where are you?"

"Where are you?"

"I'm in a dorm room at Missouri State with Bud."

"Well, I sure wouldn't've guessed that one."

"We think we've found our female victim. She's been missing for several days. We think her DNA's gonna match up with the girl in the oven."

"Good. I'm still in the air, about fifty miles west of the lake. Want me to touch down there and pick you up?"

"You cut your trip short?"

"After I gave my speech, I got bored, so here I am."

"I gotta get a piece of evidence to Buck, then I've got to turn around and come back down to Branson tomorrow and interview her parents." As usual, Bud was gesturing and interrupting me, so I said, "Just a sec, Black." I held one palm over the phone in case he was going to say something embarrassing about Black and me, and said, "What? I'm trying to talk here."

"I'll take Buck the hairbrush. You and Black can stay down here somewhere tonight and interview the parents tomorrow. That'll save you a lot of driving time. Maybe Buck'll have the tests by noon and you can give the notification while you're in Branson."

"Lucky me. You just don't want to have to do it."

"Can't argue with that."

"I guess that would work, but I don't think Buck's going to have time to match the hair. Lemme see if Black's okay with it." I put the phone back to my ear. "Wanna spend the night with me in Branson and then take me to interview the missing girl's parents?"

"I was hoping you'd ask me something like that, especially the first part."

I smiled. I had missed him, too. "You don't have any important meetings in the morning?"

"Nothing that can't be rescheduled. Does Harve have Jules Verne?"

"Yeah. I think you miss that dog more than you do me."

"Well, he does lick me in the face and other places."

"As if I don't."

Black laughed, and it sounded sexy as hell. "There you go, turning me on. Where do I pick you up?"

"I guess you can put down out at Springfield-Branson Airport. We'll have to rent a car. Or we can stay tonight here in Springfield and drive over to Branson in the morning. It's late, and it's just a thirty-minute drive."

"Okay, have Bud drop you off at the airport, but make it at the General Aviation Complex next door to Springfield-Branson. I'll be there in twenty minutes."

I flipped the phone shut. "Okay, Bud, we got about ten minutes to interview Doofus Dee out there and then you can drop me at the airport and drive my car home. I'll pick it up tomorrow when I get back."

Bud nodded. "Man, I'm with you on this girl, Li He. There's just something about her. I hope she's not the one. She looks way too young and defenseless to die this way."

"Yeah." But my gut was telling me she was the one, and now all we had to find out was the why. And who was monster enough to cook some poor innocent nineteen-year-old girl alive.

Here Comes Trouble

After Lotus's suicide, Tee was careful to act all torn up, like all the other kids in his group. He did one hell of a job on that front, too, but he wasn't upset in the least. She'd been ignorant to do herself in just because he had his way with her. Even if she hadn't liked it the first time, she would've learned to enjoy it, eventually. But he'd play the morose game because he liked it here at this clinic. He liked it a heck of a lot better than being at home with his whining, sobbing brothers and sisters, moaning about not having a mom anymore.

The therapy group session turned out to be what he really looked forward to the most. Every single day, he learned more and more personal things about the other kids and how to manipulate them. All were damaged goods; all were on the edge and only a slight little shove would push them over it and into utter despair. On top of that, he watched and learned how these supposedly expert psychiatrists worked with their patients, especially their techniques to break through and help the poor saps. Talk about a dream job. Messing with people's minds. He loved it. He had always been able to do it, anyway, since he was a little kid. But to get paid the big bucks to do it was a whole different ball of wax.

There was one doctor that he liked the best. An older guy, Asian, Chinese, actually, like Yang Wei, and Tee found out he was another reason so many young Asian patients kept showing up. It turned out that he was a defector from China, too, and sometimes when Tee was in a private session with him, the doc would tell him tales about what it was like to live in China and how much he missed his family. But more interesting to Tee, he also told him that the Chinese had become masters at mind control and had used their own citizens in Frankenstein experiments, especially convicts and dissidents. He had escaped the regime and found refuge in the United States, but not before he had been forcibly involved in many of their covert psychological programs.

More than fascinated, Tee began to search for that kind of stuff on the Internet, and he got all kind of hits. In truth, he began to admire the Chinese government and how it worked. He played up to the Asians in house and started hanging around with them. There was a couple of girls who liked him and didn't seem to mind that he was screwing them both. They were good friends, believe it or not, and both were mentally shaky. He started learning Mandarin Chinese from the doctor and loved it.

Things ended up going so well for him that he decided he'd go into psychiatry someday when he went off to college. He could also major in Asian studies and languages, and then he would see if he could travel to mainland China and study at one of their universities. His professor knew some people there, and things had begun to warm up between China and the United States. Tee was already pretty good at the language, so it would be a snap.

Yeah, his plan for his future was pretty awesome, all right, and he dived into it with great enthusiasm. His dad was pleased to see how happy he seemed now, and so were the doctors. He started working hard to get his high school diploma, right there on the premises, and it wasn't hard to excel in all his subjects with his keen intelligence. He managed to ace his classes with flying colors. Next he persuaded the doctors into possibly giving him an assistant's job right there at the clinic, so he could continue his private experiments on the kids. And he was getting better at it. In fact, it was almost like taking candy from a bunch of larger than normal babies.

Buddy, his roommate, was already a basket case, so it didn't take much to get him started down that road. Buddy was scared of just about everything. Tee tortured him regularly by implanting doubts and fears in his head, and decided to do it now, while Buddy was lying in bed reading a book about alien abductions.

"Know what, Buddy? I believe in those alien abductions you're reading about. I do. I'm pretty sure I've seen them myself."

Buddy sat up in bed. He already looked terrified. "Seen them? Are you kidding me?"

Tee shook his head. "Nope. I've seen them around here. They come at night when everybody's asleep. You ever see that movie, *Close Encounters of the Third Kind*, where that spaceship plays those loud notes?"

"Yeah, a long time ago when I was little."

"Remember when they got that blond-headed girl's little kid, and the light was really bright and shining through the cracks of the house and everything was shaking and she was all panicking and stuff?"

Buddy really looked uneasy now. He was looking at the darkness outside the window. "Yeah, that was scary."

"I saw that same thing happen one night about a week ago. Right here at the clinic."

Buddy smiled a little. "No way. You're lying, Tee. Cut it out."

Tee shrugged. "Okay, if that's what you wanna believe.

Forget it. I should've known you wouldn't believe me. I was just trying to warn you, 's all."

Tee went back to his computer screen, ignoring his roommate, but it didn't take long for Buddy to go for the bait, just like Tee knew he would.

"Where'd you think you saw them?"

"Out by the tennis courts." Tee swiveled his chair around again and stared Buddy in the face, very solemn now. "It really scared the shit outta me, too, Buddy. That's why I didn't tell anybody. I just jumped back in bed and pulled the sheet over my head, But it wasn't a dream. It was for real."

Seemingly relieved that he wasn't the only frightened one, Buddy swung his legs over the edge of the bed and put his hands on his knees. He had on black and red plaid boxers and a white T-shirt. "How did you happen to see them? Did you just wake up? Or was there some kind of noise, or something? Like in that movie."

"I dunno for sure what exactly happened. I just opened my eyes and then I noticed a funny reflection up on the ceiling right over your bed. I looked at you, but you were turned over toward the wall with your back to me, and I could hear you snoring."

Buddy's eyes were so wide now, it almost made Tee laugh. "What did you do?"

"I got up and tiptoed over there to that window." He pointed to the one beside Buddy's bed. "And I saw this big white glow back through the woods by the tennis courts. It really freaked me out, Buddy, and I got back in bed, really scared. The next morning I went out there to see what it could've been, but there wasn't any sign of anything, so I started reading about all this kind of alien stuff. And guess what?"

"What?"

"They say that's how the abductions start out. You know, they sort of come around when everybody's sleeping in the dead of night with their big, advanced laser beams, and then they pick out the specimens they want to take up in the ship and experiment on."

"Holy crap. You think they've chosen one of us kids here at the clinic for their tests?"

"Yeah, I do, but we'd never remember anything about it, even if they chose you or me. They have this mind control thing, see, that makes you forget everything they do to you when they've got you. Maybe we were taken outta here that night I saw them and don't even remember it."

Buddy began to shiver a little, and Tee looked down at Buddy's hands. Now he was gripping them tightly together to control his shakes. He sometimes did that in group when he was talking about his fears. His file was pretty detailed about his childhood. It said his dad liked to sneak up in scary Halloween masks and frighten him out of his wits when he was little more than a toddler, and sometimes would even put on a mask and snatch Buddy out of bed when he was asleep and beat him with a flyswatter. Poor Buddy had been scared of his shadow ever since. And look at him now—he was trembling like a leaf.

"Now, look, Buddy, calm down. Maybe they picked some-body else that night. Maybe they even picked one of our shrinks. Or you know what? Maybe one of our doctors *is* one of them. Maybe they all are aliens from another planet. Maybe when he does that hypnotherapy routine on you, he's really taking you up in a spacecraft and sticking probes down in all your orifices. Sure wouldn't surprise me."

And that's all it took. Buddy was terrified from then on and couldn't sleep at night. All he thought about were little gray people coming to get him, the poor slob. He was so nervous, Tee could make him get hysterical by dropping a heavy book on the floor behind him. Tee had a lot of fun with it for a while, but then Buddy started following him around every-where he went and wanting to be protected. That soon became a major problem, especially when Tee wanted to be alone with one of his girlfriends.

TWELVE

Slouched in a comfortable, bittersweet chocolate-colored leather chair in the waiting room of General Aviation Complex, I picked up the dull rumble of an approaching aircraft. I was expecting Black's Lear, but this sounded a whole lot like his Bell 430 helicopter. I could always hear the roar of rotors before the chopper gained visibility, so I walked outside the terminal building and watched the dark sky. The night was overcast, a slight drizzle with the damp smell of rain and mist clinging to the hot asphalt, but not enough inclement weather to cause flight delays. The airstrip lights revealed the tarmac and landing runways, and the tarmac stretched out into the misty darkness, the tower alight and bright, and far off to my left. The glow of Springfield's heavily trafficked streets bounced with a mysterious pink hue off the low-hanging clouds, a far cry from the inky black quiet of my lake house, where you could count a million stars nearly every night.

Suddenly the chopper swept into view, and my heart did a little glad-dance of sorts, one that pretty much embarrassed myself. I stood and watched the pilot expertly set the throbbing craft down on the tarmac about thirty yards away. When he motioned me to come, I headed out toward him, cold drops wetting my hair until the blast of the blades sent the rain spiraling off me and wildly away. With a jerk, I pulled open the passenger's door and found that tonight Black piloted his own luxury helicopter. I climbed in, shut the door, and handed him the large Styrofoam cup of coffee I'd bought for him.

I yelled, "Here's a little present. You're gonna need it to get through the night."

"Oh, God, what now?" Black took the coffee and took a gulp as if he needed one, but kept on his headphones and didn't turn off the rotors. The reflections of the rain speckling the windshield also speckled his tanned face, and his eyes glinted so blue, sometimes I just couldn't believe they were real and not a pair of cheesy electric-blue contacts.

I put on the headphones he handed to me. I said, "Nothing much. Just wanted to boost your energy so you can keep up with me in bed tonight."

Black flashed me a quick grin. "I won't need anything but you, trust me." He turned back to his dials and began his flight discourse with the air controller.

A slight shiver coursed through my more intimate spots, and I inwardly agreed. The man did it for me, that was for sure. I had missed him a lot, and it hadn't even been that long, for Pete's sake. And though he'd called and we'd talked, his physical presence at night in bed was something I had grown accustomed to, and that was probably not a good thing. People in my life hadn't lasted long in the past, and Black and I had been together quite a while. For all I knew, the end was in sight. Not that I was a pessimist, or anything.

"What's with the chopper? Thought you were in the jet."

"I changed my mind and had my pilot set down at the lake first. We can land at Taney County Airport outside Branson."

"That'll save us some drive time."

"I brought you something from New York," Black said, glancing over at me while he waited for permission to take off. "It's right behind you. Grab it and see what you think."

Leaning around the seat, I got a hold on the handles of a big dark blue gift bag and opened the top. Under some pale yellow tissue paper was a large red purse made out of what looked like alligator skin. I guess Black chose it because of his Louisiana bayou heritage. Or maybe he made a side trip to LaFourche Parish and gunned down a big red reptile for my luggage needs.

"Wow, a big red alligator bag."

Black laughed at me. "It's crocodile. And you wanted something to carry your extra ammo clips in, right? Buckle up, we're cleared for takeoff."

I did so, and we lifted off and banked up in the opposite direction of the terminals. Once we were flying high over the beautiful spectacle of the light-spangled city but under the heavy, crouching cloud bank, Black said, "The bag's a Hermès. The Grace Kelly line. They've got a waiting list for this design, but I pulled some strings. I got it for you because I think you look like Grace Kelly when she was young and making movies. There's a picture of her with it. Take a look."

Vaguely I remembered Grace Kelly, but I wasn't a movie buff. I did recall, however, that she was a real-live princess and that she looked like a bride in her coffin, which was a bit macabre so I didn't mention that to Black. I held the little cardboard picture up to the dashboard lights. "I don't look anything like this."

Black leveled a sidelong look. "It's not an insult, Claire. She was a beautiful woman."

"I can't see the resemblance."

"Open the bag, Claire."

I did so, and inside I found a new leather belt holster for my Glock 9 mm, all oiled up and ready to go. It had fancy embroidery on the edges and I hoped to God it wasn't my name, or worst, my initials entwined with Black's. Black was a sucker for personalized stuff. "All right, Black, now you're talking. This a Hermes, too?"

Grinning, Black said, "They're not into munitions yet, but trust me, that's the best quality leather in the world. Thought you might want to carry your weapon on your belt for a change."

"Thanks. I love it. This bag's good, too. I'll just dump Jules Verne in when I'm taking him to Harve's."

"That'll work. They have designer dog carriers now, if you really want one." I thought that sounded a little ridiculous as Black took a couple of minutes to talk turkey with somebody on the radio. A second later, he said to me, "We can get a car at Taney and I'll drive into town."

"You are one on-the-ball fella, Black. Handy to have around, even."

"I also had Booker do some checking on that psychiatrist with the book you were asking about, Dr. Collins. I've met him but don't know him well. Guess what I found out? He just happens to be hosting a seminar at the Chateau on the Lake resort in Branson. Thought you might want to stay there and try to get a word with him so I booked us the Presidential Suite."

John Booker was Black's old army bud and a hell of a good private investigator. "They told me up at the clinic that he was gonna be down in Branson around this time, but this is just lucky as hell, a real break, but I've heard of serendipity, meant to be, and all that. I'll say it again, Black, you're handy to have around."

"I'm always at your service."

"Right back at you."

"I'm holding you to that, Grace."

I smiled at that, but very soon it was time to set down, and I thought about how we ought to proceed with the investigation. I didn't really want to approach the girl's parents until I knew for sure that she was our victim, but drats, I just might have to. I hoped Buck could match that strand of hair in the morning so I could get the interview and notification over with and be back at the lake by nightfall. Not that I minded a day or two alone with Black in one of Branson's premier vacation accommodations. Worse things could've happened, I admit it.

Black somehow managed to have us a plush black Lincoln waiting, of course, and he took the wheel, and off we sped to Chateau on the Lake—resort, spa and convention center. I'd heard about the luxury high-rise resort overlooking Table Rock Lake, but hadn't ever been inside, or outside, either. Built in the design of a European castle, it rose about ten stories, had lots of lights and pools and high-end customers. About fifteen minutes later, we turned right into a steep entrance road and rounded a curve replete with cascading waterfalls with lots of overflowing plants and flowers inside the circle drive. At the door, three uniformed valets jumped to attention and gave us great big, welcoming smiles. They fought each other to open my door, no doubt recognizing Black as a big tipper. But they were friendly and seemed disappointed that Black only had one leather knapsack that he was carrying over his shoulder. Knowing him, it was probably full of cash.

We pushed through some lavish cut-glass doors and looked around. "Isn't this place big-time competition for Cedar Bend Lodge?" I asked Black.

"Yeah, but the owner's a friend of mine. We're friendly competitors. I've been trying to get him to let me buy it, but he isn't biting." Black grinned, but I wasn't sure if he was kidding, or not. He did so love his hotels.

I looked around, rather impressed, actually. Off to my right was some corpulent furniture, mostly leather and velvet-looking stuff. At the far end, I could see a fireplace with tables and chairs around it and a marble bar. While Black strolled over to the registration desk to our right, I moved deeper into the lobby.

It was quite the place, all right. A small high-end golf shop was to my right, but the interior atrium was what caught my attention, and everybody else's. There was a huge tree at the bottom of it below three glass elevators zipping up and down. The tree was fake, but you had to look close to find that out. There was a little casual café nearby and more cascading waterfalls and lush greenery and a couple of seven-foot-high birdcages with cockatiels in them. Almost as good as the Bass Pro Shop, but not quite. I could hear a couple of those birds calling back and forth to each other, probably making plans to break outta the place and fly to Brazil where they belonged. I stood at the railing and looked up ten stories, all the floors with railings decorated with ivy-draped flower boxes.

"What do you think of this place?" Black said, coming up behind me. I knew what he was after, so I obliged him.

"It doesn't hold a candle to Cedar Bend," I said, the diplomatic gal pal. Truth was I did like Cedar Bend better, maybe because Black lived there. This place gave it a run for its money, though.

"You're right, but the Chateau's not bad. Doesn't have the privacy of the Lodge, though."

I wondered if there had been any celebrity murders here like at his place, but that really hadn't been his fault and I'd solved it, so there you go. "Yeah, lots of families lolling around in here."

"They've got an excellent restaurant over there." He pointed to some fancy doors back to our left.

"Ooh, it looks almost as fancy as yours, too. Maybe they've got those delicious snails you like so much."

Black said, "We'll try them out, but we're having room service while we're here, providing we have time to eat."

Now that sounded damn good to me. Not that I hated crowds, of course, but I did hate crowds, of course. My stomach growled to show its displeasure at being owned by somebody like me who forgets to feed it. I should have made a play on some of Harve's fried fish that Bud scarfed up in a minute flat on the drive down from the lake.

I ignored irritated belly sounds and said, "Before we go up, let's see if Collins's seminar's still going on. That easel sign over there says it's tonight and in the Heidelberg Room."

"I guess we can do that, if we have to. I spent last night and most of today sitting through these kinds of lectures."

We turned and walked past the railed atrium and the Chateau Boutique, in case I should have an urge to spend thousands of dollars on a pair of shorts or sequined top, which I wouldn't, and into a huge and equally plush convention center. There were lots of doors lined up with ostentatious names over them like Versailles, Windsor, and Madrid and great big chandeliers that looked French country style and a lot like upside-down circus tents.

As it turned out, Collins's program was still in progress, though nearing the end, much to Black's relief. We slipped into the door at one side of a gigantic conference room and sat at a table with a pristine white linen tablecloth replete with fancy crystal water goblets and place settings for ten. Too bad there wasn't any food on the plates. Behind our table was a gigantic mural about twenty feet high and almost as wide. It was a picture of a castle and a body of water.

Black said, "All these meeting rooms have replicas of paintings of European castles. This one's the Chateau de Chillon in Switzerland. You know, like in Lord Byron's epic *The Prisoner of Chillon*."

"Yeah, that's what I figured," I said to humor him, but I was more interested in Collins. He was standing at a podium against the far wall in front of a large screen. He was giving a little PowerPoint show and the four big tent chandeliers like the ones out in the hall were dimmed way down so nobody at all the other tables much noticed our better-late-than-never arrival. I leaned forward, trying to look like I had even a pinprick of interest in psychiatry but really just getting a good gander at the man standing in the spotlight and droning on about hypnotism.

The good doctor appeared to be in his early thirties, maybe even late twenties. He wore a navy blue blazer and khaki pants, and he looked fit and muscular under his white shirt and red tie, like he worked out a lot. And he was very tanned, which made his sun-streaked brown hair look lighter. He was a lot younger than I had expected, but then again, until I met Black, I thought all shrinks wore white beards and looked like Sigmund Freud. Collins was discussing his specialty, hypnotherapy and suicidal psychosis, which was pretty damn apropos, if you ask me. Not to mention, heavy on the ear.

Black sat back and crossed his arms and looked more interested than me, but that wasn't hard. After all, he was a shrink and kept up with all this hocus-pocus and heal-my-mind-physician stuff. I listened and slowly receded into a bored, trancelike state, because the speech was way too technical and touched on things I'm sure I would hate if I understood what they meant. The speech was going on way, way, way too long, too. I leaned close to Black's ear. "Does he know what he's talking about?"

"Oh, yeah. He's pretty good. I've heard about this new book but haven't read it yet. I'll get him to sign one for you before we leave. His specialty is depressed teenagers with suicidal tendencies."

"Oh, wow, that's upbeat. Must give him one jolly holly disposition."

"That's his expertise. What can I say?"

"How long you think this's gonna go on?"

Black pulled back his jacket cuff and glanced down at his gold Rolex. "Supposed to last till nine. It's ten minutes to."

"Okay. After he shuts up, let's go up, meet him, get that book unless it's the one I already have, and let me set up an interview. Otherwise, it's no telling how long he'll put me off."

"Please tell me you don't want to talk to the guy now?"

"No, I wanna go back to Oak Haven and snoop around when I talk to him. Speak to some more of Mikey Murphy's friends in the program. Instincts tell me that something happened up there, something that triggered Mikey to hang himself under that bridge. Or someone else to hang him under there."

A couple of ladies sitting at the table directly in front of us turned, oh, ever so slightly, to alert us that we were rude, yes, even unruly saps who spoke too loudly about people hanging under bridges. I nodded politely to them and hushed such gory talk and listened to the good doctor wind down his presentation. He was a good speaker, I guess, had a low bass voice, good eye contact with the audience, and was relaxed, confident, pompous, but in my estimation, he was still mucho into the bore factor. I wondered how he'd be in a one-on-one session with clients. If he'd charm the pants off them like Black did, and I don't mean that literally, although he did manage that in my case, or if Collins would be the fatherly type, or maybe in his case, the caring and protective older brother.

Finally, he stopped with the lecture, the lights came up, and people flooded up front and surrounded him like he had just cured cancer. Black and I threaded through the crowd that was pouring out the exits, all of them probably hungry, too, and made our way to the spot at the lectern, where Collins was shaking hands with his admirers. When he glanced up and caught sight of Black, who stood above most of the crowd at six foot three, he waved to him and looked genuinely pleased to see such an esteemed colleague in attendance. He excused himself from the small knot of smiling well-wishers and walked over to meet us. I wondered if he'd look as pleased when he saw my badge.

"Boyce, it's good to see you," Black said, reaching out to shake hands.

"Yes, that it is, Nick. When was the last time? San Francisco, maybe, last year?"

"Probably was. Boyce, I'd like to introduce Claire Morgan. She's a detective with the Canton County Sheriff's department over at the Lake."

I was glad he didn't say my girlfriend, or even worse, my woman. Dr. Collins smiled at me, his long-lashed, big brown eyes very warm and friendly, and I couldn't help but notice that he had the remnants of a bruise on his right eye. Now where would a pansy doctor pick up a shiner like that? Then I saw my name ring a bell inside his head, which seemed to be going on a lot lately. Guess I was gonna have to start wearing disguises. "Oh, the lake, that's where they found Mikey Murphy. Marty called from the clinic and told me you needed to set up an interview. Is that why you're here?"

For some reason, I decided that yes, sir, I was. "Would that be convenient for you, sir? To sit down with me a few minutes right now?"

Black frowned and looked more than displeased, but I pretended not to notice his ire. The case had to come first, he knew that, and I was just itching to get my hooks in this smooth-talking guy. He was so slick, in fact, that his clothes probably slipped off at bedtime without provocation.

"Well, actually, and I'm terribly sorry to have to put you off, but it's not a convenient time. I would be glad to, of course, but I've got to catch a plane to Nashville within the next ninety minutes over in Springfield, and I'm barely going to make it now. But I am eager to discuss this case with you. Mikey was a fine young man. I was just sick when I heard what happened."

"How did you hear what happened?"

"The clinic called me. Marty. He said you'd been up there interviewing people and needed to talk to me. He indicated that you'd call and make an appointment."

"That's right. It's important that I talk to you. Perhaps we could set up a date now?"

"Of course, if you like. He did tell me that you talked to

some of the patients. Mikey was very popular with all the kids. Who did you interview?"

"So far, just Cleo and Roy, but I need to go back. Do you have a day we could agree on in the near future?" The friendly, accommodating detective butters up the target.

"Sure, but I need to check my calendar first. How about I give you a call? I hope the staff was cooperative. This is just such a terrible, terrible thing. His parents must be devastated."

Well, mom hadn't cried me a river. "Yes, it's sad, but we'll find out who did it soon enough."

Collins smiled down at me. He was pretty tall, too. I'm five foot nine, after all. "I like your confidence, detective."

"Thanks." But I wondered if he really did like it. I was trying to figure out if this guy was for real but wasn't quite sure. I'd have to get him alone and pull his chain some, which sounded like a fun time, at least for me. "When do you think you'll be available, Doctor? I can drive to Jeff City again as soon as you give me the day. This is an urgent matter. I hope you understand that."

"Yes, I do. I completely understand that. I'll be in Nashville overnight and then in Memphis for a book signing, but after that, if you give me a call when I'm back at work, I'll make time to talk as long as you want." He fished a white business card out of his inside coat pocket. "Here's my card. You can call my receptionist, Mary, for an appointment, or you can wait and decide with me a date that suits us both."

I took the card. Dr. Collins was quite the agreeable sort, but I had only been pitching softball questions at him. Wondered how he'd react to some fastballs. I drooled at the thought. Nothing more rewarding than making a calm and collected shrink stutter and get all rattled. I tried that once upon a time with Black, but he usually maintained his sang froid and made me feel silly. I had a feeling this guy wouldn't be so lucky.

I said, "I see you got a bit of a black eye there, Dr. Collins. You been fighting with your patients?"

Collins laughed, not in the least offended, I guess. "You should've seen it a week ago."

I wasn't about to let it drop, "What happened?"

"I got elbowed in the eye in a pickup touch football game with some of the kids. Purely accidental. Hurt like the devil when it first happened, though."

"Try witch hazel. That's what I put on all my bruises."

Dr. Collins smiled but had enough of me, I assume, because he turned to Black and ignored me. Graciously, he signed a book for us, a different one from the one I had, and this one had his picture on the front, after which the two of them had a pleasant discussion about psychosomatic illnesses that was absolutely so titillating that my eyes slightly blurred. Black's great, but shrink-speak was like watching paint dry. So I watched Boyce Collins's face as he spoke. He seemed an up-front enough guy, but I wasn't quite sure. He kept glancing at me and smiling unnecessarily, which made me uncomfortable, suspicious, even. I didn't think he was coming on to me, though, not in front of Black, so maybe I just had a piece of fried crappie stuck in my front teeth.

Minutes later Collins took his leave in a big hurry, and for good reason. Traffic was horrendous in Branson when the late shows got out. He'd be lucky to make his flight.

"You should've offered him a lift to the airport in the chopper," I said to Black as we stepped inside one of the sleek spotless elevators and let it whisper-whisk us up to the top floor.

"I've got better things to do than squire that guy around."

That sounded like good news to me, and those better things Black had to do started the minute the door of the VIP penthouse Presidential Suite clicked shut behind us. Black jerked off his lightweight black jacket, then stripped off my sweatshirt jacket, then my shoulder holster, then ripped my polo shirt right off the top of my head, as if he'd had plenty of practice. Which he had.

"Cool your engines, boy, we've got all night."

"You shouldn't've given me that coffee. Now I'm wired."

That made me smile and so did the way he disposed of my bra in nothing flat, but after that I got into the act, too. I helped him take off the sweet little .38 snubnose strapped to my right ankle under my boot-cut jeans, which is always a turn-on, and then I kicked off my tennis shoes, while he stood above me and slipped his black polo shirt off over his head. I enjoyed looking at the ripple effect of hard, tanned muscles until he fell on top of me and away we went.

"Wait," I managed, holding his mouth off me with both hands, "I want you to tell me everything you know about Boyce Collins."

"Yeah, right," said Black, and then his mouth closed over my right nipple and I bid adieu to all reason and hello to pure-D erotic fun and games. Nobody could beat our reunions, no where, no how, and even better, I knew I had this to look forward to all night long in that fancy Chateau on the Lake sleigh bed under all the expensive, rustly 1,000-thread-count sheets. Of course, at home, Black's were double that and hand sewn in Egypt. Yes, it's sad but I'm becoming Black-conized and know all about linen thread counts and other such fluff.

THIRTEEN

The next morning around nine o'clock, Black and I sat out on a really skinny balcony that barely held our two chairs and a little table and looked straight down ten stories to a sparkling blue pool, hot tub, two tennis courts, and a playground for the kids. More impressive was the view, a beautiful, 180-degree vista of Table Rock Lake. I watched a couple of early morning speedboats leaving strips of white wakes in that blue water, but I preferred my own lake. Nothing beats Lake of the Ozarks in my book. The lakes around Branson weren't half bad, though, all three: Table Rock and Taneycomo and the ultra-clear Bull Shoals. Missouri does boast some awesome lakes, you can bet on it.

A lovely breakfast of prepared oranges, strawberries, kiwi, and fresh pineapple chunks were arranged on a big white platter alongside crispy croissants, chocolate donuts with pecans on top (Black ordered those just for me), and giant fresh-baked bagels were sitting on the glass-topped table between us, as well as a mouthwatering display of cheese Danish, cinnamon rolls, cherry turnovers, and miniature blueberry pancakes with some kind of chef's special mango sauce.

Black had finished eating and was working on a speech he was planning to give at his next scheduled seminar, which was going to be held in Houston in a couple of weeks. He was dressed casually in jeans and a dark blue polo shirt with the Cedar Bend logo, which was a little jab at the luxurious Chateau on the Lake digs we now enjoyed, I suspect. He was writing on a yellow legal pad in longhand script. I watched his strong brown fingers hold that beautiful gold fountain pen for a while, then said something on impulse that surprised even myself.

"Something happened last night that I wasn't expecting."

Black didn't look up but kept writing. "Uh hmm. What's that?"

I hesitated a long moment, then I said, "I had dinner with Harve before I drove down to Springfield with Bud."

Still concentrating on his work, he said, "That's nice. How is Harve?"

"He's good. I was glad to see him." I hesitated. "Joe McKay showed up, too."

Black quit with the writing and looked at me. Oh yeah, he did get pinched by jealousy from time to time, unreasonably, of course, especially where Joe McKay was concerned.

"Joe was there?"

"Yeah."

"And you said something happened that you weren't expecting?"

"Yeah. I didn't plan on it happening but it just did. I'm not sure what I think about it, is all."

"Yeah? Don't keep me in suspense, Claire. What the hell did you do with McKay?" Black gave me his full attention now. He put down his pen, leaned back, crossed his arms, and stared expectantly at me. Genius that I am, I knew what he was thinking.

"I held Lizzie on my lap for a while."

First, he looked surprised, but that turned swiftly into relief, and then he smiled. He knew I'd had trouble being around little kids since Zach had died, and he'd been trying to help me deal with it. He hadn't had much luck.

He said, "That's good, that's really good, Claire. Was it your idea or hers?"

"Hers. She just came over and climbed up onto my lap."

"And it didn't upset you?"

"At first, I was just startled she did it, but then, no, that's what surprised me, I guess. I don't know. I guess I'm trying to say it wasn't as bad as I thought it'd be."

Still smiling, he nodded and looked very pleased. "That's a breakthrough for you."

I guess I had figured that out. Since Zachary had died, I could barely stand the thought of touching a baby or child because when I did, everything came barreling back and I'd relive the terrible night he died in my arms and I lost the most precious thing in my world forever.

"Want to talk about it?"

"No, I just thought I'd mention it to you." Suddenly, I felt stupid and emotional and needy, so I shrugged and said, "I wasn't expecting it to happen, and it did and threw me a little. I don't know why, I just wanted to tell you about it."

"I'm glad you told me. When and if you ever want to talk about Zach, just say the word. I'm here for you, Claire, you know that."

Suddenly I felt smothered by the subject and didn't want to talk about my dead son, and was sorry I had brought it up. I didn't want to talk about little Lizzie saying Zach's name out of the blue, either. So I changed the topic to something safer. "Hand me the newspaper and let me see if we can catch a performance of those Beijing acrobats while we're here. I'd like to get a feel for Li He's parents before I interview them."

Black picked it up and gave it to me, and I sifted through the pages one at a time, hoping to get a chance to watch them perform before I talked to them. Heck, maybe I was just putting off a very disagreeable obligation. I hadn't heard from Buck's office on the hair match, but after thinking about it, I decided it might be better to interview them before they got hit with some very disturbing news, if indeed, Li He turned out to be the girl in the oven.

Maybe miracles did happen; maybe their kid had just run off for some kind of romantic tryst with some suave, sweet-talking college guy, and the two young lovers were sitting around in some hotel like Black and me, enjoying a little alone time together. I could certainly recommend this kind of break, now and then, anyway, especially in the middle of an intense case. Not that I ever took breaks much, and wouldn't be here if I didn't have interviews to conduct. In any case, I felt top of the morning, sated, rested, and ready to roll. So did Black, by the satisfied *Me-Tarzan-You-Jane-McKay's-out-of-the-picture* look on his face. I guess his possessiveness was complimentary, as long as he didn't try to order me around, which he didn't.

Sipping his coffee, he looked at me over the rim of a fancy white Chateau cup. "I do like having you across the breakfast table for a change. Unarmed and stark naked under that terrycloth robe. A perfect start to any day."

"I liked the way we started the morning out, too, but trust me, I'm rearming the minute we walk outta this room."

"That's nice, sweetie, whatever makes you happy," said Black, but he grinned as he took the newspaper from me and immediately found the Branson showtime schedules. He reads more newspapers than I do, so he knows where to look. "The Chinese acrobats go on at three o'clock. We can enjoy our morning, have lunch sent up, and then see the show. I'll have the concierge call and get us front-row seats." Sounded good to me and also put off meeting the parents, so we went inside, got into bed, and had more fun than a barrel of monkeys.

Later, after lunch, I got dressed in the change of clothes I kept stowed away in that leather knapsack in Black's chopper just in case he whisked me off someplace, which included a clean pair of jeans and a dark green T-shirt with the Remington logo on the pocket. We ordered the rented Lincoln brought around, climbed inside, and headed out into the fun, fun, fun of Branson, Missouri. Outside, it was 96 degrees and humid as hell, and I wished I'd stowed some workout shorts aboard, instead of the jeans.

Tourists strolled around everywhere we looked, and I mean, everywhere. Darting across busy streets, waiting in line at the myriad of theaters lining the strip. Lots of families with lots of elementary-aged kids, retired Baby Boomers, and teenagers in love, who were holding hands, kissing, and more. I declare, get a room like we always do. Black fought traffic and mumbled Cajun curses under his breath when the guy in the car in front of us missed the light because he was reading a brochure. The theater we were looking for wasn't that far away from the Chateau, although we didn't know that, so we fought our way through miles and miles of traffic during Black's supposed shortcut. No wonder he drove a Humvee and preferred limos most of the time.

The Beijing Acrobatic Troupe's parking lot was crammed with cars behind the big white theater, making me wonder how Black had gotten front-row seats at the last minute, but then again, Black had a way of getting what he wanted when he wanted, so I didn't even ask. By the looks of the place, however, this show was a popular attraction.

Hurrying out of the broiling sun, we walked around to the front, looking for any kind of shade from the hot glare. Double doors edged by big scary-looking stone dogs on each side led us into the coveted relief of air-conditioned comfort that felt pretty darn good. The lobby was pretty much a scaled-down version of a plush Chinese palace in the Forbidden City, or someplace equally mystical and elaborate and over the top, but with a ticket counter, tiny corner gift shop, and the strong smell of popcorn. We spent a few minutes pre-show, wandering around admiring giant beach-ball-size red lanterns hanging across the ceiling, lots of red, black, and white Oriental masks hanging on the walls, ebony fans with painted dragons, stuff like that, and this little singing rock thing that was drawing a crowd and lots of oohs and ahs. Actually, it was pretty awesome. Even I thought so.

Black hauled off and bought me a little jade bracelet with a tiny Chinese coin hanging off it, one that cost $18.95 and was supposed to be lucky. Just what I needed. And I mean that. Black had a habit of buying me good-luck talismans, and for good reason. Too bad they didn't usually work.

The bracelet made me think, though, of the bracelets on poor Mikey's wrists, and when I pulled the beaded bracelet that I'd taken from the crime scene out of my just marvelous and much-sought-after red crocodile Hermès Grace Kelly bag and showed it to the smiling middle-aged Asian woman behind the counter, she shook her head and told me in broken, barely decipherable English that they didn't carry any. But I wasn't sure she understood my question or that I understood her answer. Unfortunately, Black didn't speak fluent Mandarin, either, so he was no help.

We crossed the lobby and stood in front of a wall hung with large color photographs of famous sites in China, including the Great Wall, the Forbidden City, and even more surprising, Tiananmen Square, which I wasn't quite sure did them any good as far as bragging rights were concerned.

"Know what? I might like to go to China and see these places," I said to Black.

He said, "I'll arrange it. It's nice in the fall."

Gee, I didn't even have to snap my fingers. Whoo hoo, Dr. Nicholas Black was a real catch, yes he was. "You've been there, I take it."

"Yes, several times. I've done some business in Beijing, and I was invited to speak at a couple of conferences. I especially wanted to walk atop The Great Wall."

"And is it great?"

"You bet it is, an amazing sight. It's a beautiful country. You'll like it, but you won't be able to carry your weapons there. They've got tight restrictions."

"Then cross that jaunt off my agenda. I've got enemies worldwide. China probably isn't an exception." I was sort of kidding, but who knows? Trouble seems to find me.

"I doubt if the worldwide category holds, but you've had your share, I have to admit. There's the last call for the curtain. Let's find our seats."

Well, lawsy, not only were we front row, we were *smokin'* front-row-center. Black was amazing with his ability to make impossible things happen and mucho handy to have around at Branson shows, not to mention in big hotel sleigh beds. The Beijing Acrobatic Troupe performance began with a flourish of sound and music and about twenty pretty Asian girls spinning plates on long sticks under vividly colored spotlights that showed up beautifully in the darkened theater. They wore yellow and pinks and purples, and one after another, truly amazing feats followed their act and never really stopped. It was an entertaining performance, I must say, with all the dazzling acrobatics, mystical music, and elegant Eastern dance. There was even a smattering of magic, a beautiful aerial ballet, playful dances, each one fast paced and exciting. And did I mention the acrobats in yellow leotards who built human towers twenty feet high? Their brochures aren't bad, either.

Early on, I scanned the program to see when Mr. and Mrs. He were slated to come onstage. Their act came near the end of the show. As it turned out and what really piqued my interest was that our missing girl's parents were master contortionists and could they ever contort, geezo peezo and wowza. But that theatrical ability fit nicely into my nasty little equation, too. The unfortunate girl in that pizza oven had folded herself up like a freakin' aluminum lawn chair.

After reliving that less than enjoyable visual image of said kitchen murder, I quit with the enjoyment of colorful tumbling acrobats and drumming drummers and sat beside Black and thought long and hard about my case. I was eager to talk to the two small, ultra-agile people I'd just seen up on that big bright stage and delve behind their wide theatrical smiles. The show had to go on, no matter what, even if you had a teenage daughter gone missing. So smile they did as they made pretzel makers look like amateurs.

When the finale finally faded away and a large curtain closed, the lights came up and we bucked the audience flood toward the exits and made our way instead to a door that we presumed led backstage, mainly because of the black-and-white PRIVATE—DO NOT ENTER sign. Flashing my badge to a Chinese security guard standing nearby and dressed like a real-live Ninja in black pajamas, I summarily took care of that roadblock.

Insisting we stay put while he informed the Hes of my interview request, the security guy was back inside five minutes with a resounding okay. We followed Ninja Joe down a long corridor, crowded now with a multitude of talented acrobats in their shiny, tight-fitting spandex outfits and enough makeup to almost satisfy Pamela Anderson's requirements for one day. Prop men were everywhere, all chattering together in runaway Mandarin or some other Asian tongue, I sure wouldn't know the difference, and looking at us curiously, as if they'd never seen real-live Americans backstage.

Ninja knocked, announced us first in Chinese then in his heavily accented English, and I walked inside, pretty much dreading this meeting worse than a dose of strychnine, with Black right behind me, no doubt feeling a similar reticence. Li He's parents were sitting side by side on a small but plush damask love seat on one side of the small room. It was the color of a ripe eggplant. The walls were red. Lots of stuff in this theater were either eggplant purple or red. Must be lucky colors in China. There was a low black lacquered coffee table and a bookcase along the wall with a small television sitting on the top shelf. There was a makeup table, and it was long enough for both of them to slather on foundation together, with its multitude of bulbs all lit up and glowing. The two acrobats still wore their makeup and yellow and red satin costumes. They looked smaller in person than they had onstage, but everybody looked small when Black was around.

"Please sit down," said Li He's father in English, but his speech was heavily accented. They both gazed at us, their faces garish with the heavy makeup. I felt like I was interviewing two Japanese Geishas or twin Bozo the Clowns, take your pick.

We sat down on a couple of black wicker chairs that seemed a bit on the miniature side. Black's creaked under his size and muscular physique. I showed the couple my badge, just a courtesy, but one that usually opened doors and mouths. After which, they looked scared of me. I smiled to show I didn't bite, and said, "I'm Detective Claire Morgan from Canton County at Lake of the Ozarks. That's about an hour northeast of here. This is Nicholas Black."

Black didn't appear to like my abbreviated designation of him, but too bad. What was I gonna say? This is my expert and superendurance lover boy, or maybe, superrich boyfriend?

The dad clown said in that thick Chinese-accented English, "How do you do. Do you have news of daughter, Li?"

"Do you know where Li is?" Mom Clown leaned forward and watched me closely. I was a little unsettled by their white pancake makeup and black-lined eyes. It gave them the look of intense-eyed aliens. No, the kind from outer space. It was hard for me to ascertain just how old they were, but they weren't that old, forties, I'd say.

I sure hoped I hadn't found their daughter, but I didn't make that little tidbit known. Not yet. "I'm afraid I don't have any new information on the disappearance of your daughter, Mrs. He. But I do have some questions to ask you about a friend of hers. When we examined Li's dorm room at Missouri State, we found a man's name in her address book. His name has come up in a recent investigation at the lake, and we're hoping you can tell us something about his relationship with your daughter. His name is Michael Murphy. Do you happen to know him?"

Mom spoke again and her accent was even thicker than Dad's. "Oh, yes. He is good friend to Li, very good. He takes her on . . ." She struggled, certainly not as proficient in English as her husband, "Date, is that seeming word?"

I nodded. "So Li and Michael Murphy were dating each other. For how long? Can you tell me?"

Mr. He said, "She like him much." He spread his hands about a yard apart, as if to make us understand just how much she liked him. "Li go to him regularly at his pizza eat at your lake. She knew him from around first of your celebrate New Year."

Okay, so his English wasn't much better than hers. Li was shaping up very fast to be our female victim, all right. I swallowed hard and forced down my wave of regret. Black said nothing. The Hes waited and watched my face. I tried to keep it straight and noncommittal.

"Did you ever meet Michael Murphy, Mr. He?"

He nodded. "He came to see act three times. He came to our home for meal one time. He is nice boy."

"So he and Li got along well."

"Yes, she say he good but had many bad lucks."

Okay. Time to zero in and get to the gist of this thing. "Did she go into detail about these bad lucks?"

"She say he not have good family like Li. She say he did not good with mother and father."

Mrs. Li cut in. "It is terrible thing not to be good with mother and father. Li said his father talk to him on phone but mother hate him. She say he was hurt in here," she gestured at her heart, "and Li try to help him."

"Did she tell you why he didn't get along with his parents?"

"Li say they make him do thing that not pizza eats and he did not like. She say parents want him be in law work, but he wanted cook and own eat place."

"Did Li ever meet Michael's parents?"

"She say she went one time to house and it was like palace. She say very uncomfortable house."

"Did she notice anything strange or unusual about the Murphy family? Or about Michael's habits?"

This time Mr. Li shook his head. "She say he wished know

about China and want to go there and maybe start pizza eats. She say he want go far away and not come back."

Mrs. He said, "That bad. Bad omen for son to hate family. We far from home but we together."

Around that point, Mrs. He remembered they weren't exactly together, that Li was missing. She bowed her head, and I had this awful premonition slither and slide down my throat into the pit of my stomach.

"You know nothing about what happen Li?" asked Mr. Li.

I told him the truth, had to, I just left a few pertinent things out. "Not yet. But I know the Springfield police are doing everything they can to find her. And I promise you that I will do everything I can to help them."

They both nodded and looked satisfied, and I felt like a dirty, lying dog. My gut was all twisted up and telling me bigtime that Li was the girl in that oven, but I did not want to believe it. And I sure as hell didn't want to tell them the grotesque manner in which their beloved daughter had met her death. Or her strange behavior that made it happen. I was ready to end the interview and get out of there, but then I remembered the blue beaded bracelet and mysterious key. I pulled them out of my new red crocodile, Grace-Kelly-who-looks-like-me-NOT bag, that reputedly had a long waiting list and was probably a big-ticket item on eBay. Not that I'm obsessed with this bag, or anything.

I said, "By the way, would you happen to know anything about this kind of bracelet?"

They nodded in tandem and looked like two painted-up Chinese puppets manipulated on marionette strings. "That call evil-eye bracelets. Li has many. Her friend, also."

I said, "Do you have any idea where they got them?"

Mrs. Li's head bobbed in the affirmative. "Li say hers at Khur-Vay's Studio and Gift Shop up on main road. Madame Khur-Vay teach yoga and belly dancing."

Now that was a interesting combination, but I guess you have to be limber to belly dance. And the name Khur-Vay had come up before when I was interviewing at the clinic. Mr. He handed the key in the plastic bag back to me. No dice there.

I said, "Do you know why they're called evil-eye bracelets?"

Together, they shook their heads, a real duet act, these two, almost as good as Bud and I were. The dad got out of character then by shrugging his shoulders. "We not have in China. Madame Khur-Vay tell you. She Li's friend."

Now there was some good news in a case that wasn't running over full of it at the moment. Maybe it was time I had a belly dancing lesson or two. I already knew how to do yoga.

"Well, thank you very much, Mr. He, Mrs. He. You've been very helpful. I'll let you know if I find out any new information about Li."

They stood and bowed together, a very polite couple. I gave a little bow back but didn't do it as well.

Black spoke up then and said, "We enjoyed your performances very much. I had the pleasure of visiting your country on several occasions. It is really quite amazing. I plan to return there soon." He gave me a significant glance to alert me that I was going, too, gun or no gun.

The Hes discussed briefly with Black which provinces he had visited and what he had seen, but throughout their short chat, Mrs. He kept looking at me, as if she knew I knew more than I was telling her. I tried to smile reassuringly but don't think it came off like gangbusters. They bowed again as we left, and I waited until we were outside in the fresh air and blazing sunshine before I spoke.

"It's gonna be her, Black. I know it in my gut. Li He's gonna be our vic."

"Let's hope not. You want to go find this Khur-Vay woman and see what she knows?"

"Yeah, let's do it while we're down here. My hunch tells me the bracelets are going to lead us to something pertinent. Maybe this Khur-Vay woman can tell us how they fit into Mikey's murder."

Here Comes Trouble

Enthralled by the power Tee could exert on everybody around him, and so easily, too, he began obsessive Internet searches for mind control and brainwashing techniques. As he expected, he found a wealth of good sites expounding on his favorite new subjects. Bowled over by all the interesting stuff listed, he first searched hypnosis and was very pleased that there were so many how-to pages, actual word-by-word demonstrations, even. He was especially interested in controlling the mind, because truth was, that's what he really wanted to do. This was gonna be a cinch, it really was. And did he ever have a group of needy geeks to experiment on.

So the days passed, and then months and months, and he pretended to still have problems over his mom's death so he could stay and not go back home. He didn't care if he ever went home. Then again, he studied hard, memorized, and absorbed every single, solitary thing he could get his hands on regarding psychohypnosis and psychiatry and brainwashing. It was fascinating; a huge challenge. Bigger than any he'd had in a long time, in his life, actually. And he was winning over the doctors. They thought he was just great. He was their special little protégé, and he loved it.

Everything was proceeding like clockwork. The doctors were so gullible and gladly lent him their textbooks and notes, even sat down and discussed theories and treatments and dangers. He especially liked the latter. They told him he was a brilliant student, but that wasn't exactly news. Memorization remained extremely easy for him. He read it once; he knew it forever. And he was charismatic, too. Nobody had to tell him that. People were drawn to him like flies. Which was a good analogy, because he was going to catch them in his web, bet on it. His master plan was working out just hunky-dory in the extreme.

After a while, he decided to hook some other kids into his scheme. He already had two girlfriends, both at the same time, too. One went by her clinic name Blossom, and he'd just found out recently that she was a half sister to Lotus and Yang Wei, and then there was Orchid, a real looker with great titties. Neither seemed to mind that he had both as girl-friends; they just seemed happy the most popular guy in the school liked them. And there was always Buddy, of course. All three of Tee's flunkies already tagged along after him like a trio of beagle puppies.

Tee needed more test subjects, however; he knew he'd have to perfect his techniques over time. The way to do that, he decided, was to invent a new, exclusive, by-invitation-only secret club. He'd make the members think he'd found new and better ways to treat them, better than the doctors, and most of all, that it was an honor to have him choose them to join aka use them in his experiments. He'd learned some techniques to help them think what he wanted them to think, so it wasn't hard to entice them. They were like lambs to the slaughter.

On one well-planned night, he instructed the chosen ones to sneak to his room after Maggie and the other night nurses and orderlies settled into the night shift, and the place became as quiet as a tomb. So they did; they crept into his room, one at a time, mostly wearing pajamas and robes and slippers. He looked around the circle at the eager young faces and the feeling of power that washed over him was intoxicating. *How stupid you are*, he thought, *weak and dumb losers.*

"Enter, my friends, into our own secret world. You are the elite of this hospital. The cream of the crop, the smartest, the best. That's why you've been chosen. But first off, you've got to prove your loyalty to me and to this group. We're gonna take an oath, right here, right now, that we'll never reveal the secrets that transpire inside this room. Do you understand that? If I ever catch word that anybody here confided our meetings to a nonmember, then you're out, plain and simple. I'll deny everything you say. And if I do, who do you think the staff here will believe? Buddy, tell me. Will they believe you guys or me?"

"You," said Buddy as if already in a trance.

"Of course they will. More important, I can help you. I can help you get over whatever it is that is bothering you, whatever it is that sent you to this clinic. I really can. Do you believe me?" The kids in the group nodded, all of them, and Tee laughed inside as he continued. "I've found new techniques and ingenious ways that really work, and I promise I'll work with each of you, one by one, one-on-one. That way, I can concentrate completely on the person I'm treating and give that patient my full attention. Does everybody agree to this? Are you ready to trust me and work with me?"

Tee looked around at all his little handpicked crazies. Everyone raised their hands, just like they were in school answering a teacher's questions. Sometimes he even amazed himself at how he could make people do stuff. But now he was going to venture onto a new frontier; he was going to try to control the human mind, and he was going to start by playing around with some plain old Hypnotism 101.

"Okay, now we will swear our oaths. Please raise your right hand and put your left hand over your heart. Repeat after me. I will never reveal information about this meeting or the names of the members therein."

They all repeated it in low, awed voices. Man, this was gonna be a blast.

"On pain of death, I will never reveal anything that Tee has said or told me about our secret society."

Again, they intoned the words, as if he hadn't even mentioned killing them if they told. Hey, this was going to be even easier than he thought. They were like big lumps of wet clay that he could mold any way he wanted. They were like Adam and Eve. And he was like God.

"Okay, then this is the way it's gonna go down. I will tell each of you when I'm ready to work on your case. It will be done like we did this tonight, late and by candlelight. None of you will know, or ask, what happens in my sessions with the other members. It will all remain completely private and confidential. I will never tell any of you what any of the others say to me or what goes on here in this room. I will not take notes or film our sessions. Do you understand?" The part about the filming was a lie; of course, he would film it to study later.

They all nodded and looked mightily impressed by the sheer gravitas.

"Okay, who would like to go first?"

Everybody raised their hands. Now, that was a good sign.

"I am so pleased that you all understand the importance of secrecy. It will be a hard decision, but I will now choose my very first subject from our group." Tee looked around as if weighing the matter, but truth be told, he'd already decided who the first victim would be. He was going to choose Girlfriend #1, Blossom, because he was in the mood to have sex, and she was always willing. They could do it afterward, after he'd gotten into her head and created a bit of havoc.

The kids sat around, awaiting his decision with bated

breaths. He let the suspense linger a moment, then smiled and said, "Blossom, I'd like you to stay tonight. The rest of you may go back to your rooms. Make sure you're not seen and that you never mention this meeting to anyone. If we should have to meet again, I will send Buddy around with the notification."

Idiotically, Buddy grinned with pleasure at being chosen the messenger.

"Buddy, you'll have to sleep somewhere else tonight. You aren't allowed to observe my session with Blossom."

"Okay, Tee. I'll sleep in Denny's room." Denny was another studious little nerd that Buddy liked to hang around with. Denny collected butterflies for a hobby and glued them to his windows so he could see sunlight come through their wings. A real psycho goner.

The group gradually melted out the door, and after they were gone, Tee walked to the door and turned the lock. Blossom smiled when he approached her, but it was a nervous smile.

"You scared, Blossom?"

"No. I trust you."

"Good. Okay, here's what I want you to do first. Take off all your clothes and lie down on my bed."

Blossom obeyed, and he was a tad shocked that she did. She was a pretty shy girl most of the time. Every time he'd screwed her, it had been in the dark and under the covers. In the candlelight tonight, though, her smooth tan skin glowed and her long dark hair was spread out on the white pillow around her head. Asian girls were so little and gorgeous. He had to fight for control. He wanted to jump her and do the deed now, but that would come later. This was his first go at real hypnotism. He was eager to get started and see what happened.

"Close your eyes, Blossom. Relax every muscle in your body." He paused, then went through the memorized script slowly, allowing her to take time to follow each command.

"Start at your toes, relax them completely, then move up to your feet, then your ankles. Now move up farther to your legs. They're so relaxed they just flop open. You are feeling so good now, so very relaxed and comfortable. Now you're relaxing your stomach and your arms and fingers. This feels so good to you. You're calm and quiet and you feel so happy. You are going to enjoy everything we do together. Now we're at your neck, Blossom, all relaxed, next your chin and nose and forehead. It's gonna make you feel so free and happy and relaxed. It's going to make you forget all your troubles." Except me, he thought, and I'm big trouble, the biggest you've ever seen.

Blossom obeyed, just like that. He could see her muscles loosening all through her body, and her eyes remained closed. She was breathing deeply, just like she was supposed to. Hell, he might not even need to apply hypnotism with this girl. She was like a trained monkey, panting to please.

Before the kids had arrived at the meeting, he had placed a hidden video camera and a bunch of short vanilla-scented candles on his bedside table, and while Blossom lay relaxed in front of him, he lit each one with his cigarette lighter. According to his research, lighting was important. The room where the session was held couldn't be too dark, but not too light, either, but he had a feeling the candles would do the trick just fine. It also gave the whole thing a sense of romance and mystery, and he wasn't above playing the romance card. His CD player was on a oak shelf right above the bed, and he turned it on.

One suggestion he had learned for hypnotizing a willing subject was to play music with a beat that mirrored the human heartbeat, like a song that repeated the same refrain over and over. He wasn't sure exactly what to use this first time, actually was experimenting when he chose Enya. A song called "The Orinoco Flow." The music played softly, and it was one of Blossom's favorite songs. Blossom relaxed some more. He could actually see her going under.

"Blossom, you are now so relaxed that you feel light. You feel light enough to float up, way, way up, above the clouds. You're completely safe here. I won't let anybody hurt you. Let your mind wander. Think about your favorite place in the whole wide world. Think about being there when you were so happy and laughing. You told me about that pretty lake in your neighborhood. Let yourself go there, float on a rubber raft in that soft green water, float through all those reflections of trees with dark green leaves. Now you can hear waves breaking on the shore with soft, soothing ripples. You can hear the branches rustling above you, and the soft breeze feels so good against your bare skin. It feels like a soft caress. It makes you relax and feel wonderful and secure, safe and happy and content."

Tee stopped there and watched her naked chest rising and falling. Her breathing was deep now, slow. He became intrigued by her pink nipples. Man, she was built, even more than Lotus had been. She was just lying there, unmoving, maybe even unconscious. By God, he'd done it. And on the first try, too. But why wouldn't he? He'd studied the how-to technique long enough. He'd practiced it in a recorder, rehearsed this first time for hours.

"Blossom, can you hear my voice?"

"Yes."

"Tell me where you are, Blossom."

"I'm down at the lake."

"What are you doing there?"

"I'm on a raft and I'm floating on the soft green, beautiful water."

"Is there anybody with you?"

"No, just me and the birds singing up in the tree branches. One robin."

"Have you been there before?"

"No. My father never would let me get in the water."

"Oh, that's too bad. Did it make you angry with him?"

"Yes."

"Did you love him?"

"Yes."

"Did he love you?"

"I don't know."

"Why not? Didn't he ever tell you?"

"Uh uh."

Tee had looked into her files but the doctors had made little progress with the root of her depression and suicidal fantasies. Looking down over her nude body, he saw that her nipples were growing hard now and it occurred to him what her inner demons just might be. He reached out a fingertip and placed it on one nipple. He rubbed around in circles.

"Did your father ever touch you like this?"

"Yes."

Aha. She had a pervert for a father. No wonder she was so promiscuous. He'd read that about sexually abused women, that some of them really got it on when they grew up, with just about everybody, too.

"Did he ever hurt you?"

"No, he never hurt me."

"What did he do?"

"He caressed me and said he wanted to give me good feelings and make me feel good."

Very interesting. He had to say he'd never heard stuff like this before. "And how did you like it?"

"I liked it. I thought he did it because he loved me."

"Did he make you do stuff to him?"

"No, he made my half sister do that."

"You mean Lotus?"

"Yes."

Okay, now he was gonna get into why Lotus had committed suicide so precipitously. "He made Lotus touch him?"

"Yes. He didn't love her like he loved me."

"How do you know that?"

"Because he hurt her. I could hear her crying and screaming when he took her down into the cellar."

"Is that where he took you?"

"Yes, but he didn't beat me or hurt me. Just her."

Frowning, Tee stared down at the motionless girl. This was very strange but pretty fascinating, too. He thought about things for a moment.

"Where was your mother?"

"She died. He killed her."

Now that drew Tee's heart to a standstill. "He killed her?"

"Yes, but nobody knows but me and Lotus."

"How did he kill her?"

"He knocked her down and she hit her head on the garden wall."

"And that killed her."

"Yes."

"You saw this?"

"Yes."

"What happened next?"

"He dragged her out into the woods."

"Did you and Lotus go, too?"

"Yeah, he made us carry lanterns and hold them for him while he dug a hole to put her in."

Whoa. This guy was a lunatic but a man after Tee's own heart.

"What did other people say?"

"They didn't know. He told them she had gone off with another man and left him with the children."

"Nobody ever came around asking questions?"

"No."

"Is that when he started taking you and your sister to the cellar?"

"No, he didn't have to hide it anymore. He just came to our room and made one of us watch."

Man, this guy was a sicko, all right. No wonder his daughters turned out to be basket cases.

"Where is your father now?"

"Dead."

"How did he die?"

"He took me out in a rowboat with him. He stopped in the deepest part, and then he said to me, 'I love you, daughter.' "

"What happened next?"

"He took a chain and wrapped it around his body, then he tied it to a big concrete block, and then he picked it up and jumped in the water with it."

"You saw that?"

"Yes."

"What did you do?"

"I looked down in the water, and I could see the top of his head going down, down, down into the darkness. Then I rowed the boat back to shore."

"Have you ever told anybody about this before?"

"No. But Lotus knew about it."

"What about Yang Wei? Did he know about it?"

"No. Yang Wei was taken from home when he was pretty young and put into a training academy for Olympic basketball because he was so tall. Lotus, too, but later."

Tee felt a sense of power that he'd never experienced before. None of the doctors had wormed this story out of this girl, but he had. On the first attempt, too. He decided to use a different technique he'd read about on one of his favorite Internet sites. "Okay, then, Blossom, I want you to pretend you have a big red trunk and it's hidden down in the cellar of your house where nobody ever, ever goes. I want you to put all this stuff you've told me about your father inside it, then slam the door and fasten all the padlocks. There's about . . ." Tee shrugged and then said, "Twenty of them. Lock it up good and tight, and then run away, far, far away where you'll never have to see it or think about it again."

Blossom did not respond.

"Have you done that, Blossom?"

"Yes. I am still running."

Tee laughed. This was awesome, man. He was having so much fun. "You can stop running now."

Now for some of those posthypnotic suggestions he'd read about. It would be very interesting to see if that could work.

"Now, Blossom, I want to tell you some things and I want you to listen very, very carefully."

"Okay."

"Whenever you hear my voice, you'll feel safe and happy and want to please me. You'll know that if you do, it'll make you feel good all over." Tee stopped and grinned. "It'll make you want to have sex with me. Any time I say that I want it."

"Okay."

Wow. He wondered just how much he could get away with. He had read a long document on posthypnotic suggestions just the other day, and he decided to try out a more specific one. "There's some words I'm going to tell you, Blossom. A secret phrase, and when I say it, only me, my voice, you will become so turned on that you will have to have sex with me, you will have to have it, understand? You'll crave it, want it, will do anything to get it. Do you understand?"

"Yes."

So far, so good. He thought about a word, and he thought about how much sex he was gonna get any time he wanted it. But the word couldn't be something that he used often. Or that anyone else used often. It had to be something he rarely said, if ever, then he thought of a song by that favorite hard rock band of his, the one out of Germany. They were unknown to most people, but he really dug them.

Smiling, he said, "The words are 'Enter Evil.' When I say 'Enter Evil,' you will do what I told you to do."

"Okay."

Okay was right. And it was never too soon to try it out.

"I'm going to wake you up now, Blossom. When I do, you won't remember anything that happened during this session or anything that we talked about. Do you understand? And you will not remember what will happen when I say 'Enter Evil,' but you will do what I asked you to do, willingly and at once, but you won't remember the words I said or why you are doing it."

"Okay."

"All right, then I'm going to count backward from five and when I reach one, you will open your eyes and you will feel better than you've ever felt in your entire life." He got all that right off a legitimate psychiatrist's Internet site, or at least, he hoped it was the real thing.

"Five . . . four . . . three . . . two . . . one . . ."

Tee held his breath, halfway afraid she wouldn't come out of it and then there would be hell to pay with the doctors. But she did. She opened her eyes and said, "When are you going to hypnotize me?"

Holy crap, this was way fun. "Enter Evil."

Blossom looked at him. "What?"

Uh oh. "Enter Evil."

"What's that supposed to mean?"

Well, shit. He'd done something wrong. "It's just the name of a song I know."

Blossom frowned and pulled the sheet up over her. "I'm cold."

"That's the truth. Wanna have sex? That'll warm you up."

"Sure."

Pulling his shirt off, Tee got under the covers with her. Okay, back to the drawing board. Good thing Blossom was usually willing to have sex anyway, or he'd be really disappointed that his very first attempt at posthypnotic suggestion did not work so good.

FOURTEEN

Khur-Vay's Studio and Gift Shop was located on the Branson strip, along with just about everything else in town. So, of course, there was a horrendous line of traffic backed up while tourists gawked at the theater marquees and other shops lining the street, especially the ones that carried all those fascinating hillbilly T-shirts, I Heart Branson coffee mugs, and Dolly Parton wigs. We parked about a block down from the studio, and then walked the distance and stood staring at the rather large sign hanging inside the window.

I said, "It says 'Belly dancing lessons. No Men Allowed.'"

Black said, "I'm not sure that's legal."

"It's printed in two feet tall, bold black letters, Black, so Khur-Vay's obviously serious about the subject. Looks like I'm going to have to handle this little gal on my own."

"I'm not sure they can keep men out of a public establishment."

"You just want to see some belly dancers."

"I do find belly dancing erotic, at times."

"How about I take a lesson or two to spice up our love life?"

"You won't get an argument out of me on that count, not after what I watched you do on my boat the other day." Black smiled, showing some deep dimples and that he was just kidding.

"Well, now I'm offended."

"See if they offer pole dancing while you're in there," Black suggested.

"I don't do poles, not for you, not for anybody," I said, but he was still teasing me and I knew it.

Black checked the time once again by his elegant, chic, and yes, gaudy Rolex, then glanced across the busy street where traffic inched along like snails to the backyard mud puddle. "All right, if that's the way it has to be, I'll see if there's a driving range around here and hit a few balls while you're inside."

"You play golf?" I was surprised, I admit it. Wouldn't of thought he'd like it.

"I don't usually have time, but I give it a try when I can."

"I can't believe I didn't know you played golf."

"I've got a few secrets left. Not as many as you do, but a couple."

"Okay, I'll come find you when I'm done. I don't know how long this's gonna take."

"I've got to make some calls, too. Business. Take your time. I'll be back and keep an eye out for you."

I watched him for a moment as he threaded through stalled traffic, talking on one of his cell phones while squeezing between a silver Ford minivan and an old model burgundy Cadillac with three white-haired couples, men in the front seat and women in the back. Turning back to my newly discovered and exotic destination, I considered Khur-Vay's place. The plate-glass windows along the front were covered with some of those special window shades that you could see out of but not in, no doubt to protect the identities of the pretties, who were no doubt baring bellies while gyrating to tinkling drums and flutes. There was a six-foot-tall sexy rendition of a particularly well-endowed belly dancer on the door, her braceleted hand up and beckoning me gracefully inside her lair. A spider and web impression came to me, and I got a little shiver down my spine. Nah, that case was long over.

I sighed, took a deep breath. Oh, boy, was this ever gonna be fun. I pulled open the door and was hit immediately with the pungent odor of sandalwood incense and jangling music straight out of Mustafa's Bar in some narrow Baghdad alley. I shut the door quickly so no males would dare get a peek inside at the ten to fifteen ladies twisting their bodies about the floor to the beat of twangy notes. The studio portion of the shop was off to one side, divided by a low quarter wall and taking up almost three-fourths of the large room. Cobalt blue walls sported less than realistic scenes of palm trees and mosques and more cavorting midriff-bared Arab women with those little handkerchief thingies that covered their nose and mouth but revealed their heavily henna-lined eyes.

The dancers before me definitely did not have on burkas. In fact, they were baring more skin than Mariah Carey, some doing so a helluva lot better than others. Most looked in their twenties or thirties, a few in their forties, a couple more with one foot in the grave. Maybe even one foot and a half. Khur-Vay herself was looking particularly enticing, with an ultra-toned tanned body that might, or might not, be sprayed on, a pretty face that looked Asian but was almost hidden by way too much makeup, and a myriad of flowing sheer scarves in rainbow pastels hanging off a gold sequined belt riding just below her waist. Her feet were bare and pedicured with fire-engine-red toenail polish, with bracelets on her ankles, bracelets on her hands, and in truth, I wondered if she weren't Fatima waiting for the sheik of the burning sands like in that old song. More bracelets adorned her upper arms, and I couldn't help but notice that many of them were of the same type Mikey and his poor girlfriend had gone so bonkers over. So okay, bingo.

Khur-Vay gave me a friendly wave but did not stop with

the hip rotations long enough to say anything. Oh, my, she did have some impressive abs going on and could swivel her hips to beat the band when she went up on one toe. She reminded me of those bouncing dolls in grass skirts that people stuck in the back window of their cars. Glancing around first, I made sure nobody was hiding behind a palm tree ready to jump me, and then I walked back to the gift shop and a counter with a cash register located at the rear of the dance floor.

Every conceivable kind of Middle Eastern attire hung on racks, even flowing white desert robes like Laurence of Arabia swept around in, plus all manner of trinkets, castanets, jewelry, and belly dancing CDs offered to Arab-inspired folk, and beautifully displayed, at that. I quickly found that one entire glass case held the blue and white beaded bracelets and amulets I was interested in. Now I was cooking, yes, now I was getting somewhere.

Browsing some more, and curious despite myself, I found T-shirts advertising Khur-Vay's voluptuous figure and face, Oriental aromatherapy bath salts and candles, feng shui books and candles, various shapes and sizes of crystals, wind chimes made out of Chinese lucky coins on red cords, embroidered white Muslim skullcaps, and all manner of other New Age gadgets and gimmicks. I found the source of the thick, sweet aroma filling the room, and it was emanating from a black Buddha sitting in his own special little alcove, one very similar to the one adorning Mikey's apartment. Suddenly I had a distinct feeling that Khur-Vay was going to figure prominently in my investigation. How, I did not know. Yet.

After poking around in gold and red sequined outfits sans any midriff, I sat down on an uncomfortable black iron bench near the CD player and watched the fun. Now the ladies had added little finger cymbals to their thumbs and forefingers and were clacking away and twirling their see-through scarves about, happy as little flamenco dancers in a Barcelona square.

Actually, down deep, I thought they looked sorta cool and to my own amazement, wondered if I should take a lesson, or two, just to surprise Black with a dancing girl costume, thus garnering some dancing ability and newfound sexiness, to boot. It might go okay with my guns and holsters, and maybe it would teach him a lesson about comparing me to that Elaine girl who couldn't dance on TV, whoever the hell she was.

Fifteen minutes later, the lesson was over; the dancers were breathless and seemingly elated. They laughed and chatted together awhile, mostly telling tales of how well their lessons were going over with their boyfriends, husbands, and significant others. Some sexual details emerged that were entertaining but belonged behind closed doors, believe you me. Mouths had been washed out with soap for less. Most of the ladies slipped their bare feet into rubber flip-flops and left with scarves wafting behind them and bellies bare, but a few more conservative lasses donned shorts and Khur-Vay T-shirts over their skimpy attire.

"Hello to you. Thanks so much for waiting. I'm Khur-Vay." The owner had approached me in a swirl and wash of exotic perfume and held out her hand with a friendly smile. I returned it. She was Asian, or partially so, had an accent that I couldn't place, and an unusually sweet voice, almost like a little girl's. And up close and personal, Khur-Vay was even more Curve-Vay than I had first thought. She was well built in all the right places, head to toe, but not that anorexic look so common among starving Hollywood starlets, instead she looked all healthy muscle and sinew. This girl lifted weights, you can bet on it.

"No problem. I'm Detective Claire Morgan from Canton County."

Her vivid green eyes widened. Black's beauteous ex-wife and model, Jude, had green eyes. Khur-Vay's were not sultry and jade and almond-shaped like hers, but wide and honest and the color of summer grass. I could detect no guile in their depths, which surprised me in a belly dancer. Ingrained prejudice against women fixated on their navels, I guess. Man, she wore a lot of makeup, though. It seemed to be prevalent in the people I met nowadays.

"Am I in trouble, Officer?" She raised both hands, then laughed. It was infectious.

I smiled but remained suitably official. "Not yet. But I have to say you give a smokin' hot dance class."

"Thank you. Would you like to sign up? You have the figure for it."

I considered. Black would be pleased. Really, really pleased. Nah, he didn't need any extra encouragement. Neither of us would ever get any work done. "Not at this time. But you are very skillful with all those scarves and little teeny cymbals."

Khur-Vay raised both arms and did a graceful little clicking show for my enjoyment, then laughed again. I liked her immediately. How rare.

"You should try it, really, Detective. Everybody makes fun of belly dancing classes, but it's a real turn-on for men. You know, it brings back all those fantasies of sheiks stealing women out of desert tents in the dead of night. Rudolph Valentino, and all those guys. Very, very sexy."

I had seen *Lawrence of Arabia*, and that guy looked pretty awesome in his white robes and shiny curved scimitar, and all, but this Rudolph guy's screen credits had alluded me. Maybe I'd make a trip to Hollywood Video and check him out. But, okay, enough chitchat, down to the business of murder and mayhem.

"Actually, I need to ask you some questions about one of your customers."

"Sure, whatever I can do to help."

I liked her even better now. Instant cooperation was not overrated. "How well do you know a young woman named Li He?"

"Oh, Li. We're good friends. She's not in trouble, is she?"

"She's gone missing. You haven't heard about it?"

Her astonishment appeared genuine, but maybe belly

dancers studied acting. Her sudden look of fear appeared pretty real, too. "Are you serious? Gone missing?"

"Yes, ma'am, I'm sorry to have to tell you about it."

"For how long?"

"Less than a week, but no one has seen her and no one knows where she is."

"Man, that's awful. I thought it was odd when she didn't show up for today's lesson. She never misses them. She's a natural, very graceful and fluid with her movements. She's a fantastic acrobat, too, did you know that? Comes from a whole family of them. They can bend themselves around like pipe cleaners."

I nodded but didn't comment. I'd seen pipe cleaners but didn't usually bend them.

"What'd you think happened to her? Do you think she's in trouble or just off somewhere and forgot to tell anybody?"

"That's what we're trying to find out. Do you have any idea where she might be?"

"Well, I guess I'd check out her boyfriend first. She goes off with him sometimes." She looked closely at me. "You know what? He lives up around the lake somewhere. Mikey Murphy's his name. Have you talked to him about this?"

I didn't want to tell her the bad news about Mikey Murphy, not yet, so I said, "Do they go off together often?"

"Whenever they want to, I guess. I've known them to do it, what, I'd say about three times, maybe even four. You know, for a weekend, or something like that." She glanced at the front door, then she said, "I don't have another class coming in for almost an hour. Why don't we sit down and I'll fix you some green tea? I have to tell you, this news is pretty hard to take. Li's a good friend of mine. You know, she comes in here all the time."

There was a small section of the studio that had a cluster of two or three high tables with tall stools around them, and a counter with a cappuccino machine, a hot-water spigot, and several glass domes covering plates of bran and blueberry muffins, oatmeal raisin cookies, and peach fried pies, all labeled with little brass plaques. Man, did I ever love peach fried pies.

"Would you like something to eat? I bake everything myself. Fresh every morning."

In answer to that, my stomach whined and threw a small tantrum. Well, it was going on noon. I was hungry again. I admitted it. "I'll take a fried pie. And give me a couple of those to go, too, for my male friend that you won't let come in."

Khur-Vay laughed. She was certainly an amiable type. I just wished she'd wipe off some of the makeup so I could see her better. She said, "Good choice. It's my mother's recipe. She's just about the best cook who ever lived." Man, everybody said that about their mom, even Joe McKay. I never knew my mother, so I don't know if I could say it about her, or not.

Khur-Vay picked up one of the half-moon-shaped fried pies with a little square of white tissue paper, then placed it on a gold paper plate rimmed in fancy black scrolls. Setting it on the table in front of me, she sprinkled a little powdered sugar on top out of handled metal shaker and told me to say when. I said when and watched her put two more fried pies in a little white pastry sack and cover them with sugar. Black was gonna be ecstatic. He loves peaches. Then she brought out a matching pair of tiny navy and gold Oriental demitasse cups and saucers on a brass tray. She placed a small tea bag inside each one and poured in some steaming water. I preferred coffee, especially vanilla cappuccino, but I was being polite. I could choke down hot green tea when I had to.

"Does your mother live around here?"

"Oh, no, we're from California. Los Angeles. I really miss her. We always have these big family celebrations with all our relatives, but I don't get to go to them much anymore."

"You're a long way from home. Why did you move here?" I was one to talk. I moved here from LA, too; had to, in fact. But that was something I sure didn't want to talk about.

Khur-Vay said, "I heard Branson was a safe place to live and make some good money. Belly dancing studios are a dime a dozen in LA. Have you ever been out there?"

Oh, yeah, I've been there but wish I hadn't. Bad memories galore. "I've seen it on TV. I even watched O. J. Simpson's slowpoke car chase."

Khur-Vay smiled, but her eyes were looking me over pretty good. "Yeah, I watched that, too. When I get homesick I just watch the movies filmed out there, which is nearly all of them." Frowning, she changed the subject, "I'm really worried about Li. She's been upset lately."

Aha. I sipped my tea in a ladylike fashion, or as best I could. "Do you know what's bothering her?"

"I'm not sure. Probably something to do with Mikey. They fight a lot, then make up and everything's fine. They love each other."

"Then you know Mikey personally?"

"Yeah, for quite a while, I guess. I met both of them in therapy."

My antenna quivered, then stood straight up. I swallowed my bite of peach pie and said, "Therapy?"

"Yes, there's a place in Jeff City. Oak Haven. We were in the same therapy group at one time. You ever heard of that place?"

I nodded, took another bite. I couldn't probe too much, so I waited, hoping she'd spill out some helpful information. Lucky for me, she wasn't embarrassed that she'd needed help at a psychiatric hospital.

"Yeah, I got really down in the dumps once. My husband really screwed me over, stole some of my money, got me into drugs for a while. But I'm clean now, completely," she added since I was a cop. "I mean, he really put me through hell. When we split up, he got the courts to give him full custody of my little girl. Anyway, I got all depressed and moped around until Li told me about her therapist and how wonderful he was, so I went with her."

"Do you mind telling me the name of your doctor?"

"Oh, no. I sing his praises whenever I can. It's Dr. Collins. His first name's Boyce."

"I see." But I was thinking what she said about her kid getting taken away. I knew how it felt to suddenly lose a child: the despair, the desire to go to sleep and never wake up. I wondered if she had her little girl back. "Was he able to help you?"

"Yes. He made me realize that life wasn't over, that I was strong enough to deal with it."

I had to ask, couldn't help myself. "Did you get your child back?"

Sadness welled up in her eyes. "Not yet, but I'm not giving up. Dr. Collins said he'd help me. She lives with her dad and his new wife in Hawaii, Oahu. Her name's Chloe. She's seven."

Suddenly I found myself wanting to pour out my own sordid story to her, and I was amazed that I was having the urge to do that. The inclination only lasted a few seconds, though, until the deep pain hit me between the shoulder blades and knifed down into my core. Pushing it out of my mind, I got back to business.

"One thing I'd like to ask you, Khur-Vay. I'm curious about those bracelets over there. The ones with their own case, you know? The blue and white ones with some black spots. What are they for?"

"The evil eyes? They're really getting popular. Li has them, and so does Mikey. Is that why you asked?"

"Why are they called evil eyes?"

"It's an old custom from the Middle East, mainly countries around the Mediterranean. People use them to protect themselves from envy. Most people think it's protection against evil, and in a way it is, I guess."

"How does it protect someone from envy?"

"Well, the idea is that when somebody looks at you with envy in their heart, those eyes on the bracelet reflect that envy back to them. Lots of mothers place them on their new-borns. I have the amulets for sale, too. They're to hang around your house. Some people believe they protect you from evil-doers, as well. Are you interested in having one?"

I thought about the murder cases I'd been running into lately, the insane serial killers, the mangled victims, the stays in the hospital for me and my friends. I said, "You know, I think I will. I think I'll take a couple, in fact." One for me and one for Black. Then I thought of Bud and Harve. "Make that four. Hey, make it a cool half dozen." I began to under-stand Mikey's obsession.

"Okay, come pick out the ones you want. I have gobs of different kinds."

Choosing quickly, I waited while Khur-Vay took the ones I chose and rang them up. She handed me a black bag dis-playing a pyramid with a shining eye on top. "Thanks. I do hope you'll come back for a lesson soon. Eleven, two, four, and six, every day of the week, except Sunday. She hesi-tated. "Would you let me know as soon as you find Li? I'm sure she's just off with Mikey, or maybe at some library somewhere, working on a research paper. She is very stu-dious and makes all A's. She's serious about becoming a doc-tor, you know."

"I'll give you a call as soon as I hear something."

Khur-Vay's eyes veered over toward the front windows, and she said, "Whoa, look at that guy out there."

Turning around, I expected to see some purse snatcher grabbing some eighty-year-old lady's purse but instead caught sight of Black loitering around on the sidewalk out-side. He kept glancing in the window and looking mightily pissed. I glanced at my watch. I'd been in the studio with Khur-Vay for almost an hour. Time flies when you're having green tea.

"Is he a hottie, or what?" said Khur-Vay.

I tried to be nonchalant, but a gloat threatened. "He's with me."

"Like, you mean, your boyfriend?"

"I guess. Sort of."

Khur-Vay looked at me with heightened respect. "Wow. You hit the jackpot with him, didn't you?"

I guess I did, but I usually didn't admit it to other people. "Well, okay, Khur-Vay. He looks pretty ticked, so I guess I better wrap it up here and get going. You mind if I come back here, if I've got more questions?"

"Not at all. Bring him with you, if you want. That would be no problem, believe me."

Khur-Vay laughed at her offer, and I knew she wasn't putting the moves on Black or trying to get under my skin, so I laughed, too. I really liked this girl, but I wasn't quite sure why. Maybe it would come to me if I wore some of her magic bracelets.

FIFTEEN

"Well, it's about damn time. A couple of more minutes and I would've kicked in the door and checked out Khur-Vay's oven."

Black was not exactly hiding his impatience, but I had a feeling that had more to do with curiosity about what had gone on inside and irk that he'd been excluded. People just didn't exclude Nicholas Black from anything without his permission.

"You missed all the fun. There was a whole gaggle of sexy women in there, baring everything."

"I saw them leaving. Yeah, and by the way, that was thirty minutes ago."

"I'd have waited on you, if you'd been the one allowed inside."

"No, you wouldn't."

"I'm so hurt by that remark."

He grinned. "What'd you find out? Anything?"

"A lot. Come on, let's get going. I'll tell you on the way. Here, have some peach fried pies and an evil-eye bracelet to keep you safe."

"Thanks. Maybe you should keep all these bracelets. We all know how you are."

"Multiple bracelets didn't help Mikey."

We got serious very quickly; the thought of murder victims usually brought that on. As we walked back toward the car, Black said, "I thought we'd have a nice dinner somewhere, and maybe catch another show before we got home."

"I thought we'd go straight home and have long, hot tantric sex like Sting until bedtime."

"Let's go."

The traffic was horrific, of course. Even in a very important, official looking car, people honked at us and senior citizens took fifteen minutes to make a left turn, even a right turn. Once we were finally inside the chopper, I filled Black in on my conversation with Khur-Vay, and he listened intently as he ate one of the fried pies. Then he said, "It's interesting to me that so many of these people were patients of Boyce Collins."

"My thoughts precisely. Coincidences usually add up to something in my book. Problem is, most of them were patients of Martin Young, too. Not to mention Happy Pete, who ought to advertise Crest toothpaste, he's so smiley."

Black frowned, fired up the rotors, and we both put on our headsets to continue our conversation.

"As you said, still pretty coincidental, if you ask me," his voice said in my ear. I merely nodded, always a trifle jumpy on takeoffs and landings. Black was a good pilot, I knew that, but accidents happened. Helicopters collided in midair with small Cessnas or flocks of geese. I am a pessimist at times, can't help it.

However, we lifted off the ground slowly and safely and moments later we were gliding over the treetops like a rather loud but sleek pterodactyl escaped from Jurassic Park. I said, "You think Boycie boy's involved in the murders?"

"By your plural, I take it you've decided Mikey was murdered, too."

"We haven't heard from Buck on the autopsy, but I'd bet my house on it. And you know how I love my house."

"I think the possibility bears looking into. Do you have the medical records for these kids?"

"We've requested them, but haven't gotten them yet. I'm going back up there and have some one-on-one time with good Dr. Collins as soon as humanly possible. If a warrant's necessary, I'm gonna have it in hand."

"You need to be careful on this one."

Well, surprise, surprise. Black always told me to duck and weave and watch my back and gave me good-luck tokens, but I was curious about the specifics of what he was thinking about this case. "Got a premonition, or what?"

"Because it stands to reason that somebody up there at that clinic is playing dangerous head games."

"Oh, that."

"I'm serious, Claire. If these turn out to be very clever murders and not suicides, we're talking about a psychopath, a particularly evil one. My God, he put a young and innocent girl inside an oven."

"Just one thing wrong with that. She put herself in that oven, remember?"

"What I'm saying is there possibly could be some kind of doctor/patient manipulation going on. Somehow he convinces them, or entices them, to do things they normally wouldn't do."

"You're talking about mind control?"

He frowned some more and fiddled with a dial on the control panel. Have to say again, it makes me nervous when he frowns when driving, be it a Humvee, chopper, or a rented Lincoln. But I'm a lot more so in the chopper. But he glanced at me and said, "It could very well be some kind of mind control, although that's a lot harder to accomplish than you see it done in the movies. She got a phone call right before she got inside the stove, remember? That's right out of the *Manchurian Candidate*, but actually making somebody do something life threatening like that is not easy, if possible at all. The killer could have used some kind of drug cocktail as inducement, but it would still be dicey to pull off."

"We found a cell phone at Mikey's crime scene, too. What kind of drugs are you talking about?"

"Sodium pentothal or sodium amytal. Maybe even a post-hypnotic suggestion is a viable option, but like I said, all that's pretty tricky stuff to pull off. But it's been documented that highly experienced hypnotherapists have made their patients do things they wouldn't normally do."

"You're talking about a truth serum type thing?"

"Yes."

"Have you ever done anything like that?"

"On occasion I've used hypnotherapy and found it useful, but I don't like doing it. It's playing around with people's subconscious minds and I think that's dangerous."

"Is that why I'm always hanging around with you? You gave me some kinda posthypnotic suggestion to make me do whatever you want?"

He gave a little laugh. "I doubt if you're exactly highly suggestible material, because unfortunately, you don't always do what I want. But who knows? Some people are very much so. Others nobody could hypnotize if they tried for a year. I think you're probably in the latter."

"Do you really use hypnotherapy in your practice?"

"Like I said, I don't like to and I'm not expert at it, but there are instances where it has worked with a patient when nothing else has."

While I was thinking about that and the ramifications of what Black was suggesting, my cell phone played its catchy little Latin tune. Bud calling. His voice was all hurried and excited, which instantly sent a chill through me.

"Where the hell are you, Claire? You gotta get back here fast! Where are you?"

Now I was the one frowning. "I'm on my way home with Black. What's going on?"

"The fire chief just called the station and said some girl's threatenin' to commit suicide at Bagnell Dam. They said she's standin' in one of those kiddie swimmin' pools filled up with gasoline and holdin' a cigarette lighter. She's threatenin' to burn herself up. They've cleared the traffic and are tryin' to talk her down, but it's a standoff. She says it's gotta be you she talks to, so you've gotta get here before she gets tired of waitin'."

"Oh, crap, who is it?"

"Nobody knows yet. How soon can you get here?"

I turned to Black. "How long till we get home?"

"Ten minutes, I guess. Why?"

"Bud, it's gonna be at least ten minutes. Can they hold her off that long?"

"Hurry, Claire, this is serious shit. Charlie says the KY3 news cameras were here to film a story on that houseboat accident that happened the other day and are already down there and set up to catch it all for the six o'clock news. Even Steve Grant's down there."

Steve Grant was the most famous newscaster in Springfield, a handsome, silver-haired man and a real seasoned pro. I felt a little better. He wasn't going to do or say anything stupid, that much was for sure. "Is there someplace we can put down around there?"

"I guess we'll have to clear a parkin' lot. I'm almost there now. Look for me, and I'll wave you in. I just hope to God we can stop this thing."

"You sure nobody knows who she is?"

"All I know is that she's young. Tell Black to open up on it or we're gonna have another dead body on our hands."

I hung up and said, "How fast will this thing go?"

"Now you're talking, baby," Black answered.

As it turned out, Black's helicopter could go pretty damn fast. Black so liked speed in his toys. We flew home in record time, and I explained the situation to him along the way, but time was running out when we finally reached Bagnell Dam in under ten minutes and took a quick circle overhead, look-ing for the landing zone. I picked out a small blue car on the shoulder at the intersection just before the dam and saw the girl standing at the rear of it. The scene was surrounded by police cars, officers shielded behind open doors. A fire truck was just pulling in. One KY3 satellite truck was there, ea-gerly filming everything. Not good, not good at all

A second later, I saw Bud in the center of an empty park-ing lot about half a block away. He was waving both arms at us, so I pointed him out to Black and said through the head-set. "Take us down over there. Can you see Bud?"

"Yeah. Here goes. Looks like we made it in time."

Black took us down like he was maneuvering a compact car into a parking space. He was a helluva good pilot, and he should be. He had piloted choppers in the Special Services. He'd let that slip out once when he was half asleep, and I suspect he had put down in some zones hotter than this one, and more than once.

As soon as we touched down, I opened my door and jumped out, not waiting for Black to switch off the rotors. Bud met me at the edge of the parking lot and we both sprinted toward the standoff. Charlie was hunkered behind his white SUV where it was parked sideways in the street. He had a bullhorn in his hand.

"Thank God you're here," he snapped at me. "Who the hell is this kid? Nobody can get an damned ID on her. Do you think she's got a weapon? And why the hell does she want to talk to you?"

"I don't know. Let me see if I recognize her." Peering over the top of the car, I recognized her, all right. It was Cleo, the sweet young girl I had interviewed at Oak Haven. What the hell was going on?

I hunkered down beside Charlie. "Her name's Cleo. I in-terviewed her up at Oak Haven clinic on the Murphy case."

"Why's she doing this?"

"I don't know. She was all right when I talked to her. I

doubt if she's got any kind of weapon, other than that cigarette lighter."

"Well, that's one too many. Get on this horn and talk her outta burning herself to a fuckin' crisp."

Reluctantly, I took the horn. Sucking in a deep breath, I tried to calm my racing heart, then stood up and said, "Hey, Cleo. It's me, Claire Morgan. What's up with all this?"

Silence. Then the girl looked in my direction. She called out, "Is that really you, Detective Morgan?"

"Yeah. I'm right here. What's the problem? I can help you, whatever it is. You don't have to do this."

Cleo was standing in a small blue plastic kiddie swimming pool, all right, one with little swimming goldfish painted all over it. I'd seen the exact one at Wal-Mart, out front with the baskets of blooming summer flowers. Now I could see the gasoline sloshing around her ankles when she moved. Three red metal gas cans sat on the back of her raised hatch. She had a Bic lighter in her right hand. It was yellow. In her other hand, she held a cell phone to her ear. It was yellow, too. She was talking to somebody. Oh, God, this was not gonna turn out good. I could feel it in my bones. I could feel it, and I didn't want to feel it. But I knew, I knew, and it showed in my voice.

"Cleo, come on over here and talk to me. Nobody's gonna hurt you. Nobody's gonna put you in jail, or anything like that. I promise you. You don't wanna do this. Let me help you. I can help you, if you'll let me."

My words echoed a little through the horn, video cameras rolled, everybody held their breaths. Cleo didn't say anything for a while, but seemed to be listening to the person at the other end of the line. I sure hoped it was somebody who loved her and could talk her down. A moment later, while we all watched in frozen fear, Cleo suddenly threw the cell phone into the gasoline sloshing around her feet. She bent quickly and held the lighter down next to the gasoline.

"No, Cleo, no, don't do it!" I yelled but she did it anyway. The lighter flared orange, and then there was a huge whoosh and roar as the gasoline ignited, and then her terrible shrieks as the fire engulfed her alive. The firefighters were ready, and they got their hoses on her almost at once but not before the flame reached the car's gas tank. The following explosion rocked us all off our feet. I fell to the ground on my knees and shut my eyes, not wanting to see what was left of poor little, friendly, likable, freckle-faced Cleo. God help us, we were living in a nightmare.

Here Comes Trouble

The next experiment Tee tried was something called a false memory implant. He'd read about it in some books and decided that he'd try it on his other girlfriend, Orchid. She was always teasing him with sex and stuff. She'd be a good candidate. Their session went along much the same way Blossom's did. She was easily hypnotized, too, and it didn't take long to put her under. He decided to use the same technique that he'd read about in his research.

"Orchid, I want you to go back, far back, when you were a little girl, just six years old. Can you do that?"

"Yes."

He was getting better at this every time he tried it, and it was turning out to be fairly easy. He was going to have to try something more challenging in the future.

"Tell me where you are."

"I'm in my house. In my bedroom with my sister."

"What are you doing?"

"Daddy's reading us a bedtime story."

"What story?"

"Cinderella."

He smiled to himself. Now to wreak havoc in her little head. "Do you remember what happened next? When Daddy took you out to the shed?"

"No. He's just reading the book. Then he'll kiss us good night and go up to his bedroom."

"No, he takes you to the shed and does terrible things to you. Don't you remember that?"

"No."

"Think about it. That's where he beats you with his big black belt and touches you in private places. Try to see it."

"I don't see it."

"You are lying in bed listening to his story. Your sister goes to sleep, and then he takes your hand and helps you stand up, and then he picks you up and carries you outside. You must remember it now. He carries you out to the shed and that's where he molests you."

"He molests me."

"That's right. That's where he touches you and beats you with his belt. You can see it now, if you try. He is sliding his belt out of his belt loops and then he makes you lean over this old rickety green card table. You can see it happening now, can't you?"

"Yes."

"Always, remember, Orchid, bad things happen in sheds. Always. Repeat after me, bad things happen in sheds."

"Bad things happen in sheds."

"Whenever you hear that phrase, *bad things happen in sheds*, you will remember how your father took you out there and beat and molested you. You will remember the pain of the strap biting into your flesh and the way he touched you. Do you understand?"

"Yes."

Three days later, he decided to test out his very first false memory implant during a regular group session. The doctor was listening to everybody tell how their day was going. Tee decided to get things fired up a bit. What they needed was some excitement around this place.

When it was his turn to speak, he said, "I remember there was this old shed in our backyard. I was really afraid to go down there because it was in the edge of the woods and had a bunch of spiderwebs and grapevines growing up all over it. Our handyman always worked there, repairing furniture and stuff."

"Why do you think you were afraid, Tee?" the doctor asked.

"Bad things happen in sheds," Tee answered, not looking at Orchid.

He didn't have long to wait for the fireworks to start. Orchid let out a little surprised groan, and then her face crumpled with pain and fear, and then she burst into tears. Everybody looked at her as if she'd gone nuts, but she wept inconsolably into her palms and kept saying, "Daddy molested me in the shed, he did, he did, I just remembered it. He hurt me."

The doctor stood up, very alarmed, but said quietly, "Orchid, try to calm down. There's no need to be so upset."

Orchid wasn't listening to his platitudes. "Yes, he did it, yes, he did it, I remember it now, I can see it. I can see his big black belt and feel his hands on me." Her tears increased to near hysteria until the doctor had to call a nurse to take her back to her room and give her a sedative.

Somehow Tee kept a straight face, but inside, he was laughing his head off. Triumphant, too. He had done it; he had actually done it. He'd gotten inside her head and changed things all around. He was God Almighty. He really was.

SIXTEEN

On the day Dr. Boyce Collins and I agreed to have our interview at Oak Haven Clinic, I arrived thirty minutes early and solo, hoping to get a shot at snooping around inside his office before he got out of his therapy session. Bud was back home, unhappily handling the press morons for the sheriff, who were all insanely obsessed with Cleo's terrible suicide at the dam and demanding answers and now digging up facts on Mikey, too, but luckily not the girl in the oven, at least, not yet. I had tried, but unsuccessfully, to block out that picture of Cleo holding that lighter to the gas each time it rose up in its leaping flames and agonized screams inside my head. So I did that again now, and concentrated on why I was here at Oak Haven Clinic, armed and ready for battle. Mary, the contrary receptionist, remembered me and trusted me not to snoop, I guess, because she directed me down to Collins's office and went back to her detective novel. Wrong move. A snooper I am, and from way back, too. Trained in the art, even.

So all by my lonesome and free to roam wild, I made my way down the quiet corridor to the designated office, taking a gander into the door window of every therapy room I passed along the way. To me, they looked a lot like advanced college classes, with kids sitting at individual desks, drinking sodas or bottles of water and doodling on five-section notebooks while their teachers droned on. It was hard to imagine they were all emotionally challenged in one way or another. They looked so normal. But so had Cleo. I shut that down again and proceeded on.

Collins's office was unlocked, lucky, lucky me, and deserted, at that. I went in like I had every right to, which I actually did, shut the door, checked my watch, and dug in with relish and gusto. But first, I checked all the bookshelves for the obligatory hidden cameras and found several tucked away, here and there around the room. Filming private therapy sessions seemed quite in vogue, but I couldn't completely condemn them, not after hearing Black agree the films were both necessary and helpful to most shrinks.

So I moseyed to my heart's content, trying to look innocuous and slightly bored by having to wait, just in case there was a camera running that I didn't locate or a two-way mirror and/or picture frame disguised as something else. Yes, I am getting big-time paranoid. I just had this itchy hunch about Boycie Boy that would not go away.

Along one wall, there was this big glass case filled with lots of trophies and awards. Some went as far back as high school and college, track meets and swim team awards. There were several MVP player awards, not a few Student Athlete plaques, but mostly there were tall gold statues with either a swimmer, golfer, or baseball player swinging a shiny gold bat perched on the top. The guy was proud of his athleticism, proud of his body, too. And he should be, the guy was buff, not that I usually noticed things like that.

Truth is, I hate guys who are too girly-man in the way they strut around and thrust out their molded pecs, especially the ones who wear those thin wife-beater shirts just to show off their bod. Black is the exception to that rule, of course, not that he'd be caught dead in a wife-beater under-shirt. Actually, I like his chest in anything he wears, or doesn't wear. I had stuck a small tape recorder in my jeans pocket, just to see if Boycie would object to being taped for an eventual court trial, I hoped. Maybe if he did agree, Black could listen to it and verify Collins was a well-educated, psychiatric but psychopathic, fruitcake.

Strolling nonchalantly around behind his desk, I quickly checked for the on-off button, and, of course, found it. I guess all the offices were set up the same way, a fact to file away. The desk was quite orderly, paper stacked in neat piles or in stacked wire baskets to the right of a telephone with three lines, none blinking. Nobody ever seemed to be calling Oak Haven. I picked up the receiver and punched through the caller ID list of incoming calls. There was one from me, but I had blocked my number out. There was a couple to the Murphy residence in Jefferson City, which I found more than interesting. I'd have to pump my man Collins for details about that connection.

On the other side of the room was a very large, rectangular fish aquarium with two chairs sitting directly in front of it. Odd decorating touch but no doubt a Collins-inspired relaxation technique. There was some kind of strobe effect flashing periodically behind the fish, very slowly and in various colors, and I wondered if it gave his black mollies and the single red Chinese fighting fish some headaches or nervous gills. I checked to see if they were swimming sideways or around in circles in need of therapy. They all were bobbing near the top and looking bored. So was I. Maybe they were just waiting to get fed.

Sitting down in one of the deep swivel armchairs covered in navy velour, I stared at the flashing lights a while, analyzing if I felt all goofy and hypnotized, and whatnot. I didn't. Hypnotism intrigued me, however, always had, and Boyce Collins had delineated some pretty far-out ideas of mind control in that book of his. I'd skimmed through it briefly and found it interesting as all get-out, I had to admit. I was mainly curious about just what could or could not be done while a patient was in a trance.

The LAPD departmental shrink had wanted to put me under and examine my subconscious after the incident that had taken Zach's life and injured Harve, but I had refused, resigned, and left LA instead. For some reason, I'd always had this penchant for being in command of my senses. I'd toyed with the idea of letting Black hypnotize me, now that I knew he did that sort of thing, thinking he might be able to clear out some of the grief I've got hiding out so deep inside my gray matter. Then it occurred to me he might make me into a Stepford Wife who followed his commands twenty-four/ seven. Probably not, he obviously didn't like compliant women, but who knows? Sometimes he got very frustrated with my independent streak and desire to do my own thing and live in my own house.

There were several sections of the room that I definitely felt were hypnotic-inducing booths, areas, mind twisters, or what have you. One was hidden behind a screen, a movable, padded wall, the operative word being padded. I walked around behind it and discovered a rather big rectangular light box attached to the wall. It was not turned on. The chair sitting right in front of it had a taller back than the fish tank ones, and was a deeply cushioned, dark brown suede rocker. On a low white table in front of the chair was a eighteen-inch laptop computer with a set of lightweight earphones plugged into it. Okay, I am bad, too curious, all that rot. I know that well.

Moving over to the light box, I flipped on the toggle switch on its right edge; it immediately began pulsating with lights, a regular fireworks show with lots of slowly moving designs, kind of like you would see when turning the cylinder of a child's kaleidoscope but faster. I picked up the headphones and cupped one to my left ear. Strange sounds emanated, obviously weirded-up frequencies. Rather annoying sounds, truthfully.

"Want to try it out, Detective?"

I jumped at the voice, very close behind me, then turned and found Collins standing at the edge of the screen. I hadn't heard him come in, which was not like me. I make a point to know who's doing what in every room I'm in. He was a stealthy little critter.

He laughed at my reaction. "Oops, sorry, I didn't mean to scare you, Detective."

"You didn't scare me." That was a lie, of course, he had startled me a little, but I didn't like him laughing at me. I put the headphones down on the table. "I take it that this is the new technique you write about in your book, correct, doctor? Sound waves and posthypnotic suggestions, all that kinda stuff."

"Well, I can't take all the credit. Dr. Young started experimenting with this procedure long before I did and really is much more accomplished than I, but I do find this therapy completely fascinating. That's why I pursued it for my doctoral dissertation, thus the book Nick so kindly purchased."

Wow, was that ever a mouthful. Smiling all friendly like, even inside his eyes this time, Boyce Collins said, "Please sit down. Let me show you how it works. You might find it interesting."

I remembered Black's rather pointed warning and heeded it. "I'm sure I would. But I don't have a lot of time, but I do have lots of questions to ask you."

"Oh, come now, Detective, loosen up, bear with me. Let me show off my wares."

Wares? Who did he think he was? Simple Simon? And that was an odd way to put it, but let's face it, Collins was an odd duck. I threw caution to the wind, which is where I usually threw it when somebody irked me as much as Boycie Baby. I got smiley, too. "All right, if you promise not to make me do something stupid, like pretend I'm a monkey or lick my paw like a cat."

Collins didn't laugh, but he did crack a smile. It might've been a charity one, though. He shook his head. "Ah, that old wives' tale rears its ugly head again. Let me be clear, Detective, I can't make you do a single thing you wouldn't ordinarily do. Certainly nothing against your own personal moral code. Something tells me you wouldn't be a good candidate for hypnotism, anyway."

That's exactly what Black had said, but I played dumb. "Oh? Why do you say that?"

"I don't know you well, of course, but you appear to be a strong, capable woman, determined, if I have read your personality correctly. You're a police officer always in search of the facts. You're trained to seek out the truth and know when people are lying. Actually, that's not so different from my job. Here, sit down a minute, and let me explain how this contraption works."

Okay, I'd play along, humor the good doc. I sat down in the rocker. Collins took my place at the light box and fiddled with a few knobs, punched a few computer buttons. The light got brighter and flashed on and off in a sporadic fashion. "This is all very experimental, you understand. Nobody is using it yet, except for Dr. Young and myself, but it's gotten a great deal of interest since my book was published. It's registered for patent, and I'm happy to say I've had some success with a couple of our patients."

"Why don't you just tell me how it works? That would be faster. We're both busy people."

"Certainly, if that's what you wish. You are looking at the light box, of course. All it is, basically, is a repetitive light spectrum with multicolored icons blinking in random sequences."

"Right. Looks like a kaleidoscope," I said, trying to urge him on. I could humor him and his therapeutic toys for a while, but I had other things to do.

"That's right. Every child loves those, you know. Adults, too. You'd be surprised how many grown men and women find it fun and relaxing to turn the end of a toy kaleidoscope. I find it fascinating myself. Do you?"

"I guess so. I haven't done it since I was three."

"Here, put on these headphones and listen to the sounds." He held them out to me, his smile openly challenging me to play along, which I had usually found meant it was something I should not do. This time, however, curiosity killed the cat. "Okay, but I reserve the right to stop this brainwashing attempt at my own discretion."

Boyce Collins grinned and looked very boyish and charming all of a sudden. He couldn't be very old. "Anything you want, detective. Just take the headphones off any time you've had enough. No problem. But I think you'll like it. Most people find it incredibly relaxing. Many even fall asleep."

Right, I'm sure it was gonna be a real party. So I put on the headphones but kept my attention glued on his smirking face. He turned back toward the box, punched more buttons on the computer, and peculiar soft sounds flooded into my ears. I watched him lean against the wall beside the light box and watch me so I transferred my focus to the shifting yellow, green, blue, and red shapes flitting, spinning, and melting into each other in front of me. Almost immediately, I felt my muscles relax. I tensed them again, just in case I was more hypnotizable than everybody seemed to think, which I can tell you, I am not. But I had to admit, this could relax a person big-time, even one wound as tight as most of his patients no doubt were.

More than curious about the sounds, or sound waves, if I recalled the explanation correctly from Collins's book, this whole therapy had a lot to do with frequency, different levels affecting the mind in different ways. In his book, he had compared the effect with how crystal singing bowls affected the chakras of the body. What are chakras of the body? Got me. But believe it or not, I know something about crystal singing bowls, but only because once when Harve and I were on patrol in LA, we had been called to a robbery at a Buddhist novelty shop and that was the day I heard my first crystal singing bowl. The owner's wife was trying to calm herself down after the robber took off and was doing it with these clear crystal bowls of various sizes that made truly beautiful and haunting sounds when she dragged a soft mallet around the rims. I know, that sounds crazy, but it's the truth. I'd have to pay Khur-Vay a visit and let her explain to me how they worked and what the sounds meant and what a chakra was. If anybody would know that sort of stuff, I had a feeling she would. Maybe she even had some in her storeroom that Black could buy me for my birthday.

Leaning my head back, I rested against the soft pillowed cushion and pretended to shut my eyes, but I really watched Dr. Jekyll from under my lashes. Just in case he pressed another button that pierced my brain with gamma rays and turned me into a vegetable or various and sundry other zombie-like creatures, you understand. He just stood there, however, smiling at me as if he knew what I was doing. All of a sudden, he looked a lot more relaxed than I felt.

After a couple of minutes of the catchy, alien-craft sounds, I said, "Well, that was just as fun as fun can be, Doc. I enjoyed it. All I need now is a cot and a blanket and maybe a pacifier."

Expression all serious now, Collins took off my headphones and placed them back on the table. "You joke around a lot, Detective Morgan, but guess what? I just put you out and found out all kinds of personal things about you. I told you not to remember it when you woke up and you don't, do you?"

"Yeah, right. Ha ha, Doctor. You're a regular Will Ferrell in a white coat."

Smiling knowingly, he flipped off the screen and turned back to face me. "Look at your watch. You'll see that you've suddenly lost fifteen minutes of time. That'll prove what I said just happened."

I looked at my watch, which said the exact right time. I think. I didn't know for sure or precisely how long I'd been in his office. And he could have messed with it, anyway. So I bluffed. "Sorry to disappoint you, Dr. Collins, but none of my time is missing. Maybe you need a new battery."

"But what if I told you when you were under what time would appear correct to you?"

I stared at him for a second, not sure, and then he laughed at me, and said, "Got you, Detective."

"Oh, I get it. Shrink humor. Gets me every time." But I was not amused. Suddenly I didn't like this guy, or his perpetual, condescending jokes, and I wouldn't put it past him to pull some kind of dirty trick like he'd just described. On me and on his patients, too. And I didn't like the way he was looking at me now, either. His next words put some nasty icing on that cake.

He said, "Oh, yes, that's right. You're Nicholas Black's newest squeeze, aren't you? You probably know all our professional jokes."

Whoa, fella. All of a sudden he was getting down and dirty, personal, even. I examined him at length and with hard eyes, not liking his description of me but well aware he had chosen his insulting words for a reason. A more pertinent question, though, is why? Baiting me, perhaps? But I couldn't see a good reason for that, not yet. We didn't know each other well enough to feel hatred, but extreme dislike might be in the cards. I was feeling a rising degree of that already.

I bit, just for the heck of it. I said, "The truth, Doctor Collins, is that I'm nobody's *squeeze*, new or any other kind. Now if you don't mind, I really need you to quit playing around and answer my questions. "

"I didn't mean to offend you."

Oh, yes, you did, you big jerk. Our budding relationship

was not off to a tremendous start. In fact, it was cracked in half and going down as fast as the *Titanic*. I was gracious. I said, "No offense taken."

He said, "I can tell that I offended you. I know you're upset with me."

"I don't upset easily. Shall we get started?"

Collins suddenly became Mr. Gentleman Extraordinaire. "Please sit down. May I get you something to drink? I have coffee over there on the counter. Water, tea, soda?"

These Oak Haven docs had a veritable Starbucks operation going on in their offices. "I'll take a bottle of water. It's so much better for your health."

"That's very true. I think I'll have one, too."

Retrieving them from a small fridge just like his cohort, Marty Young's, he handed me one with condensation on the outside. Surreptitiously, I checked the bottle for tampering, not trusting him any more than I did Young. I was thirsty, too, though, so I twisted it open and drank some of it. My parched throat thanked me. Or maybe we'd already had enough of each other and were making excuses not to talk to each other any more. Or maybe it's almost a hundred degrees outside and we're just thirsty. At least we didn't make a toast and tap our plastic bottles together.

"Okay, Doctor, if you don't mind. We need to cut out all this pleasant chitchat and delightful refreshment and get down to business."

Collins grinned at me. I waited for him to round the desk and sit down, the gentleman in me coming out, I suppose, then took a seat on his soft leather couch after he was safely in his chair. I put my Ozarka on the table and pulled out my pad and pen. "You treated Michael Murphy, correct?"

"Yes, ma'am."

I looked up to see if he was taunting me. I couldn't tell. I was pretty sure he was. My *I-hate-your-guts-worse-than-poison* meter spiraled upward in alarming fashion, but I do have overreactions at times, I admit it.

"When did you start Mr. Murphy's therapy?"

"I guess it was about two years ago. Yes, it was almost exactly two years ago."

"Michael would have been around nineteen then, correct?"

"Yes. Your own Nick referred him. We were pleased a doctor of his stature showed such confidence in Oak Haven." He paused. "Are you sure I didn't offend you? I really wouldn't want to think I did. I was only joking around."

I ignored the *your own Nick* crack. Actually, Black referred Michael to Oak Haven at the request of Mikey's parents, who would have done it anyway because of their kinship to Martin Young, but I wouldn't bring that up. I said, "Trust me, okay? I have skin as thick as a walrus. Can you tell me about your initial therapy sessions?"

"Well, we do have confidentiality clauses here at our place. I'm sure you understand that."

"Yeah? Well, we have warrants over at our place. I'm sure you understand that. I can show you one, if you like."

He chuckled, found that marginally amusing, I guess. I stared unblinkingly at him. He was trying very hard to either annoy me or charm me. I was just having trouble figuring out which it was. Why he was going to the trouble was another good question.

"All right, Detective Morgan. No need to obtain a warrant since the patient is deceased. What would you like to know?"

Glad he wasn't going to be as difficult as he was hilarious, I asked, "What was his major problem when he arrived here for treatment?"

"He presented with clinical depression. Apparently because a girlfriend threw him over for a good friend of his. He thought at the time that he was in love with her."

"It sounds as if you don't think he was in love with her?"

"He thought he was. That's what was important for us to understand."

"Did he come here willingly?"

"I think his parents pretty much required him to check himself in. You can ask Dr. Black if he presented on his own cognizance to his practice."

"Thanks, I will. Do you know the name of the girl who jilted him?"

"Her name was Sharon. I'm not comfortable giving you her second name."

"Maybe you should get comfortable with it."

"Richmond. Sharon Richmond."

Well, that sounded like a real name and not one made up off the cuff, so I didn't push it. Maybe I'd get a warrant for all his files, too, and see if there really was a Ms. Sharon Richmond. "Did you ever speak with her about Mikey's problems?"

"Once. Over the telephone. Mikey agreed that I could talk to her, after she moved down to Tennessee. A little town called Dyersburg."

"What was her take on this situation?"

"She told me that Mikey was a really nice guy but they didn't have the right chemistry to make it in a serious relationship. She wanted to move home and live closer to her parents. Mikey didn't want her to be so far away."

"I thought you said she ended up dating his friend."

"Actually, she was seeing his friend first. Mikey asked her out and they were a couple for a few months, and then later she got back with the first guy. He's from her hometown, too. When she went back there, they ended up getting married. Mikey took it harder than he should have. Felt rejected, of course."

"I see. How did he fare under your treatment?"

"He did well. That's why this has come as such a shock to all of us here who treated him."

"Did he get along with his family at that time?"

For the first time, Collins hesitated, and then he turned his gaze out over the grassy lawn, where three boys in shorts and T-shirts were tossing a Nerf football around. A group of girls sat on a concrete picnic table and watched them, waiting for them to get done so they could flirt, I assumed.

Collins said, "Have you ever met Mikey Murphy's parents, Detective?"

"Yes. I had the unfortunate assignment of notifying them of Mikey's death."

"Ah, a very unpleasant task, I suspect."

I nodded but didn't speak.

Collins went on. "He was close to his dad in some ways. He and Mary Fern didn't get along as well."

"Are you aware Dr. Young is Michael Murphy's first cousin?" I asked him, wondering why he hadn't brought that to my attention. It wasn't like it was a secret, or anything.

"That's right. Their fathers are brothers."

"Does Dr. Young's family live around here, too?"

"Yes. They live in Lebanon, Missouri. That's just down the road from here."

"I've been there." Actually, I played a hooker in a prostitution sting at a truck stop there once upon a time and happened to run into a couple of ignorant farm boys who tried to have their way with me and lived to regret it.

"Is that the reason that his parents wanted Mikey admitted here?"

"I suspect so. They're very private with family matters because of Joseph's close connection to the governor. This all happened during the last campaign, and they didn't want it to get out to the press or the voting public."

"It's gonna come out now, trust me."

"Yes, that's probably true. Marty says some reporters have already contacted them. I guess you know how that feels."

"Meaning?"

Again, he looked surprised, as if he didn't realize he was poking a hot fireplace poker into the tender underside of my private life, or at least, that's the way he wanted it to appear. I kept getting this overwhelming notion that he was planning out everything he said, trying to manipulate me or throw me off balance. "Meaning that you've had some high-profile cases lately that plastered your picture in newspapers all over the state. Not to mention the sheer notoriety of dating Nick Black."

"You seem to know an awful lot about me, Dr. Collins."

"No more than anybody else. You're a memorable lady, especially to anybody's who's had the pleasure of meeting you in person."

Steadily, I held his gaze with my own. His eyes were all warm and fuzzy, and yes, he looked pretty silly and flirtatious. I am a direct person, so I said, "Are you coming on to me, by any chance, Doctor?"

Collins then looked taken aback but didn't show it long. "You've a tendency to be rather blunt, don't you?"

"Yeah. Blunt's my middle name."

"Okay, want to know the truth? I'd ask you out for a cup of tea, if I didn't respect Nicholas Black so much."

Wanna know the truth, I thought, I wouldn't go out with you for all the cups of tea in China. Then I stopped a moment and considered why I was reacting to him so strongly and negatively. Then I remembered he was an obnoxious prick.

"Well, I'm very flattered by your attentions, doctor. Now, can you tell me what kind of therapy you practiced on Mikey? Did you happen to use that newfangled gadget of yours sitting over there behind that screen with all the whistles and bells?"

His narrow lips turned up on the edges, which might've been a smile, but this time his eyes didn't follow suit. Oh, no, he probably didn't want to take me out for a cup of tea anymore. Boo hoo, I'm crushed.

"Actually, I did. He was a very good subject for both sound therapy and hypnotherapy. Easily induced into a trance. About thirty percent of subjects are very susceptible to hypnosis, you know."

"And what did you tell him once he was helpless and under your spell?"

"He wasn't exactly helpless and under my spell, but to answer your question, I asked him what was troubling him. In fact, it was a bit of a group effort. Mikey was one of the first patients we used my experimental techniques on. Dr. Young and I usually worked together, and Pete works with us most of the time, as well."

"I see." So Happy Pete was involved, too, huh? I jotted down something to that effect on my notepad, then asked Collins, "Tell me how it works on a patient. Can you, you know, in plain layman's English?"

"Of course. Once Mikey was relaxed and in trance, we would ask him questions about his fears. We mentioned Sharon and left suggestions that she was happy where she was and that he should be happy for her and move on with his life, just as she was doing. It seemed to work. He acted fairly quickly and began dating other people."

"I see. Who did he date? Can you give me a name?"

"Not really. I know he dated several Asian girls who worked in some theater over in Branson. He liked women of the Orient, thought they were beautiful. Can't tell you anything about them, though. Maybe some of his friends here can tell you more."

"How many patients have agreed to talk with me?"

"Just about all of them. Dr. Young and I both actively encouraged them to cooperate with you in any way they could. They were all very fond of Mikey. He was quite popular with his peers."

"Did he have any other friends that might be relevant to my case?"

"Yes, actually, there is a woman in Branson that goes by the name Khur-Vay. She sold him those bracelets he liked to wear. He said he liked her, that she was a good friend, I do recall that."

That checked out with Khur-Vay's story, but she was factoring in this case more and more. I played dumb. "Khur-Vay, you say. That's an unusual name. What can you tell me about her?"

"She was here for a time because she lost custody of a young child and couldn't cope with it, but that was before I came aboard."

His words hit me like a plummeting brick, and I stared at him, making sure my expression didn't change. Again, I was thinking how I'd lost a child, too, not in custody but forever, and so I'd had lots of practice burying those memories, had it down to a science, in fact.

Collins paused briefly, then continued, "She was a different sort of woman than Mikey was usually interested in, a little older and wiser than Mikey, perhaps, but they really seemed to hit it off. She got on drugs, and the court gave full custody of her daughter to her husband and his new wife. She has no contact at all, and she blamed herself, refused to eat, almost perished from starvation before we got her here and in treatment. She was one of the best subjects on our light/sound wave therapy." Looking at me, he went on, "Your little boy died, if I recall from the news accounts, so I'm sure you'll understand how it can tear a person apart."

I stiffened but tried not to show it. People usually didn't come right out and dredge up my broken heart, then thud a pickax into the center of it. I felt the ghost of Zachary coming in hard at me and this time I couldn't stop it. I didn't want to ask the next question. Collins just sat there, as if he knew what I was going through. As if he'd brought it up on purpose to distress me.

"You're telling me Khur-Vay's therapy was successful?"

"Oh, yes, she responded beautifully. She's living a normal life and happily, I believe."

"She's coping now with the absence of her child?"

"Yes, for the last year, or so. She's like a different woman."

"Can you explain how her therapy worked?"

"Well, we gave her helpful suggestions to overcome her despair at not being able to see her daughter, you know, encouraged her to look at the child's pictures and even set them out around the house, touch her belongings, talk about her to people who'd listen and understand. Most mothers find that extremely hard to do, you know. She responded beautifully to Pete. He's a very caring individual."

Inside, I felt a quiver of fear at the mere thought of doing those things with Zach's baby things. I tried to shake off the effect of where this conversation was going, but without much luck.

Collins was still elaborating. "Basically, she needed to just face the facts and accept the loss. Of course, we have our own techniques to help her achieve those goals without undue suffering." He stopped there, and I was glad he did. "Is Khur-Vay also involved in this case?"

"I really can't divulge the facts of our case, doctor. I can say she sold Mikey the bracelets he was wearing on the day he died."

"You are talking about the blue and white beads? I did notice that he began to wear lots of those things after he was here a while. There's some kind of cultural tale behind all that, I believe. I'm sure Khur-Vay could tell you. Do you know where to find her? I think I have her address and could pave the way for your interview."

I wondered then why he wanted to know all that. Almost as if he wanted me to interview Khur-Vay. Very interesting and suspicious, but then again, I thrive on suspicions, that's why I'm a detective. "I can find her if I need to."

Collins examined me with seemingly new interest. "It appears to me that you are doing an unnecessarily extensive investigation for a suicidal death. Is there more to this case than I know about?"

As if I'd tell him something like that. "That seems to be the primary question, Dr. Collins."

"So we're back to formal titles, I see."

"We were never anywhere else, Doctor."

"Again, I hope I haven't made you angry."

"Not at all."

"Good."

I didn't really want to bring up the next subject, think about it, either, but I had to. "What about Cleo? Did you treat her?"

For the first time, Collins looked sad, oh, so sad and morose. "That was horrible. I still can't believe she did something so drastic."

"Not only did she do it, but she did it on live TV."

"I know. I had no forewarning that she was about to snap. She was doing very well."

"Not that well, it seems. Did you use your new techniques on her?"

"No," he said, but his slight hesitation before speaking alerted me that he was probably lying.

"You sure about that?" I said.

"Of course."

I still didn't believe him. "A warrant will include her records, you understand that, don't you? In case you decide to release them of your own cognizance because she's now deceased, too."

"Of course."

"Would you mind to check and see if Dr. Young has a list of the patients willing to talk to me? My partner will come up later and interview them."

"Of course. I'll have Mary give him the list when he arrives."

I stood up. Collins stood up.

I said, "Thank you for your time, Doctor."

He said, "It's been a pleasure chatting with you. I wish I could be of more help."

"Well, you can, Doctor, now that you mention it. You can make me a copy of your office notes and any other information about your treatment of Mikey, including videotaped sessions and therapy files. Especially the light/sound therapy. That would be of great help."

He didn't even look alarmed. "All right. I'll see to it."

"Maybe I could take it with me when I leave. And Dr. Young's files on Mikey as well?"

"It'll take more time than that to get these things together. As for Dr. Young's files, I'll have to check with him."

"I happen to have a warrant right here for all these things. Would you like to see it?"

He gazed at me a moment. "Yes, I would."

I handed it over, and he glanced through it a second or two, then said, "I'll have them faxed to your office or sent by FedEx as soon as they can be gathered and copied. Is that acceptable?"

"That'll be fine. Again, thanks for seeing me."

His phone rang, which gave me an opportunity to steal my bottle of Ozarka and ease myself outta there without further ado. The man had brought up Zach, and he had no right to do that. I didn't want to think about that right now, couldn't. And he'd called me Black's latest squeeze. The guy ticked me off, all right.

Here Comes Trouble

His next project was a guy named Jeff. Jeff was using his real name, and he was a little bit of a smartass. Everybody liked him, though. Even Tee liked him. He was funny, made you laugh, in spite of yourself. Especially in group, but the doctor's file on him said that he hid his pain behind laughter. His major problem was depression, maybe some kind of bipolar disorder. Jeff did have his high moments, that was for sure.

Tee had chosen him because Jeff just loved to smoke weed. Even better, Jeff had a supplier out of the nearby university town of Columbia. Jeff and his supplier would meet out by the tennis courts in the dead of night and make their deals. More important, Tee had found out on the Net and in some of his reading, that cannabis helped intensify the suggestibility in willing subjects. And all Tee's subjects were willing. Dying to be experimented on, even. They were getting mad because he didn't choose them fast enough. Life was so good.

At the moment, Jeff was lying on Tee's bed, holding a roach clip and sucking in the pot with one long drag. He held it in as long as he could, then coughed. He had smoking dope down to an art, all right. It didn't take him long to get high. Tee had his little exhaust fan in the window on reverse and it was drawing out the smell of the marijuana very nicely. The hall nurses rarely checked on him anymore, anyway, since he was such a model patient. He had most of them snowed.

"Okay, Jeff, you ready to start?"

"Yep. I'm feelin' pretty fine."

Tee walked to the door. It was already locked and all was quiet outside, so he turned off the overhead lights. Then he sat down on the edge of the bed. He picked up the strobe light he'd ordered after he'd read about it on the Internet. The World Wide Web was turning out to be just about the best thing that had ever happened to him. Some of the sites he visited were bogus, wannabe psychiatrists and such, sure, but lots of them weren't. Lots of them were based on scientific theory. He'd even found training videotapes and DVDs about how to put people under hypnosis.

His dad had given him a credit card in his own name for his last birthday, and even better, kept paying the bills because he still felt so guilty that his poor son had witnessed so many family tragedies. Like clockwork, his dad brought the whole bunch of siblings out every Sunday to visit Tee, but Tee found he had no desire to return home and live with them. He had his own personal little playground here with his own personal little playmates. Just like he'd seen on the latest DVD he'd watched, Tee said, "Okay, Jeff, I want you to focus your eyes on this strobe light after I turn out the lights."

"You got it, Tee."

Jeff's file said he was quite suggestible, so Tee had some pretty high hopes for the guy. Jeff just might be the break-through he'd been waiting for. Tee was disappointed in his experiments with posthypnotic suggestions, and all four of his attempts had failed. But now, with Jeff, and with the addition of the marijuana, he just might get lucky.

"Lie back and relax, Jeff."

"I can't get more relaxed than this, man." Jeff giggled like a girl.

"All right, here we go. Remember, watch the light. Keep your eyes on it. Don't blink and don't close your eyes."

"Gotcha, man."

The bedside lamp was beside Tee, and he reached over and switched it off, then hit the button on the strobe. He watched Jeff's face in the blinking illumination and the way his pupils were dilated. Jeff was stoned, anybody could tell that, so Tee just sat there and waited. In a little while, Jeff really zonked out and then his eyes suddenly closed.

Waiting a minute or so, Tee turned off the strobe and sat there in total darkness, hoping everything would go down right, for once. He finally said, "Jeff, can you hear me?"

"Mm hum."

"How do you feel?"

"Good."

"Where are you?"

"Nowhere."

"Look around, find a place to go. Someplace that means something to you."

Jeff lay still and did not answer.

Tee frowned. "Where are you now?"

"I'm in the barn."

"What barn?"

"*The* barn."

"Why did you go there?"

"Because it's safe in here."

"How old are you?"

"Nine."

Tee sat straighter. Excitement started welling up inside him, then rushed into his head and almost made him dizzy. He had regressed this kid, by God. Without even trying. Wow, this was gonna be a real breakthrough.

"What are you doing in the barn?"

"Just kneeling down and hiding behind a hay bale."

"You alone in there?"

"Yeah. The others are up at the house."

"What are they doing?"

"Smoking pot."

So that's where Jeff got his love of drugs, Tee thought, not to mention his capacity to use them. "You don't like that, I bet."

"No. They make me smoke it, make me do stuff I don't wanna do."

"Who does?"

"My mom and her boyfriend, Jazz."

"What'd they make you do?"

"Touch them, get in bed with them. I don't like it."

God, what a sick world this is, thought Tee. Even poor Jeff was sexually abused. Was that kind of perversion this prevalent? Good God, it made his house and friggin' family look like the Brady Bunch.

"Do they ever come looking for you?"

"No. I hide too well. And they're too stoned to remember me, after a while."

"Tell me about your mom."

"She's a junkie and shoots whiskey all day. She brings men home and they go to bed, then they give her money and she buys more dope."

"How does that make you feel?"

"It makes me feel like I hate her guts."

Tee leaned back in his chair and thought about the situation for a while. He knew by reading Jeff's file that his mother had died one night while Jeff was with her in the house. He knew by looking at Jeff's wrists once when they were eating together in the cafeteria that Jeff had scars on the inside of his wrists. That seemed to be the favorite suicide method around this place. Nobody was creative anymore.

"Did you try to kill yourself?"

"Yeah."

"What did you do?"

"I took my mom's razor and slit my wrists."

"But you didn't die?"

"That's right. But she did."

"Who did?"

"My mom."

"How did she die?"

"I killed her."

Tee's jaw actually dropped. Damn, he had not expected that one. He could barely contain his excitement. His voice almost shook with it.

"You killed your mom?"

"That's right. I cut her wrists down to the bone right before I cut my own. She didn't deserve to live after what she put me through."

"How come you didn't die?"

"The DFS lady happened to show up because the neighbor lady called and said they were beating me again. I told her that mom had cut me and then herself."

"You're pretty clever."

"Yeah. Nobody believes I have it in me, but I do."

"What do you have in you?"

"Evil. Pure evil. I like it. I liked killing her. I'd like to kill some more people."

Whoa, man alive, was this ever getting good. Maybe Jeff would turn out to be an assassin. Maybe he'd be Jeff the Impaler. Better yet, maybe he'd be Tee's own personal assassin. He thought about that a minute, then said, "Do you really like to kill people?"

"Oh, yeah. It gets me off."

"Then I want you to kill somebody for me. Will you do that?"

"Sure."

A little chill ripped up Tee's spine. Jeff's response to the idea of murder was as cold as ice. Who would've known? Good old friendly Jeff was a killer. But who around here could Tee have him kill? Who was expendable?

It came to him then, and he smiled. "I want you to kill that nurse named Maggie, who's always on my case. You know the one with bleached-blond hair in a ponytail. The one who wears the bifocals with the red frames. She hates my guts, and vice versa. I want you to wait until she goes to the break room at the back of the dormitory building after her shift and picks up her purse and coat. I want you to wait until she comes out of the break room onto that balcony, then I want you to shove her down those steep steps leading to the parking lot. Then it will look like an accident, like she tripped and fell."

"Okay."

And that was that. Leaning back in his chair, he thought about what might go wrong. His studies had alerted him that the experts believed that people really wouldn't do anything under hypnosis that they didn't want to do or was against their moral fiber. This was a real lucky break for Tee. Jeff was obviously a natural-born killer. Jeff wanted to kill, liked it. But would the posthypnotic suggestion work? He decided to give it a trigger, then lay back and see what happened.

"Jeff, can you still hear me?"

"Yeah."

"I want you to kill that blond-haired nurse named Maggie in exactly the way I said when you hear me say the words 'Enter Evil.' You understand me?"

"Yeah."

"And you won't remember that I told you to do this or that you pushed the woman. You must make sure nobody sees you and that you get back to your room and in bed before they find her. Understand?"

"Yeah. No problem."

The purest wave of elation filled Tee, and a sense of the most unbelievable power washed over him. My God, if this worked, and it probably wouldn't, but maybe it would. My God, think what he could do, think how he could control people. This was a gold mine, a gold mine he was going to get rich with. He'd wait awhile, see how Jeff reacted, see if he showed any signs of knowing what he'd been told or any signs of anxiety. If all went well, he'd have the kid kill the lady two days from today.

Smiling in anticipation, he brought Jeff out of the trance.

Jeff said, "So? What happened?"

"Nothing much happened. You did good, though."

"Well, sure, why wouldn't I?"

Jeff rolled over on his side and faced the wall. He went straight to sleep, still drugged up and heavy limbed. Tee got into Buddy's bed and figured out all the details on killing Maggie the Witch. It was rare for an adult not to like Tee because he made it a point to butter them up. But nothing he said or did worked with Maggie. She didn't like him, watched him all the time, in fact, it seemed as if she saw right through him, as if she knew he was always up to no good. And this time, he was, and she was the main attraction.

SEVENTEEN

On the way home from Oak Haven, I found myself taking the long way around, driving down rural blacktop roads north of the lake. Then to my super surprise I was suddenly turning onto the dirt road that led up to Joe McKay's place. Don't ask me why. I sure didn't plan it; it just seemed to happen. The last time I crunched over this gravelly overgrown track, I was with Black in his Humvee, and Joe McKay took off running the minute he saw us, which led us straight to a whole bunch of rotting corpses in black plastic bags. This time I didn't have to worry about that. This time I was more worried as to why I suddenly felt the urge to pay him a call. Funny thing is, I don't remember making a conscious effort to go psychic visiting.

Joe McKay lived in an old farmhouse, but I could see he had spruced it up quite a bit since I last chased him through his cornfield. He had painted it sky blue, of all things. In fact, when I pulled up and cut the motor, he was still painting up on a ladder near the front porch. I couldn't help but notice that he had his shirt off and had been lifting about a million weights, judging by his muscle tone. He had his long hair pulled back into a ponytail at his nape and his dimples were flashing.

As I got out of the car, he climbed down the ladder. A few feet away, in the shade of a large, big-boled oak tree, Elizabeth played in a sandbox. She had on a pink-striped sundress and little white sandals. McKay had cinched up one of his ball caps and set it on her head in an effort to shield her face from sunburn, I guess, but it had two red Cardinals sitting on a bat so it passed muster with me and everybody else in Missouri.

"Okay, Officer, I give up." McKay put his palms on the side of the house and leaned on them, legs apart in frisking position. "Pat me down and make it thorough, please."

"Ha ha, McKay."

Grinning, he turned back and approached my car. He was sweating, his bare chest glistening in the sun. I looked away, considering Black's feelings and the slight jump in my pulse.

"Wow, Detective, I never thought I'd see the day. To what do I owe this pleasure?—and I do mean pleasure. You look sexy as hell with that big police logo on your T-shirt, by the way."

"Yeah, right."

We stared at each other. Both waiting.

He said, "Well, welcome to my humble home. What can I do for you? Or is this just a social call?"

I found out quick enough that I didn't have an answer to that. So I made up one. "I was just in the neighborhood. Thought I'd drop by and see how Lizzie was doing."

McKay laughed. "In the neighborhood? What were you doing? Coon hunting?"

He was right, of course. There was not much going on this far out in the boondocks except dense woods, wild animals, and Joe McKay, who might be considered a wild animal now and again.

"Thanks, McKay, you're making me feel like I'm not welcome around here."

"Au contraire, Detective."

Au contraire? "Getting all fancy on me now, aren't you, McKay?"

"Yep, want you to know how cosmopolitan I am. Learned that on shore leave in Marseille." He smiled and then said, "So? How about a cold beer?"

"Can't. I'm on duty."

"So this is an official call?"

"No." I glanced around, remembering the snow and the wild chase across the fields and all the horrible stuff that had followed over the next few days. "Truth is, I don't know why I'm here. Just found myself turning in at your mailbox and decided to go with it."

McKay's eyes narrowed, brow furrowed. "That doesn't sound like you, Claire."

Surprised he'd called me that, I decided to change the subject. "Nice color on your house there. Bit unusual, though."

"I tried to match your eyes."

"That's lame, McKay."

"Yeah, most of my come-ons are."

We laughed a little. I said, "How is Lizzie? I think about her a lot."

"Well, c'mon and see for yourself. She's talking more all the time. She keeps saying she wants to go see that dog of yours, old Jules Verne. Remembers his name, and everything. I think I'm gonna hafta get her a pooch of her own."

"Hey, that's really great, Joe."

"Yeah. I think she's on the way back. She's gettin' to be quite a chatter bug. Hey, sit down in my new lawn chairs. I got this whole table set on sale at Lowe's for two hundred bucks, umbrella not included."

I obliged and rocked slightly in one of the red and green flowered, comfortably cushioned chairs. McKay reached into an ice-filled cooler and pulled out a bottle of Corona. He dug me out a Pepsi and handed it to me. I took it, cracked the lid, and took a deep swallow. It tasted good, revived my spirits a bit. I watched Lizzie toddle over to her daddy, and he gave her a Pepsi, too. I watched her drink, gripping it with both hands without spilling. She looked at me over the top, but this time she didn't show any reaction.

"Say hi to Claire, Lizzie. You remember her, don't you?"

"Hi. Where Jules at?" She looked at me, as if I had the dog hidden in my purse.

"I'm sorry, baby. I left him at home, but you come to see him soon, okay?"

The child actually smiled. "Okay."

"See what I mean, Claire? Things are gonna turn out all right, after all." Smiling and proud, McKay lifted the toddler up onto his lap, and I watched the dappled sunlight making light patterns across his face and Lizzie's blond hair. And then his little girl became Zach in my mind's eye, and the gushing torrent of pain almost sent me reeling. What was going on with me?

"What's the matter?" asked McKay, pretty observant himself. He looked intently at my face.

Clamping my jaw, I moved my attention out over the pasture, trying to get a grip on myself. "It's peaceful out here. You still gonna pack up and move to Springfield?"

Nodding, he followed my gaze. "I'm set to close on that Victorian next week. I just jumped in and did it. I'm gonna keep this place, too. I grew up here. It's my roots. Lizzie's, too."

Roots. Wish I had some, but I didn't. Wish I had my little boy back, sitting on my lap and drinking Pepsi, too, but I didn't. My throat clogged up thick and squeezed shut. I stood up.

Frowning, McKay stared up at me with a *what-the-hell's-going-on-with-you* look. "Relax, Detective. You're making me nervous here. I do something wrong?"

"No. I need to get back to work. I'm just wasting time out here."

"Thanks."

"No offense. My case is going nowhere."

"Sit down. Give me your hand. Let me help."

Considering him and wondering if that's why I showed up out here, to get a bit of psychic insight. I sure as hell needed it. If he could help me get a lead, it wouldn't hurt, maybe would even help. I sat back down and held out my hand. He took it between his big work-roughened palms and closed his eyes. I knew the drill well. Sometimes he hit; sometimes he didn't.

A few minutes later, he opened his eyes and let go of my hand. "You need to be careful, Detective."

"Oh? What'd you see?"

"Nothin' good. I gotta flash of you struggling in the water and it's dark, nighttime, but that's all I saw. Except, and man, I hate to tell you this, I really do, but I saw a picture of your little kid, clear as day, in a little white Winnie the Pooh frame. And I just now felt lots of tension in your body, too. You comin' down with something, summer flu, maybe?"

Staggered by what he had said, I stared at him and then tried to shrug it off with a joke. "So now it's Dr. McKay? Black nags me enough about that kinda stuff."

"You should listen to him. You might have some kind of health problem. Sometimes that's what it turns out to be when I read this kinda tension."

"Physical or inflicted."

"Either or both, knowing you. How's the foot, by the way?"

I'd gotten a minor gunshot wound in my foot during my last case, another in my shoulder, both not more than nicks. "Both healed up and good to go."

"Good."

"Well, I gotta go. You take care of Lizzie, hear me?"

"She's my life." He'd uttered it simply, and I knew he meant it. He was a good dad, better than most.

"Okay, I'm outta here. See you around."

"Next time, come for dinner. I'll bake you another one of those delicious apple pies."

"You still giving Mrs. Smith a run for her money, huh?"

"You bet."

As I left, he boosted Lizzie onto one hip and carried her up onto the front porch. She was tired, ready for a nap, leaning her head against his shoulder, her little legs hanging down on either side of his hips. More memories flooded me, and I shut my eyes a moment to block them, then fired up the Explorer, turned it around, and got out of there.

All the way home, I thought of nothing but Zachary. The dams and locks I'd built to keep his face buried were being swept away; my defense mechanisms were disintegrating under the onslaught of his sweet little face, the nightmare of him in his tiny coffin, his long black lashes down on eyes closed to me forever, his soft blond curls falling over his forehead, his well-worn blue Winnie the Pooh blanket over him, his little brown teddy bear that I'd tucked under his right arm the way he liked to carry it. And the frame that McKay had described to a T.

And I remembered the dread I felt, the deep, bottomless guilt when I walked off and left him all alone in that vast, grassy, shady, lonely cemetery in west Los Angeles. I'd never been back there since that day; never allowed myself to dwell on him being buried away under the ground. Now I couldn't seem to think of anything else, and my heart grew to the size of a basketball inside my chest.

When I finally made it to my gravel road, I stopped at Harve's and found him in his office. When he saw me, he waved and smiled but turned back to his conference call. He told somebody at the other end to hold just a minute, put his hand over the phone, and then said to me, "Hey, Claire, good to see you. Sorry, got some East Coast clients on the line."

"Hi Harve. Listen, I don't want to interrupt your call, but you know that trunk I left here when I moved in at the cabin? I need to pick it up."

"Oh, yeah, okay. It's in the guest room's closet. Up on the top shelf, I think. You sure you don't want to hang around and have some dinner? I'll be off here in, say, twenty minutes."

"No, not this time. Go ahead with your call. Black's supposed to be waiting down at my house, anyway."

"Okay, if you're sure."

"I'll take a rain check. See you later, Harve."

Harve's guest room was large and painted colonial blue with white woodwork and lots of red and white around. An American flag folded in a triangle was displayed in a glass case above a dresser. It had been on his father's casket when he was gunned down while on duty at the LAPD. His father was as much a hero in that department as Harve was.

I reached up and retrieved the little red trunk, trying not to think about what was inside. It wasn't heavy, and I carried out to the Explorer, raised the rear hatch, and stowed it inside. I'd open it later, if I opened it at all.

A few minutes down the road my house loomed up, and I was super pleased to find Black's Cobalt 360 bobbing alongside my little dock. I didn't see him, though. I pulled into the garage, alerted at once when I didn't hear my little pooch, Jules Verne, yapping his shrill but welcoming poodle yap.

"Hey, Claire! Down here!"

Black's voice came from out in the water, and I saw his head bobbing in the lake, about twenty yards out. Jules Verne's little head was right beside him. That made me laugh, which was what I needed, so I headed down there and strode out to the end of my rather rickety little dock.

Black swam in closer. I could see Jules paddling to beat the band. Luckily, there was a little beach where the dog could climb out by himself, but Black usually boosted him up on the deck. The man loved that dog. What can I say?

Black called to me, "Come on in, the water's fine."

Considering, I smiled because Black looked good with his black hair wet and slicked back, blue eyes glinting with challenge. It was the edge of night, deepening dark, and the water was calm, not a boat in sight and none likely this time

of evening. Still hesitant, I decided it was safe enough to dis-
arm, had second thoughts about that, considering my recent
brushes with Mr. Death, but then began to unbuckle my
shoulder holster. I wound the straps around the holster, placed
it on the dock near the edge where I could get it fast if need
be, then followed suit with the .38 revolver strapped to my
ankle. I unlaced my high-tops and pulled them off.

"Come on, you're stalling," Black called out.

I dove in, fully dressed, and swam under the surface to
where Black was treading water. I came up against his chest,
and he said, "Now this is the life."

"The water feels good."

"So do you." His mouth was on the side of my neck and
his hands were busy unzipping my jeans.

"Hey, I paid eighteen dollars off the sale rack for these
Levi's, and I'm not leaving them on the bottom of the lake."

When he got them off, with not a little trouble, either, he
tossed them up on the dock, then got my T-shirt off even
quicker. It went onto the dock with a wet plop, and our skin
slid together, then our mouths, and finally all the morbid
thoughts of Zach took leave and I thought about Black and what
he was doing to me, and what I was doing to him, and how
good it felt to be doing it in cool water, crickets chirping, full
moon coming up in the night sky behind us, and the two of
us all alone for a change. I went with it, and so did he, and it
was really good.

EIGHTEEN

At 3:30 A.M. I jerked awake out of a horrendous nightmare and bolted upright in bed. Sweaty, afraid, heart hammering against my rib cage, my skin was cold and clammy. I'd dreamed of Zach again. He died in my arms, again, for the millionth time. Gritting my teeth, I pulled the sheet up and wiped sweat off my face. For a few moments I sat on the side of the bed in the darkness, trying to let the overwhelming emotions dissipate and roll off me, but it just wasn't working anymore. Black called them my defense mechanisms, but what had happened to them? Why had they broken down? Lately, all I could think about was Zach, whether I was awake or asleep, in the car, in the office, anywhere. Why now?

Behind me, under the covers, Black slept soundly on his back. So did Jules Verne. The dog was nestled up against Black's right side, stretched out full length, all four paws in the air. Both dead to the world. Glad I didn't have to explain myself, I stood up and remained motionless beside the bed. I let my breaths return to their regular cadence. There was a little whirlpool of nausea swirling inside my belly. Black usually awoke, too, when I had a nightmare, but this time he only mumbled something and turned over, facing away from me.

Picking up my weapon off the bedside table, I carried it downstairs. I didn't turn on the lamps. White light from the full moon flooded through my front windows, misting up the living room and painting skinny slanted patterns across the couch and kitchen cabinets. Outside in the dark night, the lake looked like a brilliant white mirror, slick and calm and beautiful and beckoning. I needed to run, get out the tension. Get some exercise. Fresh air.

I put on some shorts and a T-shirt and my Nikes and strapped the .38 on my ankle with a lightweight Velcro strap, then took off down the beach. I had beaten a trail there on all zillion of my prior jogs, and I followed it in the moonlight, sweat drying on my skin in the cool night air. It was quiet, just the lap of very gentle waves, and I ran to my one-mile point, then turned and retraced my steps. I sprinted the last hundred yards and collapsed down on the grass behind my beat-up picnic table. I stared up through the tree branches at the moon, a great white orb floating in the blackness and knew what I had to do.

The time was right, and somehow I knew it. Tonight I had to do something I swore I'd never do, but I felt a deep, tangible need for inside myself. Maybe if I just did it, walked straight into the house and faced the demons head-on, I could sleep again at night, without the tortured dreams, without Zach haunting my mind, the memory of his baby face and sweet smile shredding bloody strips off my heart.

Pushing to my feet, I opened the garage door and got my Maglite out of the Explorer. The garage was pitch black and silent. Even Jules Verne hadn't sensed my absence and come looking for me. But that's the way I wanted it. I wanted to be alone with this. I had to be.

At the back of the Explorer, I quickly raised the hatch before I lost my nerve. The beam of my flashlight settled on the little red trunk. A chill of foreboding turned my flesh into a blanket of goose bumps, but I took a deep breath and set the light down where it angled on the trunk. I opened the lid. My heart actually shuddered, a constriction so tight and so consuming that I took a step backward away from it.

Steeling my nerves, it took a few seconds, but I finally reached in and picked up the baby blanket lying on top. It was still as soft and blue now as it was the day I bought it. I lifted it to my nose and inhaled the sweet scent of Zach, baby powder, milk, Johnson's baby shampoo, all the wonderful infant smells I remembered with such incredible pain. It was still there, like he was still wrapped up inside it, and I felt tears burn behind my lids for the first time in years. Beneath the blanket were the pictures. Portraits I'd had done in Wal-Mart or Penney's, different ages, six months apart, but only four before he'd been taken from me. I picked up the Winnie the Pooh frame, so perfectly described by McKay, and my throat squeezed shut, and I heard my own low, keening, guttural sound of agony.

When the door to the house suddenly opened and caught me in a swath of light, I was down and snatching my weapon and beading it in on Black so fast that he raised his hands defensively in front of him and said, "No, don't, Claire, it's me."

I began to shake then, all over, head to toe, but I lowered the .38 and let it hang down beside my leg. "Get out of here, Black. Leave me alone."

For one or two beats, there was complete silence, then he said, "Okay."

I watched the door close, watched the darkness swallow me again. And liked it better that way. Tears burned some more but didn't fall. I had learned long ago that I could not let it go that far, not without going to pieces, so I forced them back, swallowed them down, forcibly controlled myself.

So there I stood, alone, gulping breaths, waiting for control to return. But something was different now, something I didn't understand, something I needed to understand, had to. I picked up the trunk and carried it under one arm to the door. Inside, Black was in the kitchen, making coffee. I could smell the strong, fragrant aroma, could hear the drip of the water into the glass canister.

Turning to me, Black leaned a hip against the counter and said, "You okay, babe?"

"Yeah. I'm sorry. I'm real jumpy."

He just nodded and then waited for me to speak, but that was what he always did at times like this, times when I was facing my ghosts and my demons and my horribly dysfunctional past. He wouldn't interfere, wouldn't push his professional judgment on me, much less treatment, but I knew that's what he thought he needed to do. I was grateful that he didn't, that he let me make those decisions, good or bad.

Finally, he broke the silence but nonchalantly, as he filled up a mug with coffee. "So, what's in the trunk?"

"Nothing."

We stared at each other, both aware of that great big, feeble lie, then I moved to the tan suede sectional and sat down at one end. I held the trunk on my lap, both arms around it. He got out another mug from the cabinet over the sink.

"It's got Zach's things in it. The only things of his I kept."

Black drew up in the motion of filling the mug, then put the coffeepot back on its warmer. "I see. It's a painful thing, looking through possessions of somebody you've lost."

No shit, I thought, but I just said, "Yeah." My voice didn't sound like me, sounded like some clogged-up, hoarse, grieving, emotional mother. Embarrassed by that, I looked down, but I didn't have to. Black wasn't staring at me like I was some kind of specimen. He looked out the front windows at the lake as he drank from his cup.

"I didn't mean to intrude on your privacy. I wouldn't do that," he said.

"I know." But I appreciated that he said it, that he seemed to understand, if anybody could who hadn't lost a child.

Still clutching the trunk against my chest, I remained silent, and so did he. He brought my coffee to me, placed it on the table in front of me, then sat down beside me. "Do you want to be alone for a while? Just say the word."

I considered that, then said, "I don't think so."

"I can go back upstairs if it would make things easier."

"No. Stay."

In silence, we sipped our coffee, and then smiled a little as Jules showed up on the steps, looking sleepy and perturbed that we'd left him all alone in the bed. He jumped up on Black's lap, and Black stroked his soft white fur.

Then I said something that I'd never thought would pass my lips. "Would you like to see a picture of Zachary?" Then I added lamely, "My son."

"I'd like that. Yes."

Opening the lid again, I pulled out the blanket and held it protectively close against my chest. I picked up the last photograph I'd had made of Zachary. It was the one in the little white frame with Winnie the Pooh painted around the edges, the one McKay had envisioned. Zach had loved Winnie the Pooh more than anything.

Black took it, and then I was the one who swiveled my gaze out on the moonlit lake.

"He's a good-looking boy," Black said. "He looks like you."

"Yeah." Black had spoken in present tense, not past, and somehow, for some reason, that meant a lot to me. Stupid, I know, but it did.

Sighing, I realized I wanted him to tell me what was going on inside my head. Maybe that was what this was all about. Why was I suffering Zach's loss all over again now, and with jacked-up intensity as cutting as on the day it had happened? Why couldn't I stop thinking about him? What was wrong with me?

I heaved in a deep breath, let it out. Black waited.

"I think about Zach all the time lately. I mean it, Black. I used to be able to keep that kinda stuff locked away, down deep inside in some kind of mental box, but I can't do it anymore. I dream about him every time I shut my eyes. I wonder what he'd look like now, how he would've looked when he lost his baby teeth, if he would've liked going to preschool, how tall he'd be now. I think about teaching him how to swim, swing a bat, be a good sport even when he didn't win, all of those things, everything, all day every day. I can't stand it, not if it keeps up like this."

Black put his hand on top of mine. "Maybe it's just that you're ready now. Ready to accept what happened to him. Maybe this is a good thing. A sign that you're beginning to heal."

"It's not a good thing." Agitated, I jumped up and began to pace. "It can't be a good thing. It's driving me crazy. I can't control my mind anymore. Images of him come at me in waves, over and over, all day and all night. Something's wrong with my head. I know it is. I can't think straight half the time. I can't concentrate on my case. I can't let this go on."

"Nothing's wrong with you, Claire. You're as strong as any woman I've ever known. You know that. You know that you've faced horrible things your entire life, but none of it has broken you. You keep getting up. You keep doing your job. But facing the loss of a child is one of the most difficult things life can throw at you. Some people never accept such a tragedy, never get over it. Some do, in time. I think this is a good sign. A sign you're ready to stop hiding from it and start dealing with it."

I looked back at him. "I'm not ready to deal with it. I hate it. I hate that it's getting to me now, after all these years. Tell me why, Black. Why now? Why all of a sudden am I turning into a basket case?"

"First off, you're not a basket case." He hesitated. "I don't know why you're having this problem right now, but we can talk it through, if you like. Get everything out, stop bottling it up inside. Often that helps things look better."

Turning away, I stood at the window, gazing out at the water, which used to calm me and make me feel normal. Not tonight. I felt a storm roaring inside my chest, ripping its way through my vital organs and down my nerve endings. I wasn't ready for this, but it was happening, whether I liked it or not.

"I don't think I can do this, Black."

"Yes, you can. Let's talk about Zach. Tell me about him."

Black got up, came behind me, put both arms around me, and pulled me back against his chest. I closed my eyes. I should tell him. I should tell him that Zachary was the best little baby in the world, before or since or ever, but I couldn't find the words, couldn't bring myself to utter anything.

Black must've sensed my inability to act because he said, "Do you mind if I look through the trunk? I'd like to get to know your son a little, if you'd allow it."

I nodded and felt his warmth leave me, and I crossed my arms over my chest and hugged my shoulders. When he sat down, I turned and watched him pick up the blanket. "This smells good."

I said nothing.

Black dug out a little blue teddy bear. Zach's favorite thing in the world. He'd had it with him the night he'd died in my arms. There was a spatter of his precious blood on the bear's right foot. I had never tried to wash it out, and I knew it was there and I couldn't throw the bear away, not with part of Zach still on it.

"He's a cute one. Did Zach have a name for him?"

I bit my lip. Tell him. This was good for me or Black wouldn't be doing it. He was a super shrink, after all. "Winnie." I hesitated, swallowed down the lump in my throat. "He named all his stuffed animals Winnie. Every single one."

At that, Black smiled and sat the bear upright on the coffee table. He looked at me. "Why don't you come over here and sit down beside me?"

I shook my head. I was better off to keep my distance,

somehow I knew that. Black picked up a miniature story-book. *The Velveteen Rabbit.* Zach's favorite, too.

"My mother used to read this to me when I was a kid," Black said. "Did you read it to him?"

Every night, I thought, every single night of the world, but I didn't say it. "I can't do this, Black. I can't. Put that stuff back inside and shut it. I need to take it back to Harve's."

"It's good that you brought it home. Maybe subconsciously you knew that."

"Maybe for you."

"I'm talking about you."

"I know that."

We were quiet. Neither of us moved; just stared at each other. Black tried again. "Painful as it is, this is a very good sign, Claire. You've got to think of it that way. Thinking about your son isn't bad. I know it's painful, but it's good. It'll help you cope. End your internal suffering."

Picking up my mug, I took a drink of the coffee, just for something to do, something else to think about. It tasted good. Black had made it strong, and for good reason.

"Was he walking yet?"

I saw Zach toddling everywhere, laughing when he sat down hard on his bottom. I saw him running into my arms when I came off duty, squealing with babyish delight. I couldn't speak. Didn't even try to.

Black was still taking articles out of Zach's trunk. "You kept a pacifier. Was he the kind of kid who wanted to keep it for a long time?"

"I hung it around his neck with a piece of yarn so he wouldn't lose it."

"I guess it got kind of frantic when you couldn't find it for him."

"Yes, but he always helped me look."

"He was a good boy."

"The best." I wanted to tell him more, but there was a niggling feeling inside me that I shouldn't do that, that it would be sacrilegious and a betrayal. I tried to tamp it all down inside, like I used to, and this time, I managed it somehow.

I said, "Let's go back to bed. We've got to get up and drive up to Mikey Murphy's funeral in the morning."

"Yeah, we do. You want me to put this away for you?"

I nodded, grateful to let him pack away Zach's things, while I picked up my weapon and headed upstairs. I snuggled under the covers and waited for Black to come back to bed. I could hear it when he shut the lid and snapped the latches. It sounded like some kind of ending, all finished and done with. But I knew it wasn't done, wasn't finished, wasn't over. The light downstairs went off, and then Black was back, under the black satin sheets with me. He wasted no time pulling me into his arms, and I went willingly.

"I'll never pretend to know how it feels to lose a child, Claire. But I'm here for you in all of this. I'm here to help you figure it all out. I'm here now, and I'll be here as long as you want me."

I didn't respond, didn't say anything, didn't have to, but I was comforted by his words, and the way his strong, hard body felt pressed up against me. We didn't make love but shared the warmth and the intimacy, and it took a long, long time before I finally went to sleep and dreamed again of Zachary, his little round face and big blue eyes, his blond hair with curls in the back that always blew in the wind, his chubby little arms and legs that could run so fast to be so short. There, for a little while, though, in those dark dreams, I got to hold him again and play with him again and kiss his little flushed cheek again, and in my dreams, I could weep long and hard, holding him close, in the way that I could not do in real life, never, ever again, and in my sleep I could mourn all that was gone and all that I had lost.

Here Comes Trouble

On the appointed night, Tee and Jeff sat in some thick hydrangea bushes that hid their presence close to the back of the dormitory. Maggie the Witch always strutted around during her shift on a set and rigid schedule, which made it easier for them to plan their attack. Never changing her routine, she always double-checked to make sure Tee was in his room because she had made it crystal clear to everybody that she didn't trust him or his big smiles. And he was in his bed when she did her second check right at eleven o'clock, but now he wasn't. Now he was ready for payback and lots of it.

Jeff was oblivious to the momentous occasion. Relaxed, his back propped against a nearby tree trunk, he took a deep hit on a joint. Tee had been pretending to smoke it, too, when they passed it back and forth, but he wasn't, of course. He'd experimented some when he was younger, but once he realized that being mentally impaired was bad for his safety, he stayed away from all kinds of drugs, especially now when he was conducting such important experiments. He intended to be in full control of his faculties and able to remember exactly what went down so he could write it all in detail in his secret journals. Jeff was pretty fucked up but not enough to mess things up. At least Tee hoped not. This was a big break-through. If it worked.

Precisely two minutes after her late shift ended, Maggie pushed through the doors of the first floor corridor and made her way up to the staff lounge, where her locker was located.

"Okay, Jeff, listen up. There she is."

"I hate that bitch," said Jeff. "You wouldn't believe the shit she got me into with my doctor, telling them she smelled pot on my clothes."

"Oh, yes, I would. She's vindictive as hell and she hates me worse than anybody else."

Okay, now the time was at hand. Tee was really excited, and he started trying to relax his muscles, which were all drawn up and tight. Okay, here goes. All or nothing. He waited for Jeff to take another hit, hold it inside his lungs for twenty or thirty seconds, and then blow the smoke up into the tree branches above them. Tee hoped the odor of the pot didn't drift on the wind to Witch Woman and alert her to trouble.

Tee took a deep, cleansing breath, and then he said, very low but very clearly, "Enter Evil."

Jeff didn't hesitate. He jumped up and started running across the lawn toward the steep stairs.

"Oh my God," Tee whispered to himself. "This's really gonna work. It's gonna work big-time." He chuckled softly, then raised the night goggles his dad had bought him, sup-posedly for bird-watching at night—God, his dad would be-lieve anything—and focused them on the high landing where Maggie the Witch always took time to smoke a cigarette and unwind a little before she started her long drive home for the night.

Jeff reached the bottom of the steps, and Tee watched him creep up to the top landing and melt into dark shadows lin-ing the wall. Tee shook his head, slightly incredulous that this was really going down and all according to his plan. He was intrigued by the potential of posthypnotic suggestions for immoral acts, but all the literature said it wouldn't work. But it was working. At least so far. But he was nervous. Something still might go wrong. And then they'd both get caught. And that was not good.

Tee's heartbeat sped up when the hated nurse stepped out onto the landing. She put her coat over the rail and took a Bic lighter and a pack of Camels out of her purse, then she walked over to the head of the steps and lit up while she leaned back against the sturdy metal railing. Tee marveled at how predictable some people were. He never did anything in any kind of order, consciously made sure he didn't. The only habit he maintained consistently was his unpredictability.

Maggie didn't see Jeff, of course, and Tee knew that Jeff was waiting for her to finish the smoke and pick up her purse before he moved against her, just like Tee had instructed him. Anxiety and pressure under Tee's breastbone built up until he could barely breathe. This was just possibly the true breakthrough he'd been after. The most efficient way to control people around him, especially ones who had an evil streak in their makeup, and lots of people did. He was finding that out. The way he looked at it was that some people were born for him to use, and anybody else needed to be kicked out of his way, by one method or another. Maggie the Witch was about get herself kicked out of his way. He grinned, pleased by the very thought.

Then it happened. Maggie stuck her cigarette in a metal cylinder of sand, picked up her purse, and headed down the stairs. After she'd got a couple of steps down, Jeff ran at her from the darkness, but then Tee stiffened when he realized it wasn't gonna go down as expected. Maggie the Witch heard Jeff coming up behind her. Half turning, her right hand on the rail, she was holding on when Jeff hit her from behind and shoved her as hard as he could. She did stumble backward and fell about a third of the way to the bottom, but she managed to hang on to the bannister and break her fall. Bad thing was, though, she was screaming her bloody head off the whole time.

Frightened by his miscalculation, Tee jumped up but kept himself hidden in the shadows. Now Jeff was just standing at the top of the steps, staring down at the screaming woman, as if he couldn't quite figure out what had just happened. And Tee hoped to hell he couldn't. Maggie couldn't seem to get up and lay upside down on the concrete steps, but there wasn't anything wrong with her lungs and she shrieked for help over and over to come quick because Jeff was trying to kill her.

It didn't take long for every freaking person at the clinic to rush to her rescue. A couple of orderlies rushed out the door and grabbed Jeff, but he didn't struggle or try to get away. Tee could hear Jeff's voice now, and he was saying over and over, "I didn't do nothin', I didn't do nothin'."

Maggie the Witch was saying different and loud and clear, too. "Jeff tried to kill me! He pushed me off the steps, he tried to kill me, I'm telling you! And if I hadn't been able to hold on to that rail, I'd be dead right now!"

Tee breathed a lot easier then, because Jeff wasn't saying a single word about Tee being in the bushes or that Tee was in on the plot. He didn't remember any of that, just like Tee had instructed while he had him in the trance, and he wouldn't, if Tee were lucky. But anything could go wrong, so Tee needed to hurry up and climb back in his room's window and come out in the hall all sleepy-eyed and confused like all the other kids, just to have a convenient alibi, if he should need one.

Encouraged by his almost success, however, even if it didn't turn out exactly the way Tee wanted, he was glad to see Maggie loaded onto a gurney and an ambulance called out from Jeff City. At least, they'd be rid of her and her constant suspicion and persecution for a while, and that made the whole thing worthwhile. Maybe she'd even end up with spinal damage, or something, and have to give up her job. That would be great. Tee could only hope.

*   *   *

As it turned out, Maggie only broke her hip, something about osteoporosis and brittle bones. She was pressing charges on Jeff, though, and Jeff was denying everything, and so credibly that the doctors weren't sure if it had been an accident or not. So things were turning out okay. There was talk of Jeff having to go to a secured ward at a mental hospital for a while, but that was okay, too. Jeff had served his purpose. Let him serve his time somewhere else. If he ever did come up with the memory of his hypnotism at Tee's hands, all Tee had to do was deny, deny, deny. And he was very good at that. Had lots of practice.

The most important thing was that he was on the right track with his experiments, one that would lead him successfully to his own ends. Mind control. He even loved the words, loved the way they rolled off his tongue. All he could think about was what he could do if he could perfect that art of manipulating others. And there were still plenty of kids around that he could use as his guinea pigs. Someday maybe he could even sell his techniques to other shrinks, make a name for himself. Maybe he could even join the CIA and use his skills in espionage, like in all those conspiracy flicks he'd been watching on cable. Maybe he could work for them, break into the minds of mortal enemies of the good old U.S. of A. Yeah, that's what he'd do. He'd be a huge covert hero of his country. Even the president would admire him and give him medals on the sly.

NINETEEN

The only thing I had to look forward to the next day was Mikey's funeral, and guess what? I wasn't exactly in the mood to attend the services of somebody else's dead son. And there was another funeral coming up, too. Poor little Cleo. Somehow she had gotten to me, even more than the others. She had been so young, so sweet and innocent. Her death had been declared a suicide, but I didn't buy that, not for a single second. Someone had been on that yellow phone of hers, talking to her, egging her on, just like someone had egged on Mikey and Li He, and I was going to find the bastard and put him away if it took me till doomsday.

On top of that, I was emotionally unnerved by this sudden, inexplicable onslaught of grief over Zachary, and the way my mind couldn't handle it anymore. Even with Black gently showering me and my psyche with all kinds of tender shrink love and care, my head was like a black hole, bombarded with morbid thoughts and awful memories all swirled up together and sucked down into my sliced-up bleeding heart. But something about my so-called breakthrough last night must have had an effect; I was functioning again at least and could put my case on the front burner better than I had the last couple of days.

The funeral was held at one o'clock in an old, quaint, but exclusive Presbyterian church in Jefferson City. The building was made of gray granite, two bell towers rising on both sides of the front door and lots of carved stone crosses. The bronze plaque beside the front door said 1914. It was mere blocks from the capitol building and the Missouri River. Black and I stood outside in the fresh air—I was not thrilled with the idea of smelling the inevitable carnation and rose sprays that always permeated such places of death—so we just loitered outside like a couple of well-dressed street people, or at least Black was. He had on a crisp charcoal suit, gray shirt, and darker gray tie, suitably somber and unflashy.

I had on a new, equally staid black pantsuit that I'd broken down and bought at JCPenney since it appeared funerals were going to stay on my future list of *stuff I hated to do but had to so buck up and get it done*. Mourners arrived by the carload, most wearing black, most with dour, pitying facial expressions, and hurried past us and into the long rows of bleached oak pews. I realized the two of us had begun attending a lot of funerals together since we hooked up, actually one of the few formal occasions we deigned to attend, but duty did have a tendency to call.

After a while, and at the very last minute, just after the depressing music faded, we walked inside the church and stood at the open doors that led into the cavernous sanctuary. When the family finally filed in from some kind of side holding room, however, I couldn't help but notice that Mikey's mom wore all white. Looked like some kind of tacky statement to me, oh yeah. Or she thought she lived in China, where white was the in color for funerals. Black knew a lot of the people in attendance, most notably the governor himself, and when Edward Stanton arrived, Black walked over to the side door to greet the great man where he was waiting to make his grand, gubernatorial entrance. I watched the two men shake hands and smile as if they were buddies, then converse in low tones, surrounded all the while by a whole bevy of Missouri Highway Patrol officers and other security-conscious guys in dark suits, much like my own, dutifully pledged to protect The Most Powerful One in the State of Missouri.

When the organ music aka sorrowful dirge dwindled off into hushed reverence, Black skedaddled back over to me, after which we slipped as inconspicuously as possible into the back row, my favorite place at nearly any event. You know, for surveillance, my back to the door for bad guys with knives or blow darts, that sort of thing. The governor was not one for shy, private kind of entrances, however. He strode down the wide center aisle with his security entourage, like he was the real star of the show. I was pleased to find a big white pillar blocked my view of the casket. Trust me, it's better that way. I'd seen too many, and I knew it was open, and that's the worst kind, at least in my book.

The church was dead silent now, forgive the unfortunate pun, everybody somber, still, sick with grief, and a bunch of other S words. A man got up to speak, the first in a long line of friends and family who wanted to say a good word about Mikey Murphy. Fun memories, what a cute little boy he was, how he learned to walk at eight months, how he became a successful businessman, made the best pizza this side of Naples, you get the drift.

After a while, I quit listening and began to observe the people sitting around us, many dabbing at tears with tissues. It was quite a gathering, I decided. Leaning out a bit into the aisle, I located the governor sitting near the family. Now I could see his pretty and well-known, well-groomed, ash-blond first lady, who had preceded him inside earlier, alongside a nice showing of their governmental assistants/secretaries/lackeys/office workers, the number of which verged on Madonna- or Elvis-sized entourages. Governor Stanton's wife's name was Violet, but everybody called her Vi, and she wore a large black hat, the biggest one in the sanctuary. I noticed that Debbie Winters was there, too, sitting three rows back, looking cute in black, of course. Bud should've come instead of weaseling out on me. He was supposed to be looking into Khur-Vay's background, but he was probably still asleep in bed, with a pillow over his head, thereby missing out on the beauteous Deb, so there you go with the early bird gets the worm stuff, not that Ms. Winters is a worm.

Time passed in dragging-an-elephant fashion. Finally, Black leaned very close to my ear. He whispered, "There's a funeral buffet at the governor's mansion after the burial at the cemetery. He asked us to come, and I said we would. Any problem there?"

"No, that's someplace I definitely want to be." Mainly because it would give me an opportunity to go gleaning for information I did not have. I wished again Bud was here because his charm worked really well at these sort of things; he was quite the Lothario at wedding receptions, too. But maybe he was up already and finished with Khur-Vay and off to St. Louis as planned to find the elusive roommate, Melanie Baxter of Fenton, who had not shown up back at MSU or answered any of the voice mails we'd left for her.

Also, Buckeye Boyd was supposed to get hold of me today and tell me if he'd come up with a DNA match from that hair on Li He's hair brush and the one from the deceased girl from the oven, which was taking way too long. The lab also had the melted cell phone from the Cleo crime scene, which I didn't expect they could get anything off, but there was always that outside chance. Then, if Buck came out with some awful, unwelcome news on the hair match, either Bud or I would have to take the trip over to the poor kid's parents' show in Branson and break their hearts, so I heartily hoped Bud got back from St. Louis first and got that gig.

Glad I was seated in the back, I craned my neck until I could see Mikey's younger siblings and found out quick enough they were collectively taking things pretty hard.

Very Mom-unlike. This woman, this mother, was an enigma to me, and an annoying one, for sure, but what did she know about Mikey that no one else seemed to? What was it about the kid that froze her heart into a lump of dirty ice? Maybe that alone could be my afternoon quest? Get Momma Bear alone and manipulate her into spilling her guts. Sounded like something I could get my teeth into. And I mean that both literally and figuratively.

The service ended at long last, and I decided to forgo the full-fledged joy of trudging in a line to the front of the church so I could view the poor boy's remains and stare pityingly at the poor grieving relatives. I'd gone through that horrible ordeal, sat in a similar front-row pew, and looked dead, too, as my fellow LAPD officers and a couple of friends filed past one tiny little white casket with a kneeling gold angel on top. I shut my eyes and fought the agony unlike any other. How could Mary Fern Murphy not feel some kind of grief for that poor boy lying in that satin-lined coffin?

"You okay?"

Black was right there. Oh, yeah, he was watching me like the proverbial hawk. He knew how close I was to the edge, leaning over, even. "Yeah, I'm fine. I just hate funerals. I'm going outside. I need some fresh air."

Black followed me outside, and we stood together in the deep shade of a big elm tree that grew near and cooled the portico of the church. We could smell the cool, earthy dampness of ground moss and the ivy covering the tree trunk. I could hear the distant blare of a boat horn somewhere on the Missouri River, and the noisy chatter of a flock of birds feasting in a wild cherry tree across the street. Mourners began to file out around us, talking together in normal tones now. They headed for their cars to join the funeral procession to the nearby cemetery.

Black and I had driven up in my Explorer; his giant Humvee just didn't fit the bill for a funeral service, being bigger than the hearse, and all. I beeped open the locks, sat down in the driver seat, then flipped open my phone to see if Bud had called. He hadn't. No one had, in fact, which was a bit unusual. Maybe things were running smoothly in Canton County. That would be a nice change.

The drive to the cemetery was not long, and we got out and stood beside my SUV parked on the blacktopped road, rather than walking down the grassy hill to Mikey's final resting place. We didn't say anything or discuss the reasons why, though both of us knew them. We just watched in silence. The governor was standing beside our snowy-adorned momma, his arm around her waist. I thought that was a little suspect, since Mikey's dad was weeping openly and Momma was more than holding her own. Then the governor placed his hand on Joseph's shoulder, too, and all was well.

Finally, about twenty minutes later, we were in the Explorer again and on our way to the governor's mansion for the luncheon. I parked the car about a block down at the curb in front of an old two-story clapboard house painted lemon yellow with an upstairs balcony decorated with white gingerbread trim. Walking back up the hill, we paused briefly to admire the big bronze fountain dedicated to children in front of the mansion, then followed a knot of chitchatting women up the steps onto the front porch of the official residence of the governor of the State of Missouri. It was located next to the capitol building, which was more than handy, I suspect. Red-bricked, Victorian, with a square turret atop the roof, which probably gave a helluva view of the wide and rolling Missouri. It was truly a beautiful old house.

There was security manning the front door. Missouri Highway Patrol officers aplenty, but I didn't recognize any of them. The women in front of us showed their funeral card with Mikey's picture on it, but I just flashed my badge. Just so they'd know. Nope, I wasn't checking my guns, not even for the guv. A big bald guy with muscles good and plenty leaned down and looked my badge over, and then examined my face like I was Lizzie Borden in search of an ax. Then he perused Black's driver's license like he was Jack the Ripper in custom-tailored attire. Black assumed this little peeved look on his face but said nothing belligerent. He didn't get carded often, if he ever had. Most people recognized him, anyway.

Waved inside, we entered what I'd heard was denoted as the Great Hall. It was a hall, all right, and pretty great, too, as far as I could tell. Pale yellow walls, beautifully carved dark woodwork, and shiny parquet floors. The ceilings looked what? About twenty, thirty feet tall, and there was a plethora of antique furniture, including this rather large table surrounded by red tufted chairs in front of a fireplace affixed with a gigantic mirror atop its mantel. You know the kind of chairs I'm talking about, the ones that everybody's scared to sit on. Thus explained the groups of guests standing as they admired the place. Double chandeliers hung from the ceiling and were turned on because the room was pretty dim, and they both had lots of large round glass globes with crystal dewdrops under each one. Yes, ma'am, this was quite the State Palace, all right.

Adopting our awestruck faces, we wended our way through milling people, most of whom had regressed to semilow tones but occasionally burst into laughter that rang in the big room with echoes and made everybody jump. That was something I had trouble understanding, but I guess people think being jovial and laughing uproariously now and then helps the bereaved get their minds off their dead loved one, now lying cold in the ground. Don't think so.

Off to our left we found what seemed to be a library, done in a silky green and gold color scheme. Very Victorian. Another marble fireplace with its own big mirror reflecting an equally large chandelier. There were several antique cabinets full of books, first editions written by erudite Missourians, no doubt. Mark Twain came to mind. There was a couple or two in there, husbands and wives, just looking at everything. The room on the right side of the great hall was a double parlor, of sorts, done with pale rose walls and more red Victorian furniture. Maybe Victorians didn't like any other color on their furniture.

I did like one piece of furniture in there; it was pretty cool, actually, like a round couch divided off into seating areas on four sides. Another chandelier hung over it. I'd seen some of those divided chair things in old Alan Ladd cowboy movies, you know, *Shane*, maybe, in 1800s hotel lobbies, but can't tell you what they are called. Several big gold and white marble columns divided the rooms, and people were actually sitting around in small groups in front of windows sporting elaborately fringed draperies. I still hadn't seen Joseph Murphy or any of the Murphy family. Maybe they went home and said to hell with it.

We headed for the dining room, which Black knew was at the back of the Great Hall, and there we hit pay dirt. The room was big and blue and chandeliered like crazy and mirrored and set with a heavily laden buffet table with every imaginable type of food. Black said, "I'm hungry. Let's get in the line."

Geez, Black was getting as bad as Bud about foodstuffs. Maybe I brought that out in men who hung around me. Actually, I was hungry, too. I hadn't eaten breakfast, or lunch, or dinner the night before, so I grabbed a fancy red and white plate and followed a group of four legislative assistants around the buffet table. They were whispering, and I tried to eavesdrop, knowing that secretary types usually knew all the dirt on everybody in the office, be it governmental or private or sheriff's department. And they knew it first, of course.

"Poor Joseph," said one of them. "He's just not handling this well at all."

"Yes," her friend's voice lowered, which really perked up my ears, "but did you notice Mary Fern? She hasn't shed a single tear, not that I've seen."

"Everybody grieves differently," said a third, the more

understanding sort. There's one in every group. She probably didn't know Mary Fern personally. "Mikey wasn't her biological son, after all, and he did bring lots of trouble down
on them."

I remembered that Happy Pete had mentioned that out at
Oak Haven. Maybe that might explain her lack of emotion.
Then I wondered how many of the Murphy kids were not
Mary Fern's own children or if Mikey was her only stepchild.
I hoped he was. Jeez, Cinderella had a better row to hoe with
her Wicked Stepmom. I forked up a piece of honey-baked
ham, a spoonful of potato salad, a crispy croissant, and some
black olives. Black forked up everything else. We sat down
at one of the round tables covered with white linen and
arranged very close together around the edges of the room.
Good, all the better to eavesdrop that way.

In time, I found the family. They were all sitting together
at a rectangular table set off a little from the others. The kids
were there, sitting mute and red-eyed from crying, some still
sniffling. Joseph sat between the governor and his wife, no
longer crying but looking like he wanted to. Mary Fern sat
on the other side of the governor, all white and composed.
Our eyes met, and she stared at me a second, then just barely
nodded her head in acknowledgment. I had a feeling I was
lucky to get that much.

Black said, "Are you going to try to talk to them again?"

"Oh, yeah, count on it. Especially Mary Fern."

"She's handling it well, it looks like to me."

"Too well, it looks like to me."

"Mind if I sit in?"

"No, but I have a feeling she might mind. She has to talk
to me, but you don't count."

Black said, "Thanks."

A young girl dressed in a uniform of black slacks and a
starched white shirt with a black bow tie swept up to us and
offered us a selection of iced tea, coffee, or a goblet of white
or red wine off a silver tray the size of an extra-large Pizza

Hut Special. I selected coffee; Black opted for red wine. I sipped the hot brew, savoring the caffeine and craving the whole pot, maybe two, as I watched and listened while Black enjoyed the food, which he said was exceptionally prepared. I thought the ham tasted okay but a little too clove-y.

When I got a chance, I motioned over one of the big Highway Patrol security officers standing around and trying to look unobtrusive. He was six foot, graying at the temples, and appeared like he could handle himself just fine. Probably a longtimer who'd earned the plumb governor's detail and got to hang around this very comfortable house all day every day. I presented him my badge, explained my deal, and asked him to approach Mary Fern and ask her if she'd be willing to talk to me for a few minutes before I left. He said he would be delighted to be of service. I wasn't sure if he was being sarcastic or not, but he did smile, so I guess he wasn't.

Watching the officer move toward her, I expected her to get angry or freeze up in an even harder glaze than usual. Surprisingly, she listened to him, looked across the room, and nodded in the affirmative. She spoke softly to the guy and when he came back to our table, he said, "She said she'll talk to you, but alone, just the two of you, up in the ballroom after the children are finished eating. But she told me to tell you that her husband is just not up to another interview, not yet."

"Okay. Sounds good. Where exactly is the ballroom?"

"Third floor. She said she'll seek you out when she's ready and show you upstairs."

Well, now, Mary Fern was awfully familiar with the governor's mansion. "Thank you very much."

The man nodded and moved away.

Black said, "Well, at least, she's being cooperative."

"Or pretending to be."

"You suspect she's got something to do with this?"

"I'm not saying she put the noose around Mikey's neck, but she's the type who could've driven him to do it."

Black glanced over at Mom again, new interest in his eyes, like she was a rare, homicidal butterfly he'd caught in a net and was looking at through a magnifying glass. I wonder if she sensed there was a huge, magnified blue eye looking down on her. He had gazed at me like that now and again, like I was his newest head case, especially when we first met, sometimes he still did, like last night in the garage and this morning over coffee.

"Looks like you're outta the picture again, Black, just like at Khur-Vay's place. The lady wants to deal with me, up close and personal and one-on-one. Probably doesn't want witnesses when she cusses me out."

"You are wearing your weapons, right?"

"Yep. All of them. I'll be safe. I'm bigger than she is, anyway."

Black smiled at that but then a good-looking young thing with flat-ironed, ultra-straight red hair who happened to be sitting at the table on his other side touched his sleeve. "Pardon me, but aren't you Nick Black, the psychiatrist who's on *Larry King* so often?"

Black nodded in the affirmative but looked a bit wary. "Yes, I am. Have we met?"

"No, but I can say I really enjoy listening to you on television." She tossed that fiery mane and her big brown eyes added, *At which time I stripped you down to the buff and played out all my secret sexual fantasies with you.* You see, I'm observant that way.

I stopped listening to their conversation, getting used to women admiring Black's sex appeal, I guess. Just so she didn't touch him, I'd be cool. They were now chatting about her weird uncle Sammy, who was bipolar and threw boiled peanuts at her cat, so the conversation wasn't exactly one so titillating that I had to hang on every syllable. I leaned back in my chair and observed in my keen-eyed, policewoman way. Mikey's brothers and sisters were talking some now but they all looked white and haggard and like they were living in a horror movie. I needed to talk to them, too, maybe the two oldest ones, but I doubt if Mamma Mia would agree to that. Unless they weren't her biological kids like Mikey, then she probably wouldn't care if I traumatized them or if they hung themselves under a bridge.

My observational endeavors ended after about eleven minutes, to be exact, because I started watching the big antique clock swing its pendulum at 3:30 P.M. Not that I'm a clock-watcher but at precisely 3:41 P.M., Mary Fern Murphy approached me in a rustle of white linen. Leaning down close, she gave me a dose of Red Door perfume and said, "Are you ready, Detective Morgan? Vi's given us permission to retire to the ballroom."

"Okay," I said, the easy-to-please detective but nowhere close to retiring.

TWENTY

The ballroom was on the third floor and Mary Fern didn't even look for the elevator but took the stairs, three long flights of them, to be exact, and at a clip that was impressive, if not ridiculous. Mary Fern obviously wanted to get this done and rid herself of the pesky police person dogging her. She was in pretty good physical shape, too, probably had a personal trainer and everything, but hey, I wasn't breathing hard, either. We didn't say a single word on the way to the top, didn't smile warmly at each other, didn't hold hands or kiss cheeks or share ditties, either.

When she led me into the ballroom, I was mightily impressed. It was vast and massive with another set of pricey antique furniture. She walked over to a table and some chairs and sat down. Wondering if that was allowed in this museum, I sat down two chairs away from her, not that I didn't like her, or anything, but sitting that close to ice might give me a brain freeze.

Mary Fern said, "Now, in here where it's quiet, we will have some privacy."

"Yes, it does looks that way," said I.

"I know you don't like me, I can tell." Gazing at me, she dared me to reject that naughty notion.

"Not at all." I realized she could take that a couple of ways, and I did mean it the worse way, so there you go.

"I know you don't like me."

Hey, didn't she just say that? "My personal assessment of you, Mrs. Murphy, isn't the issue here. I want to find out who killed your son and why, because I'm not convinced he was alone under that bridge."

"Stepson," she corrected quickly.

Now she tells me. And alas, she had no comment on my theory that Mikey was murdered. "Yes, I am aware that Mikey was not your biological son."

Mary Fern looked down at her hands. Her fingers were long with nails painted a pearly pale pink, manicured to perfection. I wondered if they were real or applied by an expert manicurist. I'd bet on the latter. She wore a large black-faced watch with a black leather wristband. She had on a big diamond wedding set that sparkled under the chandelier like all get-out but no other jewelry, not even earrings. Her ears weren't pierced, either. Her hair looked great, lots of layers, all precision cut, every single hair in place and highlighted beautifully.

"I gave him every opportunity, I really did, Detective."

"What do you mean by opportunity?"

"To be a member of our family. To fit in with the other children."

"I see." I got out my pad and pen, set them on the table, which always gave me a second or two to think of ways to harpoon her. "And he couldn't do that to your satisfaction, I take it?"

"He was a strange boy, haunted by things, I guess, just a very different and disturbing kind of individual."

"Disturbing in what way?"

"He did things. You know, hurt people on purpose, was generally a bad influence on my own children."

"How many of them are yours?"

"The three youngest are mine. The other three are Joseph's with his first wife. Plus Mikey."

Poor Mikey, even now an afterthought.

"Do any of your other stepchildren disappoint you?"

"No. None of them display Mikey's rude behavior."

"You said he was a bad influence? How is that?"

"He was a terrible role model in every conceivable fashion. He hurt them."

"By that, do you mean physically?"

"Sometimes, but he always blamed it on accidents. I hate myself for saying these things about Mikey, now that he's gone, but I can't help it. You want the truth, and I want to give it to you. I couldn't stand him, detective, I really couldn't. Before when you and Detective Davis were questioning me, I couldn't tell you the absolute truth, not with my husband sitting right there listening to my every word. He loved that boy, did everything he could to make him grow up and act responsibly. But nothing he did helped, nothing."

I watched her face. Now it was actually emoting. That was progress. "Were the two of you, Mikey and you, openly antagonistic?"

"Sometimes, it just couldn't be helped. He was a constant irritation in my life, from the moment I married Joseph. He was like a thorn under my skin that I couldn't work to the surface and dispose of."

Nice way to describe a child. Mary Fern wasn't gonna get Mother of the Year with this kid, uh uh. "Did Mikey ever get into serious trouble?"

Mary Fern presented me with a look that could only be described as wry and patronizing. "Not that his father couldn't get him out of."

"And you're talking about . . . ?"

"Well, one time he stole some money out of my friend's house when we were there for a dinner party. Georgia's husband caught him up in the master bedroom, going through their bureau drawers."

"And the police weren't called?"

"No, Joseph handled it. Smoothed it over and blamed it on Mikey's breakup with his girlfriend. That's when we finally made him go to Oak Haven."

"And he improved at Oak Haven?"

"Yes, or I guess he did. Everyone thought so, or they wouldn't have let him out, I suppose. I never believed it, not for a single second. Not since he tried to drown our baby kitten once in the swimming pool. I was shocked and appalled and never trusted him again."

"You saw him drowning a cat?"

"Well, I didn't really see it, but I saw him hanging around the pool just before the other kids found the kitten struggling in the deep end."

"So you didn't actually see Mikey do it?"

Omigosh, such offense rising in her patrician face, such disbelief that I had questioned her veracity. She also huffed. "No, but I know he did it."

"Okay."

"I hope you believe me. Nobody else ever seems to."

I decided to change tacks. "Okay, Mrs. Murphy. Let me ask you this. Do you believe your stepson committed suicide? As I said, I'm not sure he died at his own hand. I think maybe he was driven to it, maybe even helped along the way."

Her answer was immediate, her expression unswerving. "No, I don't, and I never have. I think somebody killed him for something terrible he'd done to them. Probably one of the drug dealers he hung around with."

"Can you give me their names?"

"No. They all went by street names."

"Do you remember any of their street names?"

"No. But when I realized he was dealing and having these low-life bottom-feeders come to our house, to my house where my other children lived, that's when I asked him to get out and find someplace else to do his dirty business. I will not have drugs exchanged on my property in front of my own children. And for once, Joseph agreed."

"Others have reported that he seemed to do better after he opened his pizza place."

"Yes, better, but I don't know how much better. Like I said, and I'm sorry to say it, I really am, but I never trusted him."

"What about his girlfriends? Would any of them have a motive to kill him?"

"I don't know. I refused to meet them, so he never brought them around after he left."

"And you never met a girl named Li He?"

"No, never."

I wrote some of this down, thought about it, realized I wasn't getting much out of her except vitriol venting about the young boy she loathed in a gargantuan manner. "Is there anything else you'd like me to know? Anything you don't want to say in front of your husband or children?"

"I just want you to know that Mikey wasn't normal. Something wasn't firing right inside his head. He was depressed a lot and had these bursts of anger sometimes that really frightened me. And once, the worst thing—"

She stopped, and for the first time looked more than a little hesitant. I watched her face, saw the conflicting emotions flicker inside her eyes like forked lightning in the night sky. It took a long time for her to decide if she was going to tell me, but she finally blurted it out, voice low, eyes downcast.

"There was one time, just after he turned eighteen. Joseph was on the campaign trail with Ed. It was really late, well after midnight, when Mikey dragged in. All the other children were sleeping."

I waited some more. This was coming out hard. I wasn't sure if I wanted to hear it, either, but she went on, and I had no choice.

"He came up to the bedroom and told me he wanted to

say good night but he wanted more than that. He'd been drinking heavily. He reeked of alcohol and some kind of drug he'd been smoking."

I cringed, pretty sure now I knew what was coming. I was right.

"He came on to me, sexually, I mean, and when I refused, he pushed me onto the bed and got on top of me and held me down. He said he loved me, was in love with me, all kinds of awful things like that. He tried to kiss me and rip off my robe, but I slapped him in the face, and he slapped me back, hard. I'd never been slapped in my life, Detective. I panicked then and managed to fight loose and lock myself in the bathroom. I was terrified."

For good reason. Now, finally, I had a good reason for her hatred of her stepson. Providing her story was true, and there was no other witness to the alleged attack except for Mikey Murphy, and he was dead and buried. "Did you call the authorities, Mrs. Murphy?"

"No, I heard him get in his car and squeal the tires all the way down the driveway."

"What about your husband?"

"I told him about it, but he said the boy was just drunk. That he'd talk to him."

Well, that was big of him. "And did he?"

"Yes, of course, but Mikey denied every word of it, and nobody else was awake that night to verify my side of the story. All I had to prove it was a little bruise on my cheek."

Thinking it interesting that she denoted it as *her side of the story*, instead of the truth, I jotted some more notes, my mind racing. I just didn't know where it was going, was all.

I said, "That must have been very difficult for you."

"Lots of things in my life have been difficult for me. I despised Mikey after that and made sure we were never alone in the same room, but it was harder to forgive my husband for blowing off the fact that his son had attacked me in my own bed."

We stared at each other for a long moment. I could hear the traffic outside, and a squirrel chittering to his bushy-tailed friends high in a giant tree right outside the window. Mary Fern was right, that was one hell of a difficult thing to overlook. I looked for tears and subdued emotion, but her eyes remained dry. On the other hand, her eyes held mine in an honest, unblinking gaze that didn't usually lend itself to lies and damned falsehoods.

As our eye lock continued, she said, "I was afraid he'd try to molest my girls. I couldn't allow that. I didn't sleep easy until he was out of our house and into that psychiatric hospital. I thought the doctors there could help him. Especially his cousin. They were always very close friends. Mikey looked up to him, I think. They became even closer after they worked together at Oak Haven for a while. He told us he thought Mikey was going to be all right after he bought the restaurant and settled down a little. He said the girl Mikey was dating then was also a resident at the clinic and was good for Mikey."

"I see. You are talking about Martin Young, right?"

"Yes, Marty's a nice man, really wanted to help Mikey get well. I hope you believe me, Detective. I am telling you the truth, I swear to God." She waited for me to reply, but I didn't, because nearly all the people I interrogated swore to God, so she said, "I suspect Mikey made lots of enemies among his drug addict friends. And again, I agree with you, I don't believe he'd ever commit suicide. That was my husband's biggest concern, that Mikey would kill himself rather than go on living, but I don't think Mikey ever even considered it. He was very self-absorbed and egotistical. It was his good looks and intelligence. He always thought he was smarter than everybody else."

Somebody must've been smarter than him. Somebody who managed to kill him and pass it off pretty damn well as a suicide by hanging.

Mary Fern waited for the next question, the picture of cooperation now, but my cell phone rang and interrupted us. I pulled it out of my red crocodile bag, flipped it open, and read the caller ID. Buckeye Boyd at the coroner's office.

"I'm sorry, Mrs. Murphy, but I've been waiting for this call. I'm gonna have to take it."

Standing up, she smoothed her skirt down over her hips and said, "I really need to get back downstairs and be there for my children. Some of them are taking this awfully hard. Could we finish this later?"

I wondered if she planned to be there for all the children or just her own. "Yes, of course. I think I've got all the information I need at the present time. I'll call you and set up an appointment, if I think of anything else."

"Thank you, Detective. I hope you understand me a little better now."

Yeah, but so what?

"By the way, that's a nice bag you've got. It's Hermès, isn't it?"

"Yeah, thanks."

Yes, Mary Fern was well versed in expensive designer bags. Why wasn't I surprised? After she turned around and headed across the vast polished floor, I punched on. "Buck?"

"Yeah, it's me."

"Hold on for a sec, will you?"

"Sure."

I stood and waited until Mary Fern disappeared into the hallway and then I moved to a window overlooking the lawn. About thirty people were outside, milling around, carrying plates and cups or goblets. I didn't see Black; he was probably still counseling the ditzy redhead with the crazy uncle.

"Okay, now I can talk. What'd you get on the girl?"

"I got something, but you probably won't like it."

"Well, that's nothing new."

"We ran tests on that hair out of the hairbrush and compared it to the one I took from the charred body."

"Yeah?"

"It didn't match. Your victim is not Li He."

"You are kidding me." Yes, I was stunned.

"That's what I said, too. I don't know who she is yet. There's always the possibility that someone else used her hairbrush, but all the hairs in the brush were identical, which makes that a remote possibility. Did you verify the brush was hers?"

"Yes. It was inside her room, and her roommate, Dee, identified it as hers. Did you find anything else?"

"The vic's Asian. She's definitely young, but her DNA did not match anything in the database. I got a fingerprint, but it's probably distorted by the burnt skin. You might be able to use it in AFIS. I'm working on the report right now. Want to come by or should I fax it to your office?"

"Fax it to Black's office. I'm in Jeff City, but I'll be back at Cedar Bend later tonight. I'll go over it then. Damn, I thought we had her ID'd, and now we're back to square one."

"'Fraid so."

"What about Mikey?"

"Death was caused by a ligature around the neck. Asphyxiation. He died from the hanging itself."

"That all you have?"

"Yeah. But I've still got the girl from the gasoline explosion to do. I'm not gonna find much on her, I can tell you that in advance."

"Okay."

"Gotta go. We're busier than hell down here. Good luck."

I gave him Black's fax number, and about the time he clicked off at the other end, I saw two kids I recognized immediately as members of the Murphy clan standing at the other end of the ballroom.

Walking toward them, I said, "Hello. Can I help you?" Or can you help me was a better way to put it.

"Yes ma'am," the girl said. She looked down the hall behind her. She was nervous, and so was her brother. My gut was telling me big-time that whatever they had to say was going to be useful to the investigation. They hesitated some more, looked at each other uncertainly, but it was the girl who was the designated spokesperson. "I'm Mitzi Murphy, and this is my little brother, Robert Murphy."

"I'm not either little," said Robert.

Truth was, he was little, both in stature and in age. He looked about twelve. His sister looked about sixteen or seventeen. She ignored his comment. "Mom doesn't want us to talk to you. She said it'd be too hard on us. She called your sheriff and told him that she didn't want us kids interviewed about"—she hesitated, looked away—"about, you know, what happened to Mikey."

Her eyes filled up. So did her brother's. They had loved him, no doubt about it.

"I'm really sorry about your brother."

They said nothing, so I said, "It's a tough thing havin' to go through something like this at your age."

"Yeah," said Mitzi.

"Maybe your mom's just trying to protect you from the pain of talking about your brother." I suggested it, but I didn't mean it. Mom was as cold as Frosty the Snowman's carrot.

"Maybe, but she's awfully strong. She didn't even cry when she told us about it."

Lo and behold. Why wasn't I surprised? I bet the woman had never shed a tear about anything, except maybe a broken fingernail. "Do you have something to tell me, Mitzi? Something important to the case?"

"I dunno. I just know I want to help you figure this out. Daddy said you're a really good detective and that you'd crack this case wide open in no time flat."

"You sure you want to do this?"

Both nodded. "All right, let's sit down and talk a minute, okay?"

Once we were settled, I looked at the door to see if Guard Mom was coming for me. She wasn't. "When was the last time you saw your brother?"

"The weekend before he, well, died."

This conversation was very stressful for them, and getting worse. It was written all over their young faces. They hadn't learned how to hide their emotions yet. Maybe the Ice Queen was right, maybe they shouldn't be talking about it. "Where was this?"

"At his pizza place. We'd drive over to his pizza place whenever we could and hang out with him and his girlfriend. Mom didn't like us being around him, though, so we had to sneak over without telling her. We didn't really lie, we just didn't tell her."

"Why didn't she like you being with him?" As if I didn't know.

Robert spoke up then. "She said he'd made lots of bad decisions and caused the family embarrassment it didn't need. But Mikey wasn't that bad. He was always real good to us. Gave us free pizza and Cokes. Took us down to Bagnell Dam and let us play at the arcades. It was fun."

"What was his girlfriend's name?"

"Li He. She's a Chinese girl, and real nice, too."

My heart sang. Everything had pointed to Li He being our vic, but now she was not and I didn't have to tell these two nervous, grieving children that she was dead, too. All I had to do was find her, which was suddenly high as a kite on my agenda.

Mitzi said, "Yeah, she's really nice and pretty, too. Real little, you know, petite. She barely comes up to my chin. Mikey's just crazy about her, or was, I mean. She's gonna take this real hard when she finds out. Have you told her yet?"

I shook my head and took a right turn in subject. "I haven't interviewed her yet, but I will. Did the two of them get along well together?"

"Oh, yeah, they're in love. Li told me she was gonna marry him someday, but that he hadn't come right out and asked her yet. She said that when he did, she would find a preacher real quick before he changed his mind. Yeah, we were real pleased because we weren't sure Mikey'd ever get over Sharon." Mitzi grinned slightly, but it faded away soon after.

Sharon Richmond, I presumed. "And who is Sharon?"

"That was his very first girlfriend. You know, his first true love. They dated for a long time. After they broke up, she went back to Tennessee and got together with this other guy. I think she even got married to him."

"What was Sharon's last name?"

"Richmond."

So far so good; all was checking out. "What was her new boyfriend's name? Do you remember?"

She shook her head. "I just know Mikey wanted to kill himself when she left." Stricken, she realized what she'd just said.

I changed the subject on a dime. "Li He goes to school at Missouri State, right?"

"Yes ma'am. She's a sophomore over there."

I said, "Where did the two of them meet?"

The kids looked at each other again, debating on whether or not to tell me, I sensed from their reticence. Mitzi said, "They were both patients at the same time up at the Oak Haven Clinic. They met there."

"Why was Mikey admitted there?"

"He just wasn't ever the same after Sharon left him. That, and sometimes, for no real reason even, he'd just get real down in the dumps and upset about his life and the way things were going without Sharon, and then he'd lay in bed and say he hated himself and everybody else and Sharon most of all. He was always fighting with Mom and Dad, and they were always picking on him and telling him he was a messed-up kid, especially Mom."

Robert said, "Yeah, they told him he was a bad influence on the rest of us kids, but he wasn't."

"A bad influence in what way?"

Mitzi said, "They said he smoked pot and got himself in trouble all the time and we'd all start doing it, too, if we hung around him."

"But everybody does that, sometimes," said Robert. He blushed then and looked guilty as hell.

I said, "Well, it's not a good idea to use drugs of any kind. It'll screw up your life and land you in jail, or worse."

"We don't do it. Uh uh."

I wondered about that, with their mother to live with, and all, then I said, "Well, I guess I don't have to arrest you."

They laughed, but it sounded real jittery. They weren't quite sure how to take me. I looked at them, each in turn, trying to assess what was really going on here. They had gone to all this trouble for a reason but were reluctant to spill it out. I wanted to know what it was. I am Detective Straightforward so I said, "Okay, let's hear it. What do you have to say to me that caused you to climb all those steps out there?"

More indecisive looks. I just waited. They wanted to spill the beans; they just had to drum up the nerve.

Mitzi finally stepped up to the plate. "Mikey said he thought somebody was out to get him."

Okay, Lord amercy, now we're talking. "When did he tell you this?"

"That last weekend when we were in a booth down there eating pizza."

"What else did he say?"

"He said he felt like somebody was watching him and he'd seen somebody following him."

"I guess he didn't say who it was or why it was happening?"

"No, he just said he didn't really see them, but he just sensed it. Li was with us, too, and she said she'd had the very same feeling. She got him a bunch of those blue and white bracelets to protect him."

"Evil-eye bracelets, right?"

"Yeah, that's what she called them. You know about those?"

I nodded. "So he was pretty upset about that, huh? Had he had a break-in at the pizza place, anything like that?"

"No, I don't think so. But he was always saying that too many friends in his therapy group died, and he was afraid he was gonna be next."

I said, "He has a lot of friends who died, patients at Oak Haven?"

"Yeah. See, it was a group for kids like that, you know, kids who were saying they felt like killing themselves. Some of them tried it, too. Mikey said the same thing sometimes, usually to my mom, that he wanted to die, stuff like that, but I don't think he ever really would've done it."

Robert said, "Yeah, once I started crying when he was saying that kinda stuff up in his room when he still lived at home, and he came into my room later and told me he'd never do it really, he was just talkin' trash to Mom. He said not to worry, and then he promised me he wouldn't. He put his hand on a Bible and promised to God, he wouldn't."

The boy welled up again, and this time tears ran down his cheeks. I put my hand on his shoulder. "It's okay, Robert. Cry if it makes you feel better. This is a real bad thing that happened to your family."

I turned to Mitzi. "Do you remember who his doctor was? Up at Oak Haven?"

"Yes, his name is Dr. Young. He's our cousin. But Mikey saw a lot of those doctors out there."

"Did Mikey ever talk specifically about Dr. Young? Say whether he was a good doctor, or not? Anything like that?"

"They were pretty good friends. Mikey said Marty always sat down and talked to him when he needed him to vent about Mom and Dad, and stuff. Li liked the doctors up there, too. She told me that they helped her understand how she felt."

"Do you know why Li went there?"

"Mikey said that she threatened to commit suicide if she

had to go back to China after her parents finished their stint in that acrobatics show over in Branson. She wanted to stay here with Mikey and get to be an American citizen. He said he'd help her and get her a lawyer, and all that."

"Did your parents know that he was going to help her stay here?"

"Oh, no, they wouldn't've liked that, either. They didn't like Li, or Mikey going with her. They wanted him to marry somebody more suitable."

"Li is suitable," said Robert. "She's real nice."

It looked to me like Robert and Mitzi had turned out okay, despite their bizarro parents. When we finished up, they hurried back downstairs before their mother got wind of where they had been, and I just hoped they would get through this tragedy, because they were both hurting inside big-time and it wasn't gonna go away. Believe me.

About two minutes after they fled, Black showed up in the doorway and looked around the ballroom.

"Not exactly shabby up here, is it?" he said.

I walked toward him. "Get tired of the redhead and her uncle?"

"Fairly rapidly. I was making sure you didn't take off without me."

"Now, would I do that?"

"You have, if I recall."

"Only in emergencies."

"I'm ready to get out of here. What about you?"

"More than ready. Did you pick up anything interesting downstairs?"

"No. Nobody mentioned Mikey much. They all talked about what good people the parents are and that they didn't deserve this to happen to them. Mikey didn't come up in any conversation I was privy to."

"That seems to be the consensus. Wonder where all Mikey's friends are?"

"My guess is they're locked up at Oak Haven."

I realized then that none of them had shown for the funeral. Not Doctors Young or Collins. Not Happy Pete, not the inmates. That was a little odd, but everything about this case was a little odd, if not a lot odd. We exited the mansion quickly, walked to my Explorer, and got the heck out of there. For once, I was going to be pleased to contact this girl's parents, or maybe Bud would get that pleasure. This time we had good news. This time I got to tell them that their daughter was not dead and burned to a crispy crunch. Unfortunately, I also had to tell them I didn't know where the hell she was, either.

Here Comes Trouble

Tee began to study his books and search the Internet more intensely. He was hungry for new methods of mind control and brainwashing. He was obsessed with it, and very pleased by all his success. As a beginner, he was doing quite well, really. He could make all his flunkies do just about anything he wanted, any time he wanted, and nobody was ever the wiser. Not even the trained psychiatrists running the place could figure out why everyone's conditions were deteriorating. Most of his friends now had been prescribed mood-controlling drugs. That made Tee their only real success case at the moment, and the doctors damn near doted on him and his progress. They weren't exactly Einsteins, either, that was for sure.

One night around three in the morning, Tee hit the jackpot when he happened on a man in one of the psychiatric chat rooms he frequented. The man was from China and an expert in the field of indoctrination. They exchanged e-mails often, and Tee eventually earned his confidence by way of extreme regard and constant compliments. That's when the guy e-mailed him copies of some of his experiments with extreme mind control techniques, many of which were not legally recognized. He was a Chinese scientist who worked with prisoners and dissidents inside Chinese prisons, the people that Yang Wei had told him about so long ago, and apparently had been given permission to do anything he pleased by the government. He didn't share everything, said he was afraid of what would happen to him if he did, but Tee read all his writings and read his one published book, which was an obscure little pamphlet he'd written while in graduate school. It was enough to propel Tee into high gear.

He was hooked and intrigued and encouraged, and knew his life's purpose. When he finally decided to let the doctors know he was okay, he left the clinic and his worshiping co-horts and went to the best university he could find with a good program of psychiatry. He reveled in all his courses, psychology and aberrant psychology, and then specialized in hypnotherapy. He obtained his degrees quickly, and found it easy to do with his high IQ. He worked hard to get all the de-grees and diplomas he needed as quick as humanly possible, and all the while, he continued on his own top-secret experi-ments in mind control. He gradually got better and better at it, and then one day, he was offered a spot at the very clinic where he had gotten his start. How perfect could it get?

It was great. He loved it. He was looked upon as the au-thority of leading-edge theory in hypnotherapy and group therapy and was given access to nearly every patient's file. Things couldn't have been any better if he'd ordered them off a favorite things menu. Then a couple of his experiments went all wrong. His subjects began to question his methods, began to spy on him. Then one day everything went to hell when they stole some of his secret tapes. He had to get rid of them, and that wasn't the hard part. He had already had them both under hypnosis and had implanted the necessary trig-gers. They both offed themselves, just like he'd planned, one by hanging, one inside a timed oven, which was a nice, unique touch that burned up all the evidence in one fell swoop. All was well after that, except for the fact that he never found the tapes they'd stolen and worse than that, the police became involved. That's when he met up with one very slick female detective. He hated her intensely almost at once. She reminded him of Maggie the Witch, although she was a helluva lot better looking.

It didn't take Tee long to realize that this woman was smarter than the other people he'd screwed around with, and that she obviously suspected him of some major wrongdoing. So slowly he began to plan how to knock her out of his way before she really did uncover all the things he had been doing. First off and after their first meeting, he researched her on his trusty, invaluable Internet. And whoa, mama, she had some kind of sordid past. She had to be a loony tune case extraordinaire inside that pretty little head of hers. According to the news stories, there were lots and lots of dead relatives and other traumatic events strung out along her life's path, lots of gruesome cases, so there had to be lots of pent-up anger. She was a dream come true for an evil scientist like him. When he'd found out she'd lost her only child, a little toddler, the die was cast. He knew he had her.

And he searched and planned and got to her when she least expected it. Tricked her, slick as a whistle. She had come in to the clinic to interview them, and he watched her poke around the place through a well disguised two-way mirror. She was obviously intrigued by his revolutionary techniques and asked around with lots of questions about how they worked. That's when he got her. It was so easy; a lot easier than he'd expected when dealing with a woman as strong willed as she was. He offered her something to drink, an innocent enough gesture, and she accepted a bottle of water, as if she'd been cued.

What she didn't know was that he had injected a syringe of sodium pentothal for use on one of his young patients that he was experimenting on. Little Miss Policewoman was a goner now, and never even had a clue that he'd managed to implant a number of false memories and worries deep inside her mushed-up brain. Most effective by far was the suggestion that she should dwell on the death of her baby boy, and that she did. Second, he'd gotten another kid to commit suicide at Bagnell Dam, which would be a major distraction for her and another case on her desk. It had been spectacular, too. He'd watched Cleo blow herself up on KY3. Man, it rocked.

Best of all, though, he implanted a very good way to get rid of Miss Detective for good and forever. If she got too close, messed up his plans too much, all he had to do was give the trigger and she'd be dead and gone. And, if he was any judge of character, she wouldn't give up until she nailed him. So he would just have to nail her first.

TWENTY-ONE

The big digital numbers on the clock on the bedside table showed 3:30 in big green numbers. Blinking away sleep, I reached out, turned it toward me, and peered blearily at it again, just to make sure I was reading it right. What was with this three thirty crap? It seemed every time I looked at a clock it was three thirty. Black slept beside me, but this time we were in his gigantic bed in his gigantic penthouse at gigantic Cedar Bend Lodge, and I wished I was asleep, too, because it didn't take two seconds before Zach's face came barreling down the darkest corridors of my memories and blasting into my brain. Okay, get up, think about the case, figure it out, add it all up, forget about Zach, forget about wondering why he was constantly on my mind now, after so many years of lying dormant and repressed under a misty shroud inside my soul.

Man, Black was really out of it, and he should be after the wild and uninhibited lovemaking we enjoyed earlier that evening. Certain parts of me were still tingling. Yes, we dug each other considerably. You'd think our sexual spark would diminish after time, but it was only getting stronger, roaring up into bonfire levels, in fact. But that was definitely a good thing.

Black didn't move, even when I sat up on the side of the bed, and I knew he had a long day tomorrow with patient rounds and several important business meetings and a transatlantic phone conference or two, and that's the primary reason we stayed at his place instead of mine. So I eased carefully out from underneath the black satin sheets and tried not to disturb him. Jules wasn't in bed with us, which was a little odd, but sometimes Jules was an odd little dog. I didn't hold it against him, though. He likes to explore Black's palatial digs; it had more nooks and crannies than my cozy little cabin on the lake. And the furniture was softer and had plusher fabrics with names like chenille and damask. Jules is French, you'll remember.

Both autopsy reports, the one for the oven female victim and the one for Mikey Murphy, had come in on the fax before we got home from the funeral, and I'd skimmed through them and didn't find anything that jumped out at me and solved these bizarre crimes. Poking one arm into my robe, I picked up my Glock 9 mm and headed downstairs. Sorry, but even in Black's security conscious, super-protected hotel, I didn't go unarmed. You just never know.

I found Jules asleep, perched atop a pile of velvet tasseled pillows, to be exact, and he didn't particularly like the fact that I was switching on lights and disturbing his slumber on that very soft and luxurious black velvet and damask sofa. He got up, yawned, stretched in dramatic fashion, made a couple of rounds on the mound of said pillows, then plopped down, shut his eyes, and gave a put-upon sigh. I wondered what Zach would have thought of the funny little dog, then was sorry I did. My baby would have loved him, loved playing with him, loved everything about him, just like Lizzie did.

I found my way into Black's immense, luxurious kitchen with all its shiny stainless-steel everything and lustrous cherry-wood cabinets and black granite counters, went over to a fridge that would hold, say, about six months of food for a military Antarctic expedition. I leaned on the opened door and stared at the bottles of water, not the Ozarka that we used at the sheriff's office and that I'd found so plentiful at Oak Haven Clinic, but some hoity-toity brand imported from some super, and no doubt especially clean and clear, creek in the high meadows of the Alps. I figured that's where it came from by the bearded yodeler in lederhosen on the label. There were also lots of bottles of apple juice, orange juice, pomegranate juice, which is really yucky, believe me. Where the hell did he keep the Pepsi? I could call downstairs to the restaurant and have them bring me up a cold six-pack, but hey, I wasn't going to rouse the night shift just because I was thirsty for a soda. I'd make do with healthy stuff, just this once, since I had to.

I grabbed a small bottle of V-8 juice, twisted the cap, and dribbled some into a white coffee mug stamped with the Cedar Bend logo. It tasted good and cold and healthy. Maybe this would make up for the twenty-one days I'd gone without eating vegetables. Black liked fruit and vegetables, had even brought over a fruit basket to my house. It was still sitting on the counter with the yellow cellophane shrink-wrap intact. Black worried too much about my stomach and vitamin intake.

Switching on the fancy track lights over the shiny black kitchen table, I sat down and spread out the two autopsy reports in front of me. Maybe I'd missed something. The crime scene photos were not pretty to look at, none of them. Especially the female vic's. We were back to square one on that one, and I wondered if my new friend and suddenly potential suspect, Khur-Vay, might be able to help me out. She seemed to know the Asian population of Branson, each and every one and by heart. There was something about her that bothered me, but I couldn't put my finger on it, especially since I had liked her initially. Usually, I could pick out jerks and murderesses and dislike them from the first second—not so in her case.

I read through both reports once, then twice, then three times, because I still wasn't the least bit sleepy. I wondered if Bud was having any luck with his end of the investigation and started to dial him up, then realized what time it was. The thought of Bud made me hungry, so I got up and walked over to the counter. There were lots of large glass apothecary jars full of snacks. Black liked snacks you could pick up in your hand and toss in your mouth. Unfortunately, most of them were healthy and thus unpalatable to me. I looked at flavored rice cakes and grapes and pecans and trail mix and then I zeroed in on the Oreos and packages of M&M's and miniature Snickers all thrown together in one big jar at the very end, just for me, no doubt. Okay, now you're talking, nothing better than chocolate after an eight-ounce dose of celery and tomato juice. A sugar fix was called for, all right. Maybe it'd cheer me up.

I dumped a whole pack of plain M&M's into my palm, tossed back a couple of them, and heartily enjoyed the taste of one of my favorite things. I do love my M&M's, almost as much as my Snickers. I looked up when I realized Black was standing at the kitchen door.

"I heard your phone ring," he said. "Something else happen?"

"No, you didn't. My phone didn't ring."

"The phone rang. It woke me up. You answered it. I heard you."

"No, I didn't. You must've been dreaming."

Black frowned and looked annoyed, so I held out my hand with the M&M's as a peace offering. He was cranky; he just woke up. I could be understanding.

"No, thanks, I don't need any. I feel fine."

I had to laugh at that one. "Well, I don't need any either, but they sure taste good."

Black said, "What the devil are you talking about? And

how many of those things are you going to take? You must have one doozy of a headache."

We certainly were not connecting on the same wavelength here. I tossed another piece of candy into my mouth. "I'm in the mood for chocolate, what can I say? You know I always eat the whole pack."

"What chocolate?"

"Black, get with it. Splash some cold water on your face. "

When I picked up another M&M, Black grabbed my wrist and stopped me.

"You've had enough, Claire."

"For God's sake, Black, give me a break here. So I like freakin' M&M's. Since when are you the food police?"

"What the hell are you talking about? Those aren't M&M's, they're the Darvocets I gave you for pain, and you're taking too many."

"Darvocets?"

He took my wrist and held my palm toward my eyes. "Yes, Darvocets. Your hand is full of them."

I stared down at my open hand, shocked to see the small white tablets piled inside my palm. "Where'd those come from? What happened to the candy?"

"There's no candy, Claire. What the hell's the matter with you?"

We stared at each other a long, silent moment, then he turned my hand downward over the sink. I watched the pills bounce on the bottom of the shiny stainless-steel sink. Black ran water over them. "You planning to take the whole bottle and check out, or what?"

"I thought they were M&M's, I tell you. They tasted like chocolate."

Black said, "Who was on the phone?"

"It didn't ring."

"Why are you saying that? I heard your cell phone ring. I heard your voice talking to somebody, just a few words, and then you hung up."

Laughing a little, I shook my head, but it wasn't much more than an uncertain chuckle, believe you me. This little episode was freaking me out. "I don't understand."

"Me, either. But I can tell you one thing, M&M's sure as hell don't taste like Darvocets. Let me see your phone."

Handing it over, I leaned against the counter and watched him punch up recent calls. "The last call is from an unknown caller."

"What?"

"It says the call came in exactly six minutes ago."

"You're kidding me, right? This is some kind of joke."

"Not even close."

I took my phone back and thumbed in the last call. I took a few paces away, a bit unnerved, oh yeah.

"So what's going on?" Black asked me again.

"I don't know. I just woke up, at three thirty again, as a matter of fact, which fits into this *Twilight Zone* episode, and came down here to look over the autopsy reports."

"And you don't remember the phone ringing or taking those meds?"

"No, I don't. It didn't happen."

Black came around the counter and picked up the bottle full of Darvocets he'd given me when I'd had that gunshot wound in my foot. I hadn't taken them because I hated taking any kind of drugs, but I'd kept them in my purse, just in case. He shook the bottle, then opened the top. "Well, it doesn't look like you took very many, not with the ones you had left in your hand. It's still almost full. I guess we won't have to pump your stomach."

I decided to make light of this until I figured it out. I grinned. "Well, that's good to hear. They ought to take care of any aches and pains I have till I solve this case."

Black decided to make dark of it. He frowned. "This is not normal behavior, Claire."

"I've never been a normal sort, true, but this is a little freaky, even for me."

Black sat down on one of the high mahogany and black leather stools and stared at me, or maybe it was a glare. Yeah, it was definitely a glare.

I shrugged. "Hell, if I know, Black. Maybe I was sleepy and not paying attention and picked up the wrong thing. I'm distracted by the case and was concentrating on the reports."

"Yeah, that's a good theory, except for the fact that we don't have any M&M's right now, and you said Darvocets tasted like chocolate. I have a pretty good idea what might be going on with you, and it's not good. I don't like it."

"I don't like it, either, but go ahead and hit me with it."

"You're acting like somebody who's been hypnotized."

I smiled at that one. "Come on. I've never been hypnotized, ever."

"What if you just don't know it? You've heard of posthypnotic suggestions, haven't you?"

"Well, sure, that's what Collins's book's about, but there's no way. I would've known. I'm not stupid, Black, and I won't even let you put me in a trance."

"Think about this, Claire. If I hadn't heard the phone and come down here, you might've eaten that whole bottle of pills and never even known you'd done it. It's the only explanation."

"I am not hypnotized. That's downright stupid, impossible"

"Tell me about your meetings at Oak Haven. That's their whole thing out there. Did any of the doctors do anything strange or have you do anything unusual?"

"No, of course not." Hesitating, I said, "Well, you know about Collins's new play toy, you know, the one with all the lights and sound waves."

"You interacted with that?"

"Yes, but not long enough to be put under. Trust me, I'd know."

"It doesn't take long."

"Why would he do that?"

"Claire, you're still not seeing this for what it is. You could be dead, if I hadn't come to check on you when I did. You could've died from an overdose of pills, and we would've called it an accidental overdose or a suicide."

I began to see the whole picture then, and it didn't have roses coming up in it. "He wouldn't have the guts to try this. Not on a police officer."

"Yeah? Think again. And just wait till I get my hands on that sonofabitch. If he did something like this, I'll have his license and make sure everybody in the United States knows he's a fraud and a quack. And then I'll beat the holy hell out of him."

"If this's true, which I still don't believe, what could he have done to me?"

"Remember that movie I told you about, Claire, *The Manchurian Candidate*? There's two of them, an old one with Frank Sinatra and a new remake; both concern brainwashing and hypnotism and making patients commit murder."

"I haven't seen them. Bud liked the new one, I remember. Denzel Washington's in it, and he's Bud's favorite actor."

"Damn it, Claire, forget Denzel Washington. This smacks of mind control, pure and simple. The Chinese have been researching this kind of stuff for decades."

"The Chinese? That fits in with my case pretty good. My God, is that how they got Mikey to hang himself? And the girl in the oven, that could explain why she climbed inside like she did?"

"Yeah, true to all, maybe. They've been experimenting out there with all sorts of untested drug and light/sound therapies. It's difficult, if not impossible to do. It's unlikely, but it's the only explanation for what just happened. I'm more concerned about you and how this affects you. If he was able to control your mind, having you do something like this to yourself tonight, he might be able to make you do anything he wants."

I frowned, still skeptical of the whole scenario. "I still can't believe it. This could've been an accident. I might've just been sleepy and got mixed up. Can you prove he messed with my head?"

"I don't know. I'm more concerned that you did these things and don't remember and are trying to pass it off as something else. What if it happens again and I'm not around to stop you?"

I sat down, no glib answers for that one. "Come on, Black, this is all just a little too far-fetched to believe. You know good and well that nobody's gonna hypnotize me without me knowing it. I was very careful not to stare at his light box too long. I wouldn't fall for something like that."

"About a third of the population is highly suggestible. You might fall into that group. Another third is fairly suggestible. Another is unlikely to go into a trance at all."

"Trust me, I'm behind door three."

"This is not funny."

"I know."

"There are whole shows in Las Vegas centered around this kind of thing. Entertainers who pick audience members out of the crowd and make them do stupid but harmless things. There's a show in Branson that does that, too."

"Really? Then maybe I ought to put them on my suspect list and check them out."

"I want to see if I can put you under and deprogram you, if necessary."

I shook my head. "No way. I'm not going under hypnosis."

"You don't have much of a choice. If he got to you, he may succeed next time he decides he wants you to kill yourself."

"Well, that's putting it pretty plain, Jane."

Waiting, he said nothing.

"You're really serious, aren't you? I can't believe you think he could've manipulated me like that."

"What harm can it do to let me see if I can find out? All I want to do is see if you can remember more about what happened when you were out there. What he did to you, if anything. Maybe he didn't, maybe I'm wrong, but why take that chance? Think about Mikey. Think about that poor girl in the stove, whoever the hell she was. We wondered why she would put herself in that oven, didn't we? Well, she wouldn't, not unless she was programmed to think it was something else."

When I didn't jump at the chance to let him enter my mind and putter around, he added, "I can film your session with me, and you can see and hear exactly what I say and what you say. You trust me, don't you?"

"Yes, but I know he couldn't've done it. There wasn't time. I remember every single minute I was there. And I was watching his every move because I didn't trust him."

"Claire, let me do this. What harm can it do? We'll see just how suggestible you are."

"This is crazy."

"Humor me. It might save your life."

"Why would he want to kill me?"

"Because you're getting close to uncovering that he's using mind control on the patients out there. If he was behind Mikey and the two girls' deaths, you can put him away forever. If he's making people commit suicide, that's first-degree murder."

"You've been a shrink too long, Black. Nobody's gonna get into an oven and burn themselves up because some doctor gave them some kind of posthypnotic suggestion."

"I've read plenty of studies in medical journals that say just the opposite, depending on the drugs used and temperament of the subject."

Hesitating, I shook my head, unable to believe it. "How come I've always heard that nobody could be hypnotized without their consent?"

"That's right, that's the general consensus, but they can

make people do things that they think are innocuous. You didn't think you were killing yourself with those pills. You thought you were having your favorite chocolate candy."

As much as I hated to admit it, it was beginning to make sense. Even more important, it lined up pretty well with my case. And as much as I hated being a guinea pig, I needed to know if it were possible. And if I trusted anybody, it was Black.

"Okay, but I'm telling you that you're wrong this time. Maybe he got into Mikey's head, and those girls, too, but he couldn't have done it to me. I was just there once and not for that long. And I was very careful."

"If he could make you take those pills, he could also make you forget what happened, as well as what he said to you under hypnosis."

"No way."

Black didn't answer; he just held up the pill bottle.

"Okay, but don't do anything funny when you're inside my head."

"Come on. Let's make sure I'm wrong and I'll rest easier."

"This is ridiculous."

"We can do it in my office. I've got cameras already in place."

Ten minutes later, I was sitting in a chair in Black's plush office waiting to play some hocus-pocus with him. He sat down in a chair just across from me.

"You are trained in this, right, Black? You aren't going to turn me into a Muppet or a nymphomaniac, or anything?" Smiling, the joke fell flat. Neither of us were in a happy-go-lucky mood.

He didn't crack a smile. "The latter's not a bad idea. Maybe you ought to try to relax. You're as stiff as a board."

"I'm as relaxed as I'm gonna get. Told you I'm not made for this kinda stuff."

"Okay. Just stare at the light above you and listen to what I say."

"This is so gonna fail."

"Listen to me, Claire, block out everything else, hear only my voice."

"There isn't anything else. Maybe you should turn on the radio, or something."

"You're not trying."

"Okay, but don't blame me if I fall asleep."

"Just do it, Claire."

Sighing, heavy and resigned, too, because this really was ludicrous, and I don't mean the rapper. I listened to his deep, soothing voice and all that silly stuff about how relaxed I was, how loose my muscles were, etcetera, etcetera, blah, blah, blah.

When I woke up, Black was sitting where he had been. I was relaxed back into the chair, so I sat up.

"I told you. Didn't work, did it?"

"Yes, it did. You're highly suggestible. Sorry."

I stared at him but I believed the serious expression on his face. "You mean you put me under?"

"That's right. But I didn't get much out of you. Do you want to see what happened?"

"You bet I do."

He walked to the DVD recorder, got out the disk, and put it in a player on a big-screen plasma television behind his desk. I watched the film come on and then I was sitting there while Black was doing all that soft, sweet, soothing talking to me. Suspicious, I listened as he asked me my name and where I was born, all of which I answered correctly. I stood up and walked closer. Now this was just weirder than weird.

The camera stayed focused on me, but I could see Black's legs and hear his voice. He went through more of the relaxation stuff then after a while, he said, "Are you comfortable, Claire?"

"Yes," I said, but I didn't remember that question or answer.

Wonderingly, I looked at Black. "I don't remember that."

"You're under big-time. Watch."

Onscreen, Black said in that same very low, gentle voice. "I want you to go back a few days ago, go back to the day you are visiting the Oak Haven psychiatric clinic."

"Okay," I said on the screen.

I shook my head. "Man, this is making me nervous."

Black was speaking again. "What did you do first?"

"Bud and I went in and asked to see Dr. Young."

"Was this the only time you were there?"

"No, I went out there another time."

"What happened the first time?"

"We held some interviews."

"With whom?"

"Dr. Young and Happy Pete, and then Cleo and Roy."

"Did one of the doctors put you under hypnosis?"

On the film, I was silent. "I don't remember."

"Think back. Were you ever alone with any of the doctors?"

"I don't remember."

"Was Bud with you the whole time you were with Dr. Young?"

"I don't remember."

"Did he ask you to look into any kind of lights?"

"I don't remember."

"Did he give you any kind of drugs?"

"I don't remember."

"Did he tell you not to remember."

"Yes."

"Who told you not to remember?"

"I don't remember."

I looked at Black. "Oh, my God."

Black's voice sounded again. Sounded angry now. "What about your second trip to that clinic? Did anything happen that time?"

"I went alone. I didn't like Boyce Collins. He came on to me, wanted to ask me out for a cup of tea."

"Really?" said Black's voice on tape. "What did you say?"

"I asked him if he was coming on to me, and then he said he'd like to take me out, but he knew I was with Black."

"Good. Did he do anything unusual during the interview?"

"He explained his theories with the pulsating colored lights and sound waves."

"Did he ask you to help him demonstrate?"

"I don't remember."

"Did he tell you that he would call you and tell you what he wanted you to do."

"I don't remember."

"Did he touch you?"

"He put his hand down my shirt and fondled my breast."

I gasped and jerked my gaze to Black.

Black hit the pause button and said, "Yeah, and I'm going to make that bastard pay for that the next time I see him."

Facing Black, I shook my head. "That can't have happened. I'd never have allowed that to happen."

"I hope to hell it didn't. Unfortunately, we can't prove it, one way or another."

"This is unbelievable, Black. I cannot believe any of this is happening."

"Hypnosis can be very disturbing and dangerous in the wrong hands. Now all we have to do is prove he's doing this kind of stuff to his patients."

"Do you think it's Collins?"

"Yes, but it could be Young. You never said which one of them. They'd blocked that out of your mind. Who knows, it might've been both of them. They've always been thick as thieves."

"You think he films his victims?"

"I'd be very surprised if he didn't."

"I'll get a warrant, and we'll have them."

"Based on what? This tape? I don't think any judge is gonna sign off on it. You don't remember enough, and what you do say doesn't really mean anything."

"I want to hear the rest of it. Hit Play."

Refocusing on the DVD, I listened to myself speak, supposedly while in a trance.

"Did he tell you to think about your son and dwell on his death? About Zach?"

"I don't remember."

My jaw dropped, and I knew then this all was making perfect sense. I put my hand over my mouth and watched the screen.

Black said to me on the tape, "Claire, listen carefully to what I say. I want you to forget anything any doctor has told you to do, other than myself. Just go back and remember what they said and erase their instructions from your mind. If you receive a phone call and hear their voices, or any voice telling you what to do, you will hang up the receiver without listening to them. You understand me? You will never do anything they ask you to. Do you understand what I'm telling you?"

"Yes."

"Okay, I'm going to bring you back now. I'm going to count backward from ten, and when I reach one, you will open your eyes."

I watched it happen, shocked to my deepest core. Flabbergasted, I was.

"Will that last stuff stop me from doing anything to myself or anyone else?"

"I hope so, but I can't guarantee it. I can't guarantee anything. This is very dangerous stuff they're messing with."

"I said I couldn't remember. Maybe that just means it didn't happen."

"Maybe. Maybe not."

"You're scaring me, Black."

"You ought to be terrified. You need to find a way to search their homes, if not for this, then for something else illegal. Find a reason, anything. If we can get hold of tapes where they manipulate you or their patients, you can nail them for malpractice, if nothing else."

"I can do that."

"Do it soon."

I sat down and stared at the dark screen. This fit very well with certain aspects of my case, but proving it was going to be damned near impossible to do.

"I'm going to get that pervert," I said, anger clenching my teeth as I realized just how vulnerable I was, if this turned out to be true.

"And I'm going to help you, if I don't kill that guy with my bare hands first."

I glanced at Black to see if he was kidding. He was not kidding.

TWENTY-TWO

The next afternoon Black had an emergency with a patient in counseling at Cedar Bend. He didn't like having to leave me on my own, but he had to, and Bud was in Fenton seeking out Dee's third roommate, the elusive Melanie Baxter. I didn't tell Bud about what happened last night with the Darvocets when we talked on the phone, hadn't wanted to think about it myself, but it was pretty much controlling my every thought. The Darvocets I'd taken had ended up giving me a pretty deep and dreamless sleep when Black and I had hit the sack again. Still, I was nervous and unsettled about the state of things, so I decided to go to the office, sit at my desk, and spend the afternoon surrounded by a dozen or so other armed sheriff's deputies, while I went over every fact we'd uncovered, which didn't amount to a whole lot.

Most of the guys knocked off around six, and the station was practically deserted after that, except for the night duty guy on the desk. When it began to get dark outside, I switched on my desk lamp and wrote up more reports on the Mikey Murphy murder investigation, knowing Charlie was two seconds from yelling at me for not turning it in. I also read through Cleo's autopsy report, for really fun reading. It didn't take long for me to decide that if our three victims were murdered by one of their doctors, that someone sure hadn't left any incriminating evidence lying around for me to trip over.

The evidence box was tucked out of sight under my desk, and I took out the plastic bags with Mikey's personal effects inside them. My eyes focused on the unknown key in its plastic evidence bag. I got it out and laid it on the blotter in front of me. I stared at it. Nobody knew what lock it fit. We'd done the research, had asked every single person I had interviewed who might have been privy to that information. Nada. Maybe I should just start going to every bank, every bus station, every gym or fitness club and start trying it in the lockers. It beat sitting here wondering about it. I put it in my purse, if worst-case scenario came to pass.

My cell phone began to sing, which made me jump, afraid a psycho doctor was calling. I grabbed it and flipped it open, hoping it was Bud with some kind of good news concerning Li He's missing roommate. It wasn't. Caller ID said M. F. Murphy. Icy Dearest was on the line. Great.

"Claire Morgan."

"This is Mary Fern Murphy."

"Yes, ma'am. What can I do for you?"

"You said to call if I heard anything, or if anything else occurred to me that might help you in your investigation."

Okay, I did say that. "Yes, ma'am."

"Well, I don't know if this will be of any value to you, but I did recall something I heard a couple of weeks back that might be helpful. Maybe not. It concerns one of my son's ex-girlfriends. The one who dumped him and started all this."

Ears perked, I sat straighter. "And that would be Sharon Richmond, right?"

"Yes, how did you get her name?"

"I'm sorry, but I'm afraid I can't divulge information like

that, Mrs. Murphy. But I am very interested in anything you might have to tell me."

"Yes, I suppose you are. I understand the investigation is more or less stalled."

"I wouldn't say that. We're working very hard to get the facts."

"I didn't mean offense."

Right. "Yes ma'am."

"Well, it's not much, just a tidbit, and I got it just by chance. I was getting my hair done. I go to Cyd's Hair and Nails, because she's the absolute best around, and while Cyd was styling me, there was a lady at the next station getting her hair highlighted. She and her stylist were talking about the kids in their own children's high school graduating class and what they were doing now, and she said that she was in Branson and ran into Sharon Richmond. That took me completely by surprise, since I thought she had moved to Tennessee a long time ago."

That took me by surprise, too. "I see. Did she say where she saw her?"

"Yes, apparently Sharon's got a shop there, a weird kind of place, she said. With lots of incense and candles, items like that. That girl always was a little on the peculiar side and into drugs, too. I was glad when she took off and left Mikey alone."

I'm not going to say it. No, I won't. Oh yes, I would. "Despite the fact that she broke your son's heart and put him in the psych ward?"

"Well, of course, I didn't like that part of it."

"Did you get the address of this shop, Mrs. Murphy?"

"You know what, I didn't think to. Besides I didn't wish to appear as if I were eavesdropping."

"I see."

"But I did catch the fact that she's going by a different name now."

Was I gonna have to pry the facts out of this woman? Where was a crowbar when I needed it? "And that name was . . ."

"Khur-Vay. Whatever that means."

Whoa. Now this was some information I could dig a shovel into. "Khur-Vay? You sure that was the name, Mrs. Murphy."

"Yes, Detective. I'm positive. Who could forget a name like that?"

Not me. But our little Miss Khur-Vay must've forgotten to mention she was Mikey's former girlfriend, a fact I never would have even considered. "Thank you, Mrs. Murphy. You've been very helpful. I'll check this out immediately."

"Well, I do want to help in any way I can. Joseph's not handling this well at all. He hasn't been back to work, but Ed's been very understanding."

"I'm glad to hear that. If you should think of anything else, please give me a call."

"I certainly will."

We hung up and I dug Khur-Vay's card out of the bottom of my purse. No home address or phone number, but it did have the number for the belly dancing studio. Punching in the number, I waited while it rang six times. Then a voice recorder answered in Khur-Vay's distinctive voice.

"Hello, this is Khur-Vay. Sorry but my shop will be closed for two weeks. I'll return on August twenty-second. Please leave your name and number if you should like to sign up for lessons. See you on the twenty-second."

Wonder where Khur-Vay was heading off to so fast? She hadn't mentioned going on vacation when I was with her. Suspicious, yeah, angry, too, I punched in Harve's phone number.

"Hey, Claire. It's about time I heard from you."

"You think you can get somebody's home address and phone number for me?"

Harve laughed. "Sure, that's one of your more simple requests."

"Okay, it's this girl who works in Branson. Her real name

is Sharon Richmond, but she goes by Khur-Vay, and that's K U R hyphen V A Y. She's got a belly dancing studio on the main drag over there. She graduated from high school in Jefferson City. I'd say she's midthirties. Dark hair. Green eyes. Probably five feet six inches, hundred ten pounds, maybe less. She's Asian, I think, but if not, she's sure as hell interested in the Orient."

"Shouldn't take long."

"You're a genius."

"I'll call you back. Give me about ten minutes."

Shutting my phone, I thought for the millionth time how nice it was to have a computer whiz on my friend list. Harve's multiple Internet businesses gave him options most people didn't have. He was the best at what he did.

While I waited, I sat there and thought about this new development. When I was in Khur-Vay's studio, we talked about Mikey. If she didn't have anything to hide, why wouldn't she just come out and tell me who she was and that she had dated Mikey herself?

The patient files had finally come in from the clinic late yesterday evening. They were stacked on the desk in front of me, both Young's and Collins's. I was trying to work out a way to get a warrant for their homes but hadn't come up with a legitimate reason to do it. Maybe a nocturnal break-in was in order. It was as good a time as any to read through them and see if I could find out how they were getting by with their dirty tricks. Bud was supposed to help, but he was late coming in, still on the road, I guess. The warrant had asked for Mikey's and now Cleo's files, but the doctors had willingly included a handful of other patients who were there during the same period. I really needed those of all patients in the clinic, and two years before and after. Zero chance of that. I looked at the thickness of the file folders. Fun, fun, I had a feeling I was going to spend the whole night reading through stuff straight out of Wes Craven scripts.

Beginning with Boyce Collins's patient load, mainly because he annoyed me the most, and possibly had molested me, too, I began with Mikey's rather thick file. He was diagnosed paranoid. No kidding. Three hundred evil eye bracelets either attached to his person or amulets strung all over his house pointed to that conclusion. Obviously, and in hindsight, he was right to be worried. I read on, all kinds of therapies, but especially group therapies with his fellow patients. He was quiet, attentive, caused no trouble, but was scared of his shadow. Probably because of Ice Queen of the Universe. For once, I voted with Freud on the mother thing.

Twenty minutes passed. No Harve. No Bud. Okay, keep going. The more I read, the more I realized that an inordinate amount of these kids had committed suicide, either at the clinic or after they'd left. Of course, the place catered to at-risk kids, many of whom had already tried to take their own lives but failed. It probably wasn't inordinate for that kind of place, but it didn't exactly make Oak Haven look like a suicidal patient's lifeline. I wondered if maybe the troubled teens fed on each other behind closed doors and dared each other to pull the trigger. Many of the files had successful outcomes, I guess, but there was just something that didn't pass the sniff test with me. I knew the doctors up there were involved in these murders knee-deep.

I read on. It appeared more girls than boys ended their lives while in residence. I thumbed through the faxes, looking for Sharon Richmond. Not there. I looked for Li He. She was treated by both doctors. She was obsessive compulsive with suicidal tendencies. That explained her neater than humanly possible dorm room.

The Mexican Hat Dance song broke the silence. With trepidation, I picked it up. Maybe I just wouldn't pick up to anybody except trusted friends. It was Harve. I punched him on quickly.

"That girl was harder to track down than I thought. She moves around a lot. She lives in Ozark now. She moved there several years ago from Dyersburg, Tennessee."

Ozark was a small town halfway between Branson and Springfield. "You get an address on her?"

"Yes. She lives on State Highway W. Box number is 1550."

"Got it. I'm going down there and see what she has to say."

"Now? It's a little late, isn't it?"

"Nah. I don't have anything else to do. If I wait, she might be gone by the time I get there. I have a feeling it's a good idea to surprise the lady."

"Be careful. Where's Black?"

"Working."

"Where's Bud?"

"On his way back from St. Louis, probably."

"Well, be careful. Call if you need an ambulance."

"Ha ha, Harve."

He laughed, and then I did, but I didn't really think it was all that funny. I had ridden inside a few ambulances in my day, and I preferred Black's Humvee.

After I hung up, I grabbed my purse, made sure all my weapons were loaded, stopped at the snack room, poured me a cup of that morning's coffee, now with a consistency resembling Mississippi mud, choked some down, and I mean that literally, checked in with the night desk with instructions on where I was going and why, called Black, who was still with that patient, and told his voice mail where I was going and why, and then headed off to Ozark, Missouri, a good hour and a half drive away. Look out, Sharon Richmond aka Khur-Vay, here I come, ready or not.

Here Comes Trouble

Tee became obsessed with the detective bitch. His call did not trigger her overdose as planned, so she was still sniffing around. Oh yes, she had to go. The news articles about her were plentiful, a dime a dozen. And it didn't take him long to figure out her Achilles' heel. She had a seriously demented stalker at one time and was that a serendipitous gift for Tee. An androgynous stalker at that, one who nearly killed her before he had been put away in a mental hospital. Tee had to grin. All he had to do was set the guy free, and he'd take care of matters, and Tee wouldn't have to dirty his hands, so to speak.

The stalker's name was Thomas Landers, but he had masqueraded as a woman and had gone by the name of Dottie. Once, Thomas had been a very close friend of the detective, and if Tee had anything to do with it, Thomas would be her bosom buddy again, and real soon, too. Best of all, the man was incarcerated in a hospital located not far away, and Tee had the right credentials to gain access to him, interview him, and if he met Tee's expectations, which he fully expected

him to do, he might be able to help the psycho escape. And if
he did, and if Thomas Landers got hold of the nasty little detective again, so be it. May they live happily ever after in
hell, as far as Tee was concerned.

Tee smiled. It could happen. He could make it happen.

The interview with Thomas Landers was easy enough to
set up. Tee's colleagues at Thomas's hospital were pleased at
his interest. Thomas was such an interesting case, so intelligent, so psychologically deficient, but making progress day
by day. He was so much better, in fact, that they were considering supervised day trips. Input from another doctor of
Tee's reputation would be greatly appreciated. So he set
things in motion, just like that.

Tee got his first glimpse of Thomas in a private interview
room. His new subject was smaller than he had expected him
to be. He was sitting quietly, his fingers laced together on the
table in front of him. He didn't look like he would harm a fly,
but from the files that Tee had read, the guy would lop off a
man's head with a meat cleaver without batting an eyelash.
All the better. Nothing Tee liked better than a natural-born
killer.

"Hello, Thomas."

"Hello, Doctor. Are you here to examine my head? I have
a thing about heads, you know."

Tee laughed, thinking that rather clever. He liked his new
patient at once. Landers's voice was very calm and studied,
but he looked mildly surprised by Tee's reaction, and somehow, pleased.

"So I've heard," Tee said.

"You aren't horrified like the other doctors?"

"Not really."

"Then you must have your own agenda, I suspect."

"Yes, I do. Want to help me?"

Thomas stared at him out of big, intelligent blue eyes.
The reports had indicated his hair was bleached blond when

he went as a woman, but now it was dark brown, cut short by the hospital staff. He was very serene and unmoving, but very interested in what Tee had to say.

At length, and after a glance at the screened-glass window in the door, Thomas said, "Possibly. How can I help you?"

Tee glanced at the window, too, although he had made sure the room wasn't equipped with microphones or cameras. He said, "We have a mutual friend, Thomas."

"Indeed. And who would that be?"

"That would be Claire Morgan, or as you knew her, Annie Blue."

His words impacted Thomas. The man couldn't hide it, although he tried. He lowered his gaze, and several minutes passed before Thomas said, "You know my Annie?"

"I sure do."

"Is she all right? Nobody will tell me about her."

"Oh, she's fine. She misses you. She told me that herself."

For the first time, Thomas smiled. "I suspect you're lying about that."

"No, I'm not."

"Why are you really here? It's obvious you need me for something."

"Nope. I just think it's time you met and talked to Annie again, spent some time with her. I believe that's the therapy which would help you most. Of course, your other doctors don't agree. So we'd have to keep this just between ourselves. You do understand that."

Thomas observed him, then crossed his arms over his chest. He was very muscular and looked strong. "They won't let me out of here to see her. That's the last thing they would allow. They won't even let me have her picture in my room." He sighed.

Tee said, "They won't know. I'll think of a way to help you escape this place. We'll meet when you're outside and I'll take you to her."

Thomas said, "I worry about her. She's got a dangerous job."

"Yes, I know. I understand your admiration of her. She's quite a woman."

"What do you want me to do?"

"Just do exactly what I say, and I'll get you out of here without anyone knowing it. Then I'll get you that one-on-one meeting with Annie."

Thomas narrowed his eyes. "You got yourself a deal, Doctor. When do I leave?"

TWENTY-THREE

Little Miss Sharon aka Khur-Vay lived way out in the boonies of Ozark, Missouri. Lots of trees and hills and narrow blacktopped roads and no streetlights. I hoped she was home after I had put in such a long drive, but I sure didn't want to give her a call so she could pack her bags and flee before I rang her doorbell. Along the drive, I spent some time on the cell phone with Black, who was burning furious because I'd gone off without him. He didn't care for the idea that I was headed into the dark woods alone, either, so I gave him Khur-Vay's address and told him to come on down and join the party, if it'd make him feel better. He said it'd make him feel better, and to turn on my GPS tracking device so he could find me, and not to answer my phone to unknown callers. Gladly, I agreed to both suggestions. Phone friends, yes; phone fiends, no. Not that I considered one small belly dancer particularly threatening unless, of course, she knocked me unconscious with some serious hip swivels.

When I finally found the right box number on Khur-Vay's very dark and Cur-Vay road, it was fastened to a brand-new, shiny silver mailbox with gold reflective numbers but no

glow-in-the-dark name. There was a barred gate locked across
the entrance to the graveled drive but no corresponding fence.
Therefore, if I so desired I could just drive on the grass around
the gate and get up to the house anyway. The purpose of Fatima's gate, therefore, eluded me. However, I didn't want to
get thrown in jail on a vehicular trespass charge by my wor-
thy Ozark PD counterparts, so I pulled my Explorer off on
the shoulder. I could see lights on up at the house at the far
end of the driveway, about fifty yards up a rise. It looked like
a small ranch house inside a grove of tall pine trees. A couple of cars were parked out front.

I got out, locked my door, and waded through some tall
weeds edging the road. Hesitating, slightly gun-shy of late, I
considered calling for backup but for what? I was armed.
Sharon Richmond didn't strike me as a dangerous character
who'd pull a gun and shoot me dead, and I had pretty good
instincts about stuff like that. I was just paying a social call.
She'd told me to call her if I wanted to learn how to entice
Black with my belly. So, hey, maybe I was here to order up
some belly lessons, so enthused, in fact, I couldn't wait until
she opened up shop again.

Or, in a less Mickey Mouse scenario, she might have invited a whole bevy of evil Jekyll-and-Hyde doctors in for
green tea and peach fried pies. I pulled the Glock out of my
shoulder holster, just in case, and felt incredibly better about
the whole thing with the heft of the weapon in my right
hand.

It took me a couple of minutes to walk up to the house,
mainly because I was being stealthy and looking in the thick
shadowy bushes for murderous assailants. The driveway was
longer than it looked from the road. All was very quiet in the
dark night. About a million plus crickets were having a hoe-
down in the bushes, really giving their back legs a work out,
but nary a bird call from yonder tree branches. All gone to
Fort Lauderdale on vacation, I guess. Two cars sat in front of
the house: one, an older, rather beat-up, olive green Dodge

van and the other, a newer model white Concorde. I had the urge to keep my gun up and out in front to greet the bogeymen I usually ran into at times like this. Not a good sign, that. But I didn't get any of my innate danger vibes, the kind that really got me all nervous and riled up. I had learned to always trust my instincts. They'd done right for me so far. I was still alive, wasn't I?

I walked up the front steps, not exactly hiding my approach, but not tromping around with hobnailed boots, either. I stopped and examined the house. The front windows were lit up, all yellow and welcoming, but covered with vertical blinds so I couldn't see who was hiding inside. I opened the screen door and tapped lightly with my knuckle. It was just so dang quiet. No sounds came from inside the house and nobody answered the door. So I walked back down the steps and placed my palm on the hood of van. The motor was cold. So was the Concorde's.

A breeze tossed the top branches of the trees around the house, no doubt looking for the absentee birds. It smelled like rain was coming, the air suddenly cooler after a very hot day. Then I heard the voices, drifting to me through the wind and cricket tantrums. Okay, somebody was in the backyard doing something or other. The something or other was what I was most interested in. I eased around the corner, the Glock pointing down at the ground along my right thigh. Not that I thought petite little Khur-Vay was gonna attack me with her castanets or tie me up with her see-through scarves, or anything, but then again, her alter ego Sharon Richmond might decide to attack me with something sharp and shiny and not fun to be planted in my chest.

More overgrown and scratchy bushes lined the side of the house, and I had to wade through tall weeds that had a sulfuric, acrid stink that would probably cling to my jeans through both rinse cycles, but they cushioned my increasingly cautious advance and now I could see a strange soft glow coming from somewhere behind the house. I proceeded carefully and stopped to listen several times, a little wary about rounding that back corner and putting myself into somebody's gun sights. It's always good to know how many people might jump you before you show yourself. Still, I had no sense of bodily threat. Go figure.

Now I could tell that there were two voices, both female, both speaking in normal tones, neither yelling bloody murder or screaming in agony, which was always a good sign. The women sounded like they were just sitting around and shooting the bull, not literally, of course, that would've alarmed me. I couldn't hear what they were saying but it didn't sound particularly life threatening. Just two girls having a little chat. Always fine in my *creeping-up-on-somebody* book.

So I relaxed a little bit, that is, until I heard the soft but unmistakable click of a weapon cocked somewhere behind me and a male voice saying, "Put the gun down or you're gonna get a new hole drilled in the back of your head."

Well, okay, and shit. But a new hole drilled in the back of my head was something I didn't really care for, so I went for my best bravado and bluffed him without ado, "I'm a police detective, here to investigate a case. I'm not putting my gun down and I've got backup on the way."

Luckily, that changed his tune. "Look, Officer, I don't want trouble. Put your weapon down and then we'll talk."

"Sorry, no can do."

Rustling footsteps occurred in the dark, and then the voice again, closer now. "Do it or I'll shoot you. I'm not kidding."

Crap. "How about we talk about this some more?"

"Do it, lady, now, or I'm gonna blow your fuckin' brains out."

Fairly certain by his heavily gritted teeth that he wasn't kidding around any more and that he was polite because he'd called me lady and hadn't shot me without giving me a chance and that it wasn't a voice I'd heard before and definitely not that of any witch doctors from Oak Haven, I said, "Well, okay, if you think I should."

Slowly, I squatted down and lay my weapon on the ground, pleased as punch that I had my handy little .38 revolver strapped to my ankle in easy reach, and this guy didn't know it. I also had a cylinder of mace in my jeans' pocket, which often came in handy when accosted by strangers. Now if he just held off on shooting me where I stood, I'd be okay. Happily, the aforementioned sixth-sense antenna that usually apprised me of impending danger was still not quivering, not even a wimpy little wiggle of unease. Which made me wonder if it was broken, or out of batteries.

"Walk on ahead of me, out to the backyard, if you will."

I guess I would. Jeez, what a refined assailant I'd run into; usually they just clubbed me in the head. I did what the guy said. When I rounded the corner, I saw the two women. They were sitting on a little concrete patio with about fifty strings of Christmas lights strung all over the place, swaying in the wind and dripping rows of icicles from the surrounding trees, thus creating the ghostly or romantic glow, depending on one's mood. To me, and in my present plight, it seemed ghostly. I recognized Khur-Vay right away because she jumped up and said, "Why, it's Detective Morgan. What a pleasant surprise. What are you doing here?"

"I'm being prodded at gunpoint at the moment, Khur-Vay. Anything you can do about that?"

Khur-Vay wasn't dressed like a belly dancer anymore. She was dressed more like me in a black T-shirt and black jeans, or in her case, black denim capris. She was barefoot. I had on my high-top Nikes, in case I stepped on a snake. She looked at the man behind me, whoever the hell he was, and then she said, "Yang Wei. She's okay. I know her. She's a police officer."

My polite and prodding companion came into view, and showed me his rather lethal-looking gun. He had my weapon in his other hand. He said, "If I give this back, you won't shoot me or arrest me, will you?"

Well, ha ha, and aren't you a card? "I'll do my best to restrain myself, but it won't be easy."

Grinning, but warily, he came forward and handed over my weapon. Then I saw that he was Asian, a real tall, thin guy with long black hair tied back in a ponytail, and I don't mean pulled back low on the neck like hippies do but fastened up high with a rubber band like little preschool girls wear theirs. He didn't have a pink ribbon on it, though.

"Thanks a million, Yang Wei," I said, and meant it. He could've just shot me and asked questions later. That's the way most of my enemies do it. Except for Young or Collins or whoever was killing people out at Oak Haven. They'd probably make me shoot myself.

"You're welcome."

Nobody said anything for a moment, then Khur-Vay said, "How did you find me?"

"I've got a knack for that sorta thing."

"You must. I thought I was secure here."

"Secure?"

The second woman hadn't said a word, but then she stood up, too, and the twinkling lights illuminated her face. I realized she was crying. I realized she was Li He.

Khur-Vay immediately noted my *shocked-out-of-my-gourd* expression, I guess, because she said, "Yes, it's Li He. She's been here with me all along."

I said, "I've been looking for you, Li He. So have your parents, the Springfield police, and lots of other people." I was pissed that she'd been hiding out here, but on the other hand, I was also relieved to see with my own eyes that she wasn't the blackened victim in that awful oven. Now she was a person of interest who could answer a whole bunch of my questions.

"Sit down, Detective," said Khur-Vay. "I'll pour you some

lemonade and then I'll tell you why I've been hiding Li He out here."

"That sounds like a plan." I glanced at Yang Wei, slid the Glock back into my holster, and then I sat down at the table with the two women. Yang Wei melted away into the night to catch some more trespassing detective types. He was pretty stealthy, I'll give him that. People can't usually sneak up on me. I'm glad he's on my side, whatever side that is.

Khur-Vay said, "Actually, I'm glad you're here. I hated lying to you at the studio. What I'm going to tell you is strictly confidential. You do understand that, right?"

"Wrong. Nothing's confidential in my investigation, unless I decide it is."

"I believe you will agree, once you hear my story."

Li He kept up the sobbing. It made me wonder why, but I had a feeling I was about to find out.

Khur-Vay bustled around, pouring me some lemonade, then refilling her glass and Li He's. She pushed a plate of date shortbread cookies in front of me, the consummate hostess. "Help yourself."

I took one because I'm polite, too, and a little hungry, and not under the fear of death anymore. "Okay, let's hear it, Khur-Vay, or should I say, Sharon, why'd you lie to me and why is Li He out here in hiding?"

"She's in hiding because she doesn't want to go back home to Beijing. Yang Wei and I are helping her evade the Chinese authorities. They'll eventually come looking for her when they realize she's not coming back."

"And you are doing this why?"

"Yang Wei's a Chinese national who defected here from a basketball exchange program years ago. He helps others escape and gets them asylum, and I'm talking about the ones who aren't given clearance to immigrate by the government."

"And how did a little belly dancer like you get involved in all this?"

"Mikey."

"Mikey Murphy?"

"Yes."

"You were his girlfriend once upon a time. That correct?"

"Yes, for a while until I left the state and went home."

"Okay, go on."

"I went back to Dyersburg because of this guy I thought I wanted to marry, but when we broke up, I came back here and started my studio in Branson. Mikey came to me and asked me to help his new girlfriend stay in the United States."

"Why you?"

"Because I already knew her through the studio."

I turned to Li He. "Why couldn't you apply for immigration?"

She sobbed out the answer while dabbing at her tears with a black paper napkin imprinted with a white yin/yang symbol. She looked even smaller in person than in her pictures. "Because they won't let me stay. I've been trained since I was three years old to perform with my parents in the show and they consider me a commodity. I have to go back home."

"Mikey could've gone over there. Things are different now between our two countries."

Khur-Vay said, "Mikey was going to, but then he decided that he didn't want to live in China." Hesitating and giving a long look at Li He, she went on, "And she can't go back. She's pregnant."

Okay, now I began to understand. "Mikey's baby?"

"Yes," sobbed Li He. "And then somebody killed him."

"There, there, sweetie," Khur-Vay said to Li He. She patted the girl's back, then turned to me. "Li He is only nineteen. That's not old enough to get a marriage certificate in China. Girls there have to be twenty. Men have to be twenty-two. Without a marriage certificate, she can't get a birth certificate. If she returns to China when she's supposed to, and that's before her baby's born, she'll either have to sell it or have an abortion or pay a huge fine. That's how they do things in China. Mikey was going to pay the fine, but now he's dead and she's left with no one to help her."

"So she's gonna just disappear here in the States?"

"That's right. Yang Wei has a network set up, sort of like the old Underground Railroad but in the Asian American community. Mikey was gonna sell his pizza place and join her somewhere after the baby was born and they'd stopped searching for her."

I said to Li He, "And your parents don't know the truth?"

More crying. "No, they'll get in trouble if the immigration officials find out they know where I am. But now Mikey's gone and everything's gone wrong, and I'll be all alone here."

Khur-Vay put her arm around the tiny girl's shoulders. "No, you won't, Li He, you won't, either. Yang Wei's getting you into a good family, who'll help you start over. Nobody will know who you are or where you are. Nobody will take your baby away."

All this was fine and dandy, except for one thing. Who was the girl in Mikey's oven?

I asked those questions, eliciting more distress in my companions. Li He said, "I think it might be my roommate, Mel. I can't get hold of her since it happened."

And neither had we. "Why do you think it was her?"

"Because she told me that she and Mikey had found out some stuff about a doctor at Oak Haven when they were patients up there, and she was afraid."

"Which doctor?"

"She didn't tell me. I was already in hiding out here, and I couldn't take a chance being on the phone with anybody. Mikey, either. I didn't get to say good-bye to him." More sobbing commenced.

"Then you don't think either one of them killed themselves?"

"Oh, no, Mikey would never do that to me. We were

going to get married as soon as he could sell Mikey's Place and join me."

Khur Vay said, "We're not sure the other victim is Mel. We're hoping it's not. Do you know who it is yet?"

"No, but my partner's checking that out as we speak. He needs to know all this."

Moving away from the patio, I pulled out my cell and dialed up Bud. He answered on the second ring, and I spoke in a low voice, watching Khur-Vay and Li He so they wouldn't take off on me. Khur-Vay was now talking on her cell phone, too.

"Where are you, Bud?"

"I'm outside Mel Baxter's parents' house, and they don't know where the hell she is. She wasn't supposed to be here, there wasn't any cousin's wedding, and they haven't seen or heard from her in two weeks. And get this, they adopted her from China when she was fifteen and she's been in treatment at Oak Haven."

"I think she's our vic in the oven."

"Could be, I guess."

"And if she is, we'll need proof for the lab. Can you go back in and ask her parents if she's got a toothbrush or hairbrush we can take in as evidence? Buck's gonna need that ASAP."

Bud said, "What put you on to her?"

"Maybe the fact I'm sitting here looking at Li He, very much still alive and kicking?"

"No shit. Where'd you find her?"

I told him the story without much detail, mainly because I didn't have much detail.

Bud said, "I'll get right on it. I should be home in say, two and a half, three hours."

We hung up, and I rejoined the ladies, who had been talking together in anxious tones. They weren't yet wringing their hands but were close to it.

Khur-Vay looked at me. "We've gotta get Li He out of here tonight. It's no longer safe. If you found us, somebody else can, too."

"You're telling a sworn police officer that you're hiding an illegal immigrant. You understand that, don't you?"

"Please. She's going to have a baby. She doesn't want to give it up."

I'd heard about the One-Child Policy that China had adopted several decades ago, but I hadn't heard all the legal details before. I wasn't about to turn the girl in. Khur-Vay knew it, and I knew it.

Khur-Vay added sugar to the pot. "Maybe I can help you find out about those doctors and what Mikey and Mel knew about them. I'll help you, if you'll help me."

"How can you help me?"

"I know a lot about Mikey that other people don't know. We went together. He trusted me. Didn't he come to me for help with Li He, even though we broke up a long time ago?"

Now that made sense. It occurred to me then that she or Li He might know something about Mikey's mysterious key. I pulled it out, still in the plastic evidence bag, and showed it to them. "Do either of you know what this unlocks?"

Li He leaned forward, examined it, and then shook her head. Her face was sorrowful, her cheeks wet with tears. I had a feeling she'd been crying for a long time. "I do not know. Orchid might have known."

"Who's Orchid?"

"That was Mel's name when she lived at the clinic. Some of the patients went by fake names. The ones that wanted to keep their identities secret."

That explained some of the weird names I'd seen at the tops of Dr. Young's and Dr. Collins's files. "Did Mikey have a special name up there?"

"No, he just went by Mikey. He didn't care if people knew who he really was. Everybody got to choose what they were called."

"I see."

Khur-Vay was examining the key. "I don't recognize it, either." Frowning, she seemed reluctant to speak her next words but finally got them out, "But I know a place he used to go to. He stored some of his furniture and stuff there when his parents kicked him out of the house."

Excited and not hiding it, I said, "What place? Where is it?"

"It's an old warehouse and boat dock on the Finley River. His grandparents owned it, I think, and left it to him. Mikey said rumrunners used to unload liquor out there during Prohibition. I helped him move his stuff in. He locked it up when we left. Maybe that's what this key goes to."

"Yeah, maybe. Where exactly is this place?"

"It's not far away. Maybe ten or fifteen minutes from here. You go right by this restaurant called the Riverside Inn and over a little narrow one-lane bridge, then it's a little past there, on a gravel road that turns to the left."

"You willing to show me?"

"Yes, if you'll let me get Li He packed and out of here. I want Yang Wei to take her to another safe house tonight. It won't take long to get her ready."

"Okay, but make it quick."

Khur-Vay and Li He went inside the house. Minutes later, Khur-Vay was back outside with a fresh pitcher of lemonade and a plate of fried pies, still the hostess with the mostest. She filled up my glass and then returned to the house. I drank the lemonade and wished she would hurry up. I wondered where Black was and tried to figure out what the key I was holding might uncover. Evidence for multiple first-degree murder warrants, I hoped. I reached for my phone to call Black but stopped when Yang Wei materialized out from underneath the dark trees.

He had on a black cotton tunic and pants, Chinese style, probably trying to look like a ninja warrior when he creeped around in the dark. He joined me at the table, deciding he liked my company, after all, I guess. He just sat there, silent and unfriendly. So did I. I could be as silent and unfriendly as the best of them.

"I think someone at that clinic killed my sister. Her name was Lotus," he said suddenly, and dare I say it, unexpectedly.

"You don't say."

"I am very serious. I have always believed it."

"Who?"

"I cannot prove it, but he was known as Tee at the time. He was a patient then, but I don't know what happened to him. I only know that she slit her wrists in the bathtub not long after he arrived. It was very bloody." His facial expression did not alter with those words, but I could see the pain in his eyes before he looked away.

The gruesome scene he had just described brought back a terrible trauma from my own past, a mental image I quickly tried to shut down. All this was coming together. I was getting very close to the truth but couldn't quite get a handle on it yet.

"What did this Tee guy look like?"

"He was a big kid, athletic, brown hair, big smile, friendly. I know he had something to do with what Lotus did. I know it in here." Dead serious now, he looked deep into my eyes again and put his palm over his heart.

That description sounded an awful lot like Collins, now didn't it? And by God, if it was him, I was going to prove it. But Happy Pete and Young also fit that description, to a lesser degree, maybe, but they fit. I needed to look through those clinic files again. Most of them had included photographs of the patients. Maybe Yang Wei could identify this Tee guy for me. At this point, I'd take any help I can get. If Yang Wei was right about his sister's death, somebody affiliated with Oak Haven Clinic had been manipulating kids to commit suicide, and maybe for years. And now I was so hot on his trail my feet were getting scorched.

TWENTY-FOUR

"Look over there, Claire, there it is, the Riverside Inn. Mikey said it used to be a speakeasy back in the twenties."

On first name basis now, Khur-Vay was pointing off to my left, where a long white structure that looked like it might have been a motel in days gone by was spread out a little lower than the roadbed. Lights spilled out all the windows, and lots of cars were packed together on the asphalt parking lot. The place must have a good menu.

"They have the best fried chicken in the universe," said Khur-Vay, as if on cue.

"That's pretty good chicken," I said, but to be fair, I haven't sampled any from Mars or Jupiter, so there you go.

"Just follow the road around, then go over the bridge." Khur-Vay was getting real chatty now, nervous, even, but I couldn't blame her. We both were dealing with dangerous people playing dangerous head games here. No telling what we were going to find in that deserted warehouse of Mikey's. I shuddered to think. Hopefully, it would just be a lot of incriminating evidence that would nail the killer big-time.

The bridge was an old iron single-lane kind, and it spanned

the Finley River just on the other side of the restaurant. It was too dark to see the water below us, but it was probably up and running high because of the recent flooding in the area. I could hear the rush of the current as I navigated slowly across the narrow bridge and hoped no oncoming traffic showed up at a high rate of speed. One-lane bridges were few and far between in this day and age and for good reason, too. I wondered why this one had been left behind in the march of progress. "How much farther, Khur-Vay?"

"Not too much, I think. It's been a long time, and I was only here that one time. I hope I can still find it. The road we want turns off to the left and then curves back toward the river. I think it finally comes out at the warehouse a couple of miles upstream from the bridge."

The belly dancer's chatter was going nonstop now. I drove along the deserted blacktopped road, way out in the sticks now, my headlights flashing on the dense, dusty green brown brush and tree trunks along the sides of the road. When I suddenly began to feel funny, I hit the brake. I felt dizzy and sluggish, like my mind was suddenly slowing down. When I tried to blink that strange sensation away, it didn't go anywhere. I pulled off the road onto the shoulder and shoved the gearshift in park.

"What's wrong? Why are you stopping?" Khur-Vay was saying in a voice that seemed to spiral down my ear canals like a slow-moving funnel cloud.

Looking over at her, I tried to wake up and blink her face into one image instead of two. "I feel sick. It came on really fast." My hands were going limp, my muscles like jelly, and then I realized this was not some little dizzy spell. This was a drug effect. A drug that Khur-Vay had given to me, probably in the lemonade. Oh, God, she was part of this mess; she'd drugged me.

"Whad you give me?" I said, and heard my own words slur out of my mouth. I shut my eyes, couldn't hold them open, but I could hear her voice.

"It's just a couple of my sleeping pills. I put them in that last glass of lemonade. It's not enough to hurt you, but you'll probably go to sleep for a while. Oh, God, I'm so sorry, Claire, but I had to do it. He told me to do it or else. He made me, I swear."

I knew about sleeping pills, especially when you took more than one; Black had given me a prescription to help me cope with my nightmares. It was supposed to make me fall asleep fast but it didn't affect me so much that way, took me a long time to fall asleep, anyway. Maybe I could beat it, stay awake and get back in control, but I was feeling groggy and messed up and sick to my stomach, and her words kept echoing farther and farther away as the drug sped its way through my bloodstream. Clarity of mind was slipping, thoughts flitting around the edges of my mind like some kind of butterfly dancing. I tried to speak, ask her who made her do it, but my tongue wouldn't move anymore, felt like a thick, warm worm asleep in my mouth. I was losing consciousness, and I tried to will myself to awake. I could not go to sleep. I could not let her get by with this.

Khur-Vay was still talking. "He told me that if I didn't help him find out what you knew, he'd get to my little girl, Chloe, that he had people who could find her and kill her, all he had to do was give them a trigger. That's what he called it, a trigger. He said you were getting too close to him, that he wanted to talk to you and find out what you know. He's gonna let you go after that, Claire, I swear, he promised me. So I called him up when I went inside with Li He, and he told me he was out here at Mikey's place with some friends and to bring you here. He's not gonna hurt you. He promised me he wouldn't hurt you."

Yeah, right, I thought, that's about as likely as a spaceship landing on top of my car. Then I laid my head back on the headrest and closed my eyes.

Vaguely, fighting sleep, I heard Khur-Vay get out of the passenger door and run around to my side. I felt myself being pushed across the seat and out of the way, and ended up with my head leaning on the passenger's window as I fought to stay aware of what was going on. I could not let myself go completely out. The motor fired, and I blinked and shook my head, forcing my eyes open as she drove us along the main road for a while, then took a sharp left.

More riding, bumping down an uneven surface, gravel crunching under the tires. Branches were whipping against the windows, and the sleep took me briefly until the car pulled to a stop again. I forced myself awake enough to see a weathered gray warehouse sitting directly in the glare of the headlights. When Khur-Vay opened the door and got out, I could hear the loud rush of the river again, gurgling and splashing its way downstream. Then somebody came out the front door, and I tried to see who it was as they walked out to the car, but couldn't focus my eyes long enough, and the pills finally got me.

I woke up again when they dragged me out of the car. I was going in and out of sleep, but I was mostly semiconscious. I felt the adrenaline surge as a man's hands touched my body, picked me up, and I hoped to God I could somehow counteract the sleeping pills. Then we were inside the building, in a dimly lit room, and they were talking together, but I couldn't quite understand the words. I was dumped onto the floor, and then I felt nothing and saw nothing for a while.

Later, I don't know how long, I awakened to loud voices. I forced my eyes open, tried to focus, had a lot of trouble doing it. Now I was slumped in some kind of lawn chair, but I could make out other chairs, too, all in a circle. There were people sitting in them, but dark shadows hugging the edges of the room obliterated their faces. An old crate sat in the middle of the circle with an electric lantern on top that gave out the only light in the room. I could hear Khur-Vay now, crying. She was saying, "Please, Tee, please, don't hurt me, I did what you said. I'll do whatever you want me to."

"Yes, Blossom, you sure the hell will."

The voice was familiar, I knew who it was, but I couldn't get my mind to recognize it. But I could see the man bending down and taping Khur-Vay to a chair. He straightened up and picked up my red crocodile purse off the floor. He rummaged inside it, then pulled out the plastic evidence bag containing Mikey Murphy's key.

He laughed with triumph. "So here's the key to Mikey's little hidey hole, wherever it is. Now all we need to know is where he and Orchid hid my tapes. I tell you, Blossom, our little friend Mikey turned out to be a brave little shit. More than I ever thought he would. He never did give up the location of the tapes to me, not even when I put the noose around his neck. In fact, he threatened to destroy me even as I shoved him off that bridge support. You should've heard his neck snap, but he still kicked and twisted before he gave it up."

I tried to think clearly. My weapon was gone from my shoulder holster, I could tell that much. Very slightly, I shifted my right foot, trying to see if I could feel the heft of the .38 revolver strapped to my ankle. There wasn't any weight there; he'd taken it. When he heard me moving, he picked up the lantern and moved toward me. "Oh, good, our famous little detective's awake. I've got the surprise of her lifetime in store for her."

Then I knew. It was Pete, Happy Pete, always so eager to please. Oh, God. He was grinning like a kid with a new toy. I realized he hadn't tied me up yet, obviously thought I was too drugged up to fight back. Wrong. I blinked and tried to look dazed as I attempted to clear my head. He bent down low and held the lantern up close to my face. I kept my eyes half-closed, struggling with murky thoughts. It was Happy Pete, all right, and he was down leering into my face big-time. He was smiling, still *top-of-the-morning* and enjoying his power over me. When he stripped off a piece of tape, I tried to struggle, but he held me down and taped my forearms to the chair and my calves to the legs. Then he stood up and looked down at me.

"Just a little insurance to keep you nice and quiet. A couple fast-acting sleeping pills, not exactly enough to keep you down for the count, now is it, Detective? You should've just left good enough alone but thank you kindly for bringing me the key. You see, don't you? If those tapes of my experiments get into the wrong hands, I'd be called unethical and my budding career would be ruined, and right now, too, when I'm just now making a name for myself. Even your boyfriend seemed impressed with my therapies. They are mine, did you know that? Collins tried to steal my thunder with his new book, but he's already regretting that. Nobody double-crosses me and gets by with it."

I tried to talk, found my voice thick and drunken. "You're going down. People know where I am. You can't get away with this."

"Yeah, sure they do." He sat on his haunches beside me and chatted as if we were having a latte at Starbucks. "I Googled you, Detective Morgan, and you simply would not believe all the newspaper articles that have been written about you. It's amazing how trouble always seems to find you, and here we go again, what'd you know, trouble found you. But know what? It's not gonna work out so well for you tonight. This time you're done for. Nobody's coming. Nobody knows you're here. Nobody knows any of us are here. The chips are definitely down."

Except for Black, I thought, as Happy Pete stood up. He laughed. "You can thank yourself, you know. I never would've gotten you over here tonight if you hadn't showed up at Blossom's house when you did. Wrong move, Detective. I came down here tonight to wrap up some loose ends before I moved on, but I sure as heck didn't think I'd get a chance to get rid of you, too. Guess it was just meant to be. I'm lucky that way, always have been."

Keep talking, you bastard, waste some more time, give Black time to track me down.

"I've got another little surprise for you, Detective," Happy

Pete was saying to me, all his words sounding long and drawn out and vibrating like a kettle drum. "We're down here to have our last little therapy session, and guess who's new to the group? An old friend of yours, but first, let me introduce you all around."

Happy Pete stepped to my right and shone the lantern on the man sitting in the chair beside me. Shocked, I stared at Martin Young. His face looked blank; his eyes unmoving. He was either drugged or in a trance, or both.

Almost rubbing his palms together in glee, Happy Pete said, "I believe you've already met old Marty, right? He's been my best buddy ever since I showed up at Oak Haven. But guess what? He's been one of the best subjects in my mind control experiments. In fact, he's in a trance right now, just like everybody else in this room. My own little band of assassins, all waiting for me to tell them who to kill. We're more organized than the CIA."

He was showing off, I realized. He wanted to demonstrate to me his power over others, his genius. But that was good; it'd give me more time to stop him. Black would be getting closer. He had the GPS in the Humvee, and he'd zero in on my Explorer. Even if he went to Khur-Vay's place first, eventually he could track us out here. Not much time had passed yet, at least I didn't think so. I was waking up pretty good now. Khur-Vay wasn't crying anymore, but I could make her out in the dim light, and she looked absolutely terrified. What had he called her? Blossom?

Happy Pete was still strutting his stuff. I was feeling stronger all the time. I pulled at the tapes, but there was no way I could pull them loose. Black was gonna have to show up soon.

"Ready to meet another of my excellent successes? Roy's his name, but that's right, you already interviewed him, didn't you?"

The lamplight revealed Roy's young face, and he stared straight out into the room with the same hypnotic trance that

Marty Young had. How had Happy Pete managed this? How had he gotten them to come here and cooperate in this madness?

Seemingly reading my mind, Happy Pete answered my questions. "They all trust me, you see, agreed to let me do my therapies on them, came to me like lambs to the slaughter, poor stupid fools. No offense, but so did you. I really thought you were smarter than that. Don't feel bad, even Boyce got involved in this stuff up to his neck. He's sitting right over there. He made a big mistake when he let me do all the research and work, then cashed in on it as his own. He succumbed to my light and sound waves, too, just like you did. Remember when he was showing you the light panel, you were out so fast and then he called me in and I worked my magic inside your head. You were easy, just a few suggestions about your son and that's all it took. You were already royally screwed up, so it didn't take much.

Happy Pete smiled down at me. "Tonight, Detective, is clean-up time. Best of all, all of my friends here trust me. All I had to do was call them, give the trigger, and ask them to come down here again for another one of our special group therapy sessions. They've all been here before, and so has Mikey. He told us about this place, told me I could use it. Too bad he didn't tell me what this key goes to, but it doesn't matter now. Not after I get done here tonight. Yes, ma'am, it's a brilliant call of mine, actually, to get rid of everybody in one fell swoop. Maybe I'll even burn this place down, so it'll take the police forever to identify who's who. But first, I want you to see what I've accomplished all these years working on mind control techniques. You barely scratched the surface in your investigation. You have no idea what I've managed to accomplish."

I said nothing, but panic was lurking just beneath the surface, pushing hard, ready to come out. I wasn't sure yet what he was going to make these people do, but I knew it wasn't going to be much fun to watch.

"Oh, yeah, I forgot, one more thing. I've got my latest and very best subject to introduce to you. It's that old friend of yours that I was telling you about. You're going to be so glad to see him. Luckily, I managed to help him break his way out of the hospital you locked him up in. He can't be too pleased with you about that. He turned out to be highly suggestible, just like all of you. You see, I had to pick my subjects very well; not every patient would work for me. Your friend's in a trance right now, but not for long. You ready? It's reunion time."

Shuddering, I tensed up and waited, because I knew who he was talking about. Even so, when he turned the light on Thomas Landers's face, bile as bitter as acid slid up the back of my throat. Thomas Landers, the main star in most of my ongoing nightmares, the childhood friend who'd stalked me for years and killed my relatives and cut off their heads with a meat cleaver and almost killed me before I got away and had him locked up with other criminally insane psychos. But he was out now, staring straight ahead, handsome face blank of emotion, just like all Happy Pete's other victims. How did he do this to people? Had he done it to me? Or had Black cleansed his poisonous venom out of my brain? Oh, God, if Black hadn't done it, this maniac could make me do anything he wanted, anything thing at all. He could make me kill people, kill myself.

"You see, Detective, after reading all those newspaper headlines about Thomas, here, I realized the perfect assassin I was looking for had finally come along. I'm sure you know what I mean, right? Your friend, Thomas, just loves to kill people, does it with great aplomb, too, I've gotta say. Can't beat a meat cleaver for getting the job done. Yeah, it's rare to find a guy who gets so much pleasure chopping off heads and keeping them around for souvenirs. Uh huh, he's a real gem. He and I are gonna have some fun in the future. We'll go places together and if anybody gets in my way, I'll trigger him. Like you, you're in my way big-time. I've already told him that he can keep your head, if he wants it. He can have everybody's head here, if he wants. No skin off my nose. He told me he loves you, and as long as you're with him, dead or alive, he'll be happy. And if he's happy, I can keep him in line and killing for me. And to think that you're the one who introduced us in a roundabout way. I thank you for that. Thomas and I make a helluva killing team."

Happy Pete gave me a cold smile, and in his boyish face I saw the dark light of pure evil. Thomas Landers had committed horrible gruesome acts, that was true, but he wasn't wired right in the head, warped from years of child abuse, but not so for Happy Pete. Happy Pete was just a stone-cold natural-born psychopath.

"Okay, lemme show you how this works, Detective. You're a smart woman, I admire that in you, and I hate it that Thomas is gonna have to kill you in a minute. I'd love getting inside your head and messing you up even more than you already are, but somehow I knew I just had to let you get one last glimpse of your nemesis. Don't be afraid. He's really quite harmless until I trigger him."

Fear gripped me. What was he going to do? I was awake and scared because Black should have shown up by now. What had happened to him? I couldn't count on him anymore. It was up to me. I had to make a move as soon as I got the chance, or everybody in this room was going to be dead, and soon.

Happy Pete moved to the center of the room and put the lantern down on top of the crate. He turned up the wick to the highest intensity, and then I could see the weapons lying on the table. My Glock 9 mm, my .38 snubnose revolver, an eight-inch meat cleaver, and a garrote. Three cans of gasoline sat nearby. All the props were ready. The show was about to begin.

"I can put you under in a trance any time I wish, you do know that, don't you, Detective? But not yet. Still, I'm gonna warn you not to try anything. All I have to do is say your trigger and you'll be a zombie just like the rest of these poor folks. Here let me show you how simple it is." He turned to Khur-Vay, leaned down, and whispered something into her ear.

I watched Khur-Vay go into a trance, just like that, eyes staring straight ahead like all the others. Oh, God, he could do that to me, too. I swallowed down burgeoning terror.

"Okay, here we go. We'll start with some light entertainment, just to give you an idea of what I've been able to accomplish with my subjects through the years. Why don't you pick out our first contestant?"

I said nothing.

"All right. Let's go with Roy. He's a particularly susceptible young man. Watch and learn, Detective, because you're gonna get your turn to play soon enough."

Happy Pete picked up my .38 and emptied it of ammunition. He held up one bullet for me to see, then put it inside a chamber, spun the cylinder, and snapped it closed. "Ever heard of Russian Roulette, Detective?"

"Don't do this. Roy's just a kid."

"Yes, most of my subjects are. But he's also one of those loose ends I was telling you about. Thanks to you, things are getting too hot at the clinic with your department snooping through our files and looking for dirt. So I've decided to move on, just me and Thomas. I can't leave all these freaks around for you to put on the witness stand, now can I?" He knelt down in front of the young boy beside me and whispered and said, "Take this gun, Roy, put it up against your temple, and pull the trigger."

"Stop it, no, Roy, don't do it," I cried, but I knew he was going to do it.

Roy took the gun, put it to his temple, just like that. I shut my eyes as he pulled the trigger, and then I sagged in relief when the gun clicked on an empty chamber.

"Roy's always been a lucky bastard, I'll say that for him," Happy Pete said. "Okay, scenario number two. We'll use my pretty little Blossom for this one." He slit the tape binding her with a penknife and placed the .38 in her hand. "Take this gun, Blossom, and shoot Detective Morgan in the forehead."

I froze. Face blank, Khur-Vay rose to her feet and walked over to me. She looked at me with unseeing dead green eyes, then without hesitation put the end of the barrel against my forehead. I began to sweat, felt it pop out on my forehead and run down my temples, as I sat in mind-numbing terror and watched her finger pull back on the trigger. It clicked again, and I collapsed weakly against my bindings.

"Well, you're pretty damn lucky, too. Hell, you guys must be living right. Okay, what to do next? Let's see." Happy Pete moved back to Boyce Collins, but he was still talking to me. "Collins was one of my doctors in the beginning, too, the sap, told me he thought I was a genius, and I am, but he's not. Look where he ended up. Marty wouldn't go for anything unscrupulous with the patients, but not so with Boyce. He worked right alongside me for a long time and then stole my research for his book. Now he's just another loose end, the pretentious creep."

He said to Collins, "Go over there and shoot our old friend, Marty, in the head."

Collins rose obediently, went to Marty, put the gun to his temple, and pulled the trigger. The deafening blam rocked the room, the smell of smoke and cordite acrid in my nose and mouth, as the bullet ripped through Martin Young's head and splattered blood and brains all over the wall behind him. I gagged and vomit burned up my throat, but nobody else in the room even moved. I didn't want to look at the blood and the gore and what was left of Martin Young. Oh, God, I was really gonna die. We were all gonna die.

"This is getting a bit tedious for you, I suspect, Detective Morgan. Okay, so be it, let's just get this thing done. I think you've gotten the drift, here. Hey, Thomas, it's your turn."

He told Boyce Collins to sit down, and then he said, "Thomas, kill Collins over there with the meat cleaver."

Thomas got up obediently, picked up the cleaver off the crate. I didn't want to watch as he raised his arm high into the air and brought the cleaver down as hard as he could on top of Collins's head. The blow cleaved the man's skull from scalp to eyebrows, and Collins collapsed on his knees, then fell forward on the floor, blood gushing out of his head.

"Very good, Thomas. Just excellent, really."

"Okay, time to go, Thomas. Kill the detective first, then the others. Like I said, you can have her head, if you want it, but cut that off last, after you kill the others."

Thomas moved toward me, his handsome face devoid of emotion. Happy Pete knelt down beside me and put his fingers on my wrist. "Oh, boy, your pulse is just racing. Now you know what real fear is, don't you? Okay, Thomas, do your stuff."

This was it. I was going to die. Right here. Right now. The Grim Reaper had finally found me. Thomas was going to get me, after all, just like he'd always wanted. I watched him raise the cleaver again, high, and I shut my eyes as he brought it down hard. The scream was high and horrible, but it didn't come from me. I opened my eyes, and saw Happy Pete, on his knees, shrieking with pain and holding the stump of his right arm where Thomas had brought the cleaver down through it with incredible force. Blood spurted everywhere, and the severed forearm and hand fell on the floor. I pushed my chair away from the horrible sight, trying to get away, as Thomas brought the cleaver down again but this time in a hard, sideways swipe that took off Happy Pete's head at the neck. The head went bouncing and rolling across the floor, the gush of hot blood spraying all over me.

Panic-stricken, I fought desperately against the tape, but then Thomas was there beside me, as if nothing had happened, patting my blood-spattered cheek to console me, and I cringed away in utter horror. His face was right in front of me, and up close, he looked a lot different than he had when I'd last seen him; his hair was no longer blond and he had gained a lot of weight, mostly muscle mass. But it was him, oh, God, and he was completely insane and he had me helpless and captive again, just like he had last time. And I knew what he was going to do, what he had always wanted to do. He was going to take me to his hell on earth, wherever it was, and he was going to keep me captive there with him forever.

"Thomas, please," I got out. "Don't hurt me. Let me go."

"I'm not going to hurt you, Annie, don't you see, that's why I had to kill Pete." He was using the name he'd known me by when we were children. He went on, his face growing angry. "He thought he was so smart, that he could hypnotize me, of all people." He laughed as if that idea were so ridiculous. He still had the cleaver in his hand, but it was lying in my lap now with his victims' blood dripping off it. He was talking to me, very earnestly. "I've been studying psychiatry ever since I got put in that hospital. I know how things work, how the doctors think. It was ludicrous, all of it, to think Pete thought he could manipulate me. What a joke. I fooled better psychiatrists than him, and every one of them tried hypnotherapy on me. I knew how to pretend to be in a trance, but not these other people Pete's been messing with." I groaned in growing despair but he kept on talking like nothing had happened, as if corpses were not lying maimed and mutilated on the floor around us. "Tee did get me a key and helped me escape from the hospital, and that was nice of him. But none of that's important, the only important thing is that we're together again. How's Harve doing, by the way?"

Last time he'd gotten me in his lair, I had managed to outwit him, but this time I couldn't think straight enough to do anything but sit frozen with absolute, overwhelming, dehabilitating dread. If I did the wrong thing, said the wrong thing, I could die any minute in a terrible, horrible, gruesome way. Nobody could save me now.

"Come on, Annie, let's get outta here. We have lots of plans to make, you know, like where we're gonna live. I thought maybe Florida, Pensacola, maybe. You'll like those snow-white beaches, or maybe Alabama. People down south are real friendly. And we've got to dig up my mother, too. God, I love you. It's just been so long since I've seen you. Why didn't you come visit me in the hospital? I watched out the window for you every single day."

Sitting rigid, I watched him cut the tape off my legs with the bloodstained meat cleaver. Pete's blood had saturated my clothes now and felt cold and clammy against my skin. Thomas cut the tape off my wrists, then taped them together and jerked me upright, as I fought the terrible vertigo and dizzy residue of the drug. Dragging me with him, he took me out the back of the warehouse where the others had parked their cars, leaving Roy and Khur-Vay sitting docilely in their chairs among the dead as if he'd forgotten all about them.

Then we were in Happy Pete's spotless and fancy new white Avalanche truck, heading down the narrow road toward the blacktop, jouncing over ruts and recklessly mowing down bushes alongside the road. I tried to get the door open, but it was locked from the driver's side, and I knew my only chance was to wait long enough to make him think I was too scared to move, then go for an escape.

Excited, Thomas was talking nonstop about how great it was to be back together and how we could collect shells on the beach together, and nearly overturned the vehicle with his reckless swerve out onto the blacktopped road. He floored it for the bridge, going way too fast, and as we roared across the narrow bridge, car lights lasered through the darkness as a vehicle rounded the curve by the Riverside Inn, the headlight glare hitting us directly in our faces.

When I recognized the vehicle as a Humvee, I knew it was Black. I had to make my move now. I started screaming and hitting Thomas with my bound hands, and struggled to get the can of mace out of my pocket, but he punched me hard in the head with his fist and knocked me back against the passenger's window. Shoving the gearshift into reverse, he gunned the truck back over the bridge, weaving danger-ously from side to side. Black brought the Humvee roaring straight at us with all the power of a military tank, and Thomas jerked the wheel at the other end of the bridge and slid the Avalanche into a sideways skid, trying to turn the truck around. Black was on us again, and Thomas floored the gas pedal and brought us ramming into the side of the Humvee. The impact was violent with shattering glass and rending metal, and the sheer force of the collision sent the Avalanche skidding and careening with screeching brakes over one end of the bridge, and we went crashing down the embankment, overturning on our side just above the water.

Thrown forcefully against the passenger's window, the side of my head broke the glass as the truck teetered precar-iously back and forth for a second or two, then slowly tipped over with a whine of crushed metal and broken glass, then rolled over and landed upside down in the river. The second impact sent my forehead hard against the windshield with an incredible burst of pain, and I blacked out until cold river water revived me. I couldn't see the water pouring in, but I could hear it and feel it, cold and shocking and black. The headlights were still on, creating bright arrows of light under the water, and I could see Thomas struggling to get out the driver side window. I tried to do the same as the interior quickly filled up with the rushing current.

Weak, blood streaming down both sides of my head, I somehow held my breath in the submerged car and wrested myself free of the tangled wreckage and pushed myself out of the broken window. I floated upward and surfaced, gasp-ing for air, pushed violently sideways in the swift, swirling current. I rolled onto my back and got a brief glimpse of stars in the black night sky, heard somebody yell my name, and then I gave up the fight. It was the end. My time had come. I sank into the dark water and let it take me down the river, slowly swallowing me into its ink-black, silent depths.

EPILOGUE

Springfield News Leader—Springfield, Missouri

MURDER, ATTEMPTED MURDER
IN OZARK

OZARK, MISSOURI—The abduction and attempted murder of two women by an escaped mental patient left three prominent psychiatrists dead and a sheriff's detective in critical condition. Ozark police officers arriving at the scene said the mental patient escaped and possibly drowned when his car plunged off a bridge on the Finley River.

A female victim, Sharon Richmond of Ozark, related to officers a terrifying ordeal that began when both she and Canton County Sheriff's Detective Claire Morgan were taken captive with several other victims inside a deserted warehouse two miles upriver from the well-known Riverside Inn Restaurant in Ozark.

The three dead males identified at the scene were Dr. Boyce Collins, Dr. Martin Young, and Dr. Peter Parsons, all three well-respected psychiatrists at the Oak Haven Clinic in Jefferson City. According to a witness at the scene, the perpetrator, Thomas Landers, was attempting to abduct Morgan when their truck went into the river. Morgan suffered severe head injuries and is at the Cox Medical Center in Springfield where she remains comatose and in critical condition. Richmond and an unidentified teenager were also admitted for observation.

I wasn't sure where I was. I wasn't sure who I was. I didn't care. It was all misty gray and cool and ephemeral, like drifting inside the loveliest, quietest cloud ever created. I was just floating around, softly, swaying gently, and I liked it. It was peaceful and calm, no noise, no bother, no fear. I realized that I was anchored to the ground, somewhere far, far below, at the other end of a shiny silver tether that slipped down through the clouds mounding like giant, fluffy cotton below me. That didn't matter. I didn't want to think about it. I just wanted to be very still and enjoy the soft rocking motions of the gentle breezes. I wanted the clouds to take me higher, up very high, up into the bright white light making the clouds glow above me. It beckoned to me but I couldn't seem to make myself loosen the silver cord holding me in place so I could float up to that beautiful place.

I shut my eyes and knew nothing more until a man's voice awoke me. It was deep and husky and sounded scared and insistent and determined. I didn't like it, but the voice was familiar somehow, and somehow I knew I had to listen.

"Come on, baby, I know you can hear me. I know you can. You can come back, just try, try to open your eyes, try to follow my voice back." Then the voice melted away and there was a strangled sound, and I saw a face materialize inside my mind, with blue eyes and black hair, but I didn't really recognize it. I ignored it then and let the rocking lull me to sleep again.

The voice came often and made me weary of listening because I liked the quiet. And then other voices came, not as often as the blue-eyed face but enough to disrupt my peace and wake me up.

"It's me, Claire, Bud, c'mon, please don't do this to us. The doctors say you can recover, if you'll just wake up. You're in a coma, that's the problem, you gotta wake up to get well. Charlie's here, too. We're all here."

That voice didn't even sound familiar. Neither did the ones that came after him. I slept again, wishing they would just leave me alone and give me the tranquillity I wanted. But they didn't, they wouldn't stop, and the voices seemed to go on night and day and forever.

"It's Black, Claire, listen to me, listen, damn it, you can do this. Everybody's been here to see you. It's okay to wake up. I've got you back home now, and I'm not going anywhere until you open your eyes. You'll be all right. It's over. I've got the best doctors in the world on your case. You're healing just fine. All you have to do is come back to me. You've got to come back. Just do it. Do it, Claire."

I slept some more. The voice would not stop. Now it was reading to me. Shut up and go away, I thought. Leave me alone. That same face loomed in my mind, and he looked vaguely familiar now, but I still didn't know him. I didn't want to know him.

His voice seemed always to be there, always talking to

me. "The sheriff needs you, Claire. You love being a detective, remember? You're good at it. You've put lots of criminals behind bars. You got them, all of them. They're all dead. They're never going to kill anybody again. Charlie needs you back on the job. I need you back."

Then a long time later, another voice came in to wake her, slow and drawling. "It's Joe McKay, Claire. What you tryin' to pull? Scarin' us all to death like this. You get your pretty little butt back here. Lizzie's here with me. She wants to say hi, too."

The more I heard the voices, the closer they seemed. They were dragging me down through the lovely clouds, down to wherever the silver rope was anchored, and I didn't want to go down there. I wanted them to stop, I wanted to stay here in the soft quiet so I resisted and tried to arrest the descent and shut my ears and not listen. Why wouldn't they just leave me alone?

Then I heard the voice of a child, very indistinct and far-away. Nothing more than a whisper. "Me and Jules is sad you're sick."

A vision erupted inside me, a little blond boy with chubby cheeks and chubby arms and a fishing pole with a little perch hanging on the hook. I didn't know his name, but I knew he needed me. I haven't seen him in so long. I gotta go back and find him. I left him somewhere, but I don't know where. I've got to find him. He'll be scared without me, I know he will.

Somehow I raised myself from that lovely, dreamy, pearly white, peaceful bed and took hold of the silver rope. I began to pull myself down, hand over hand, down, down, listening for the little child's voice until the other voices came closer and closer, and the one named Black who pestered me so relentlessly, said, "Oh, thank God, she's coming to. She's trying to wake up."

Then finally, at long last, I opened my eyes.